PRAISE FOR

"A stunner of a thriller. From ⸻ ⸻ *n the Tracks* weaves a spell that only ⸻ And a guarantee: you'll fall in love with one of the best characters to come along in modern thriller fiction, Sydney Rose Parnell."

—Jeffery Deaver, #1 international bestselling author

"Beautifully written and heartbreakingly intense, this terrific and original debut is unforgettable. Please do not miss *Blood on the Tracks*. It fearlessly explores our darkest and most vulnerable places—and is devastatingly good. Barbara Nickless is a star."

—Hank Phillippi Ryan, winner of Anthony, Agatha, and Mary Higgins Clark awards and author of *Say No More*

"Both evocative and self-assured, Barbara Nickless's debut novel is an outstanding, hard-hitting story so gritty and real you feel it in your teeth. Do yourself a favor and give this bright talent a read."

—John Hart, multiple Edgar Award winner and *New York Times* bestselling author of *Redemption Road*

"Fast-paced and intense, *Blood on the Tracks* is an absorbing thriller that is both beautifully written and absolutely unique in character and setting. Barbara Nickless has written a twisting, tortured novel that speaks with brutal honesty of the lingering traumas of war, including and especially those wounds we cannot see. I fell hard for Parnell and her four-legged partner and can't wait to read more."

—Vicki Pettersson, *New York Times* and *USA Today* bestselling author of *Swerve*

"The aptly titled *Blood on the Tracks* offers a fresh and starkly original take on the mystery genre. Barbara Nickless has fashioned a beautifully drawn hero in take-charge, take-no-prisoners Sydney Parnell, former Marine and now a railway cop battling a deadly gang as she investigates their purported connection to a recent murder. Nickless proves a master of both form and function in establishing herself every bit the equal of Nevada Barr and Linda Fairstein. A major debut that is not to be missed."

—Jon Land, *USA Today* bestselling author

"*Blood on the Tracks* is a bullet train of action. It's one part mystery and two parts thriller with a compelling protagonist leading the charge toward a knockout finish. The internal demons of one Sydney Rose Parnell are as gripping as the external monster she's chasing around Colorado. You will long remember this spectacular debut novel."

—Mark Stevens, author of the award-winning Allison Coil Mystery series

"Nickless captures you from the first sentence. Her series features Sydney Rose Parnell, a young woman haunted by the ghosts of her past. In *Blood on the Tracks*, she doggedly pursues a killer, seeking truth even in the face of her own destruction. The true mark of a heroine. Skilled in evoking emotion from the reader, Nickless is a master of the craft, a writer to keep your eyes on."

—Chris Goff, author of *Dark Waters*

"Barbara Nickless's *Blood on the Tracks* is raw and authentic, plunging readers into the fascinating world of tough railroad cop Special Agent Sydney Rose Parnell and her Malinois sidekick, Clyde. Haunted by her military service in Iraq, Sydney Rose is brought in by the Denver Major Crimes Unit to help solve a particularly brutal murder, leading her into a snake pit of hate and betrayal. Meticulously plotted and intelligently written, *Blood on the Tracks* is a superb debut novel."

—M. L. Rowland, author of the Search and Rescue Mystery novels

AMBUSH

ALSO BY
BARBARA NICKLESS

Blood on the Tracks
Dead Stop

AMBUSH

BARBARA NICKLESS

THOMAS & MERCER

Text copyright © 2019 by Barbara Nickless
All rights reserved.

No part of this book may be reproduced, or stored in a retrieval system, or transmitted in any form or by any means, electronic, mechanical, photocopying, recording, or otherwise, without express written permission of the publisher.

Published by Thomas & Mercer, Seattle

www.apub.com

Amazon, the Amazon logo, and Thomas & Mercer are trademarks of Amazon.com, Inc., or its affiliates.

ISBN-13: 9781503901513
ISBN-10: 1503901513

Cover design by Kirk DouPonce, DogEared Design

Printed in the United States of America

For my father, Kirby Chase Stafford, who stood watch long ago.

And for Ronald Cree.
You are gone much too soon, my friend.

On Watch

The call came late on an August evening while Jeremy Kane was upstairs, rocking his infant daughter.

When the phone buzzed, Kane shifted Megan in his arms and pulled his cell from his pocket. An out-of-state number he'd never seen. He pressed a button and silenced the call.

Megan's breath hitched as if she would fuss, and Kane rubbed her back. She swallowed her cry and nestled into his shoulder, her tiny hand a petal against his throat.

His bum leg ached. Closing his eyes, he shifted his weight. He inhaled the baby's clean, sweet scent and listened to his older daughter singing softly in the next room.

At moments like these, the war and its aftershocks seemed very far away.

Still, Kane knew there were some things you couldn't fix. No matter how much help you had. No matter what interventions people ran on your behalf. No matter how hard you tried.

Some things stayed broken. A bum leg. A bad memory.

But he believed in work-arounds. If you had the sense God gave a goat, you learned to trim back, cut down, reroute. You accepted that no plan came with guarantees, and when life blocked one lane, you found another.

He had his family. He mostly had his health. And he had a good job as a security officer for Denver's Regional Transportation District—the RTD. The gig wasn't the life he'd dreamed of before the war. It wasn't medical school. It wasn't a bright, sunny office and a steady stream of patients and a world that admired a man's intelligence and awarded him money and accolades for his dedication.

But there were compensations. Like these times with his girls.

The phone buzzed again. Same number.

A cold thread wriggled its way into Kane's thoughts. *Lester Crowe.*

For Crowe, the war was always *right there.* In his face or on his back. In his dreams, and always on his mind. When things got too dark, he would call Kane from someone's cell or use the phone in whatever dive bar he found himself in when the shakes hit.

Kane answered with a soft hello.

"Someone's been following me," Crowe said without preamble. "Trying to smoke my ass."

An icy fear knifed into Kane's neck, right at the base of his skull.

He kept his voice soft. "Hey, Crowe, you okay?"

"I was until some fancy suit started following me. Watching me eat my food and scratch my ass. Watching me every time I take a shit, I swear. Not safe anywhere. It's fucking Iraq all over again."

A week ago, Kane would have tried to talk Crowe down from whatever mental ledge his war buddy had crawled out on. But that was before Kane began digging into the past. Before he learned just how wrong things had gone in Iraq. And how it had spilled out over here.

Maybe someone had noticed his online research. The drive-bys and photos. Maybe he'd endangered his entire fireteam.

"Crowe—"

Megan woke with a mewling cry. Kane stood and jounced her in his arm. He walked to the window, taking a sentry's position above the quiet street. "What are you talking about?"

"Some nutso shit, man."

Kane caught the rumble of a truck through the line. A horn honked. Then Crowe said, "It's like we're the heroes in a fucked-up movie. And Iraq is the monster that won't stay dead."

"Where are you? I'll come and get you. Doesn't matter where you are."

"I'm calling from a pay phone. Only way that's secure. An hour from now I'll be in another state. You hang with your family, take care of your own. Stay on watch and be careful. These guys are serious trouble. They're probably listening in right now."

Kane did not want to go down the path his friend had taken. "Crowe, c'mon. You been smoking something?"

"I'm telling you. It's Iraq, back with a mouthful of teeth. We should never have done what we did. It was wrong, man. It was so wrong."

Kane swallowed down the panic and reminded himself this was, after all, Crowe. Unstable in the best of times. Crowe had gone radio silent right after he returned to the States. And a man didn't disappear from his Marine brethren unless there was something very wrong with what was bouncing around between his ears.

But still.

Kane considered what he'd learned this last week. Covert deals, illegal weapons, faked reports. There were enough pieces missing that he couldn't yet make out the overall image. But what he could see made him think that what Crowe had going on was less PTSD than self-preservation.

"You been to see anyone, Crowe? You know, just to talk. You sound—"

"Paranoid?" Crowe snorted. "Don't give me that bullshit. These dudes will hand everyone on our team their asses and make us thank

3

them for the pleasure. It's something to do with that Iraqi kid whose mom got killed. He's in the middle of this clusterfuck."

This was a sucker punch. *"Malik?"*

"He saw something over there. Those weapons. Remember that?"

The panic clawed free and tried to pull Kane down. Megan began to fuss. He walked her back and forth across the room, struggling to pull up an image of the small boy who'd been adopted by the Marines after his mother's murder. "You think they're after you because of—"

He stopped himself, abruptly aware that if Crowe's fear was grounded in reality, someone really might be listening.

"Because of that?" he finished weakly.

"Only thing I can think of. Look, I gotta go. Stay on watch, brother. Remember what we used to say? Just 'cause you're paranoid don't mean they're not out to get you."

Crowe disconnected.

Kane's thoughts flew in a hundred different directions. No question, Crowe was crazy. He saw things no one else did. He babbled on about conspiracy theories and space aliens. He'd never learned to rest his head anywhere for more than a night or two.

Then again, given what Kane had learned, maybe right now Lester Crowe was the sanest man on the team.

A sound at the bedroom door made Kane spin around, one hand gripping Megan, the other reaching for a nonexistent gun.

His four-year-old daughter, Haley, stared up at him, eyes wide. "Daddy?"

Heart racing, Kane sucked in air and forced his hand back to his side.

"You should be in bed, Haley." His voice came out all wrong. Sharp and angry.

Both Megan and Haley began to cry.

An hour later, after Kane had gotten both girls to bed, he stood at the front window and watched until his wife pulled up in their ancient

Toyota. He waited until she was safely inside, the garage door down, the doors and windows locked. He listened to her complain about his sudden moodiness while she got ready for bed, then waited some more, until her soft breathing told him she was asleep.

Then he got out the handgun he'd hidden from her and stood watch through the night.

Crowe might be crazy, but Kane knew better than most that sometimes the monsters were real.

◆ ◆ ◆

For the next few days, Kane tried to call Tucks and Sarge, the other members of his fireteam. Neither picked up. Both men went in and out of Kane's life like it had a revolving door. So he left messages. *I might have screwed up. Watch your back.* He installed an alarm system over Sherri's protests that they couldn't afford it and insisted Sherri and the girls stay at her parents' house while he was at work.

"What's wrong?" Sherri asked as he stuffed books, bathing suits, and pool toys into Haley's Shopkins backpack. "Why are you acting like this?"

What could he say? That something—he didn't know what exactly—had happened in Iraq, and he had been looking into it. Just a little local recon during his free time, and the details he had uncovered so far indicated . . . what? Shadows, really. Whispers in the dark.

Just 'cause you're paranoid don't mean they're not out to get you. This was true, but the fact was there had been no mysterious visitors, no cars lurking at corners, no one tailing him. He was starting to think that maybe Crowe *was* crazy and that maybe some of that had rubbed off on him.

He dropped all his attempts to look into what had happened in Iraq and made every effort to prove to anyone watching that he was only a simple husband, father, and wage earner.

A week later, after dropping off his family with Sherri's parents, he bounded into Denver's Union Station, tugging on the damp uniform shirt clinging to his back in August's electric-blanket heat.

Saturday night at Union Station was Kane's favorite shift. Tonight he took in his surroundings with his usual all-in stare of a combat vet who had done more patrols than a bear had hair on its ass. He watched the swirling, restless throngs of people—window-shoppers, travelers, drinkers, gourmands, loiterers, and likely pickpockets. He studied the stores and kiosks, the nooks and corners, the doorways and high, wide windows. He inhaled the scents of hamburgers frying and coffee brewing, noted the overstuffed waste cans and the crumpled trash tossed beneath benches, and cocked an ear for the whoosh of trains and the hum of passengers disembarking outside.

He scanned for abandoned backpacks, wet paper bags, wires, and pipes, and for any man or woman who sweated and shook and refused to meet his gaze.

During Kane's first month on the job, the RTD had received twenty-two bomb threats, thirty-three call-ins for suspicious packages, two alleged suicide bombers who promised death and destruction, and one real bomb placed under a light-rail platform near the football stadium, a bomb that had been quickly detected and quietly disposed of.

The public knew nothing about it.

Kane had found the bomb—a pressure cooker filled with nails, ball bearings, and black powder with an estimated fifteen hundred–foot blast radius. After that, he understood that if the short-term memory issues caused by a head injury in Iraq meant he couldn't be a doctor, he could be a shepherd—not a fair trade, but a good one. His prize was the safety of the people—their innocence something to both envy and protect. Maybe finding and removing a terrorist or a bomb was not so very different from rooting out a virus before it could harm an otherwise healthy patient.

Kane swiped away the beads of sweat on his forehead and nodded at Mills, another security officer, who was headed in the opposite direction.

"It's a sauna," Mills said. "Ninety-four degrees at effing 1800 hours."

Kane grinned and leaned in as they passed. "Try Iraq, you pussy. A hundred and twenty in the shade."

Mills laughed and moved on.

Kane spun on his heel and headed toward the hallway leading to the north end of the station. Some part of his brain registered himself in this space—the pain in his leg from years-old shrapnel, the trickle of sweat between his shoulder blades, the weight of his utility belt, and the faint burn in his right deltoid where he'd tweaked it lifting weights.

But most of his attention stayed on his surroundings.

A scrawny teenager with a backpack and beanie studied a bus map. An elderly couple came out of the Tattered Cover Book Store, the woman's arm laced through her husband's, his free hand clutching a bag of books. Nearby, two twenty-somethings sat at a table in the bar, their heads tipped back as they laughed. A line cook slipped outside with a pack of cigarettes.

My people, Kane thought. *Mine to protect and defend.*

He turned away from the octogenarians making their unhurried way across the floor. His right hand skimmed the butt of his gun as his gaze sought the far corners. The National Terrorism Advisory System was comfortably quiet tonight. Nothing had appeared in the bulletins he'd scanned before his shift. His friend in the Department of Homeland Security hadn't heard so much as a whisper of trouble.

Kane returned to the center of the building and pushed out through the west-side doors beneath the red neon TERMINAL sign. He walked out onto the platform, where six sets of recessed train tracks stretched under banks of silvery-cool LED lights.

Most of the people standing on the platform were waiting for the local commuter trains to take them to clubs or shows. The

Saturday-night revelers wore hipster clothes or urban chic or God knew what else, most of them scrolling on their phones or taking selfies. A group of white suburban teenage boys in Thrasher hoodies and Vans high-tops hung out on the south end of the platform. They loped back and forth, sometimes goading each other into dropping to the ground and knocking out twenty push-ups before springing back to their feet with the lightness of gazelles. They reminded Kane of his own privileged upbringing before the war rewired his thinking about self-worth and what one human being owes another.

A mechanized voice announced that the next train was due in seven minutes. Kane looked north along the platform, the overhead lights throwing the tracks into high relief and casting shadows between the support columns. He narrowed his eyes. Maybe twenty yards farther down, a pile of what looked like brown rags twitched against one of the columns. Kane shoved away his immediate, war-honed reaction that a pile of unidentifiable anything meant an IED and pushed through the crowd toward what he was sure would turn out to be a transient, hunkering down for the night. Denver had its share of the homeless, and Union Station was a magnet for many of them—a place to panhandle, to find shelter, to clean up in the public bathrooms, and maybe to score a half-eaten sandwich from one of the trash bins. On bad days, it seemed like half of Kane's shift was spent rousting vagrants. He hated that part of the job—sending the most desperate people away from a place where they might find something to ease their lives.

Sure enough, as he approached, he caught the stench of days'-old sweat, and then the stinking bundle of rags morphed into a man curled beneath a weight of blankets—a full-on crazy move in the heat. Kane could make out a knot of frizzy dreads at one end of the pile and, at the other, shoeless feet so encrusted with dirt that the white skin looked gray. The rest of the man was invisible.

"Hey, man," Kane said. "You can't hang here."

The rags stirred. A head shot out, and one bleary eye opened.

"Go 'way." The eye closed.

"Come on, man," Kane said. "Get moving. Don't make me write you up."

More mumbling. The blankets shook as the man hauled himself to his knees, swayed for a moment, then bounced onto his feet with surprising agility, tossing off the blankets. He was compact and wiry, his shoulders bunched, his forearms muscular in a way you didn't often see in a vagrant. Kane's hand went to his gun before his mind followed, and he forced his fingers toward the pepper spray instead; the spray was a particularly potent blend intended to be his first line of defense.

"Officer Kane," the man said in a slurred voice.

He startled, then realized the man was staring at his name tape above his uniform pocket. Kane frowned. "You got some ID?"

The bum shook his head and spat. "Stinking pig," he said. "You all should die."

Something coiled in Kane's gut that was neither fear nor rage. It was more like the disembodied feeling he used to get heading out on patrol, when sometimes trash was just trash and sometimes it was a bomb, and you never knew which card fate would deal that day.

"You've got to move along," he said.

The man turned away and began to gather his belongings, muttering words to the effect that Kane was a son of a bitch and a mother-effing pig.

Kane let it slide.

He backed away a few steps and took his eyes off the guy to make a quick scan. A few people were standing nearby, busy with their phones or their friends. But most had seen the bum and moved farther down the platform. He swept his gaze along the far side of the tracks and stiffened. Standing directly across the tracks was a woman in black slacks and a plain white blouse. Her face was unmade, her haircut simple, her expression flat.

Her eyes met his.

What the hell was *she* doing here?

Certainty rang through his mind like the lid closing on a coffin. They knew. Somehow, they knew.

Which meant he was a dead man. Still breathing for the moment. But dead, for all that.

"Asshole," the vagrant muttered, still rattling through his things. A pot clanged on the cement. "Where'm I supposed to go?"

"Hey, it's okay," Kane said to the vagrant, not breaking his gaze on the woman. "I'll give you directions to a shelter."

The pot clanged again, and the vagrant said, clear as a bell, "Jeremiah Kane."

Kane whirled around.

He was suddenly sure what hand he'd been dealt.

The bum was already leaping for him. A knife flashed in the man's hand—Kane caught the glint of steel in the overhead lights. With his left arm, he reached out fast to knock his attacker's hand aside, stepping into the motion with all his weight to make sure the knife went wide. His right hand scrabbled for his gun. But the man moved even faster. He grabbed Kane's arm with his free hand and thrust with the knife, an underhand jab.

Pain exploded through Kane's body as all four inches of steel slid through the gap below his vest and into his stomach. The knife went in cold and hard and without so much as a whisper.

The man jerked it free and jumped back. Kane's blood poured out hot.

From somewhere, as if in another county, a woman screamed.

The man advanced again, swinging the knife in a low arc. Kane scrabbled away, clawing for his gun. He willed his legs to stand firm, his body to stay upright. But the body is a weak thing. The man caught him as his knees buckled. The knife went into his hip. Kane cried out.

"I got a little secret for you," the man whispered in his ear, his voice soft and close, as if it belonged to a lover. "It was us, the Americans, who did it. We killed Resenko. We killed the woman. We'll find the boy."

For a moment, the man held him, the two of them caught in a bizarre waltz, gliding toward the tracks, the train closing in, its brakes grinding, almost *right there*.

The train operator stood on the horn. The woman screamed again.

The man gave a little shove, and Kane dropped over the edge onto the tracks, the train ten seconds out. The headlamps flared over him. Brakes shrieked.

Kane's last thought was that the monster was very much alive.

It was the hero who wasn't coming back.

MEXICO CITY
THE SAME DAY

CHAPTER 1

Harder to find than the man who hides himself is the man who is truly lost.

—*David Fuller. The Hope Project.*

I arrived in Mexico City at 2:00 p.m. on a blazing August day with a toothbrush and a change of clothes—a lowly railroad cop and former Marine searching for a lost child.

By early evening I'd picked up a tail. A wiry man with tattoos and a chain-smoking habit had taken up residence on the roof across the alley from my hotel. In addition to an apparently endless supply of cigarettes, he'd brought a nylon folding chair, binoculars, a flask, a penlight, and a tattered copy of *Love in the Time of Cholera*, which he traded for the binoculars every time I twitched a muscle.

Just what I liked. An educated spy. Or pervert. Or whatever.

I'd noticed him earlier, in line behind me at the airport's taxi kiosk. He'd been smoking Marlboros and standing too close, the Gabriel García Márquez novel stuffed into the pocket of his carry-on. When I finished buying a ticket, he'd thrust out his tongue in a lewd gesture as I walked away. In return, I'd shot him the finger behind my back.

Now here he was.

Call it a draw.

I stood near the window, just far enough back in the shadows that he had to strain to see me. In the alley two floors below, a man careened from one side of the lane to the other like a billiard ball, his voice raised in a slurred melody of love.

"Encontraré a mi amor esta noche," he sang. *"Y la tomaré en mis brazos."*

I smiled. Good luck with that, my drunken friend.

Odors wafted in—rotting garbage, the acrid bite of pollution, roasting meat from a nearby taco stand, and the stink of the spy's cigarettes that made me wish I hadn't sworn off tobacco. Close by, horns blared, traffic droned, and sirens wailed. Even closer, someone yelled, and someone else laughed. Metal grinders whirred, and a hammer rang against steel—in *la ciudad de México,* people not only drove on the streets, they used them as open-air body shops.

Welcome to one of the largest metropolitan areas in the western hemisphere.

A rush of longing filled me for my own city of Denver. For my man, Cohen, and my Belgian Malinois partner, Clyde. What the hell was I doing here, almost two thousand miles away from all that I loved, searching for a needle in a haystack?

Because you love Malik, too, whispered a voice in my head. *The orphan you promised to care for.*

I bounced on the balls of my feet. Across the alleyway, the man on the rooftop raised his binoculars.

His presence forced me to rethink how I'd work my time here. Only three people knew I hadn't come to Mexico to soak up some culture and tequila.

The first was David Fuller. David ran the Hope Project, a nonprofit that helped Iraqis displaced by war. He had given me the tip that brought me here and was one of the most sincere people I knew.

The second was Angelo Garcia, a local postal clerk. Angelo volunteered for the Hope Project and was one of a handful of contacts Fuller trusted enough to enlist in the search for Malik. A week ago, Angelo had spotted a boy matching Malik's description in a local mosque. He'd notified Fuller, who passed the information along to me. A friend in the FBI's Denver field office informed me that Angelo was thirty-two years old, no criminal history, married with two young children. His only apparent vice was that he sometimes slipped out early from work to take his kids to a Cruz Azul soccer match.

As a potential risk, Angelo pinged my radar in the slim-to-none category. Plus, he had no reason to put a tail on me. He knew exactly where I was because he'd arranged the hotel.

The third person who knew I was here was Detective Mike Cohen of the Denver PD. While I trusted Fuller and even Angelo with my life, I trusted Cohen with far more.

So maybe the guy was a random thief or kidnapper who had spotted me at the airport and pigeonholed me as an easy mark. Or he was a Mexican Peeping Tom who parked himself on the roof every night in the hope of getting lucky, voyeuristically speaking. Which would make our presence together in this corner of the universe mere coincidence.

I didn't believe in coincidence.

There was a third option, one that made me feel like a bug under a magnifying lens on a sunny day.

Three years earlier, something terrible had happened in Iraq. Something outside even the so-called normal atrocities of war. I hadn't figured out the details. But whatever went down, it had resulted in the murder of Malik's mother—an interpreter for the Marines—and the deaths of several Americans. Now an unknown someone was working a cleanup operation to erase the past. I dubbed this person the Alpha. The Alpha was a man without a name or a face—a bogeyman I could not find or label. I didn't know who he was, what he looked like, or where his loyalties lay.

I knew only two things. That he would kill to keep the world from learning the truth. And that he believed I had something he wanted.

I didn't. But this confusion, near as I could tell, was the only reason I still had a pulse.

So maybe the man on the roof meant that someone on the Alpha's team—or the Alpha himself—had figured out that a war was on, and I'd fired the first volley by coming to Mexico to look for Malik. The Alpha had been after the boy for a long time—Malik was part of what needed to be buried.

Now it was a race to the finish line.

I tugged on the cord to the window blinds, but the broken slats refused to unfurl. I stepped backward into the arms of a dusk fading into night and resisted the desire to turn on the lamp. Shadows stretched and lengthened across my room like athletes warming up for a game. Across the alley, Rooftop Thomas's cigarette flared, and I cursed the desk clerk who'd told me in broken English that there were no rooms available on the first floor. The first floor meant an easier escape, if it came to that.

Just because you were paranoid didn't mean they weren't out to get you.

I considered my options as a single woman alone in a foreign country without a pistol or my K9 partner. I could change hotels, but if Rooftop Thomas worked for the Alpha, he would follow me anywhere I could afford. I could call the police, but according to everything I'd heard, they'd probably join my admirer on the roof. Or I could go on the rooftop myself and confront him.

Tempting. But I suspected he had a gun in his backpack. And I doubted he was alone.

The best option seemed to be to stay up all night, then have Angelo get me somewhere safe tomorrow.

Semper Gumby. Marine-speak for *always flexible*.

The good news was that if they intended to hurt me, they wouldn't have set up a tail. They'd have snatched me at the airport by using a fake cab, or grabbed me during my earlier detour to the crime-infested barrio of Tepito. If it was the Alpha, I figured he was just drawing a line in the sand, letting me know he was onto me.

Across the alleyway, Rooftop Thomas flicked on the penlight and turned a page in Márquez's epic.

I was beginning to regret my decision to stay in what was probably the cheapest hotel in the city—cheapest where a white girl would be safe, anyway. I was here courtesy of Angelo's generosity—the hotel was owned by the sister of a friend of his second cousin, or some such relation.

You'll be safest around my family, he'd told me.

Plus, another friend of mine lived in the area. Jesús López, a Mexican Marine I could call on if things got dicey.

But my room on the second floor of the Hotel Fiesta was about as cheery and welcoming as a roach motel. Which might explain the roaches. A hard, narrow bed. An equally hard concrete floor. The porcelain sink in the bathroom was cracked, and the toilet leaked at the base. A broken ceiling fan left the room in a stifling heat that raised a sheen of sweat on my skin. The slit of a window looked across an alleyway to a two-story building that hosted not just Rooftop Thomas but also a tattoo parlor that looked like it hadn't seen a paying client since the time of Pancho Villa.

The Hotel Fiesta was some party.

But the toilet flushed if you jiggled the handle, a tired stream of cold water came from the faucet, the cockroaches mostly left me alone, and the immense spider tucked behind the single chair was doing a good job of taking care of any insects smaller than a pigeon.

Count your blessings.

I reached in my duffel for the stun gun I'd bought an hour ago during a detour between the airport and the hotel and placed it on the bed. Bringing a weapon into Mexico was illegal, so I'd gone straight from Terminal 1 to the Tepito market, escorted by a man who looked like he could arm-wrestle Satan and then spit in his eye for good measure.

Jesús López was *infantería*, a former Mexican Marine I'd first vetted then chatted with over Skype before I left the States. I'd told him I was in need of a few days of sun and fun, but the prospect of being unarmed made my reptilian brain itch.

No hay problema, he'd said. *In Tepito, you can buy anything. Just as long as you leave your dignity at the door.*

No hay problema, I'd answered. Dignity wasn't one of my stronger points.

Jesús had met me outside the barrio, then stayed by my side as we small-talked our way through the so-called 'fierce neighborhood,' edging past gang members and drug dealers and God knew what else until we reached a man who sold items *que se cayeron del camión*—things that fell off the truck. *Give him your money,* Jesús said, *and don't ask questions.*

For two thousand pesos, the dealer had sold me a "conducted energy weapon," then asked if I wanted to throw in an assault rifle—a *cuerno de chivo*—for forty thousand more. I'd told him I wanted to defend myself, not start a war.

I hoped I wouldn't regret that decision.

Restless, and now leery of taking a neighborhood run, I removed the travel pouch hanging around my neck, set it on the bed next to the gun, and dropped to the floor. I did fifty push-ups, better than my Marine days, then started on the crunches. I'd been working hard to heal from the injuries I'd suffered earlier that summer during a hunt for a killer. While my VA counselor focused on my war-related PTSD, I zeroed in on the physical—strength building with weights, bands, and my own body weight. It also included as much cardiovascular as I could handle.

Throw in the fact that I was still off the drugs, mostly off the cigarettes, and down to a drink or two a day, and that added up to progress, at least in my book.

I rolled onto my stomach and held my body rigid in a plank. Then side planks. Followed by more crunches.

Finally, I stood and used a towel to wipe the sweat from my neck and face, then sat on the bed out of Rooftop Thomas's eyeshot and picked up the travel pouch. Inside were my passport, my phone, a credit card, and some cash. And two pictures I pulled free.

The first was a photograph of Malik, the child I'd left behind in Habbaniyah. He'd come home late from a soccer game and found his mother murdered. Possibly the assassins had meant to kill Malik, too, and only a game delay saved his life. He'd been taken in by the Marines after Haifa's death.

And then he'd disappeared.

The picture was spiderwebbed with creases and worn to the softness of velvet from my daily obsessive handling of it. It showed Malik standing on our forward operating base, grinning and holding aloft a soccer ball that one of the Marines had given him. He was forever eight years old in this photo, with a shock of black hair and an expression of open innocence that made my heart ache. Only the ugly scar on his arm—a memento from the night's chaotic aftermath—and a faint panic in his eyes suggested he'd had anything other than a normal childhood.

The second picture was a sketch created by a woman who specialized in age-progression drawings, which are used to determine what a kidnapped or runaway child might look like months or years later. She had progressed Malik by three years. This Malik was taller, but still lanky and still with the dark shock of hair. But the artist had also flattened his cheeks and nose, enlarged his ears, and added a layer of baby fat that blurred his features. When I'd protested, she'd shrugged.

"Eleven is not the most attractive age in humans," she'd explained. "We're gawky and awkward. In another year or two, he'll lose the fat and grow into his features. He'll be quite handsome then, if I'm any judge."

I held the pictures next to each other, comparing them. In addition to the facial changes, the artist had done a beautiful job of translating the younger Malik's bewilderment into the older boy's anguish.

Whatever nastiness had gone down in Iraq and was now spilling over in the US, Malik was somehow the key to unlocking that door and fumigating whatever horrors lay beyond. He had something. Or he knew something. I wanted those answers. But more than that, I wanted to find him, extricate him from whatever trap had ensnared him, and wipe away the misery in his eyes. If that was even possible.

The world is very good at hurting the youngest and least culpable among us. For that, we all bear some responsibility. And an obligation to try and fix it.

"I'm here, buddy," I said aloud. In the corner, the spider froze. "Mexico City, same as you. Now how do I find you?"

Only 573 square miles, twenty million souls, and one eleven-year-old Iraqi boy who looked pretty much like any eleven-year-old Mexican boy. No job too tough.

Tires squealed at the end of the alleyway. I tucked Malik's photos back in the pouch and returned to the window. A black SUV rocketed down the cracked pavement, back tires skidding, trash cans clattering in its wake. I flicked my gaze to the rooftop. Thomas was heading toward the stairs, his chair slung over his back. Two floors below, the Mercedes-Benz SUV slowed as it neared the hotel. A door opened, a man tumbled out on the pavement, then the door slammed shut and the SUV roared down the alley to the street, where its brake lights flashed before it bounced and skidded into traffic. Very faintly came the sound of rubber squealing. Was the vehicle peeling out or slamming on the brakes?

I filed away the question and craned my neck to see who'd been dumped by—I presumed—one of the cartels that operated in the city. I could make out just enough to tell that it was a man. He lay crumpled on his side, facing the hotel, not moving. Light from the lobby spilled across a face that looked like it had been rammed against a propeller.

I jerked back from the window. Even with the damage, I knew him. Angelo Garcia. The man I'd come to see.

At a faint creak in the hallway, I whirled to face the door, ears straining. There was only silence. I forced aside my horror and considered my next move. Was dumping Angelo a warning? Or an attempt to flush me from the meager safety of my room?

As if on cue, the ghostly figure of Private First Class Hart, the first Marine I'd processed in Mortuary Affairs when I was in Iraq, appeared in the room, materializing from wherever the dead hang out when they're not following me.

Not a dead man, my counselor would say. Not a ghost.

A manifestation of my fear.

Reflexively, my hand reached for Clyde's comforting presence, but my fingers closed on emptiness. Clyde was safe in Denver, probably enjoying filet mignon with Cohen.

PFC Hart tilted his head toward the window, then the door.

Right. *Get the hell out of here, while you can still do so on your own terms.*

I loaded a cartridge into the stun gun. The logo on the barrel said TASER, and although I figured the gun was a knockoff, it appeared to be in good working order. I'd only been able to get four cartridges from the dealer. I needed to make them count.

I slid the gun into the pocket of my cargo pants, slung my duffel over my shoulder, and made sure my travel pouch was secure inside my shirt. I wished desperately for Clyde, who would be able to warn me what, if anything, waited on the other side of the door.

I wasted a moment considering the fire escape before deciding a ladder hanging off the side of a building was unacceptable exposure. I had no idea where Rooftop Thomas had gone.

Then I eyeballed the phone on the nightstand. I could call the police. I'd be gone long before they arrived, but their presence might serve as a diversion for whoever was after me.

On the other hand, if things went south, I didn't want to be involved in any way with the Mexican *federales*.

I gripped my duffel. This was one of those moments I'd experienced often in war. That cliff-edge second a pilot must feel just before takeoff when something doesn't feel quite right, and you have to commit or pull back.

Whatever. Not making a decision was worse than making the wrong decision.

I peered through the peephole. Darkness. Someone had unscrewed the bulbs. They'd been burning at forty-watt glory when I arrived. I drew in a breath. No stench of Marlboros seeped through the door, so it wasn't Rooftop Thomas. Probably someone bigger. Heavier. With good lungs.

I listened for the sound of a man—it would be a man—in the hallway outside, but heard only the people down below, spilling into the alley, chattering with alarm. I dropped my bag, pulled the gun, and pressed my back against the wall to the right of the door before reaching over to ease off the chain—the only well-constructed item in this hotel—and turn the knob. I cracked the door ajar an inch and waited.

The door burst open as whoever was waiting on the other side barreled their way in. A man, tall and wide, coming in too hard and too fast; he'd been expecting me to be in his path and must have planned to use his momentum to knock me flat.

His bad.

I hit him with twenty thousand volts, holding the gun in place for the minimum five seconds required to truly incapacitate him. I followed him down as his back arced, muscles spasming, and a long, low moan escaped him. I kicked the door closed, rehung the chain, then a part of me that I resented made me bend and take his pulse. Stun guns weren't meant to kill, but if you had a weak heart, getting smacked with voltage was a very bad thing.

He was still breathing. I wasn't sure how I felt about that.

I dropped another cartridge into the gun and studied him—white, midthirties, built like a beast—then searched his pockets while he twitched and drooled. Empty. A guy with a lot of confidence in his hands and a lack of appreciation for women.

I yanked the cord free from the blinds and trussed him, then glanced toward the spider perched in the middle of its web.

"He's all yours," I said.

I grabbed my duffel, eased over the twitching man, then pulled the chain and stepped aside. I counted to sixty before I cracked open the door and peered up and down the hallway. No one except PFC Hart, who stood motionless in the hallway, a man of haunting luminescence. He nodded his approval and went ahead of me down the stairs.

At the bottom, I turned right to avoid the lobby and race-walked down a corridor toward the emergency door I'd scoped out earlier, guessing that the sign warning of an alarm was only there for show. Sure enough, the door yielded with nothing more ominous than a creak of hinges.

It opened onto a narrow lane that dead-ended thirty feet to my right. On my left, it formed a T intersection with the alley where the bastards had dumped Angelo.

I retreated back into the hallway and yanked out my cell phone.

"Were you telling the truth?" I asked when Jesús López picked up. "Are you really at a bar two blocks from my hotel?"

Jesús laughed. *"Aún más cerca. Solo una cuadra."* In English he said, "I am one block away. Pretty *señorita* like you buys a gun, I figure she might need me. A man has his dreams."

"I do need you. But it's dangerous."

"Ah, *señorita*, you make me blush. Whips and chains?"

"Bullets and blades. You up for it?"

"Am I not a Marine?"

I told him what I needed. He assured me it was no problem. *"Cinco minutos."*

I counted to sixty again, then went through the door and turned left. At the intersection, I pressed flat against the hotel wall. I drew a breath and peered around the corner.

Angelo lay near a side entrance to the hotel. The people who had surrounded him only a moment earlier had retreated back into the lobby. Afraid of being found near the body, probably. By the police or by the cartels, whichever they figured was responsible. Always a guess in Mexico.

By now, three minutes had elapsed since my call to Jesús. I wanted more than anything to run to Angelo. To take his pulse and—if he still breathed—to offer care and learn what had happened. But if I walked into the alley, the bad guys would have the perfect opportunity to pop me. There would be thirty witnesses to my death, and not one of them would be able to say what had happened.

Chances were, Angelo was already dead. By now, he'd been in the alley a good ten minutes. Better to wait for Jesús.

Then Angelo groaned. A gut-wrenching moan of the kind you would expect from a man whose face had been used as a whetting stone.

And still no sign of Jesús.

I bent my head, a form of surrender. Sometimes you have to trust the universe.

With another quick glance around, I ran to Angelo and dropped beside him. Light from the lobby revealed a face that would never be as it had been—even if he survived. Iraq reached out its claws, and for a moment I caught the heat and smell of the desert—sand and sewage and wind—and saw my lover's own broken body as it lay on a gurney.

"Stay here," I told myself, and pushed away the memory.

I gripped Angelo's shoulder. "Angelo!"

He didn't stir. His left arm was stretched out in the filth of the alley, his palm turned up toward the smog-smeared night. Three of his fingers were gone, the wounds cauterized. Gently, my own hand now bloody, I picked up his arm and laid it across his chest. I took his pulse—thready and weak.

I glanced over my shoulder at the hotel lobby, at the faces pressed to the glass.

"*¡Una ambulancia!*" I screamed. "*¡Llame a una ambulancia!*"

They stared at me as I mimed putting a phone to my ear.

"*Hazlo,*" I yelled. *Do it.*

A woman nodded and disappeared. I turned back to Angelo. From somewhere, a dog began to bark, a grating, repetitive sound.

"Angelo, it's Sydney. Stay with me, buddy."

A violent tremor ripped through his body. His remaining eye scraped open, and his gaze locked on my face.

"Go," he whispered, his voice clotted with blood. "Run."

"They're gone," I said, knowing the lie. "Help is on the way."

"They . . ." Angelo's right hand floated up, found my shirt, and gripped it. "They asked about the boy. About you."

"Who, Angelo? Give me names. Who did this to you?"

He loosed my shirt, and I caught his hand.

"They . . ." He coughed, and a fresh swell of blood leaked through his lips. "Dalton. They wanted to know . . . about him. I . . . know nothing. Why . . . do they ask?"

Dalton. It was a name I recognized. Richard Dalton was a CIA guy who'd been on our base in Iraq. The first I'd known about him was when he showed up in a photograph I found of Malik. The picture showed Malik, Dalton, and a third man—Max Udell, a.k.a. Sarge. All looking as happy together as bugs in a rug.

In another picture, Dalton had been standing with Doug Ayers—Dougie. The man I'd loved who was tortured and killed by terrorists. In the photo, Richard and Dougie had been wearing native dress. Working together, I presumed. Or at least on friendly terms.

Angelo's voice brought me back.

"I have heard . . . you cannot resist pain." His one eye, filled with pleading, found mine. "I am sorry."

I squeezed his uninjured fingers as if my hold was the only thing keeping him here, the string to a balloon caught in a windstorm. Grief and fury quaked through me. For Angelo. For his children, who wouldn't go with him to any more soccer games. And for the fact that my only link to Malik lay dying in a filthy back lane.

Urgency throbbed behind my eyes, pounding out a rhythm that warned me to flee. The space between my shoulder blades itched. I glanced up and down the alley, taking in windows and doorways. I looked at the shadowed places where no light reached. I listened for the sound of men approaching, but the night fell oddly quiet, as if the universe had drawn a breath. The dog had stopped barking. The sounds of traffic were a dull, faraway buzz. The people in the lobby were voiceless. No one spoke at all.

"Where's that ambulance!" I shouted into the silence. My voice echoed off the walls.

"La ambulancia está viniendo," said a woman in the hotel, her voice muffled through the glass. "It comes."

"Sydney." Angelo groaned.

"Stay with me, *mi querido amigo*," I said. "You're going to be all right."

His gaze drifted. He gaped at the night sky, his expression one of confusion. As if he wondered how a man who volunteered to find people now found himself in such a mess.

At the north end of the alley, men's voices rose, a few in anger, most in drunken enthusiasm. Jesús López's cavalry had arrived. A car horn blared, drowning out everything else. I waited for the flare of headlights, but then the horn fell silent, and a man shouted in English, "Move along! No cars here, no cars."

I knew that accent. As Boston as the Red Sox. It looked like my fears about the Alpha had been right.

"*¡Vete a la mierda!*" shouted a second man.

"*Y el burro en el que cabalgaste,*" cried a third.

A foul-mouthed cavalry. From the darkness on the alley's north end emerged a crowd of staggering, wheeling men who came at me with remarkable speed, given their apparent drunkenness. As they drew near, I counted eight men. Some of them sported Mexican eagle tattoos on their biceps, and several wore T-shirts with MARINA spelled out in white block letters.

The *infantería*.

I turned back to Angelo. His single eye was still open, but now it served only as a mirror to the night, flat and lifeless as an icy pond.

"Angelo!"

I touched my fingers to his neck—the weak pulse had vanished. I tilted his forehead back and lifted his chin, then pinched his nose closed and clamped my mouth over his, breathing into his lungs. Then again. When his chest didn't rise, I rose to my knees and began chest compressions. Thirty compressions, two breaths. Thirty compressions, two breaths.

Angelo remained motionless. Thirty compressions . . .

"Sydney!"

Jesús's voice penetrated the haze, and I became aware that he was crouched next to me. His men eddied around us, human shields. I checked Angelo's neck again for a pulse.

Nothing. I tilted his head back, breathed into his mouth. Tasted his blood.

Jesús placed his hand on my shoulder.

"We must go, Sydney."

I shrugged him off. Placed the heel of my hand on Angelo's breastbone.

"Now," Jesús said. "Your enemies won't wait much longer."

An approaching siren sounded, too late to offer Angelo anything more than transportation to a steel table and the coroner's scalpel. I rocked back on my heels and stared at his corpse, my eyes wide and painful in sockets as dry as old bones.

"He's gone," Jesús said. "Come. We must be gone as well."

At last I looked at him. "Where's your car?"

"The Americans blocked off both ends of the alley. We have had to improvise. And we cannot hold them off forever. Even the *infantería* know when to retreat. So come. I think you were right in saying this is dangerous."

I looked at him dully. "Come where?"

He rose and pulled me with him. "Follow me."

CHAPTER 2

Trust in God, but tether your camel well.

—Arabic saying.

We backed away from Angelo's body, then Jesús's phone lit up like a Christmas tree, and he stopped as suddenly as if he'd walked into a wall.

"Wait," he said, scrolling through a torrent of texts. Then, "Shit."

"We gotta keep moving, *sí?*" said one of his men, a guy with a jutting jaw and a body like a six-foot-five brick. "Get out of sight of the *norteamericanos.*"

"We lost plan A and now plan B." Jesús shook his head. "We got nowhere to go at the moment."

"I see doors," said the Brick. "I see windows."

"Won't work. They got guys everywhere." Jesús typed with furious speed, then jerked his chin toward me. "Make sure they can't get a sight on her."

Jesús's men closed ranks around me, and the bar stink of beer and cigarettes filled my nostrils. The men put me in mind, appropriately enough, of alley cats—scruffy and lean, tough in their jeans and T-shirts, their faces in fighting mode and their eyes signaling all systems go. The reek of testosterone could make a girl's eyes water.

But the men were no longer a merry band of revelers. They'd been silenced by Angelo's broken body. Death does that.

I looked past the shaved heads and bushy beards toward the blocky shapes of the SUVs guarding each end of the alley. The drivers had cut the headlights, but the faint hum of idling engines rumbled against the bricks. When I squinted, I could make out shadowy figures sitting in the cabs. Waiting, I presumed, for Jesús's men to get over their shock at the body and move on, leaving me alone with Angelo.

Years ago, in Iraq, Doug Ayers told me that after a hunter lays eyes on his target, his next move is to choke off all routes by which that target can flee. When the man in the hotel failed to do whatever it was he was supposed to do—kill or capture me—they'd set a trap by closing off the alley. They undoubtedly had another man inside the hotel by now, and God knew where else.

Guys everywhere, Jesús had said.

As soon as I was alone and out of the public eye, they'd spring their trap.

High overhead, the last shimmer of sun lit the tops of the buildings. Down here, the dark encroached in a relentless tide.

I swallowed my panic. "Jesús?"

He was hunched over the bright glow of his phone.

"Madre de Dios," he murmured. A glance at me. "Who the fuck are these people?"

I took the question as rhetorical and said nothing.

He kept texting. "When you called, I thought you had *un prob-lemita*. A little trouble. But this is a shit storm."

Twenty feet away, a fire escape dangled. "I'll go up and over."

"No."

"I'll move fast. You'll have my back."

"They've got men on the rooftops, too."

"Then they don't want me dead."

He glanced up at me, the lower half of his face blue white in the reflected radiance of his phone. "*Cierto*. They would have already put a round in your head. However, they may care less about my men."

To the south, the singsong wail of the ambulance had grown steadily louder. Now the siren shut off as the vehicle arrived at the mouth of the alley. Lights strobed against the deepening night, a rotating throb of red that pulsed like a heartbeat. I squinted, trying to see past the lights.

"They're blocking the ambulance," said the Brick.

"Once they let it pass," I said, "I'll slip inside while they're busy with Angelo."

"It's not an ambulance," Jesús said. "It's the *policía*. Your enemies have made themselves some very good friends. My source says those *pendejos* are moving into the area now, too."

The BIC Lighter panic I'd been trying to damp down now burst forth, an acetylene torch that shot flame up my spine. Around me, the men cursed. I couldn't tell if their anger was directed toward me or the police.

"I'll turn myself over," I said. "I'm an American. A cop. They won't hurt me."

Jesús barked a laugh. "Your badge means nothing here. No. We got this. First, you become one of us." He whipped off his black ball cap with its stitched anchor and carbines emblem and plunked it on my head. "*La chianga* instead of an American. Hide your hair." He shrugged out of his denim jacket and tossed it to me. "And your skin. Then voilà, *una chianga*."

I yanked on the jacket and stuffed my blonde braid beneath the cap. In the heat, sweat didn't so much trickle down my skin as materialize from every pore.

The Brick said, "What are they waiting for?"

"For us to move along and leave Sydney here like a *pollito* for slaughter." Jesús wiped sweat from his hairline. "We leave, and she is no more."

The Brick's jaw worked like he had a wad of chewing tobacco. "So what are *we* waiting for?"

"An open sesame from Ali Baba would be nice. But for now, just keep standing around with your dicks in your hands. And say your prayers."

"We wait much longer, we won't have any dicks," growled one of the other men.

"*Sí,*" said a third. "The *policía*, they'll spike our balls to the wall with a nail gun. And that'll just be the warm-up."

A man appeared at the hotel window, a radio to his mouth while he scanned the alley. I recognized the gorilla shoulders and the arrogance—it was the man I'd stunned. He had a bruise on his forehead from hitting the floor and an expression like he'd swallowed piss.

I needed to work on my knot-tying skills.

To the south, the SUV's headlights blazed to life. Ditto to the north. Tires rumbled against the rough pavement.

"We gotta go," the Brick said.

"I know." Jesús held his phone like it was a rosary.

"Jesús," I croaked. The word was both name and prayer.

"I *know!*" His phone buzzed with another text; he glanced at it, then pointed toward the tattoo shop. "Okay, drop your dicks and haul ass!"

Seconds later, we crowded into the tiny anteroom of the tattoo parlor I'd noticed earlier. One of the Marines closed and locked the door behind us. Doing so wasn't a simple act. He rammed home four separate dead bolts. When he finished with those, he dropped a heavy wooden bar across the door. The door itself looked like two inches of solid wood.

"The hell?" I asked Jesús.

"Safe house."

A woman stood behind an immense desk, guarding a hallway that led toward the back. She looked fiftyish, her thick black hair scraped into a ponytail, her drab blouse buttoned tight across ample cleavage, the cuffs shoved up above her dimpled elbows. A plain gold cross hung on a chain that all but disappeared in the fleshy creases of her neck.

"That everyone?" she asked in Spanish.

Jesús nodded. *"Sí."*

She tucked a plastic notebook under her arm and picked up an overstuffed messenger bag. "This way."

We moved after her, falling into pairs in the narrow hallway.

"I'd already left when I got your call," the woman said to Jesús. "Had to come back. But we got everyone out."

"Gracias, Señora Torres."

"Now, though, *hay policía* out back, along with more *americanos*. It's not good."

"That's why we—"

"I know." Torres shot me a glare over her shoulder. "She is worth it?"

"She is a Marine."

Pounding erupted behind us—someone hammering on the front door.

"Vámonos," said Torres. *Let's go.*

At the end of the hall, Torres made a sharp right down another hallway, then unlocked a door and waved us into a ten-by-fifteen room. A large, heavy desk—twin to the one up front—sat on a rug in the middle of the room. A quick glance around showed shelves stocked with water bottles, packets of food, flashlights, and sleeping bags. On the floor, cardboard boxes overflowed with clothes.

Not just a safe house. A way station. But from where to where? The trains the migrants hitched to ride north were miles from here.

From up front, the pounding grew harder. How long before they brought in a battering ram or an ax?

Torres closed and locked the door. Another series of bolts and a drop bar.

"Más rápido," she said.

Jesús and the Marines lifted the desk and set it against the door, then tossed aside the rug. Just visible in the wooden planks was the outline of a trapdoor. Jesús grabbed a crowbar from a shelf and pried at a corner until the door came loose. He and another Marine lifted it and set it aside. A whiff of cool earth wafted into the room. But underlying the sweet, loamy smell came a nauseating stench of sweat and urine and feces.

I recalled a news report I'd read, that some sections of the military were in the hands of the cartels. "Jesús?"

"Migrants, Sydney." His eyes met mine. "Not prisoners. Thirty minutes ago, we had five men and women in here. Headlamps are in that box to your right—pass them around. Señora Torres, you have a chain and padlock so you can bolt the trapdoor from the inside?"

"Sí."

The Brick gave a low whistle and jerked a thumb toward the front of the building.

"Listen," he whispered.

We froze. The pounding had stopped. In the ominous silence, the building groaned like an arthritic old man. Pipes ticked overhead, and somewhere water dripped.

There came a boom like thunder, and the entire building shuddered.

"They've blown the front door," said the Brick.

Jesús shoved me toward the trapdoor. "Go!"

More thunder rumbled, closer than the first.

"And the back," the Brick added.

I flicked on my headlamp, took a quick look down at a cramped tunnel, and, holding tight to my duffel, dropped through the opening. I landed in a pile of dirt.

Jesús dropped beside me. "Run!"

I stumbled forward a few steps and stopped. The tunnel disappeared into darkness. My headlamp picked out plywood walls, a trampled dirt floor, and a ceiling five inches above my head. The hair lifted on the back of my neck.

I don't do tunnels well, not since a month earlier when Clyde and I had been forced to walk through one I thought would collapse at any moment.

Jesús touched my shoulder. "Run, Sydney. You stay, maybe we all die."

I ran.

◆ ◆ ◆

The tunnel wound like a serpent, slithering forward, then partially doubling back on itself as it curled around an obstacle. Sometimes it sloped down before it leveled off and then, each time, climbed again. My headlamp caught scenes flickering past, like pages from a tragic flip-book.

A hollowed-out space with packed-down earth and a foul plastic bucket.

A doll of twigs and cloth, dropped on the path.

A pair of sneakers, shoelaces gone, the toes worn open.

A cross.

Behind me, the *infantería* came, silent save for the rustle of denim and the pumping of their lungs.

Seven minutes in, a third shuddering boom shook the tunnel. I lost my footing and pitched forward onto the ground. Jesús fell beside me. I closed my eyes and mouth, burying my face in the crook of my arm as dirt broke loose from the ceiling. Thick clouds of dust boiled around us.

Jesús's voice came ragged in my ear. "They've blown the door to the room. Now there's just the trapdoor."

From behind came harsh coughing.

"Christ," someone said. "How much explosive those guys using?"

"You okay?" Jesús asked me.

37

I raised my head. Blinked. The whites of Jesús's eyes stood out in the dirt and sweat on his face.

I found his cap and the headlamp where they had fallen. "Can they figure out where the tunnel emerges?"

"No." He shrugged. "Still, prayer might not hurt."

We hauled ourselves to our feet and kept running.

Another fifteen minutes, and the tunnel dead-ended. A ladder led up into the gloom. We clustered at the base, and Jesús pulled out his phone.

"Why haven't they blown the trapdoor?" someone asked.

"God is smiling on us," said the Brick.

Someone laughed. "You should be a comedian."

Jesús said, "The door above leads to La Merced. Miguel has been monitoring the police scanner. There's nothing about us and our girl. Carlos?"

"Here," answered the Brick.

"Once we're in the market, you and Juan stay with Señora Torres. Make sure she has no trouble getting home. Jorge and Eduardo, you come with me and Sydney. Miguel has a car waiting for us outside, near the *tianguis*. The rest of you, separate and start walking as soon as you reach open air. Browse. Act casual. Buy some flowers for your girlfriends so you have something in your hands. Text or call if you see anything, but don't take more than ten minutes before you hit a subway and disappear. As soon as they figure where this tunnel comes out, we're blown."

A fourth boom.

"Here they come," he said.

La Merced was Mexico City's largest traditional food market. Angelo and I had planned to meet there the next day for lunch. After Angelo suggested the place, I'd scoped it out on Google Maps. Located on the eastern edge of the city's central zone, the place stretched across several city blocks. For anyone in the business of transporting migrants, La Merced was the perfect place to hand them along; they would be invisible among the throngs of tourists and locals crowding the immense sprawl of buildings and stalls and *tianguis*—the illegal markets on the streets and sidewalks. Nearby subway lines offered multiple escape routes.

I followed Jesús up the ladder, then waited while he slid the door aside and peered out.

"All clear." He braced his hands and hoisted himself out of the tunnel, then turned back to haul me up. "Hurry, hurry."

We surfaced like panicked rabbits from a warren. The tunnel emerged in a medium-size enclosed stall almost entirely filled with wooden crates. When we were all out of the tunnel, Jesús and two of the Marines dropped the door back in place and shoved two large boxes over the opening. The cords on their necks and the muscles of their arms bulged, and I gave Jesús a quizzical look when he finished.

"Car-engine blocks," he said. His teeth were bright in his dirty face. "That will slow them down. They won't dare blow up the door while they're standing right under it."

A rolling metal service door covered the stall's entrance. The Brick—Carlos—eased the door up six inches, and Jesús took a mirror on a long handle and scoped the area outside.

"We're good."

I shoved my headlamp in a pocket of my utility pants, and Jesús adjusted the cap he'd given me. My braid had come loose, and I pushed it back under. I tugged the jacket closed; the stagnant air hugged like an unwelcome embrace.

"Ready?" he asked.

"Ready."

We emerged in an alley behind a row of chili merchants. The aromas of jalapeños and poblanos and serranos sizzled in the warm night air. Two of the Marines, Jorge and Eduardo, I presumed, took positions on either side of Jesús and me. The Brick took Señora Torres by the arm. But before she went with him, she turned to me and said in heavily accented English, "I hope Jesús is right. I hope you are worth it. That tunnel, we will never be able to use it again."

"I know. I'm sorry." I offered my hand. "Thank you for my life."

She took it and squeezed my fingers. "Your life is God's gift. Use it well."

As Jesús had ordered, we joined the throngs surging along the market's asphalt paths, filthy warriors in a dirty war, and scattered to the four winds.

CHAPTER 3

Here in America, we can mostly stay above the fray. War,
refugees, epidemics. Secret police, despots, assassinations. These
are vague terrors outside our borders. We pity the victims, but
we don't identify with them.

Then a child falls sick or we get a diagnosis of cancer. And
suddenly we are in the thick of it.

The story of the victim becomes our own.

—Sydney Parnell. Personal Journal.

The four of us reached the car, a beat-up Nissan sedan, in under ten minutes. The driver had pulled the sedan up tight against the curb near a cantina, on a side road lined with fruit stalls. I'd spotted two cops on our walk here, but they appeared to be taking only a mild interest in the people jostling around them. Maybe they hadn't gotten the word. Or maybe the Alpha had only managed to bribe a few members of the *policía*.

Jesús opened the back door, and the driver gestured for us to hurry. Jorge jumped in the front, and I followed Eduardo into the back seat. Jesús got in after me. We squeezed together in the close quarters.

The driver wrinkled his nose. "You guys been sweating a little, huh?"

"Fuck you," Eduardo said.

The driver laughed. "Still nothing on the scanner. I think we're in the clear."

Jesús gestured toward the front. "Sydney, meet our driver, Miguel. Miguel, Sydney."

Miguel reached a hand over the seat back, and we shook. "So you're the cause of all the trouble," he said.

"I'm afraid so." I glanced past Jesús out the passenger window. A man in pressed jeans and an oxford shirt had just emerged from between two rows of stalls and now paused outside the cantina, scanning the crowd. He was too well dressed for a tourist. And he carried a radio.

"Jesús," I said.

He followed my gaze. "Time to move."

"Roger that." Miguel turned the wheel and eased the car into the lane, tapping his horn at the shoppers spilling across the street. A few minutes later, he merged into traffic on the Avenida Circunvalación, heading north.

"A friend has arranged a room for you at a small hotel," Jesús said. "You'll be safe there. The hotel is located in a tourist area—lots of *güeritas* like you. You'll blend right in. At least"—his glance took in my face, my bloody, filthy clothing—"after you shower and get rid of those clothes."

I nodded my thanks.

As Miguel drove, he alternated his speed from slow to fast and back again, following a circuitous route that spiraled outward from the city center. He took a great many turns and sometimes circled back, while Jorge in the passenger seat kept an eye on the side mirror.

"I used to drive for a security company," Miguel said when our eyes met in the rearview mirror.

"Lucky for me," I said. "Jesús, I'm sorry about the tunnel."

"It happens. We shut it down, find another safe house, open it again in a year. It's part of the work we do."

"And what work is that, exactly?"

He gave me a wry smile. "Señora Torres and I are not traffickers. And we're not *polleros*, either—not coyotes. Some of the migrants crossing Mexico from Guatemala and Honduras, they need to cool their heels for a bit. They're waiting for family members, or they need money, or they're just too tired or terrified to go on. So we hide them. From the *policía* who would give them to the cartels, and from the cartels who would traffic them. Torres trains them and gives them work. Some learn to do the tattooing. Others sew or work day crews. Then, when the money comes or the spouse comes or they recover their courage, we get them moving north again. They have to keep going. They're running away from gangs or vendettas or abusive husbands. For them, to return home means death."

Headlights swam over us from a passing car and then fell away. "You're a good man to help them."

He looked out the window and shrugged. "It takes many hands. But there are never enough."

"Every soul counts," I offered, thinking of Malik.

"So now my turn. Who are these men chasing you? And why do they flex so much muscle?"

"I think they're trying to prove to me that this is too big. That I have no hope of winning. But, honestly, I don't know who they are. Not exactly." I glanced out at the passing city. Somewhere out there was one small boy. "I just know we're after the same thing."

"And what is that?"

I shook my head. "Forgive me, Jesús. After all your help, I owe you an explanation. But the story isn't mine to share."

"It's okay." He touched his heart. "We, all of us, carry others' stories. Maybe someday you can share, when this is over."

If it ever was.

Forty minutes later, satisfied we weren't being followed, Miguel pulled up to the curb in front of a weather-beaten motel with a miniscule lobby and ten rooms set along the long arm of an L. The entire street was lined with similar motels of the kind frequented by American and European teenagers taking a gap year before college—clean and safe but without any frills.

"I figured you'd want a quiet place and a clear view of the street," Jesús said. "One way in, one way out."

I nodded, pushing back a wave of fatigue that threatened to swamp me. "It's perfect."

"Wait here. I'll get the key."

When he returned, I made my farewells to the *infantería*, then Jesús and I walked together down the long arm of the L to Room 9. I unlocked the door, and we inspected the room. Nothing more threatening than another spider, this one in the bathroom.

Jesús turned to me. "I will be right outside if you need anything."

"Thank you, Jesús, but no. You've done enough. This is a good place, and we weren't followed. I'll be fine."

"You said that the last time we parted. Am I right? No, my friends and I will stay close by and keep watch. We'll see everyone who comes and goes. Anything suspicious, we'll come and get you. You focus on sleep."

I groaned. "I'll sleep—"

"When you're dead." He rolled his eyes. "Such a Marine. That day is too far away, *mi amiga*. Sleep. Even the toughest warriors need their beauty rest."

I shrugged out of his jacket and tried to hand it to him, along with his cap.

"Keep them. Souvenirs of the night you lived."

"Let's hope that wasn't a one-off."

"It never is. Until it isn't."

I laughed, but the laugh turned into something else. Another tsunami threatened to buckle my knees. I touched Jesús's cheek briefly, conscious of the blood on my palm, under my fingernails. *"Gracias, amigo.* For everything."

"It is my pleasure." He caught my hand. *"Buenas noches,* Sydney. Sleep well."

◆　◆　◆

Inside the room, I bolted the door, dropped my duffel on the bed, then ripped off my bloodstained clothes and stepped into the shower. The stall was moldy, and I had to share the space with the spider I'd spotted earlier. Jesús had lifted his foot to crush it, but I'd stopped him. No more death. Sharing the room with the spider seemed only fair, since I was the interloper.

I took my corner, and he took his, but he scurried away as soon as I turned on the tap. Fickle friend. I cranked the faucet until the wheezy stream of water was as hot as it would go and then let it burn away the surface of my skin still stained with Angelo's blood. I used every bit of soap and shampoo as I scrubbed my hair and body, then stood with my face turned into the spray and rinsed my mouth until I no longer tasted blood. My weeping mixed with the fall of water, and I could tell myself the tears were only that—a warm mingling of oxygen and hydrogen.

The minutes ticked by, and still I did not move. Then the air shifted, and the stall seemed to shrink, and, even in the heat, goose bumps ran down my back. Behind me, I sensed a ghostly presence. I didn't have to turn to picture Angelo standing with me in the small space, his ruined face awash with water, his butchered hands hanging helpless near his thighs. I kept my back turned and my eyes closed, for I could not bear to see him.

Our ghosts are our guilt.

"I'm sorry," I whispered, water leaking into my mouth where it mingled with the tears. "I didn't mean for anyone to get hurt. I didn't know they were following me. And I didn't know they would go after you."

A thick silence greeted my words.

My counselor would have advised me to turn around, to face my demons and confirm that they existed only in the traumatized space between my ears. But although Peter Hayes had served in Iraq just as I had, he had not spent long nights alone with the newly deceased. Hayes was wise about many things, but about the dead, I feared he was, well, dead wrong. If I turned, I would learn that I was not alone.

I spread my hands flat against the ancient tiles and pressed my forehead to the slimy wall. The water pounded the back of my head and neck, burned down my back, and roiled at my feet as my chest heaved with sobs.

"You have to go," I said at last. "I can't think with you so close."

By the time the water turned cold, my tears had stopped and Angelo had vanished. I lifted my chin and shunted aside the self-pity. I was here to find Malik. He was all that mattered, and I would not let myself be sidetracked by grief or guilt or fear. His mother had given her life for the Marines, and, if need be, I would do the same for her son. The life of one boy might seem a small thing against the backdrop of a still-raging war. Against the loss of so many. But if I ever came to believe that, my soul would be forfeit.

I stepped out of the shower, turned away from the mirror.

Despite what I'd told Jesús, I needed some sleep to clear my head before I could plan my next move. A good six hours, then I'd be ready for the world again.

To sleep, perchance to dream.

But not here. The Alpha seemed capable of reaching anyone—of corrupting them, or torturing them, or killing them. I had to find a different hotel. A place where no one would be at risk for the simple sin of knowing me.

I dried off with the rough towel, donned a clean tank top and my filthy cargo pants, placed Jesús's cap and jacket on the bed, then grabbed my bag and cranked up the volume on the television set.

I went out the window above the toilet.

CHAPTER 4

There are good and bad people on both sides of a conflict. The trick is in figuring out which is which. And who is working for whom.

—*Sydney Parnell. Personal journal.*

At 2:00 p.m. the next day, I sat at a table in an open-air coffee shop in the Mexico City suburb of Ecatepec with a café Americano and a plate of sugar-dusted *pan dulce*.

I'd arranged myself with my back to the adobe brick wall, my chair half-hidden by a riotous climb of brilliant-red bougainvillea and the shade cast by the eaves of the roof two stories above. The afternoon was quiet, save for the occasional rattle of cutlery and clink of glasses as a woman set the tables inside. I tried to relax as I took in the mingled aromas of coffee and baking bread and the sweet waft of the flowers nodding in a soft breeze.

Angelo had died a soldier in a war he hadn't even known was being waged. But the fact that the Alpha's men had gone so far meant they were desperate. Malik was not yet in their sights. And for the moment, at least, I'd shaken off their pursuit. Over the next hour, perhaps I would learn something that would help me find Malik. And find a way to keep him safe.

I put down my coffee and sat back. I wore a newly purchased embroidered blue blouse, a long skirt, sunglasses, leather *huaraches*, and a straw hat, bought at a market that morning. I'd dyed my hair a dark brown and replaced my usual braid with a tight chignon coiled at the nape of my neck. I looked minty and new, or so I hoped, the duffel sitting next to my sandaled feet the only outwardly tattered thing about me.

To any casual observer, I hoped to pass as a local, an idle expat housewife enjoying the afternoon while she watched the sun bake the world into a torpor.

The waiter, a friendly twenty-something, appeared at my table.

"You like the *abrazos*?" he asked, gesturing toward the pastries on the red-and-white patterned plate. "They are a warm hug, are they not? Those with the cream, they are my favorite."

I smiled and picked up my coffee. "They are very good."

"Would you like more coffee?"

"Por favor."

"I'll be right back."

The little square in the town of Ecatepec was a sleepy, sun-drenched refuge. After my trip to the market that morning, I'd taken an Uber to the Buenavista subway station, then the suburban railway to Lechería Station. From there, I'd used a combination of taxis, another subway, and a bus before walking the final stretch. When I was absolutely sure there was no one on my tail, I'd selected this table tucked into the afternoon shadows. My duffel was within easy reach on the ground, the stun gun with its remaining three cartridges sitting on top of my filthy clothes.

I was there to meet a man named Ehsan Zarif, who ran security for the Jameh Mosque where Malik had been photographed. When I called him that morning and introduced myself, Zarif had assured me the place was known only to the neighborhood locals. "You won't find it on any tourist map," he'd promised. Which made it a good place to rendezvous if you didn't want to be seen.

And Zarif and I did not want to be seen. I had my own reasons. For him, it would likely raise uncomfortable questions if he were spotted in the company of a young American woman, sharing pastries with her on a Sunday afternoon.

And meeting at the mosque had been out of the question—the Alpha almost certainly knew about it by now. Extreme pain like the kind Angelo suffered sooner or later makes everyone talk.

The waiter strolled out of the café and refilled my cup. He smiled at me, then stretched and yawned, taking in the day before strolling back inside. I was his only customer. I scooted my chair a few inches to the right to avoid the encroaching sunlight spilling across the tables and kept my face in shadow. I slid my phone from my pocket and checked the time. Still early.

Ten texts and two voice mails from Jesús. I'd sent him a text earlier, thanking him and letting him know I was all right. I ignored these newest messages and my guilt and dropped the phone back in the pocket of my skirt.

In the distance, a train blew its horn. The sound pushed against the effects of the coffee and adrenaline, and my heart rate slowed. But the sound also brought a deep desire for Denver and those I loved. If his schedule permitted, Cohen would be out for a midafternoon run with Clyde, the mountains rising in steep blue ridges beyond the park near police headquarters. Clyde would ignore the taunts of magpies and mountain blue jays, and the lure of the squirrels darting between trees. He would stay with Cohen.

I sat up when a man appeared on the far side of the square. Of medium height and build, he had a neatly trimmed gray beard and wore jeans, tennis shoes, a collarless shirt, and a black suit jacket. A black ball cap topped off the mix of casual and professional. He stood motionless as he scanned the restaurant patio. I leaned forward, into the sunlight. When he saw me, he smiled and made his way across the square.

I stood when he drew near.

"Ms. Parnell?" he asked in unaccented English.

"Sydney. And you are Mr. Zarif?"

"Ehsan. Please." We shook hands. "It's a pleasure to meet someone from my home country."

"You're American?" I asked.

"First generation. My parents fled Iran for the US in 1979, after the shah was deposed. I grew up in San Diego, but I went to college in Boulder, not far from your hometown of Denver."

Of course he had researched my background. "You speak like a native."

"You're kind. But not completely truthful. Still, I try."

"And now you live here. In Mexico."

"I still have my American citizenship. But I'm an expat. Or, as I prefer, a man of the world."

"Most people are running in the opposite direction."

The skin around his eyes crinkled. "What do they know?"

He held my hand for a moment, cupped in both of his in the Persian manner as we took a moment to inspect each other. He was not what I expected. Most people who work security are physical, almost overbearingly so, and they carry themselves with an aggressive body language designed to discourage anyone from getting close to their clients. Zarif's gentle gaze and frameless glasses gave him the look of someone more comfortable running Google searches than chasing bad guys.

But appearances could be deceiving. And there was the matter of the gun he was packing; I'd taken note of the outline of an ankle holster beneath his jeans as he approached. Possibly there was another gun in his back waistband.

He released my hand.

"Thank you for agreeing to meet with me," I said.

"Of course. Although you were very mysterious." He smiled. "But then, maybe that's why I came. Who can resist a mystery?"

"There are things I prefer not to say on the phone."

"And who, I wonder, do you think might be listening in?" He cocked his head. "You mentioned a man named Angelo Garcia."

"Please," I said. "Sit down. Would you like some coffee?"

His smile was bemused, but he nodded. "It is one reason I picked this place. Aside from your desire for privacy. Their coffee and pastries are without parallel."

He waited until I had resumed my seat, then chose the chair across from mine so that his back was to the square. Not something I'd ever seen a security guy do.

At my raised eyebrow, he said, "I trust you'll watch my back."

"Of course." But I was wondering what was up with this guy. Maybe running security at his mosque was more of a theoretical job than an actual need.

The waiter reemerged and took Zarif's order for a double espresso and more pastries.

When we were alone again, I asked, "How can you be sure you weren't followed?"

"That mystery again," Zarif said. "I did as you asked. Although my secretary will forever wonder at my insistence on borrowing her car instead of taking my own."

"She won't talk?"

"No more than usual. Now tell me what I can do for you."

I drew in a breath. Zarif hadn't been on my original list of people I'd planned to meet with. During the night, as I'd tossed and turned in a new bed in a new hotel, I'd debated how much I would reveal to him. I needed to persuade him to share what he knew—if indeed he knew anything—without giving him any more information than was necessary.

As for Zarif posing any risk to me or to Malik, I had little concern. From what I could glean online, his life seemed straightforward. He served as the head of security for Jameh Mosque. The mosque's website said he was married with two children, and spent his free time playing tennis, coaching his daughter's soccer team, and painting landscapes.

The mosque itself appeared as banal as the Presbyterian church I'd grown up with. Jameh was the cornerstone of its small Muslim community, a meeting place for the locals with not only a prayer hall but also a community room, programs for young mothers and preschoolers, and soccer teams for the older girls and boys—the Islamic equivalent of a local parish.

"I need to be clear," I said. "There is risk for you in meeting with me. Maybe—probably—a lot of risk."

Zarif raised a sardonic brow. "I got that sense."

"I'm very serious about this, Ehsan. People have died."

His expression turned somber. "After you called me this morning, I did some digging into your past. Your time in the Marines. Your work as a railway cop. You will forgive me for this, I hope. I would be remiss not to do so."

"Of course."

"I saw nothing there that would explain why you reached out to me. You have asked for my help, and because you made me curious and because I hate to turn down a woman in need, here I am. But I don't understand what help I can possibly provide."

An image rose in my mind of the woman Haifa and the Marine, Resenko, their butchered bodies arranged next to each other in a small house in Habbaniyah. And eight-year-old Malik, weeping nearby. In my memory, I once again gathered him in my arms and carried him outside, his eyes wide and wet in the moonlight.

Zarif cleared his throat, and I snapped back to the sun-drenched patio.

"For six months, I've been looking for an eleven-year-old boy named Malik," I said. "His mother was an interpreter for the Marines in Habbaniyah, in Iraq."

Zarif's brow furrowed. "Okay."

I spun the saucer under my coffee cup around with restless fingers. "When Malik was eight, his mother was murdered by insurgents. After she died, Malik spent a lot of time on our forward operating base. I think he felt safe on the FOB. Outside the wire, it was chaos. There were corpses on the street every morning, local nationals who had been kidnapped and tortured the night before."

I paused to take in the sunny, sleepy square and forced my hands into my lap.

Zarif's voice broke through. "Ms. Parnell. Sydney. Are you all right?"

"Yes." I plunged on. "Malik and I grew close. I wasn't a mother figure for him. I have no children of my own, and my parents weren't great role models. But I did my best. I worked with him on his English, let him play games on my computer, showed him how to count cards in blackjack." I smiled. "I told him that in America, thumbs-up means something different from what it means in Iraq. We watched a lot of movies together. His favorite was *The Lion King*. *Hakuna matata,* he would say to me. It means—" I glanced away and cleared my throat.

"It means *no worries,*" Zarif said. "A good idea, hard to hold on to."

I brought my gaze back. "The other Marines helped take care of him. We were all fond of him. Then, a few months after his mother's death, I was redeployed. I tried, but failed, to bring him with me back to America."

"I've heard that story many times," Zarif said. "Men and women who helped our soldiers and Marines, then were left behind when we withdrew and things got ugly. A lot of them died. I thought we'd learned that lesson in Saigon."

An old, familiar anger burned in my throat. "Not our most shining moment."

"No. But please, go on."

"After I left, friends sent me emails to let me know how Malik was doing. He continued to spend time on the FOB. Then one morning he didn't show up. No one was worried until he didn't appear the next morning. Or the next. A week went by."

Zarif raised an eyebrow. "Let me guess. He never came back."

"Everyone hoped that his grandparents had decided to move away. But in truth, a lot of us figured the family had been killed for working with us. It was not only Malik's mother who worked for the US government. One of his uncles did some sort of business on the FOB. And another family member had served as an interpreter for a special-ops team. He was killed in an ambush along with the rest of the team."

Including the man I'd loved. Doug Ayers.

"It's a terrible story," Zarif said. "So much loss."

"Yes."

He took a pack of cigarettes from his shirt pocket. "Do you mind?"

"I live for secondhand smoke."

"Sarcasm." He moved to slip the pack back into his pocket. "I'll wait."

"Actually, no. Please, go ahead."

He tapped out a cigarette and lit it. The pungent scent of tobacco filled the air. I tried not to notice how good it smelled.

"But now something has changed," Zarif guessed.

"Six months ago, a man came to see me. He believed that not only was Malik alive and well, he was sure the boy had made his way to America. But he had no leads. He thought I might know something, since Malik and I had been close. But this was the first I'd heard anything."

"This man, who was he?"

A real son of a bitch. "A fellow Marine. I didn't ask how he got his information."

"And you do not wish to share his name."

I hadn't decided what to do about Sergeant Max Udell—Sarge. I didn't know where he was or what he was up to. Sharing seemed like a bad idea. "What could it mean to you?"

Zarif tipped his head to the side and blew a stream of smoke up and away. "Nothing, I suppose."

Max Udell had been a tank sergeant in the Marines, a trusted colleague, if not a friend. But by the time he surprised me in my own kitchen, he'd fallen a long way from his time in the USMC.

"This man broke into my house and told me at gunpoint that he was working for the CIA. They'd taken the boy to use as a spy, then lost him."

As if Malik were merely a toy, carelessly misplaced.

"And what did you tell him?" Zarif asked. There was a bright rim of metal in his voice that hadn't been there before, as if he were more interrogator than bystander.

I narrowed my eyes. I'd had nothing to offer Sarge to help with his search. Not that I would have shared anything with a man who wanted to turn kids into spies. Or with someone who opened the conversation by promising to splatter my brains around when we finished.

"The truth," I said. "That I hadn't seen or heard from Malik in nearly three years."

The waiter came out and, unasked, poured my third cup of coffee and brought Zarif another espresso. If I drank any more, my heart would be leapfrogging over my ribs.

When the waiter returned inside, Zarif said, "But now something has led you here. To Mexico." His voice was mild again.

"Have you heard of an American named David Fuller?"

Zarif shook his head.

"Fuller runs an organization called the Hope Project. Its mission is to help endangered Iraqis—especially those who helped the Americans—get out of Iraq. Fuller has people working for him around the globe—the US, Canada, Europe, Mexico. When I asked for his help, he had an artist create an age-progressed sketch of Malik. Then he sent the word out, telling his people to keep watch for Malik."

"Wasn't that risky? You don't know why this man, this Marine, was looking for him."

"Fuller spoke with very few people, and only those who have been with him for a long time. People he knew would be careful. And discreet. Angelo Garcia—" *You cannot resist pain.* "Angelo was one of the men he trusted."

"Was?"

"He's dead."

I studied Zarif, trying to gauge if all this was truly new to him. But Zarif could have taken the place of a sphinx if he'd been so inclined.

"I am sorry for your friend. But what does this have to do with the Jameh Mosque?"

"Angelo saw Malik there," I said. "Last month."

Zarif frowned. "And you believe him? That this child came all that way from Iraq to our little mosque in a sleepy suburb of Mexico City. How could he manage this feat? And more importantly, why would he?"

"Angelo sent a photo. There's no question. Malik was with a man, a Caucasian, inside your mosque. As for why he ended up there . . . I don't have an answer for that."

Zarif rested his still-burning cigarette in the glass ashtray. Smoke spiraled up like a signal for help. "And now this Angelo is dead. And you must think his death had something to do with this small thing he did, sending you a photograph."

"I know it did."

"How did he die?"

The day had warmed as the sun moved into the western sky, and now the air was so heavy, I felt I could push it away with my hands. Bees buzzed among the flowers, and a flock of pigeons landed on the cobblestones nearby, cooing softly, their heads bobbing. I took a gulp of cooling coffee and let the caffeine run counterpoint in my blood.

"He was tortured to death." I laid my gaze on Zarif. "They dumped his body outside my hotel room last night. I've been on the run since."

Zarif had gone very still save for a flash in his dark eyes of what I guessed to be anger. He didn't touch the espresso, which was no longer steaming. "And now you have brought this danger to my doorstep. Almost to my mosque."

"That is why I asked you to meet me away from there."

Zarif picked up the cigarette and sucked in a long drag. He huffed out the smoke and tapped away the ash, taking his time. "Why didn't this man, this Angelo Garcia, just come to me and ask if I'd seen the boy?"

"He said he did. You told him no."

There followed a long silence as Zarif eyed me through the smoke. For the first time I noticed how weather beaten his face was, how spare his gestures. The distance he held in his eyes. I'd seen this look before, many times. It was in the eyes of the men who returned from a tour in the Iraqi desert where they'd spent their days staring through a sniper's scope or kicking down doors. Men who had been unable to let down their guard for so long that suspicion had merged with their flesh like a second skin.

Zarif blinked first. "I remember that now. I believe I also told him that we got so many visitors that I could not be sure who might have come and gone. I told him that I would ask around."

"And did you?"

"No one had seen him."

"Except, apparently, Angelo."

A faint flush crept into his face, and he looked down at his cigarette. "Apparently."

Some emotion whispered just beneath his skin, barely detectable. A white noise of reaction, impossible to read.

But one thing I did know—he was lying.

The part of me that was big into self-preservation urged me to stand up, thank Zarif for his time, then walk away and disappear onto a bus or taxi. To put as much distance as possible between the two of us. His behavior had been strange from the get-go. And now he was lying about something.

But I could not leave without learning everything I could, even if—especially if—what Zarif was lying about was whether or not he'd seen Malik or knew anything about him.

I played out a little rope. "What are you uncomfortable about, Zarif?"

He stabbed the air with his cigarette. "Tell me this. If what you are doing is honest, if your reasons for looking for the boy are sincere, why did you not come straight to me once you believed he'd been seen at our mosque? Or ask to speak to our imam? If you are worried about this boy's safety, that would make sense, wouldn't it? To ask us directly instead of wasting time?"

"Angelo tried that."

"A second request would have carried more weight. Especially if you'd said you were concerned for the boy's safety."

"Bullshit!" I slapped my palms on the table. Silverware rattled. "That's bullshit." My blood pressure took an express elevator up. "I did not come to you immediately because Malik disappeared again right after Angelo saw him. Fuller and I weren't sure who we could trust. We still aren't sure. And now you are lying to me. I'd like to know why. For all we know, he was grabbed at your mosque. And maybe you had something to do with it."

Zarif took another drag from his half-finished cigarette, the tiny flame blazing with a crackle, then stubbed it out. "What is it you want to do with the boy if you find him?"

"Why?"

"Because now I am part of this charade."

"Fuller knows people outside the US who are willing to take him in. Who *want* to take him in. Families who could give him a safe and normal life."

"A safe and normal life." Zarif leaned back and tapped his chin with a forefinger. "What does that look like for a boy who—if what you say is true—is being hunted by killers?"

Safe and normal, for both me and for Malik, resided on the far side of the investigation I was conducting. The one I'd allowed myself to be scared away from six months earlier when Sarge came calling.

But I couldn't share that with Zarif. Couldn't tell him that the key to Malik's safety possibly lay in what Malik himself could tell me. In what Malik might be able to reveal about who killed his mother and PFC Resenko, assuming he'd seen or heard anything at all. Answers he'd been too traumatized to offer three years ago, but which I needed from him now.

Answers that could mean exposing him to risk in order to save him.

"Until a family is vetted, I've made arrangements for an FBI safe house," I said.

"First you have to get him there."

"Yes."

"And what if he is safe where he is?" Zarif pressed. "What if he is safer if you don't find him? These men you say are looking for him know who you are. They dumped a dead man outside your hotel room. What kind of message is that? Maybe you can elude them here. But as soon as you return to Denver, they'll have you. They will ask you about this FBI safe house, and you will sing." He jabbed a finger at me. "Because we all sing."

As if that thought hadn't given me nightmares from the moment I decided to walk off the cliff. "What if he *isn't* safe, Ehsan? What if he's in danger?"

"And your presence will make the difference? You're that good?"

My face grew hot. "For a man who's never seen this boy, you seem quite invested in the outcome."

Zarif's look had hardened to the point where his mild spectacles made me feel as though I stood on the wrong side of a rifle scope. "He's a child. It is normal to care. But more importantly, if he really was at my mosque, he might return. I'd like to know what risk he brings with him."

"As long as Malik is somewhere out there, he will never be safe. If he returns to your mosque, then maybe you won't be safe, either."

"And you believe you and your Feds can protect him." He spit the words.

In the square, the pigeons startled, flapping heavily into the air, the beat of their wings a panicked throb against the drowsy afternoon. I jerked upright and scanned the area, but the rest of the world dozed peacefully. Zarif, apparently utterly relaxed, kept his back to the square.

"You are arrogant," he said.

"I am determined. Malik deserves a real life."

"And arrogance," he went on, "has killed more people than stupidity ever did."

"Would you choose to live your life looking over your shoulder?"

"I'd certainly find it better than a bullet in my heart."

"Ehsan—"

"There were men," he said.

"What?"

"Men came looking for the boy a week ago. Americans. Perhaps the men who killed your friend. I told them the same thing I'm going to tell you now. If that boy was ever in my mosque, he came and went without my knowledge. And he never came back, because I've been watching.

So please—" He clenched a fist but stopped short of smacking it on the table. "Please go away and leave us alone. I am sorry for your troubles. But I want no part of them."

I said nothing. There was nothing to say.

"Well, then." He smoothed his suit coat, then placed a two hundred–peso note on the table and stood. "Good-bye, Ms. Parnell. I wish you and the boy, wherever he is, good luck."

He came around the table with his hand extended. I reached out.

"I'm sorry," he murmured as he clamped his fingers around my wrist. "It must be done this way."

At a sharp burn in my arm, I jerked back. He pulled me to him as if we would embrace. I wrenched violently away and bent to grab my duffel with the stun gun. But the ground dropped away, and I staggered. I opened my mouth to cry for help, but Zarif clamped a hand over my mouth and hustled me toward the door to the restaurant.

"It's better if you don't fight me," he said as the ground stopped falling and instead rose to meet me.

CHAPTER 5

Don't be afraid of the ugly in your past. The trauma. The failures and mistakes. The what-ifs and the what-the-hell-was-I-thinking and the times someone broke your heart.

They're over and done with, a pile of bones you can use to stand tall.

—Peter Hayes, Clinical Therapist, VA Hospital.

A trace of light nudged at the edges of the world, and a man's voice dropped through the drugged depths of silence.

"*¿Cuánto tiempo?*"

A rustle of movement. Fabric.

"*Ella debería despertarse en cualquier momento,*" someone answered.

My brain labored to parse the words. *How long?* Followed by, *She should come around any minute.*

The first voice I didn't know, but it took me only a few seconds to recognize the second as belonging to Zarif. I made up my mind to kill the bastard at the first chance.

"Ms. Parnell?" he said.

I lay as boneless as the dead and worked to sort out my whereabouts without any visual cues. A warm, fading light filtered through my closed lids. Late-afternoon sun, I guessed. So I'd been unconscious a couple of hours. The surface beneath me was soft and smooth and smelled of leather. The scents of roasting meat and vegetables stirred in the warm air, accompanied by the aroma of baking cinnamon, coriander, and cumin, smells I recognized from my favorite Moroccan restaurant. Maybe I was still on the square. That gave me hope. Whoever heard of torturing someone to death in a café?

I felt no pain, save for a residual burn in my arm from the injection. And I wasn't restrained. I took these as good signs.

"She is coming back to us," Zarif said in English. "Sydney, you are safe."

I opened my eyes. Zarif was leaning over me, a furrow between his eyes.

"You son of a bitch." I threw a fist, hoping to break his nose.

But he caught my hand and then patted it, as if I were a child. "I am sorry. I had no choice."

He released my hand and stepped away as I pushed myself to a sitting position and waited for the world to stop spinning. I found myself on a leather sofa in what looked like a millionaire's living room. High, timbered ceilings, a wood-planked floor covered with woven carpets in reds and blues, and white walls adorned with carved masks and framed oils of local scenes. Each painting had its own personal spotlight, and I'd swear the door to the room was thirty feet away. Sunlight slanted through a high row of windows on the southwest wall and lay in mellow trapezoids on the floor. I was in the home of someone so wealthy they didn't care if the carpets faded.

Just visible outside were an expanse of lawn and a row of distant trees. If I squinted, I could make out faraway hills. I definitely wasn't in Kansas anymore. Or even Ecatepec.

A man in his early thirties stood behind Zarif. He wore jeans, a black T-shirt, and an expression of alarm. I narrowed my eyes at him, and he flushed, as if I'd caught him thinking things he shouldn't. Like maybe how to remove my eyeballs without getting blood all over the sofa.

Zarif took a chair a couple of feet out of swinging range. "Do you feel all right?"

"Peachy. This how you get all your dates?"

"My apologies for the rough treatment. But I couldn't let you see where we brought you. If your enemies are willing to torture you to get the answers they want, then I'd rather you didn't have those answers."

"Covering my eyes would have been sufficient."

Zarif shook his head. "My men were nearby, but even with every precaution, I couldn't be sure who was watching, or who in the restaurant might talk. I had to make it look good. For both our sakes, you and I cannot be seen as allies. Any story you tell later must be convincing." He brought his palms together, almost as if in prayer. "There is a great deal at stake, Ms. Parnell. Even more than you imagine."

"You're not just a security guy at a local mosque, are you."

The room dimmed as a cloud drifted over the sun. The younger man switched on a lamp. At a sudden pulse of pain, I pressed my fingers to my temples.

"The headache is a residual effect," Zarif said. "Would you like some water? Maybe a pain reliever?"

"Yeah. Opioids with a cocaine chaser." At Zarif's look, I summoned a faint laugh. "Acetaminophen or some ibuprofen will be fine."

"Of course." Zarif spoke in rapid Spanish to the other man, who nodded and disappeared through the door.

"You're going to tell me what this is all about," I stated. There was a fluttery anticipation in my chest—why kidnap me unless he had something important to share? Hope is the thing with feathers.

"I will tell you what I can," Zarif said.

The younger man returned with a bottle of water, which he placed on the table along with four orange capsules.

"Ibuprofen," he said.

At a look from Zarif, he retreated, closing the door behind him. I picked up the pills and washed them down with the water, then set the half-empty bottle on a coffee table the size of a city block. "I'm listening."

"Three months ago, a man came to me and asked if I would be willing to protect a young Iraqi boy."

I straightened. "You mean—"

"Wait, please. He told me he worked for the American embassy."

"He was a spy?"

"A diplomat." Zarif smiled. "Probably a spy. It's how things work. I mulled his request over for a few days, but ultimately I decided it was too risky. We Muslims must walk a very careful line."

The feathered creature in my heart went belly-up, feet in the air.

"Then last month he returned. I told him my decision. He explained that the boy was in grave danger and needed protection, and he could not think of a safer place than with me. Not at the mosque, but in my personal home. Once again, he asked if I would be willing to help."

"And?"

"That is why we are here."

A little heartbeat fluttered beneath the feathers. But hope is a dangerous thing, easily crushed. Trying to make it last, I asked, "Why you, Zarif?"

He spread his hands. "He suggested I might be related to the boy. My family, like this boy's great-grandparents, came from Shiraz, near the city of Parsa—better known to the world as Persepolis, ancient capital of the Persian empire. So . . . perhaps." He shrugged. "This man also asked because he knows my home once belonged to a drug trafficker. It is remote and easy to guard. And this little town where I live, it is not too small, not too big. Like Goldilocks. It is not hard to hide one small boy here, with all of my security detail on hand. Especially when that boy can blend with the locals."

My head buzzed with questions. Like how the head of security for a small mosque in a small town could afford the former home of a drug lord. And a security detail. And how his possession of such a place could be kept secret.

But all that could wait. I looked at Zarif with eyes naked with need. My voice came out a whisper. "He's here."

"The hadith says that whosoever alleviates the need of another shall have his own needs lightened by Allah. Last month, this man brought Malik to me and placed him in my protection."

I stood so suddenly that I knocked the table. The uncapped bottle of water tilted over and rolled onto the thick carpet. I stared blindly as water glugged onto the floor.

Zarif reached around me and picked up the bottle.

I was shaking. "Show me."

Zarif rose smoothly to his feet. "Come."

He led the way through the vast house—down innumerable hallways and past innumerable chambers—until he reached the back of the house and we entered a large room with a wall of glass on the far side overlooking a pool and garden. Outside, brilliant light from a western sun spilled across the tops of trees and slanted into the grounds, illuminating a riot of shrubs and flowers and making the water of the pool glow an incandescent blue. I followed Zarif across the room. He slid back a glass door, then gestured for me to go outside.

I stared out into the half-groomed, half-wild place. Some part of me was thinking that if Zarif intended to shoot me, the garden would be the perfect place to do so. I could return as next year's daisies, or whatever grew here.

He rested a hand on my arm. "I know you have many questions for him. But remember, he has been through a lot and is still very troubled. He gets angry. He is often fearful. His nightmares are terrible."

I nodded, still staring into the garden, waiting for Malik to appear. Zarif stepped in front of me and took my shoulders.

"You are here not for yourself but for him," he said. "It's important that he knows you didn't intend to abandon him. But your presence here could also open old wounds, raise bad memories. Tread lightly, and ask only what you must."

"I can't make life safe for him if I don't understand what happened."

"It is for that reason that you're here. He deserves a chance at a normal life, and you seem to be a critical part of that hope." He loosed my shoulders. "But your presence is also a danger to the privacy I've worked so hard to establish. Which is critical in an entirely different way. One hour. After that, two of my men will drive you to the airport. There is nothing more for you in Mexico City. If you are afraid to go home, then go somewhere else. And if you are captured, try to kill yourself before they can torture my name out of you. Those are my conditions."

Panic rose in my throat. "It's not enough time."

"I applaud your goals. But I won't sacrifice Malik for a quest that might turn out to be as futile as the hunt for El Dorado. As far as I'm concerned, he can stay here with my family until everyone who means him ill has grown old and died." The expression in his mild gray eyes turned flinty. "Will you comply?"

I nodded stiffly.

"He's waiting with his tutor just down that path. I sent him a photo of you, as a final verification that you are what you claim. He knows you're coming."

He stepped aside, and I walked through the open doorway. The warm air draped itself like a shawl around my shoulders. I didn't look back when the door slid closed behind me.

Humid air descended like a benediction after the stench of the city, filled with the not unpleasant tang of chlorine from the pool and the earthy scents of flowers and trees and rich soil. Minus the chlorine, this must have been how Eden smelled, before the fall. On the far side of the pool, a brick-paved path as wide as two people led into a dense forest. Pink bougainvillea hung nodding from shrubs taller than my head while, high above, the fronds of palms stirred in a light breeze that didn't reach the garden.

I reached for Clyde, needing him beside me. But he was almost two thousand miles away.

I shook out my hair and rewound it at the nape of my neck, smoothed my wrinkled clothes, then skirted the shimmering pool and started down the path. As soon as I stepped beneath the trees, the temperature dropped as the still-fierce sun became a golden haze glinting through an emerald screen. Two minutes of brisk walking brought me to an open space. I stopped at the edge.

A boy sat on a bench next to a woman in a long skirt and a hijab. At his feet was a soccer ball that he scooted forward and back with the flat of one foot. He had a book open in his lap and was reading aloud in a high, clear voice while the woman listened. A poem.

My eyes went to his left arm, searching for final proof. There it was—a long, puckered scar, a souvenir from the night his mother was murdered.

Malik.

I pressed my hand to my mouth and watched him.

He was six inches taller than the last time I'd seen him, still thin but even ganglier than before, all elbows and knees. His hair was shorter than I remembered, with a cowlick that stuck up stubbornly in the back. He wore navy shorts, a white E Street Band T-shirt, and sneakers without socks. On his left wrist was a braided leather band, on his right a neon-orange bracelet of the kind usually used to support a cause.

He fidgeted on the bench, his foot rolling the soccer ball as he read.

He was just a kid. A regular kid.

Of course, how many of us wear our traumas on our skin for the world to see?

His voice broke on a word, and he paused and shook his head, as if to say, *Not my fault.* The woman murmured something, and he returned to the reading.

And still I watched, my heart pressed tight against my ribs so that drawing a breath felt like lifting a car.

Would he blame me for leaving him? Blame me for whatever hardships he'd endured since his mother died?

What if he didn't remember me at all? Maybe I was just part of a crazed past of grief and terror he'd rather not revisit.

I lifted my chin. None of that mattered. *I* did not matter. Only Malik did. And if my being here could help him in any way, even if it amounted only to letting him know that someone cared, then that was enough.

I cleared my throat and stepped into the sunlight.

Malik and the woman glanced up. The woman placed a hand over her eyes to shade them, but Malik stared straight at me, unbothered by the light, desert child that he was.

He stood, and the woman rose. The woman whispered something to him, squeezed his shoulder, then came toward me. She nodded and walked past, heading toward the house.

My pulse roared in my ears as I waited for Malik to say something, waited for a light of recognition to go on in his face.

I took a few steps toward him. Somewhere overhead, a bird punctured the quiet with a long, single trill, then hushed again.

"Malik," I said softly, my voice tentative. "You are—" My voice broke. "I am . . . I am so very happy to see you."

He remained motionless by the bench, the book of poems still in his hand, his finger holding his place. I approached him the way you would a wild animal, my hands raised, palms toward him, as if he might take flight.

The book slipped from his hand and hit the ground with a soft plop. "Miss Sydney."

"Yes."

"Is it really you?"

"It's me."

"Your hair is different. Dark."

I laughed a little. "Yes."

"You are not a jinn?"

"Oh, Malik, I am so sorry. I never meant to leave you. I never, I've always—" My throat filled, and I struggled to speak. My voice came out as a jagged whisper. "Yes. I am real."

He nodded. But other than that quick, light gesture, he made no move.

"And you?" I asked. "You are real, too?"

"Yes."

"Not a ghost?"

"No."

"So here we are."

I opened my arms, and he ran to me. We held each other as tightly as we could, and soon my shoulder and his hair were wet with our tears.

CHAPTER 6

Don't apologize for what you do to survive. Anyone would do the same.

—Sydney Parnell. Personal journal.

We held each other for all too brief a time before Malik pulled free. He picked up the book of poems and placed it on the bench, then grabbed his soccer ball. We stared awkwardly at each other.

"You want to walk?" I asked.

He raised his shoulders, then dropped them. Classic preteen. "Sure."

The path I'd come on continued on the far side of the glen. Malik led the way.

"In Iraq, I thought you would come back," he said. "Every day for weeks, then for months. Even after the American spies came and took me away, I thought you would come for me."

Go slowly, I reminded myself. *One thing at a time.*

"I tried to bring you with me," I said. "Do you remember?"

"I didn't understand why I couldn't just get on a plane with you."

I laid my hand on his shoulder. "I want you to know this. I tried harder to take you to America than I have ever tried to do anything."

He shrugged me off. "But you didn't."

Give the boy a knife.

"You're right," I said. "I didn't. I hope you will forgive me."

"I thought you'd changed your mind." His voice trembled between anger and anguish.

"Never."

"I thought you didn't want me."

"Oh, Malik, it was my failing, not yours. It's important you know that."

He stopped and regarded me through eyes that were no longer too big for his face, but still huge, with fine brows and thick lashes. Even cut short, his hair tried to find its way into curls. The sketch artist hadn't gotten him exactly right. He was already handsome.

At the moment, his measuring gaze was unnerving for one so young.

I cleared my throat. "Do you like it here?"

"Yes." His voice was fierce, as if he expected me to doubt his answer.

"It's a long way from Habbaniyah to Mexico. And very different."

"Different is good."

I wanted to ask him about family. About friends. About all the things we'd talked about in Iraq. But time was water, spilling through my fingers.

"Malik, I'm trying to figure out some things. Trying to get answers so I can stop the men who are looking for you. You might be able to help me with some of it. Then you won't have to hide anymore."

"That's why you came? After all this time? So I can answer your questions?"

"No. Yes." Dear God, this was hard. "I came to see you, Malik. But also to try and understand what happened. So maybe I can make the world safer for you."

I sounded like a B-grade superhero—one without a cape or any powers to speak of. Malik gave my words the response they deserved. He stayed silent.

"A lot of bad went down in Iraq. I mean, not just the war. And not just—" I hesitated a beat, then plunged on. Pretending something hadn't happened didn't erase it. "And not only your mother's death."

He flinched.

Go easy, Parnell. "You know there are men after you. I want to find those men and stop them."

More silence.

"Do you know why they want you? Are they—I have to ask—are they the same ones who were there when your mother died? Did you see them that day?"

His eyes slid away. "Strider said I shouldn't talk about it. Not to anyone."

"Strider?"

"My friend. My real friend. He brought me here."

"To the mosque?"

"Yes. To Mr. Zarif."

Strider must be the man in the photo taken by Angelo. "Strider—that's his last name?"

"It's not his real last name. He said it was better to never use his real name."

"Do you know what his real name is?"

His gaze came back. "No."

"Do you know where he's gone?"

"No."

"Malik—"

"It's the truth. He wouldn't tell me."

The only Strider I knew about was a character from one of my favorite books, *The Fellowship of the Ring*. Strider had helped hide the hobbits from the dark riders. Maybe there was a clue in that. Or maybe this guy fancied himself a lost king.

"Is Strider one of the spies who took you away from the FOB?"

"No." Malik began walking again. He shifted the soccer ball from under his right arm to his left. "Those men were very bad. Strider was good. He took me away from them."

If he'd driven a stake through my heart, it would have hurt less. "Bad in what way?"

His shrug was elaborately casual. "They thought I would spy for them. Strider said I was just a tool to them, not a boy."

"A child should never be a means to an end."

"Strider said that, too."

Well, the mysterious Strider and I had one thing in common.

"So this Strider, he took good care of you?"

"He was kind. He protected me. He never abandoned me."

Maybe committing seppuku would help me feel absolved. I murmured something sympathetic. I wanted to push. To ask all my questions. *Tell me about these spies. How did they find you? How did Strider take you away?*

What kind of life have you had for three years?

And most immediately relevant, *What did you see or know that makes the Alpha so desperate to find you?*

I forced my mind to let go of those questions for the moment. It was like dropping into second gear while still doing seventy. "You still like soccer, I see."

"I'm really good now."

"I'll bet."

"Mr. Zarif says if I keep practicing, keep working at it, I'll be able to play for El Tri."

Meaning he would stay in Mexico. I forced a smile. "That's wonderful, Malik!"

We came to a gate, which Malik opened and led me through, still following the path. The riotous forest gave way to an immense emerald-green lawn where it would have felt right to see peacocks and a group of Victorians playing croquet. In the distance, fifteen-foot walls demarcated the property. Now that we were out in the open, I could see dry, scrubby hills all around. I got the sense that we were up high, among those hills.

The lack of cover would have made me uneasy, but I'd already spotted men with radios and guns moving near the walls. No doubt there were also cameras, infrared detectors, and multiple alarms. A former cartel home, Zarif had said. Again, I wondered at the source of his money. And his need for security.

Malik dropped his soccer ball, kicked it high, then raced after it before it could reach the ground. He smacked it with his head, then when it landed again, caught it on the bounce and juggled it back and forth on his knees.

"Bravo!" I said.

He kept juggling. "Did you bring Clyde?"

"You remember him? He's staying with a friend."

"That dog went crazy after he lost his partner. That's what you told me. You wouldn't let me near him."

"He and I both went a little crazy after we lost Dougie."

Malik let the ball drop and trapped it under his foot. "But you got better."

"And so did Clyde. And you're getting better, too, aren't you?"

He reached out and snatched a hibiscus from one of the bushes lining the walk. He handed the bright-red flower to me. "For your hair."

I tucked the flower behind one ear and let the question go while I searched for more innocuous things to ask.

"Do you go to school?"

"Not public school. Mr. Zarif says it's better that we have a tutor."

"We?"

"Javad and Azar. Mr. Zarif's children. They're twins."

"How old are they?"

"Eleven. Same as me."

"That's good, isn't it?"

"Sure."

When I'd first seen Malik, crying in his mother's home, I'd thought he was older. I'd been surprised to learn he was only eight and tall for his age. Goes to show what I know about kids. Or maybe trauma had aged him beyond his years.

"Do you like them?" I asked.

"Sure." He went still, staring off at something only he could see. "They don't understand things. They think I'm weird. But they don't know very much. They're just kids."

Which Malik, perhaps, wasn't anymore. War steals childhood as readily as it takes lives. "What don't they understand?"

"All they know about is stupid parties and video games and Netflix. Azar plays with plastic horses. Javad collects comic books. He acts like they're so important." His gaze remained distant, putting me distressingly in mind of some of my fellow Marines. "They've never, you know, seen people get blown up. Never seen anyone die. They ask me stuff about it, but I don't answer."

"Malik, I'm so sorry."

He blinked, his long lashes glistening. "Javad asked me if I killed anyone."

I didn't know what to say to that. Even as an adult, I'd felt that frustration with my fellow Americans. Whenever someone learned I was a Marine and asked if I'd killed anyone, I was tempted to say, "You'll be my first."

Malik swiped at his eyes. "It wasn't until I came here that I learned war isn't everywhere."

He'd been five when we invaded Iraq. "Do you miss home?"

He shook his head violently. "I hated it. Not on the FOB. I felt safe there, even after the bomb killed Fal Mohammed. But everywhere else . . . it was not good."

"*Fal* Mohammed. Meaning he was your uncle."

"My mother's brother. Before he died, he told me to leave Habbaniyah. To go with my grandparents. He said if I stayed, the bad men would find out what happened. Then they would kill me, too."

What did *happen?* I wanted to scream. I was picking my way through a minefield. "Did he mean the spies who took you from the FOB?"

Malik shook his head. "Fal Mohammed didn't even know about them. They came later."

"Then who?"

"He meant the men who killed my mother and PFC Resenko. Fal Mohammed said they were coming for him, too. And me, if they found out I'd been there. Then he died."

I pressed my hands to my stomach, processing the names. And the hurt.

"So these other men, the ones your uncle said might . . ." I paused.

"Kill me," Malik filled in.

"Did you *see* them that night? The night when they hurt your mother?"

"I heard them. I was late coming home, and I heard them and I hid outside. Two men."

"They were insurgents?"

"They were Americans."

I stopped walking. "What?"

"Americans killed my mother and Resenko. They had other men killed, too. Other Americans. My uncle said they sent your Special Forces into an ambush and made sure they were shot by members of the al-Mahdi militia."

"Malik, are you sure? That doesn't make any sense. Why would Americans want other Americans dead?"

He frowned and tapped the ball along the grass. "I asked my uncle the same question."

I kept pace with him. "What did he say?"

"He said it was because of his truck."

I closed and opened my eyes against the vertigo. "What truck?"

"The one he used to deliver things for the Americans."

"He had a hauling business?" To prevent American casualties, the US government outsourced a lot of noncritical tasks. In Iraq, most supplies were brought in by international companies. But local contractors were sometimes used, hauling cargo to the bases in so-called jingle trucks. A lucrative, if dangerous, business. This was the first I'd heard that Malik's family had an interest there. "Tell me about your uncle's truck."

"He was very proud when he got the contract. He called it—" Malik stopped and closed his eyes. "His future."

"His future? Running a truck like that would have made him a target for the insurgents every time he left the FOB."

"He paid the Sunnis protection money." Malik shrugged. "It was always like that. It was safer than being an interpreter, like my mother. But people were still afraid to go with him. So I did. I sat in the front and held his gun."

I tried not to shudder at the picture of an eight-year-old kid riding shotgun across the desert. "But something went wrong?"

"Men from our village came to my uncle. They asked him to go to our border with Iran and bring in a special load. They said if he refused, they would kill him."

My brain fired shutter clicks as things began to fall into place. "What was this special load?"

"Men and weapons. A lot of Iranian soldiers were coming across the border, taking over villages, telling people they would hurt them if they talked, giving them money to stay quiet. Fal Mohammed wanted nothing to do with this, so he went to talk to an American on the FOB. I don't know who. The man told him to bring in the soldiers and take them wherever they wanted to go. In this way, he said, the Americans would know how to find the Iranians. Then they would capture them."

That struck me as crazy. But what did I know about military strategy?

"So your uncle brought them in."

"Yes. He was very afraid. Afraid of the Iranians. And afraid of the Iraqis who made him go. That is why I went with him. So he wouldn't be afraid."

I stopped walking. Malik turned to me.

"He let you do that?"

"No." For a moment, Malik's expression brushed against gleeful. "I hid until we were many kilometers from Habbaniyah. By then, I knew we'd gone far enough that he wouldn't have time to turn around."

"You were brave."

Malik shrugged. "He was my uncle."

"So he kept driving?"

"He was very angry with me. But he had no choice. We picked up the men. One of them told me he was Quds and asked me if I knew what it meant. I said no. He laughed and gave me a coin. A Persian coin. He said our countries would someday become one, *inshallah*. Which means if God wills it."

I nodded. Quds. I didn't know much about Iran, but I'd heard of the Quds Force. Someone had described them to me as a hybrid of the CIA and Special Forces, and the deadliest fighting group in Iran. They were responsible for all foreign operations and had been designated a terrorist organization by the United States.

Maybe that was why someone on the FOB had green-lighted Mohammed and Malik's trip to the border. Capturing a member of Quds would have been a major coup.

But why give an American team a mission to capture the Iranians and then betray those same Americans?

"They had a lot of weapons," Malik went on. "It took two hours to get everything into Fal's truck. Then we drove them to a village and left them there. I took a video. With my camera. They never knew."

The shock of that fell like a blow. Was this what the Alpha was after? "A video of what, exactly? The trucks?"

"Yes. And the men unloading the weapons."

"Malik, that video is very important." My heart thudded in my ears. "Can you show me?"

But he shook his head. "After my uncle was killed, I gave my phone to Sergeant Udell. I didn't want anyone to know I had the video. But I was scared to delete it. I knew it was important."

I was breathing hard now, as if running a race. An eight-year-old kid dealing with this. But dammit, of all the people he could have given that to. "Why him?"

"Because I knew he would protect me. He's a Marine. And Marines don't do bad things." His eyes were on me. "Except when they have to."

Or when they themselves have gone bad. I was willing to bet a bottle of Blackadder whisky that Sarge had already given the recording to rogue elements in the CIA or the Alpha. Or more likely a copy; he'd want something for himself. If so, then the video wasn't the intel Sarge had been sent to my house to find. Or the reason they were hunting for Malik.

Unless Sarge *hadn't* turned it over, and they'd learned about the video from someone else.

Maybe the Alpha believed the video had ended up in my hands.

"Malik, who else knows about this video?"

"I told my mother and Sergeant Udell. Maybe they told people. I don't know."

I ran down the list. Mohammed and Haifa had known about the video, and they were both dead. Haifa had probably told PFC Resenko. He, too, had been murdered.

"Okay. Okay." I'd follow that later. "What happened after you dropped off the Iranians?"

"Nothing. We never heard anything else about them. But pretty soon after that, people started dying," Malik said. "First my mother and the Marine. That was the night you found me. Then came the ambush, when the Special Forces men were killed. Fal Mohammed said the bad Americans killed all these people because they didn't want anyone to know about the Iranians and their weapons. A cover-up, my uncle said. And since of course he knew, he was also in danger. He told me the bad Americans didn't know about me. Not yet. Not back then. But that was why I couldn't keep the video."

I gawked at him. "You're telling me that *Americans* murdered everyone who knew about the Iranians and their weapons."

"Yes."

The world gaped open at my feet, a sudden and unimaginable abyss. What Malik was suggesting, without knowing it, was that there had been a traitor on our FOB. And not a small-time, slip-me-some-cash traitor.

This was high treason.

"Malik," I said gently. "Is it possible your uncle was wrong? Could he have been working with the Iranians? Maybe he decided on his own to pick up these men and their weapons, and the Americans found out? That would explain why he was afraid and why he wanted you to leave."

"No! It wasn't like that. Fal didn't want to do it. It was the American who told him to go."

"And you have no idea who this American was?"

"No."

"Did your uncle say anything about him? Anything at all?"

Malik shook his head and scowled. The expression transformed him—he was suddenly a cranky preteen.

"I don't want to talk about it anymore," he said.

The burden of time sat heavy. A single hour to unravel years of mystery.

"Just one more question." I weighed my words carefully. "You were close with two men on the FOB. Max Udell, the man everyone called Sarge. And Richard Dalton."

He nodded.

"Did you ever see them again? After you left, I mean. Did they ever contact you?"

"That's two questions."

"Malik—"

"No." He gave the ball a hard kick. It soared into the air, striving toward escape velocity. "Never."

The back of the house had come into view. Zarif stood near the pool. He raised a hand and waved for us to join him.

The last grain of sand had dropped.

Malik watched the ball land but made no attempt to pursue it. "Mr. Zarif says you have to leave today."

"That's what he said."

He didn't look at me. "You will come back?"

"Yes."

"And then you'll take me with you?"

"I'll come back to see you. It will be your decision whether you want to stay here or go with me to America."

"But you promise to return?"

"I promise, Malik." And then, even knowing that the most sincere promise couldn't keep me alive, I dug as deep a hole as I could. "No worries. I will come back."

"*Inshallah.*"

The child was wiser than the woman. "Yes. *Inshallah.*"

He ran to the ball. He kicked it toward the house and started after it, pausing only to give me a long stare under his thick lashes—a look half of defiance, half of plea—before he fled.

CHAPTER 7

*War was the longest period of my life. I was twenty when I
enlisted. But by the time I mustered out three years later, I
felt ninety.*

—Sydney Parnell. *ENGL 0208 Psychology of Combat.*

When I reached the patio, Malik had disappeared into the house. I
wanted to call after him, but I knew our moment—for now at least—
had come and gone. It would be easier for him if I let him go.

Zarif was sitting at a table next to the shimmering pool. The day
had eased into a bruised dusk, and evening birds called from the trees.
A row of citronella candles flickered on the table, scenting the air with
lemon.

He handed me a newspaper as I approached. "You might be interested in this."

I took the paper and unfolded it. The *New York Times.*

"Page A12," Zarif said. "It's a sidebar to a larger story on American
railways."

I laid the paper on the table and flipped the pages.

RTD SECURITY OFFICER KILLED BY TRAIN

A security guard for Denver's Regional Transportation District died Saturday night when he was stabbed, then pushed in front of a commuter train at Denver's Union Station.

Witnesses say the guard, Jeremiah Kane, a US Marine Corps combat veteran, had approached a homeless man on the main platform. After a brief altercation, the man stabbed Kane, then shoved him in front of an inbound train. According to the Denver Medical Examiner's office, Kane died instantly.

The Denver Major Crimes Unit is conducting a search for the suspect, who fled the scene.

My knees gave out, and I sank into a chair across from Zarif. My pulse roared in my ears as I tried to process Kane's murder. With a shudder I realized he must have died within an hour or so of Angelo. Two warriors in a long-running war, and the Alpha hunting all of us down, one by one.

Why now, three years after things went down in Iraq?

And who else was the Alpha after?

Sergeant Max Udell wouldn't be on the list because he'd gone to the other side. That left me, once the Alpha had the intel he wanted. And Tucker Rhodes and Lester Crowe, who, along with Kane, had been on the same fireteam with the murdered PFC Resenko. All three men were present when the Sir and I arrived to take away the bodies of Haifa and Resenko. Our orders had been to cover up how the pair had died so that we could prevent an escalation of violence between American troops and locals.

Or so we were told at the time.

I read the article through again, trying to process that Kane, the Marine who had risked his life every day in Habbaniyah, had made it home only to be murdered by a vagrant.

Kane had a wife and daughters. A home. A life. He'd been a friend to Tucker and, perhaps unwisely, to Udell. The last time Kane and I had spoken, he'd been planning to return to college at some point and work on his dream of becoming a doctor.

This was how it ended?

And which one of us was next?

A bat flitted overhead. Zarif lit a cigarette and watched me. The tang of tobacco burned through the citrus of the candles. "Wasn't he in Habbaniyah when you were?"

"What if he was?" I found the strength to rally a wishful protest. "Kane was killed by a homeless man. It was a horrible fluke. A tragedy."

Zarif raised an eyebrow. He'd removed his suit jacket and rolled up the sleeves of his white shirt. His forearms were muscular. They probably hadn't gotten that way playing golf.

He stared out over the garden. "Do you believe in coincidences, Ms. Parnell?"

"No."

"Then perhaps this death is more than a horrible fluke. Perhaps it is how it begins."

"It began a long time ago." I closed the paper. "If Kane died because of what happened in Iraq, it shows even more the danger Malik is in."

His eyes came back to me. "Did you learn anything?"

"A few things. Enough of an opening to get my fingernails in. But Malik is—"

"—as safe here as he could be anywhere. Nothing changes."

I rose. "I need to get home."

He stood as well. "Your flight leaves later tonight. One of my men will take you to the airport. You will be blindfolded until you are in Mexico City."

"Just don't stab me with anything again." I picked up the newspaper. "I'd like to keep this."

"Please."

I folded the paper and tucked it under my arm. "Who are you, Zarif? This home. All these men with their guns and radios and patrols. This isn't because you work security for a mosque."

"No. But I am not at liberty to say more."

"How did Strider find you?"

"I did not ask him."

"But you vetted him."

"Actually, no. I don't know anything about him."

I shook my head. "You're bullshitting me. You wouldn't take an unknown child from an unknown man. Either you know more about him than you're sharing, or someone you trust asked you to do it."

"Someone did. A friend of yours."

I blinked. "Who?"

"Hal Beckett."

My breath hissed between my teeth. "Hal's involved in this?"

Zarif's shrug was eloquent.

I said, "He was the one who approached you about Malik."

"That is correct."

Hal had been one of Dougie's closest friends. After Dougie died, it was Hal who helped me bring home his military working dog, my partner, Clyde. It was Hal who kept me upright at Dougie's funeral and who checked in with me now and again—probably a promise he'd made to our mutual friend. Still robust at sixty, gentle, and smart, Hal was something of a distant father figure for me, offering the attention I hadn't gotten from my own dad.

But thinking of him this way had been a mistake. Hal worked for the CIA. And if the CIA was after Malik, then trusting him was impossible. I was furious with myself for not taking a closer look at Hal Beckett as soon as Sarge mentioned the CIA.

Had Hal brought Malik to Zarif to keep him safe? Or to hide the boy until he was ready to use him?

Or was there something more?

"Do you know where Hal is now?" I asked.

"I have heard nothing more from him. He mentioned a job. Perhaps he is out in the cold."

◆ ◆ ◆

Zarif escorted me to a black Mercedes SUV. Before I got in, he blindfolded me.

"Your duffel is in the passenger seat," he said. "Hamid will ride in the back with you. To make sure you are comfortable."

"And to make sure I don't peek."

"That, too." He helped me into the vehicle and closed the door.

I fumbled for the button to lower the window. "Zarif?"

"Yes?"

"Tell Malik I'll be back. When it's safe for him."

"*If* it is safe."

He had that right.

For what seemed like hours, I sat in silence with the equally silent Hamid, bracing myself first against a series of hairpin turns as we descended out of the hills, then along a string of roads that eventually led, judging by the smoothness and sudden acceleration, to a highway.

I spent the time thinking over everything I'd learned that day. The enigma of the Iranian, Zarif. The men and weapons Malik and his uncle had brought in from Iran. I threw out theories about why a loyal American would invite enemies into Iraq, then hide their presence, but came up with nothing that made sense. I thought about the man who had helped Malik escape, then brought him to Zarif. Strider was only one fly in the ointment, but I spent a lot of mental energy on him.

To Strider's credit, Malik trusted him. Then again, by the time Strider found him, Malik would have been desperate to believe in anyone.

Finally, I turned my thoughts to Jeremy Kane. Sarge had told me that the Alpha wasn't interested in going after the others involved in the cover-up in Iraq—Kane and Tucker and Crowe. But Sarge wasn't exactly a man I trusted. And maybe something had changed. As soon as I arrived home, I'd get the details of the murder and start peeling back the corners. The death would be handled by Denver Major Crimes. But no one would question my interest in the murder of a fellow transit cop. And no one but an ass would refuse my help.

The car slowed, then accelerated. The engine revved.

Had I started a war by coming to Mexico? Were my own hands stained with Kane's blood?

I pressed my palms together, almost in prayer.

Whatever the cause, the battle had begun. And it had already cost two lives—Angelo Garcia and now Kane. Maybe others I didn't know about.

Six months ago, when I'd learned that the Alpha was trying to erase the past, I'd been so afraid of losing everything that I'd risked my own soul to remain silent.

But I was done with that. No matter what it cost me—my job, my GI Bill, even my freedom if my actions in Iraq came to light and I was court-martialed as a reservist—I would see it through.

The Alpha—whoever he was—would pay for his treason.

Long after we left Zarif's home, Hamid said, "You can remove the blindfold."

I tugged off the scarf and let it flutter to the seat. Outside, day had surrendered to night, and all around us city lights blazed against the darkness. We sped along a highway through a river of traffic.

"We're in Mexico City?" I asked.

"Yes."

"How much farther to the airport?"

"Forty minutes, give or take."

I pulled out my phone and glanced at the time on the digital display. Cohen would be in bed, but probably not yet asleep. I typed a text.

You in bed?

Cohen responded immediately.

With the fur ball

I smiled and typed. Something I should know about?

He smells bad

Stop feeding him steak

We live like kings when the queen is away

I miss you

Miss you too. Things OK?

I debated, then typed, Good and bad

Home soon?

Tomorrow early

Didn't work out?

Not sure

What's your flight #? Clyde and I will be at the curb.

I'll get a taxi

We'll be there. Then he typed, Love you.

Before I could think of a response, another text popped up on my screen.

No pressure. See you soon.

I felt a smile on my face as I slid the phone back in my pocket.

The driver pulled up to the curb at departures. Hamid hopped out and came around to open the door.

"You have a few hours to wait," he said. "My apologies that I couldn't get you an earlier flight."

I grabbed my duffel and stepped out of the SUV. "It's fine."

"The driver will park. I'll stay with you until you go through security. Mr. Zarif expressed his concern that the Americans might be watching the airport."

I opened my mouth to say no, then thought better of it. If I wanted to live long enough to help Malik, I would be a fool to fight alone.

"Thank you," I said.

The Benito Juárez International Airport was bustling with crowds of tourists and businesspeople. Hamid carried credentials of some kind, because he was able to get me to the front of the ticketing line. Even so, by the time we finished and walked to security, there was a mob at the gate.

Hamid pointed toward a restaurant. "Miguel's. They have excellent red mole. Would you like to wait there until the line goes down?"

I nodded. In truth, being on the other side of the security gate made me feel trapped. A leftover from my time in the Marines, when we couldn't leave the FOB.

Miguel's was dark and moody, heavy on the oak and brass, more British pub than Mexican cantina. Despite the crowd at security, it was almost entirely deserted—there was only the bartender and a middle-aged couple in a back booth. My lucky night—Hamid wasn't the chatty type, and the quiet and solitude suited my mood. We both ordered a Negra Modelo at the bar, skipped the glasses, and carried our drinks to a booth where we could keep an eye on the room.

Hamid set his beer on the table across from mine. He sat, but when his phone buzzed, he glanced at the screen and frowned.

"I am so sorry," he said. "I must take this call. I'll be right back."

I watched him head out the front door, then pulled up the *Denver Post* site on my phone, hoping to learn more about the murder. The article in the *Post* was longer than the story in the *Times*, but there wasn't much that was new. Just some filler on Kane's background and the fact that the police had set up a hotline and were pursuing all leads.

Next to the article was an artist's rendering of the suspect. Wide and angry eyes stared into mine, a wild halo of hair framing a face stretched tight with fury. The eyes were empty of everything human but rage.

I startled when a presence loomed over the table, and a man slid into the booth next to me.

"Don't make a sound," he said. "Or I'll gut you."

Something sharp pricked my side, and I glanced down. The man turned his wrist enough to show me a blade.

I stayed silent. But inwardly, I cursed myself for my carelessness. Where the hell was Hamid?

I said, "My guard just stepped out. He'll be right back."
The man laughed. "Not in this lifetime."
My skin went cold at the implication. "What did you—?"
"Use your imagination. Now me, I'm just here with a friendly word
of warning. Relax. Take a sip of your drink."

I did as he said, swallowing hard as I moved my eyes enough to
glance around the bar. The bartender had vanished. The couple in the
booth were still ogling each other, oblivious to anything around them.
A man in jeans and a hoodie staggered through the door and made his
way toward the bar, clearly drunk and as oblivious as the couple. He sat
down and rested his face in his arms.

"None of these sheep will help you," the man said. "But there's
no need to be afraid. I won't hurt your pretty little skin, as long as you
listen."

There was the faintest lilt of an accent—Canadian, maybe. He
smelled of soap and sweat. I could just make out a knee encased in
green khaki and the sleeve of a tan shirt. My gaze fastened on the hand
holding the knife. The hand was large and pale and puffy with big
knuckles and neatly trimmed nails. A desk jockey's hand, I told myself.
Not the hand of a killer.

I rolled my eyes sideways, trying to catch a glimpse of his face.
"Tut-tut," he said with a dig of the knife. "Eyes forward."
I complied.

Across the table from me, Gonzo's ghost slid into the booth. Gonzo
was a Marine buddy who'd been blown apart by an IED. I'd processed
his body, and because of that he liked to show up in my life sometimes.
Now he shook his head at me, apparently amazed at my ineptitude.
Pretty critical for a dead guy.

"Be smart," he mouthed.

"See, we think you've gotten a little confused," the man beside me
said. "You and us—we're on the same side. We all want to put Iraq
behind us."

A woman came in and approached the bar. *"Hola!"* she called.

The drunkard's head stayed down. The bartender didn't emerge. I kept watching for Hamid.

Beside me, the man lifted his arm—the one without the knife—and draped it over my shoulders. Another large, pale hand came into view. This one had a smear of blood on it.

"Snuggle," he said, then sighed when I went stiff.

"Hola!" the woman called again. She glanced at her wristwatch and left.

"As I was saying," the man went on. "We want to lay Iraq to rest. The boy is secondary. Give us the intel Doug Ayers gave you, and the boy won't matter to us. We'll go away. You'll be safe. The boy will be safe. It will all be done with."

The intel again. It was the same request Sarge had made of me.

I'm here for the intel, girl. Then I gotta take care of you.

When I'd truthfully protested that I didn't know what he was talking about, he'd left bruises trying to get me to talk. It hadn't helped. I still didn't know what he was talking about.

Turn over whatever it was Ayers gave you, he'd said, *and I promise it will be quick. A single shot to the temple.*

But Dougie hadn't given me anything that could qualify as intelligence. A compass. A ring. A broken heart.

No video of men smuggling weapons into Iraq.

Perhaps taking my silence for refusal, the man said, "If you don't agree, then think of your friend Angelo as a warning. A taste of things to come."

"Deal," I whispered. "I'll give you what you want. But I require guarantees. Some way for me to know we'll be safe."

"We all want guarantees." He leaned in, brushing his cheek against mine. I didn't suppress the shudder. "But you got nothing to bargain with. If anything comes out about Iraq, you got as much to lose as we do."

"How do I know you won't kill the boy and me after you have what you want?"

"Your deaths would not be our first choice. We prefer not to draw attention to ourselves, if we can help it."

"Hasn't stopped you so far."

"Even so, we're not in the business of guarantees. That's as much as you're going to get."

I decided to see how far I could push this. And I wanted my capitulation to sound believable. "And I want money."

"Even the noble warrior has a price, eh? How much?"

"Two million."

The blade broke skin and trailed along my ribs. A line of fire followed the knife's path through my flesh, and a trickle of blood ran down my side. On the other side of the table, Gonzo shook his head. *Not your day to die,* he told me.

"You're a greedy little shit," the man said.

At the bar, the drunkard lifted his head. He didn't look our way.

"A hundred thousand," the man said, twisting the knife. "That ought to pay off that dump you live in and maybe buy your granny a nice casket."

In for a penny, in for a pound. "Two fifty."

The tip of the knife withdrew. My side continued to burn.

"Deal. You have twenty-four hours. After that, we assume you're not going to deliver without some additional motivation. Should we start with the boyfriend?"

My thoughts flew apart.

Panic kills, Gonzo said.

"That's not enough time." I scrambled to find a reason. "I can't access the intel that quickly."

"What, you hid it in Fort Knox?"

"A safety deposit box. But my access is limited." Was there even such a thing? "I set it up that way. Because of you assholes. I can't open it again for a month."

"You're shitting me."

Totally. "No."

Across the table, Gonzo gave me a thumbs-up.

The man said, "Did you forget how much you have to lose? Because if you did, we can remind you. One person at a time." The knife dug back in. "Give us everything Ayers gave you. Every nickel and dime, every photograph. Every piece-of-shit junk he gave you. And forget that month bullshit. You've got forty-eight hours. Figure it out."

He slid out of the booth, then leaned back in. When I went to turn my head, he grabbed my chin and held me still. "Go home to your boyfriend. And your mutt. Two days. We know where to find you."

"If anything happens to someone close to me," I said, "the deal is off. I'll take the intel and go straight to the Feds and the devil be damned."

"Such a little shit."

He released me, and I caught a glimpse of close-cropped blond hair and a pockmarked cheek before the back of his hand slammed into my face. Tears sprang to my eyes, and blood flew from my nose.

"Bit of advice," he said. "Don't piss me off. And don't try your hand at poker."

He straightened and walked away. The drunk staggered after him. Maybe they'd been in cahoots. I pressed a napkin to my nose. When the bleeding stopped, I lifted my blouse to check the damage. The wound wasn't much more than a scratch. Or that's what I told myself. But it was deep enough to bleed like a mother. I grabbed another cloth napkin from the table, folded it, and pressed it against the wound, then tucked my shirt back in, grateful it was dark enough to hide the blood.

Then I yanked out my phone and shot a text to Zarif.

Assaulted at airport. I think Hamid killed.

A response came immediately. You OK?

Still breathing. *Okay* was relative. I was alive.

I sat in the booth for a while longer, until the bleeding and shaking stopped and the wild rage banked down to a slow smolder. Gonzo sat with me.

Good job, he said. *Live to fight another day.*

"That why you volunteered for the mission that got you killed?" I asked, trying on snarky.

It fit better than fear.

◆ ◆ ◆

I was halfway through the security line when I came out of my fog enough to notice a flurry of activity outside the passageway leading toward the terminals. The passenger line stopped moving forward as security agents closed crowd-control ropes and spoke into their radios. On the far side of the cattle chute, two *policías* went by at a run.

Around me, people—tourists, mostly—chatted in nervous voices.

"I heard some dude was killed," said a guy in a Hawaiian shirt. "In the men's bathroom."

"My sister is out there," said a woman, looking at her phone screen. "A guy was knifed. She got the news from an airport employee."

My phone buzzed with a message. I pulled it out. A text from an unknown number. The hair rose on the back of my neck, as if I already knew I'd find something terrible.

Hamid, I thought.

I opened it.

A blond, acne-scarred man wearing a once-tan shirt and green khakis sat slumped in a rain of blood between a toilet and a tiled wall. His large-knuckled hands lay in his lap, the fingers of one hand curled around a knife.

My tormentor.

Someone had slit his throat.

CHAPTER 8

*How, one might ask, does a regular citizen get caught up in
the shadow lives of men and women who live by subterfuge,
conspiracy, assassination, and treason?*

All it takes is a single wrong step.

—*Sydney Parnell. Personal journal.*

I shuffled onto the plane as if my feet were shackled. The ticket Zarif
had purchased was for the window seat in the front row—first class.
The attendant took one look at my bloodied shirt and wounded face
and maybe came to her own conclusion about the kind of company I
kept. But she was kind, offering a pillow and a stiff drink. I accepted
both and tried to shut out the image of the man with the bloody second
smile beneath his chin.

But my mind kept circling around the thug's death, wondering who
had seen fit to eliminate him from the equation. Wondering who else
had a dog in this fight. If I was lucky, there was someone aside from
me and Zarif who cared about Malik's survival. Maybe the mysterious
Strider, the rescuer Malik had mentioned.

If I was unlucky . . .

I shifted in my seat, all too aware of forces swirling invisibly around me.

Did I still have forty-eight hours? Or had that deal died along with the man?

A businessman took the seat next to me. He gave me a polite nod, then leaned back with his own drink, a set of noise-canceling headphones, and the *Wall Street Journal*. Maybe he was a businessman. Maybe he belonged to Zarif, or to the Alpha.

At this point . . . whatever.

As the plane lifted into the air, I leaned my forehead against the window and touched my fingers to the cold whiskey glass. I watched the lights of Mexico City spread out below me, pinpricks in an ocean of darkness.

Malik, falling away from me while I sat at an impossible distance. I went to Mexico hoping to save his life. But all I'd had to offer was a handful of promises.

Try taking that to the bank, young man.

An icy breeze wafted through the cabin, as if someone had opened a door. I gripped the arm rests and turned in my seat.

Behind me sat two dead men, staring at me with molten eyes. Two of the six men whose lives I'd taken months earlier, while on an investigation with the Denver PD. The men had been killers, rapists, torturers. But they'd also been sons, brothers, husbands. And I'd killed them.

Our ghosts are our guilt.

You failed, one of them said, his lips a ruin.

You will always fail, the other sneered.

They scowled at me, their presence an accusation I had no way to refute. How do you apologize to the dead?

"Can I get you a blanket?"

I jerked back around. The flight attendant stood in the aisle, a crease between her blue eyes.

I nodded, and she handed me a soft square of cloth before offering a compassionate smile and moving on.

You'll never be warm, a voice breathed from behind.

My own set of Greek furies. Furiae. Erinyes. The infernal ones. Their presence cast me as the tragic hero of my own story, an Odysseus doomed to wander forever without peace.

I forced away my self-pitying thoughts and returned to more practical matters, back to the man who had been murdered at the airport. I wanted to believe I had a guardian angel, even if I'd prefer a less violent one. But I suspected the truth was darker. I figured there were multiple parties involved in whatever was going down, and someone had just upped the ante.

At least the risk wasn't all one-sided.

What I felt about the man who'd died was a sense of satisfaction. And that scared me more than anything. As soon as you are no longer bothered by death, maybe even approve of it, you've lost yourself on a dark path.

I slammed down the rest of the whiskey and reclined the seat. The lights dimmed. I pulled the blanket to my chin and let my eyes drift closed as memories swam to the surface.

The boiling sun set over Iraq, yielding to the silver knives of moonlight that carved up Camp Taqaddum, slicing through the barracks and the rec center and the motor pool. Outside the barricade, someone fired an AK-47, the rounds echoing in the empty desert around us.

Insurgents.

I touched the sidearm in my thigh holster to make sure it was still there. Combat—24-7-365.

"We're safe," said Corporal "Conan" Tomitsch.

"You think?"

"Sure, Lady Hawk." My own nickname.

I ducked into my tent and curled into a fetal position on my cot, breathing in kerosene fumes from the canvas. I must have finally slept, because sometime later I was startled awake by my commanding officer, the Sir, who knelt next to my bed, the red beam of his flashlight illuminating his face. He pressed his finger to his lips and tipped his head to indicate I should go with him. I reached for my uniform, but he handed me a pair of sweats and a hoodie, and I noticed that he was dressed in civvies. Uneasy, I pulled the sweats on over my T-shirt and shorts and followed him, weaving my way past my sleeping tent mates. Outside, the warm wind threw dust in our eyes while overhead, the Milky Way glittered like treasure from Ali Baba's cave.

The Sir said, "I'm going into Habbaniyah, Corporal Parnell, and I could use your help."

"This an order, sir?" Knowing something was off by his manner and our clothes.

"No, Corporal. Your choice."

He knew damn well I would crawl to Baghdad if that was what he needed me to do.

"Should I get Ayers, sir?" I asked. "For security?"

He regarded me with sudden alarm.

"No," he said. "No one can know about this. Especially not—no. Do you understand, Corporal? You can't tell Doug Ayers."

"I won't, sir. But, sir, you're giving me a bad feeling."

"Want to back out?"

"No, sir."

"I trust you, Parnell. It's why I chose you."

"Yes, sir. You can trust me." I trust you, too.

"This way, then."

◆ ◆ ◆

After a layover in Dallas where I went through Immigration and Customs, then boarded a different plane, I awoke a second time when we touched down in Denver at zero dark thirty. A text greeted me as soon as I switched my phone out of airplane mode: Cohen and Clyde were in the cell-phone lot, waiting for my text.

Once off the plane, I found the nearest bathroom and cleaned up as best I could. A bruise had bloomed across the bridge of my nose, edging toward my left eye, and there was no hiding that. The bleeding from my side was now only a seep. I reapplied paper towels and tucked my blouse to hold them in place.

I checked myself in the mirror one more time. Bruises. Check. Bloodstains. Check. Glowering rage with a side of panic. You bet. Everything I needed to make Cohen wonder what the hell I'd been up to.

No chance to dance around it any longer. It was time to tell this good man the truth. Even if it drove him away.

"Grab those bootstraps," I whispered to my reflection, "and pull hard."

Back on the concourse, the tourists streamed around me, talking sleepily. I shot Cohen a text, then called Hal Beckett, damn the hour. I'd tried to reach him while I was waiting to board the plane in Mexico and then again in Dallas.

As before, his phone went straight to voice mail. This time I left a message. "It's Rosie. We have to talk."

Hal was one of the few allowed to use my middle name. Father figure. With a caveat.

I snorted and wondered if this was how Luke felt about Darth Vader.

As I walked through the eerily quiet airport, I worked over how I would tell Cohen about my secret life. But as I fumbled over possible segues into my checkered past, I found no gracious way to tell him that I'd gotten myself eyeball deep in some serious shit. And that, through no fault of his own, he was hip deep in the cesspool with me.

Not for the first time, I reflected on the fact that if our roles were reversed, if he'd been the one who spent our time together getting all "I can't tell you or I'll have to kill you" on me, I would have walked out months ago.

I startled when a ghostly figure emerged from a janitor's closet on my right. The Sir.

The truth shall set you free, I imagined him saying.

"You're probably right, sir." Probably far freer than I wanted to be.

The glass doors leading outside whooshed open, and I stepped onto the sidewalk, leaving the Sir behind. A deep, joyous bark echoed from somewhere farther down the passenger pick-up area, and then there was my partner, my war buddy, my best friend, bounding toward me, the handful of travelers parting before him as if he were Moses dashing across the Red Sea.

I dropped my duffel, squatted, and braced for impact. Clyde sailed over the last few feet separating us and bounded into my open arms, planting his front paws on my shoulders and sending me staggering. We were eyeball to eyeball for all of two seconds before I squeezed my eyes shut, and he mopped the tears from my face with one sweep.

"Good boy!" I cried in the high singsong voice he loved. "Good Clyde!"

I wrestled him to the ground and onto his back, ignoring the pain from my injuries. His tail thumped against the sidewalk, his back leg spasmodically kicking as I rubbed his belly beneath his service vest. Then he rolled back over and sprang at me again, and this time we both went to the ground.

"You'd swear I kept him chained in the basement, barely alive on dry kibble," Cohen said from somewhere above us.

I wrestled out from under Clyde and let Cohen pull me to my feet.

We took each other in for a moment. He processed the bruise and the dark stains.

"Rough landing?"

"You should see the runway."

His thumb brushed my bruise, then his hand drifted to my hair. "Suddenly a brunette?"

"Think of it as getting to sleep with another woman."

But he shook his head at me. "You could shave your head and dye your scalp orange, and I'd be good with it."

"I'm saving that for when the Broncos go to the Super Bowl."

He stared at me a moment longer, then wrapped me in his arms. I pressed my face to his shoulder and inhaled his scent. For a few long moments, words ceased to matter.

If only we could stay this way.

At the car, he opened the back seat for Clyde while I got into the front. Clyde shoved his head between the seats and tried to get to work on my face again. Gently, I pushed him back.

"I'm clean enough now, thanks," I said.

He doggie-grinned.

"You want to stop at a doc-in-the-box?" Cohen asked as we left the airport and hit Peña Boulevard, heading toward I-70. Maybe he'd seen me wince when I got in the car.

For a moment, feeling a fresh seep of blood, I considered asking him to drop me off to see my Grams. She was a nurse who'd tended to more than her share of traumatic injuries. Plus, it would give me a chance to warn her and my honorary aunt, Ellen Ann Lasko, about the Alpha.

Then again, right now nothing connected the Lasko residence to me. Grams and Ellen Ann were safe for tonight as long as Cohen and I didn't unwittingly lead someone there.

Cohen's voice broke in. "Sydney? Make a stop?"

"Nah. I just need a bandage and some lidocaine."

"That I can handle. With a Marine in the house, I've learned to stock up."

"Glad I'm doing my part for disaster preparedness."

Our playful schtick wasn't going over well in Peoria. Cohen tapped the steering wheel twice, then said, "I didn't expect you back so soon. You get done what you'd hoped?"

"Some of it."

I caught an angry flick in his eyes. Cohen possessed the patience of Job. But even Job had his limit. I reached out and ran the tips of my fingers across his knuckles and around to the flesh of his wrist. His skin was warm, familiar, beloved. A sudden image rose in my mind of those hands on my body. On my shoulders and ribs and waist. On my breasts. Everywhere.

I snatched my hand back. "I'm ready to talk, Cohen."

"What?" He actually laughed. "I didn't even have to waterboard you. Say it again. Wait, let me turn on a recorder."

"Laugh while you can."

He glanced over with the look on his face that I loved. Open, curious, eager. Mingled in was relief. And a tenderness that wouldn't last once I started talking.

That's right, Detective Cohen. Make what I have to say even harder.

"Sydney, don't you get it? Whatever you have to tell me, it won't change anything. I'll still—"

"Stop." This time my hand went to his lips. "Don't say anything you'll have to take back. Once you know what you're dealing with, then you can decide how you feel about me. Just give me a few minutes to figure out how to say what I have to say."

He breathed out a sigh and nodded. His posture went soft, as if he'd just settled into a comfy chair. Might as well let him enjoy it while he could.

It lasted the few seconds it took us to get from I-70 to I-225, and then his shoulders came up again.

"You probably haven't heard." He reached out and took my hand. "I'm sorry to tell you. Jeremy Kane was killed yesterday."

And there we were. The opening I both wanted and dreaded. Cohen knew that Kane and I were acquaintances—I'd talked to Kane during the Elise Hensley case. But he had no idea what really tied us together.

"I saw an article in the paper," I said. "The case is yours?"

"Most everyone is on deck for this." He put both hands back on the wheel. "A lot of footwork involved. Lead is a detective named Bill Gorman."

Gorman and I had worked together briefly on a theft case before he moved to Major Crimes.

"He's a low-hanging fruit kind of guy," I said. "Or did I miss something?"

Cohen stayed silent as he merged with the westbound traffic on the interstate. It was answer enough.

"How'd he get the assignment?"

"He was up in the rotation."

I stared out the windshield. I was pissed, but in truth, a lazy or lousy cop made my task less difficult. He was likely to let me work on angles and not ask too many questions. The fact that Cohen was only peripherally on the case made it both easier and harder. Easier because I wouldn't have to keep him embroiled. Harder since I also wouldn't have access to much information. Cohen often shared his cases with me because, as he generously put it, my view of the world was warped.

Sometimes I fit perfectly.

He took the I-25 ramp heading north, then exited at Hampden and turned west. In the back seat, Clyde lay down. But he kept his head on the console, and I continued to rub his ears. As always, his company was a solace. I figured he felt the same way about me.

That's what it means to have a war buddy. No one gets it like those who've been there.

I wondered if Cohen could understand what I was about to share. He'd hunted gangbangers, gone undercover with drug dealers, and as a murder cop, he'd peered into the darkest recesses of the human soul.

But he'd never been to my kind of war.

◆ ◆ ◆

Michael Walker Cohen lived in Cherry Hills, a neighborhood where the houses cost more than what I'd make putting in forty years on the job. My first glimpse of the place had made me feel like I'd landed on Mars. I'd warned myself not to get involved with a man who could start and finish each day in a bubble so rarified it almost demanded its own supply of oxygen.

But when I learned it was family money and he was every bit as uncomfortable with it as I was, I overcame my hesitation. Now, well . . . I couldn't say I hated it. The manicured grounds, the gourmet kitchen, the fact that no matter how much junk you had, there was a cupboard for it—it added up to something. Plus, Clyde seemed to prefer trees over fire hydrants. Cohen's deceased grandmother's library—which ran to history books and noir mysteries—along with a wine cellar that held mostly whiskey stored upright in glass cases like museum specimens . . . these things helped ease the transition.

So far, I'd worked my way from Ken Bruen to James Cain and, with Cohen's help, through most of a bottle of Ardbeg Renaissance.

The money also told me what made Cohen such a great detective— he was motivated by his sense of justice, not a pension.

That counted for a lot.

The family mansion loomed before us, our headlights illuminating gables and flashing off leaded glass windows. His grandmother—the only other Cohen to venture west of the Mississippi—had lived in the house until her death. Now, the only people going in and out were the cleaning staff.

Cohen lived in the carriage house out back.

As he took the curve around the manor and approached the carriage-house driveway, the headlights caught a small security sign planted near the stairs to the front door.

I raised an eyebrow. "That's new."

Cohen shrugged self-consciously. "Had a break-in the day you left."

A ghostly hand pressed fingers to my neck. I forced my voice to remain casual. "Here in the land of entry-coded gates and a roving security force? You've destroyed my faith."

The garage door sensed his vehicle and opened obligingly. Welcome home, sir.

He said, "The insurance guys told me they'd keep my rates down if I bought into a security service. Makes sense. But it's embarrassing as hell for a cop. Anyway, I wrote the security code down for you. It's by the phone in the kitchen."

"They take anything?"

"Not as far as I could tell."

"So how did you know—?"

"They left a calling card."

A ragged thread in his voice made me sit up. "What kind of card?"

"Sydney—"

"Tell me."

"They left a dog in the house."

"A *dog*?"

"Not a live one."

That shut me down. My hand reached back for Clyde, and I buried my fingers in his fur.

"Looked like a pooch they found on the street," Cohen said. "Thin and filthy. Someone strangled it. My top suspect is a guy I put away for robbery who just got paroled. A piece of work, that one. Started every job by shooting the pets. His PO is following up with him. In the meantime, I changed the locks and hired the security service."

"Where did he leave the dog?"

Cohen's eyes flicked to Clyde. "Doesn't matter. I took care of it."

We got out of the vehicle, and Clyde and I followed Cohen up the stairs. Once inside, the first thing I noticed was Clyde's new bed in the living room. I raised an eyebrow.

"That's where the dead dog was?"

An elaborately casual shrug. "Clyde needed a new bed anyway."

Clyde, at least, seemed to agree. After I removed his service vest, he gave the fabric a good sniff, then circled in place for a few seconds before plopping down. He unfurled a tongue long enough for a photo shoot at the Oscars and grinned at me.

My hands curled into fists. They could not have him. Not Clyde. And not Cohen.

Payback was going to be hell.

Cohen's phone buzzed. He looked at the number, then excused himself and went into the kitchen area. I popped into the bathroom to use the promised ointment and bandages, then took a seat on the couch and tried to spend a few minutes enjoying the pleasure of home.

Not my *home,* I reminded myself. *Cohen's home.*

The distinction was important. In a few minutes, everything might change.

The main floor of the carriage house consisted of a great room—a living room and a partially walled-off kitchen that filled the immense space. Floor-to-ceiling windows lined the front of the room. Exposed beams spanned the ceiling. Quietly tasteful furniture was arranged in elegant groupings. At one end of the room was a basketball hoop; at the other stood a fireplace that would comfortably fit a pair of roast pigs.

Opposite the windows rose a wall where people of taste would have mounted art. Instead, Cohen and I had installed two corkboards. His board had originally been downstairs, in the study; after I moved in, he kept the door to the room closed so that I didn't have to look at whatever case he was working. But there wasn't enough wall space in there for him to tack up everything he needed to see when he was actively running an investigation. I'd encouraged him to move the board to the living room. Which meant that if you leaned back from your barstool at the kitchen counter, you'd be greeted with an array of crime-scene photos. No doubt, it was an unhealthy blending of our jobs and our off-duty hours. But it worked for us. Cohen was never really off duty anyway. And often the subconscious picks up what the conscious mind has missed. Having his board within sight had sparked ideas more than once.

Now his corkboard was covered with photos from his current case—a jogger slain in Commons Park.

I leaned back on the couch and narrowed my eyes to squint at my own board, which was a montage of thirty-some photographs. Some of these were images I'd taken in Iraq—shots of our Mortuary Affairs bunker or the mess tent or the rec center. Others were more personal. My cot, looking sterile and unlived in save for the books stacked on the floor. Pictures of my fellow MA Marines playing volleyball. Photos of Malik I'd taken when he lived on the FOB.

Pinned somewhere in the montage were the two photos I'd taken from Sergeant Udell's apartment. In one of them, Sarge and Malik stood with Richard Dalton, the man Angelo's torturer had questioned him about.

Almost two thousand miles away, and I still heard Angelo's voice in my ear. *Dalton. They wanted to know . . . about him. I . . . know nothing. Why . . . do they ask?*

Dalton was the man whose ghost I'd seen six months ago when I'd gone to Sarge's apartment. In this photo, Dalton looked confident, even arrogant. He and Udell squinted into the desert sun, Malik standing between them and holding a soccer ball. All three were smiling like they'd won the lottery.

Of course, the ghost I'd seen—imagined—hadn't really been Dalton. According to two people who knew him, the man was alive and doing just fine, still on the job in Iraq. And if Dalton actually was alive, then he might be my Alpha. He was CIA, in-country at the right time, and had a relationship with both Malik and Sarge. I'd considered the theory many times, but had nowhere to run with it. The only person who might be able to feed me information about Dalton was

Hal Beckett. And Hal, according to Zarif and the evidence of my own unanswered calls, was not available to mere mortals.

As for the ghost, my counselor had his own theory.

This man—this image—is an outward manifestation of your anger and fear, he told me during one of our sessions. *At some point, your path crossed with his, and your brain internalized his image. These ghosts, as you call them, are parts of you that your core self doesn't know how to process. Over time, we'll integrate them. It's how we heal.*

Sounded like a plan to me. But so far, there hadn't been any integration. I was the woman of a hundred ghosts.

Well, fifteen, give or take.

I rose and crossed the room to the board. I reached out with a finger and touched the second picture I'd taken from Sarge's apartment. In this image, Dalton stood in front of an Iraqi market. Behind him and to his right was a second man, also dressed like an Iraqi. This man's face was in shadow and hard to make out. The first time I saw the photo, I'd recognized him by the curved Kurdish dagger he wore in his belt. He'd bought it off a bedouin coming in from the wadis of the Syrian Desert.

This man was Douglas Reynauld Ayers. Dougie.

The man Clyde and I had both loved before he was killed in an ambush. The man I suspected we both still loved.

I let my finger trail over his image, then stepped back.

I tilted my head. The pictures had been moved slightly. It took me a few seconds to realize what was wrong. The pictures had been moved to cover a gap.

The photo of Malik, Sarge, and Richard Dalton was gone.

CHAPTER 9

Before the bomb hits, there comes a shriek that splits your soul.

—Sydney Parnell. ENGL 0208 Psychology of Combat.

I stood frozen in front of the corkboard.

"Cohen?" I called.

He leaned out of the kitchen.

"Did you move any of the photos on my corkboard?"

He understood immediately. "Something's gone?"

Behind him, a kettle's whistle blew.

"I'll be right out," he said.

I rubbed my upper arms, the goose bumps like sand on my skin. I understood the message they'd sent by killing the dog. But why would the Alpha steal a photo of Malik with Sarge and Dalton? Unless Dalton *was* the Alpha, and he was covering his tracks.

Then why not take the photo of him with Dougie?

I flipped quickly through the rest of the pinned photos, making sure the one I wanted hadn't been concealed by the others. Then I checked the floor and behind the library table set against the wall.

Nothing.

The gentle sounds of Nina Simone wafted into the room. Cohen had queued up what I thought of as his deep-thinking playlist and piped it through the built-in sound system. I loved the great women of jazz. Simone, Holiday, Vaughan. But tonight I felt more Megadeth than "Don't Let Me Be Misunderstood."

Cohen joined me at the wall and handed me a mug of steaming liquid.

I scowled. "What is this?"

"Chamomile tea." At my look he added, "You'll sleep better on that than on booze."

"You get your medical degree while I was gone?"

"Shut up and drink it."

I held the mug at arm's length. "Jazz and herbal tea. What's next? Laxatives and long-term care insurance?"

"Pacifiers and a blanket."

He sidestepped my jab. I held on to the grimace, took a sip of the tea, and let my frown deepen for Cohen's benefit. But the flavor was only moderately awful.

"What do you think?" Cohen asked.

Never call me a pushover. "It's dreadful."

"You'll get used to it." He grinned. "I bought a case. It was on sale."

"You sneak in anything else healthy while I was gone?"

"Veggie bones."

"For us or for Clyde?"

Cohen's expression stayed innocent. "Depends on whether Clyde likes them."

"Well, that's a relief. He likes everything. No sense of taste." I sniffed the tea. "It's contagious, apparently."

We both glanced at Clyde, who lay sprawled on his side, lights out and snoring.

"He likes his new bed," I said.

"Memory foam."

"He liked his old one, too."

And with that, the moment passed. We turned back to the corkboard.

"Which picture is missing?" Cohen asked.

"A photo of the boy I went to Mexico to find." For the moment, I left out any mention of Dalton and Sarge. I would ease into them if I had to.

"So whoever broke in here and left the dog . . . it has something to do with this boy?"

A thought occurred to me then with a fierce and sudden burn, like the bite of a rattlesnake. I snatched up the pad of paper Cohen kept near the corkboards, jotted down a note, then turned the pad toward him.

YOU STILL HAVE THAT AUDIO JAMMER YOUR BROTHER GAVE YOU?

He cocked an eyebrow but then nodded. He went downstairs to his study and came back a moment later with a small black box. He placed it on a table nearby and turned the switch, slowly raising the volume until Ella Fitzgerald sounded like she was singing next to a waterfall.

Cohen leaned close to me. "That good?"

How can you not love a man who accepts your paranoia? I nodded.

He angled his shoulders so that he faced me, his eyes alert with that expression I loved. The one that reminded me painfully of Dougie. Cohen's look said, *I need to know everything, and yesterday was too late.*

I heard Dougie's voice in my head. *Tell me everything.*

"Sydney," Cohen said. "It's time to share."

I brushed the backs of my fingers against his cheek. He turned his head and kissed my hand.

The fear for this man that I'd been holding ever since Sarge broke into my home and threatened my life now wrapped its hands around my throat and tried to drag me to the floor. Along with the fear came a shame that went beyond guilt. Guilt was for when you forgot to call your mother on her birthday. This feeling was the kind that settled in your bones and set the marrow on fire.

All because, I finally admitted, I'd allowed myself to fall in love.

And now I was about to blow it out of the water.

I drew in a breath. "Mike . . ." Another breath. At this rate I'd need an oxygen tank just to get started. "I never meant for you to be a part of this."

"Part of what?"

"It's a long story."

He took my hand and led me to the couch. And while Édith Piaf sang "La Vie en Rose" to the accompaniment of static hiss, I took a corner on the sofa and faced him, my mug cupped between my hands like an anchor that would keep me from flying apart.

"I don't even know where to begin," I said.

"Start anywhere," he answered. "We've got all night."

Deep in my chest, where no one could see, my heart began to bleed. Too late we come to our realizations.

"It's an ugly story," I said. "And I will tell you most of it. But I can't tell you everything. For your sake and for mine. You have to accept that."

Cohen's jaw went tight, which suggested he wasn't 100 percent on board. But he said, "I can respect that."

"Close enough."

I pulled my knees up to my chest and went small. The adult version of hiding when you know you can't. I took a few more breaths until a strange calm descended.

"I'll start with the abridged version. The child I went to Mexico to find, his name is Malik. His mother was an interpreter for the Marines. His uncle also worked with the Americans. Malik was a small child at the start of the Iraq War, and he grew up around US troops. At some point, he saw something he shouldn't have. Something that involved Americans and was quite possibly treasonous. These are bad people, Cohen. They've murdered to protect their secret. They've killed

Americans *and* Iraqis to make sure they couldn't talk. Now, these same people have figured out that Malik was a witness, and they want to silence him before he shares what he saw with the world."

Cohen's expression changed from curiosity to bewilderment as he processed my words. Now he shook his head.

"Sounds like Hollywood, right?" I said.

"Did you say treason?"

"Yes."

His face cleared and a look of relief flooded his eyes. "There are people for this kind of thing, Sydney. Entire organizations. Interpol. The International Criminal Court. Truth and reconciliation committees. Hell, Congress. Let's take it to them."

I heard the plural and loved him for it. But I shook my head. "Right now I have nothing to offer them. I don't even have enough to warrant opening an investigation."

"But that's the point. Let them determine if there's a case. We can—"

I held up a hand to stop him. "Not yet."

"Don't try to protect these people, Sydney. They don't deserve it."

"I'm not!" I glanced at the audio jammer and sucked in a few breaths until I could talk without screaming or breaking things. "This isn't just about me and this child. A lot of lives are caught up in this. People have died. Not just in Iraq, but here. If I try to go public, these men will double down."

Faint flickering forms appeared in my mind's eye. Angelo Garcia. Zarif's man, Hamid. Jeremy Kane. The Alpha's victims.

"And they'll hurt this boy," Cohen said. "Malik."

"They'll kill him."

I stopped myself before I told him that I thought the boy was safe for the moment. Giving him that information was too risky. It implied we knew something of his whereabouts. And if they grabbed Cohen and forced him to talk . . .

I saw fingers chopped off. A face beaten to a pulp. Cigarette burns and cattle prods and waterboarding.

Even as I turned away from these things, a detached part of my brain ran busily in the cranial basement, coolly calculating what to share with Cohen and what to hide in the event that he was forced to talk. It was a gift from growing up in an unpredictable household—always make sure you have the right answer before you open your mouth.

I hated it, but there it was. What I didn't tell him might save us both.

"I won't put Malik at risk," I said.

"That's exactly why you need to get others involved."

"Later."

"Sydney . . ."

In my belly, something reached out a languorous paw and scratched.

Every Marine carries some form of the beast inside. We might soothe it with alcohol or numb it with drugs or teach it to play dead through counseling. And sometimes, after a few years as a civilian, the beast goes quiet.

But even when we've gone a little soft, the monster hasn't gone away. It just hasn't been fed in a while.

I pushed myself off the couch. "There's something else."

"What?"

This was the part in a movie where the music swelled to a harsh crescendo, letting us know that things had changed and there was no going back. But here, in the wealthy enclave of Cherry Hills, the only sounds were jazz and static and the light jingle of Clyde's collar as he went into the kitchen to see if anything interesting had shown up in his food dish.

I kept my eyes on Cohen while I delivered the coup de grâce.

"I played a part in that treason."

Cohen's expression went sideways, the look of a man who'd just gotten a vicious uppercut. *"You?"*

Fear and fury flooded my mouth like molten steel. "Yes. Me."

Cohen didn't move an inch. But I felt him withdraw nonetheless. As if he'd gotten up and walked into another room.

"Tell me," he said in a faraway voice.

So I did. A few fumbling words into the story, Denver vanished, and Iraq rose up around me in a swirl of dust and heat. I smelled blood and shit while all around the cries of men shattered the air. And through it, I kept talking, trying to get Cohen to understand.

After I'd agreed to help, the Sir and I went to a residential area in the town of Habbaniyah, where we wouldn't normally venture without an armored caravan. Four men with rifles stood outside a single-story mud house. The men wore street clothes; keffiyehs covered their mouths and noses. I thought they were Iraqis until I heard them whispering.

Americans. Tucker Rhodes. Lester Crowe. Jeremy Kane.

I followed the Sir and one of the Marines into the house.

There were two bodies, both in a back bedroom, both naked, dead a couple of hours. A male Marine, castrated and beheaded, his head propped next to the gaping wound near his crotch, his penis and testicles where his head should have been. Next to him lay a pregnant Iraqi female, her face destroyed, her body battered until the skin had split.

In the front room was a young Iraqi boy, rocking and weeping on the floor.

Nauseated, horrified, I clung to the wooden doorjamb for support. I couldn't understand why the Sir had brought me to this place in the middle of the night. To these deaths and this weeping child. It wasn't how we operated.

"Let's get them out of here, Corporal," the Sir said to me.

And because he was my CO, and because I trusted him, I did as he ordered. We lifted the corpses into body bags, placed them into the trunk of the interpreter's car, and took them away.

"Sydney?" Cohen's voice brought me back.

Cohen's home emerged from the darkness. I looked around. Blinked. I did not look at Cohen. I was afraid to.

Clyde padded over and rested his chin on my thighs. I set aside the cold tea and dropped my hand to his head.

"After we took them away," I said, "we destroyed the bodies. Not only because it was an order, but because we believed it was the right thing to do. The man who issued the order told my CO that members of a Sunni militia had killed Haifa and Resenko, to punish them for falling in love. This came just as we were doing our best to win hearts and minds. If word had gotten out about the killing, the fallout on both sides would have been horrendous. The Sir and I were told that if we made these deaths look like a random IED attack instead of a targeted assault against a Marine, we'd keep our guys from going all Abu Ghraib and killing everything in a headcloth. And that would keep the insurgents from retaliating and killing more of our guys. Turns out, it didn't work. Things got bad anyway."

"I . . . see," Cohen said.

There was a note in his voice I'd only heard him use with people he didn't like. Drug dealers and murderers. Weak judges and lazy cops and the unrepentant.

I was so young, I wanted to say. *Barely more than a child.* In my mind, I heard that most heinous of excuses: *I was only following orders.*

"And Jeremy Kane was there," Cohen went on.

"Yes." I forced myself to again look him in the eye. "I thought we were saving American lives. Only years later did I learn that my actions played right into the hands of a man whose behavior was probably treasonous. He gave the order. He made me part of his sin."

But Cohen was shaking his head. "Give me a hand here, Sydney. I'm trying to understand. What about their families? Didn't they have a right to know the truth?"

I said nothing. He needed to work it out. If that was even possible.

He went on. "I'm trying to line up the woman I thought I knew with what you're telling me."

This was exactly why veterans don't talk about the war. How can anyone understand decisions made under fire, or turns taken when it feels like there's no other way to go? Only someone who's been in the cauldron knows that truth has many sides.

An abyss yawned between us. The gulf that always existed between the military and civilians. A lot of people on both sides of the fence were trying to close that gap. After all, trauma isn't owned by veterans. Neither is an ability to understand war. But it's a hard argument to make with the troops. Even within the military community there is a pecking order akin to whose dick was the biggest: You see combat? How many tours? You get blown up? How many times?

Now here I was with Cohen, as if we were a microcosm of that old divide between the warrior class and those whose nearest approach to war was playing Call of Duty. Cohen had seen his share of ugly. But not war ugly.

Still, I had hope. Ask any astronomer, and they'll agree that significant things happen with the close approach of two bodies. Tides. Menses cycles. Social madness in all its forms.

Love.

"I know about the pages you stole from Jazmine's file," Cohen said.

Or maybe not.

The blood left my face. My hand slid off Clyde's head, and he nosed my palm, worried.

"I know you put them back," Cohen went on. "But it was hard for me to understand."

During the first full investigation Cohen and I worked together, I'd found references in a case file to a man I'd grown up with, Gentry Lasko, a man who was like a brother to me. He was listed as a possible suspect in a cold case. In a panic, I'd stolen the pages out of the case binder, wanting to give him a chance to tell his story before the police went to him. In my world, family did for family before they did for anyone else.

I'd felt horrible about it. But I'd done it anyway.

"How long have you known?"

"Since just before we wrapped up the case. I went to talk to your friend. I believed him when he said he hadn't touched Jazmine. And we had our killer, so I let it go." His gray eyes were hard. "But I had to work at it."

I stayed silent. A hundred excuses came to mind, but I didn't offer any of them. How Cohen chose to see me was his decision alone.

"You want to say anything?" he pressed.

"You have the facts."

"You aren't making this easy."

"It isn't an easy thing."

He sighed and shook himself. After a moment, he pushed up the sleeves of his pullover and rested his elbows on his thighs, switching modes.

"Let's put culpability aside for the moment," he said. "Who gave the order to destroy the bodies?"

"That's what I'm trying to find out."

"And you think this person is silencing everyone involved. And he started with Jeremy Kane."

"Yes."

"And he's also after you."

"They'll come for me soon enough."

"*They?*" Cohen's face went pale. "Jesus, Sydney."

I noticed for the first time that the whites of his eyes were shot through with red, and he'd missed a patch while shaving. He'd been working overtime, the way he always did when on a case.

And now I'd dropped this in his lap like tossing a grenade.

He glanced around his home. This privileged, sheltered place with its marble countertops and floor-to-ceiling windows, the leather furniture and wide-planked floors and Sub-Zero refrigerator. The ghetto-hip basketball hoop where he practiced his hook shot in a living room large enough to park a Cessna. He knuckled his eyes, and when he dropped his hands, he looked like a man who'd found that his house had been plucked from Kansas and dropped in Oz's war zone. And the witch was fresh out of ruby slippers.

His eyes came back to mine. "This man hurt you in Mexico?"

"One of his men did. Yes."

"How can you just . . . you're so calm."

"I have no choice. You're involved now, and this is about your life as much as mine." I wanted nothing more than to touch him. But I didn't move. "I have to stay calm."

He cleared his throat. "What about your CO? What does he think? He must know who gave the order."

"He died not long after that night. Mortar attack. I thought it was bad luck. Now I'm not so sure."

"Okay." He palmed a fist, rapping his knuckles. "You said one person gave your CO the order. Who is this 'they' you're talking about?"

"I think one man is behind it. I call him the Alpha. But he's got plenty of help."

"What kind of help?"

"I'm trying to figure that out, too. But I have reason to believe they're black-ops people."

He scraped his fingers through his hair. "You mean something like the NSA? Or the CIA?"

"Like that. Yes." Clyde was watching me with worried eyes, and I placed my hand back on his head. "I don't know. That's part of the problem."

"Okay. Okay." Cohen's voice was artificially brisk. "Tell me what you're thinking. What do you intend to do?"

"If I can determine exactly what happened over there and who was behind it, *then* I can take it to the authorities. And then I will grind these guys into the dirt."

"Won't that be risky for you if the whole story comes out?"

"I could still be court-martialed. You should know that. But that's the least of my worries right now. My plan is to start with Jeremy Kane's murder. Finding his killer should get me a lead to the Alpha."

Cohen narrowed his eyes. This was his territory.

"How so?" he asked. "All the evidence points to a homeless man."

"A homeless man whom all of the Denver PD can't find? Who just disappears into thin air?"

"Go on."

"That's pretty much my case in a nutshell." I looked away. "I need to know you won't try to stop me."

He was silent for a long time. A trumpet solo heralded Billie Holiday's "Strange Fruit." Cohen stood and went into the kitchen, then returned a moment later with two glasses, each holding two fingers of amber liquid. He handed one of the glasses to me.

"Last of the Ardbeg," he said, clinking his glass to mine.

We drank. The scotch burned.

He went to the nearest window and gave me his back. "I have to go to LA for a trial. The crime was committed in California, but we caught the guy here. I was going to leave Clyde with your grandmother since I fly out in the morning."

"How long?"

"At least a few days."

Relief flooded through me. "That's good."

"It sucks. But I don't have a choice." His voice was tight. "Come with me."

"You know I can't."

"I know you won't. I'll tell Gorman that Kane was a friend of yours and ask him to share what he learns."

"Thank you."

He tossed down the rest of the whiskey and without looking at me walked around the couch toward the bedroom. "I'm going to bed."

"Just like that?"

He stopped. His shoulders were a wall. "I have to think about this, Sydney. I'm grateful that you finally shared things with me. And I don't want to punish you for letting me in. It's what I've been asking for ever since we met. But it's a lot. I need time to chew it over."

"You're not even in the room with me right now," I said.

"Maybe not. But the real problem is that you have never been in the room. You never even left the doorway."

Since Cohen and I had been together, I'd wanted to make our relationship normal. Create a bond that wasn't hobbled by my past. A "how was your day at the office, dear?" kind of relationship.

But he was right. I was way too skittish to walk all the way into the room.

"I'm sorry," I said.

"It's not what you did in Iraq. As a cop, I know we're all just trying to do our best. And I know that sometimes it's impossible in the moment to perfectly draw that line between right and wrong. I get that."

My pulse throbbed in my temple. "What, then?"

"It's how you handled it with me. You've buried yourself so far behind your walls that even when both our lives were in danger, you wouldn't let me in. Wouldn't tell me what was going on. And now . . . now I don't know if I can trust you to have my back."

A needle slid into my heart. "I thought I could handle it on my own."

"That's exactly the problem. You think you have to handle everything by yourself. You should have included me, Sydney. Dammit." He turned to face me. Anger and pain and hurt swam in his eyes, eddies in a dark current. His entire body slumped, as if gravity had finally gotten a grip on him. "Can you try not to die while I'm gone?"

My eyes filled. "Marines are hard to kill."

"Apparently, not always."

Because I had no words, I tried to put everything in my eyes. Love, apology, strength. Maybe Cohen saw it. Maybe not.

"I love you," he said. "But I don't know what that means anymore. Because I don't really know who you are."

He turned and walked into our bedroom, taking my heart with him.

CHAPTER 10

Hard shouldn't scare you. Lay yourself open to the bone if you have to and take out what's weak.

—Effie "Grams" Parnell. Private conversation.

Cohen didn't stir when I came into the bedroom.

I undressed and slid in beside him. He lay with his back to me, and I lifted my hand, intending to touch him. To try and break down the barrier of flesh and bone he'd erected as firmly as a stonemason's wall. But in the end, I was too much of a coward. I rolled away and stared into the dark until sleep finally granted me the company Cohen would not.

I woke the next morning to the sound of him showering. When he came back into the bedroom, I feigned sleep while he grabbed a few things from the closet. A minute later, the garage door went up and then down, and as quietly as that, Cohen was gone.

For a few days, or forever.

I shot him a text, asking him to let me know when he'd landed. Then I tossed back the covers and hauled myself to a sitting position. Clyde came back from following Cohen and locked his eyes on mine, his brow furrowed but his tail wagging.

You're late, he was saying. He butted my knees. *Time to get our game on.*

"Ooh rah," I agreed without much heart. I set aside my pain to deal with later, preferably in the dark and with a bottle of scotch. "Let's go get the bastards."

◆ ◆ ◆

As Clyde and I left the gated community of Cherry Hills in my ancient Land Cruiser, I watched for a tail. It had to be there. But if so, the guy was too slick for me to spot. I spent fifteen minutes winding through backstreets without noticing anything, and finally accelerated onto I-25 and got sucked into the clot of morning traffic creeping north. On a good day, my beloved old truck topped out at fifty; this morning, that was ten miles an hour faster than the traffic.

I took the exit for I-70 and headed east toward Limon, away from my destination. I exited at Washington Street and took a few turns before I pulled into the parking lot of a liquor store. Still nothing. Finally, convinced we were alone, I returned west on Forty-Eighth. Once I was on the far side of the freeway, I made better time on the side roads.

Grams lived with my honorary aunt, Ellen Ann Lasko, in Denver's Royer district, a low-rent scab on the face of the gentrification occurring all around. Royer had been settled in the early 1900s as a housing district for employees of a smelting and refining company. These days, most of the people in Royer worked for the railroad. Or had until gasoline got cheap in the eighties, and the railroads downsized. Now the neighborhood boasted more long-haul truckers than railroaders, along with plenty of the unemployed. Rumor had it that railroads were about to get popular again. Maybe there would be a shift in who was using food stamps at the local supermarket.

I used to come to Royer often, hoping to score dinner from Ellen Ann and guidance from Nik. But all that had changed after Nik and

I worked a case together the previous winter and things ended badly. I'd hardly been back here since Nik died and Grams moved in with Ellen Ann. Visiting my onetime home away from home had become too painful. Plus, I'd been fearful of drawing the Alpha's attention here.

There was no reason for him to look at the Lasko residence unless I pointed it out.

Now, as I pulled to the curb and studied the house, it was Nik Lasko who occupied my thoughts. The sight of his truck in the driveway with its God and Country Will Prevail bumper sticker shafted a hurt into me that went bone deep.

Nik had been like an uncle. A father, even. Offering advice and encouragement and sometimes disapproval. But he had not been the man I thought he was.

I knew how he would have handled the Alpha, though. He would have gone in, guns blazing.

"You have to know what you're fighting first, Nik," I whispered.

I looked away, blinking, and let my gaze land on other homes, ones without the kind of memories that could gut me. When I was calm, I looked back at Nik's.

No matter what, home remains home, and even though looking at it hurt, it also satisfied some part of me to take comfort in the familiar porch, the American flag, the white vinyl siding. All the ways in which Nik had made a home for himself and Ellen Ann and their son, Gentry.

I grabbed my duffel, and Clyde and I got out. When I slammed the truck door, a curtain twitched in the window, then the front door opened. Grams unlatched the screen as we reached the top step.

"It's good to see you, Sydney Rose," she said in a voice as dry as two twigs trying to spark fire. "Thought maybe you'd lost the address."

Clyde and I stepped inside, and I embraced her. Her thin, strong arms wrapped around me, and even though she barely reached my shoulder, I felt like a child again, enfolded in her love. The house smelled warmly of lemon, and even out here I heard the kitchen clock drone its slow ticktock, as if time in this house passed differently, without the troubling madness of the outside world.

Still holding me, Grams said, "Ellen Ann's out. She'll be sorry she missed you."

"Give her my love when she gets home."

"You're back to Denver a little soon, aren't you?"

"Mexico beaches didn't suit me."

She stepped back and sized me up. Her eyebrows winged together. "You get that black eye here or down there?"

"In Mexico. I fell and did a number on myself. Puncture wound near my rib cage. I'd love it if you'd take a look, make sure it's clean."

"Girl, you've never been a good liar." Her eyes went to slits. "You weren't on vacation."

I had a mixed relationship with my grandmother. There was no doubt that she loved me and would fight to the death for me. But there was something wild and unearthly in her. Something elemental that I recoiled from, even as a child. As if a dangerous part of the Appalachian wildness was woven into her like a second skin. Grams was seventy-eight, and she hadn't aged so much as gone dry, until what was left was bone and sinew and hardened will. There was never hiding anything from her, and now I saw in her dark eyes that she would see through whatever story I tried to concoct.

"I had things to take care of," I said.

"Why Mexico?"

"I was looking for something."

"And you're going to tell me about it."

"Some of it."

She snorted. "Well, some will have to do. Come back to the bathroom. Let's fix whatever's broken so you can go off and break something else. You never were much for soft landings."

◆　◆　◆

When I lifted my shirt, Grams crabbed something about not running with scissors. But she made quick work of the knife injury. A wash, some ointment, and a bandage. She might have been less gentle than I would have wished, but I didn't figure I had much call to complain.

"You got time for coffee?" she asked as she washed her hands.

I nodded. "We need to talk."

In the rooster-themed kitchen with its blue walls and faded linoleum, I sat with Grams at the kitchen table. Clyde stretched out near my feet, ignoring Nik's Doberman, Harvey, who took up a post at the back door. Grams had already brewed coffee, and now she placed a mug in front of me on the scarred oak table.

I watched as she pulled a plate of lemon scones from the oven. She set them, wrapped in a tea towel, on the table along with butter and a jar of homemade strawberry jam. We each took a scone and ate, and I closed my eyes as the warm pastry dissolved in my mouth, the bit of jam a sweet counterpoint.

"I've missed these," I said.

"You know where to find us."

"It's still hard, coming here."

"Hard shouldn't scare you."

I opened my eyes. Grams regarded me with the unsettling gaze of an owl—wise and predatory all at once. Intelligence with bite.

"Talk to me, Sydney Rose. And don't give me any bullshit. Whatever secrets you got are as safe with me as with God."

I considered that. Nik had told me never to share anything about the war, then turned around and proved to me how fucked up it was to hold everything inside. He'd refused to talk about combat even with other veterans who would understand. But I'd already opened up to Cohen. It came easier the second time.

"Did you hear about the RTD cop who was killed?" I asked. "Jeremy Kane?"

"It's been all over the news."

"I think his death might tie in with what I'm doing. Or what I'm trying to do."

Grams studied me for a moment, then got up and refilled our coffee mugs, her movements quick and efficient. She set the coffee on the table and resumed her seat.

"Tell me," she said.

So I did. A far more abbreviated version than what I'd shared with Cohen. I told her that bad things had gone down in Iraq and that I'd played an unwitting role in some of those things. That I'd been forced to leave an orphan behind. I told her that now some very bad men were looking for that boy. And that they were after me, too.

"I'm in over my head, Grams. I don't know who these guys are, or how many of them there are." I flashed to the Mexican police. "They've got resources. And they play for keeps."

"That knife wound a warning?" she guessed.

"Yes."

"Is this why you told me a year ago not to go home?"

I nodded. "I don't think the Alpha knows about you. And definitely not about Ellen Ann. But if he managed to follow me this morning, he knows now. You and Ellen Ann have to go. Get away somewhere until this blows over. I can help pay for it."

"Comes a day I can't pay my own way, we have a different set of problems." She was quiet a moment. "There's no reason for us to stay, necessarily. And seems like there's plenty of reason to be scarce for a while. Ellen Ann has been pestering me about visiting Gentry. Might be a good time for us to finally do it." She glanced at the clock. "We can head out almost as soon as she's home. Which should be any minute."

"That's perfect. Thank you." After the Elise Hensley case, Gentry had moved away from Denver, eventually settling in a small mountain town on the Western Slope. "I'll get a message to you when this is all over."

Grams continued to study me. "You've got it back."

"What are you talking about?"

"There's something bright and strong in you again. Haven't seen it since before the war."

I pushed away from the table. "There's something rotten in me. That's why I'm in this mess."

"Don't go feeling sorry for yourself, girl. There's something rotten in all of us."

"But bright and strong?" I shook my head. "Not feeling it."

"We never do." She reached out and smacked my arm hard enough to sting. "The important thing is, can you clean up this mess?"

I looked down into my empty coffee cup. "I don't know. They want something from me, some intel they think I have from Iraq. It might be a video recording. Might be something else."

"And you don't have it?"

"Not as far as I know. I'm hoping I'm wrong. Do you remember that luggage I brought over here?"

A flicker of amusement. "Your old Superman suitcase."

"The one Dad gave me."

We both laughed, but there was a burn beneath the laughter, like still-raw skin beneath a scab. The suitcase was emblematic of a familiar battle from my childhood. My dad had pushed to let me be as "masculine" as I chose—video games, Superman comics, toy guns. My mom had been determined to feminize me, and not in a girl-power way. More a doll-on-the-shelf way. Isabel had been a poised beauty who believed that the only way for a woman to survive in a man's world was to charm the pants off those guarding the glass ceiling until they relinquished whatever you wanted at the moment. Anything from a free drink to a corner office.

In Isabel's mind, you were just being smart to utilize the only assets a man wouldn't ignore. But I still struggled to forgive her for seeing the world in such a narrow way, and for trying to get me to jump in with both feet. One reason I'd signed up with the Marines was to prove to myself that I could handle male superiors in my own stubborn, non-sexual fashion. Joining the railway police had been an extension of that.

The battle between my parents reached a low point on my ninth birthday. Isabel had given me a Barbie suitcase. Inside was a makeup kit and a little mirror and a certificate to get my ears pierced.

My dad had given me Superman luggage and a fishing rod.

Apparently my parents had agreed on what I needed. But not the form it should take.

I'd been especially angry with my mother that day because she was in one of her sloppy moods. Sloppy words, sloppy kisses, sloppy steps. It was around then that I'd begun to understand that her long afternoon naps, her shaking hands, her slurred words, all fell under a new term I'd sounded out after watching a television show.

Al-co-hol-ic.

That day, I'd made Superman my hero and refused to have anything to do with Barbie. I don't think Isabel forgave me for that.

"The suitcase is still in Gentry's old room," Grams said. "Right where you put it."

Clyde followed me down the hall. He plopped down on Gentry's blue braided rug while I set my duffel on the bed, pulled the blinds closed, and flipped on the light. Gentry had moved out of his parents' home years ago, when he went to Denver University and eventually took up law. But his room was still all boy—blue paint, plaid bedspread. Posters of rock stars and Halo on the walls. I pulled the Superman case down from the high shelf in the closet and set it on the bed. My fingers lingered over the latch.

After Sarge's visit last winter, I'd taken the few things Dougie had given me, packed them into this harmless-looking case, and smuggled it over to Ellen Ann's, where I'd repacked it, hiding the items beneath

Gentry's childhood clothes. I'd considered and rejected both Cohen's personal safe and a bank deposit box. Somehow those seemed of little use in the face of a man whose powers mystified me. I could not build a barricade against the Alpha. I could only hope to outwit him.

If the Alpha had learned about this house and sent someone to search it, I'd hoped a boy's suitcase in a boy's room wouldn't cause a second glance. My version of Poe's purloined letter.

I pressed the latch and lifted the top. Immediately visible were Gentry's childhood clothes—shorts and T-shirts and a pair of *Toy Story* pajamas. I lifted out the topmost clothes and unrolled the rest to reveal what I was really after.

What greeted me were memories from Iraq. Hours on the FOB or in Mortuary Affairs. The recovery missions when I'd driven the reefer to collect our Marines and bring back their bodies. The companionship of my fellow Marines, and the grief when some of them made the ultimate sacrifice.

And, of course, my time with Dougie.

I picked up an olive-drab T-shirt I'd worn on the FOB and pressed it to my face.

How does anyone *make military-issue clothes look hot?* Dougie had teased me once when we were on a midnight stroll.

The need to hide the truth of our relationship meant there were few opportunities for anything physical between us. Except for a few frenzied encounters, our relationship was celibate. In the absence of actual lovemaking, Dougie had pursued me with the grace I imagined had been used in medieval times when knights wooed their lords' untouchable ladies. Courtly love—love as a noble ideal rather than a consummation—became our routine. Twenty-first century style, which included barbed wire, jersey gates, and remote outhouses.

Do you get tired of this? I'd asked.

He'd raised an eyebrow. *Tired of looking at you?*

Tired of never touching.

His hand found mine. My hand rubbed against the hard calluses in his palm, my fingertips feathering the rough skin.

How do I love thee? I whispered, smitten with sonnets even then. *Let me count the ways.*

Dougie slipped his hand from mine and brushed back my hair. *All I think about, Rosie, is what waits for us when we get back to the States. We'll have our whole lives together.*

In Gentry's dimly lit room, my tears soaked the T-shirt. What fools we mortals are to think that the plans we make are anything more than a soap bubble blown against a hurricane, a frail and fleeting wish destined to burst.

The light shifted as the Sir sat on the end of Gentry's bed, luminous in the gloom, his ruined legs invisible on the far side.

Near the door, Clyde lifted his head.

I heard the Sir's voice. "Self-pity? Unbecoming in a Marine."

"Momentary weakness, sir," I muttered. But I set the T-shirt aside. "If you want to be helpful, why don't you tell me what went down in Iraq. Who gave the order for what we did? Was it really Richard Dalton, like Sarge said? Is he the Alpha?"

"Figure it out, Marine. Stop wasting your brain."

"Very helpful, sir."

I leaned over the remaining items in the suitcase and closed my eyes, breathing in the scents. Dust and oil and—another burst of momentary weakness—the unique smell that was Dougie's. Most of what I'd placed in the suitcase had belonged to him. Given to me on what would turn out to be the last time I'd see him alive.

There wasn't much.

The Sir watched while I unrolled a pair of Gentry's jeans and revealed the first item. An old WWII Wittnauer military field compass. I slid it out of its cloth case. The Wittnauer had belonged to Dougie's grandfather, and he'd carried it everywhere. Up until my encounter with Sarge, I'd also carried it, safe inside a pouch in my Sam Browne belt—relying on it as Dougie had.

The compass was simple and small, about the size of a silver dollar. It had a scratched and polished nickel exterior, stamped with **US**, and a loop through which an optional chain could go. I opened the lid. Inside was a brass face, a blue needle, and a few sparkling grains of Iraqi sand. The needle vibrated as I moved, swinging steadily north.

The night when Dougie had pressed it into my hand before a mission, I'd protested.

It's your good luck charm, I'd said. *It's your grandfather, watching over you.*

I don't need it. He'd shaken his head. *We'll let him watch over you for a time.*

My tears splashed on the face of the compass. How wrong he'd been.

I swiped my eyes with the back of my hand and studied the compass face. When I'd looked at it before, I'd noticed there was conceivably a narrow space under the mechanism in which to hide something. I'd shaken the compass, but only the needle rattled. My efforts to pry the compass free of the case had failed, and I hadn't wanted to destroy it with what might be nothing more than a snipe hunt.

I tried again to remove the mechanism from the case, but nothing had changed. I slid the compass back into its pouch and then into my canvas bag.

I unrolled another shirt. Dougie's lion's head ring. Dougie had worn it around his neck on braided leather; it was the one thing he hadn't relinquished to me that day. After his body was brought into the MA bunker, I'd glimpsed the ring around his neck before the Sir hustled me out and made me stay far away, under guard, while he processed Dougie's body. Later, the Sir had given the ring to me without the braid. I had to assume the leather was too bloodstained for him to pass along.

"Thank you for this," I whispered to the Sir, who still watched from the end of the bed.

He nodded.

Like me, Dougie had been an orphan. No family had come forward to claim any of his possessions. His fellow warriors had died on the same mission that killed him. I was all he had. Up until six months ago, I'd worn the ring around my own neck, hung on my father's silver chain.

I lifted the ring to the light sifting through the blinds and studied the carved head. The lion was noble. Protective. I'd felt safe wearing it.

Defiantly, I raised the chain, intending to drop it around my neck. But then I lowered my hands and returned the ring to the suitcase. No matter what happened to me, I didn't want the Alpha having Dougie's ring.

"It didn't save Dougie," the Sir pointed out.

"And yet, you were the one who put it aside for me."

The Sir nodded in acknowledgment.

"You want to tell me why?" I asked.

But on this, the Sir remained silent. My dead never had anything practical to offer. Their comments ran more to warnings and philosophical musings. My therapist likened the Sir to Pinocchio's Jiminy Cricket—he was my goad, my whip, my conscience. Hayes advised me to tell the Sir that it was all right for him to leave. That my conscience was, if anything, a bit overdeveloped.

But I found his presence comforting, even if it suggested an alarming degree of instability on my part.

I touched the ring again. It seemed incapable of hiding so much as secret fairy dust, so I moved on.

Next was the Kurdish dagger Dougie had purchased from a bedouin tribesman. The handle was camel bone with silver, the sheath fashioned of carved silver and brass, the blade curved steel. I pulled the knife free of the sheath and stared at the pitted blade. You could do a lot of damage with one of these. But my careful examination of the hilt and the sheath proved, as with the ring, there was no place to hide anything.

The last things in the suitcase were the memorial flyer from Dougie's funeral, which I put aside without looking at, and copies of the photographs I'd taken from Sarge's apartment, including the one that had been stolen from Cohen's home: a picture of Malik with Sarge and the man my CIA friend had identified as Richard "Rick" Dalton.

The other photo showed Dougie and Rick together. Both of them wore beards and native dress. Dougie had the dagger on thin, braided rope slung across his chest. I wondered what the two men had been up to together, and if Rick had been present on the mission that killed Dougie.

I laced my fingers across one knee as I leaned back, staring at the meager belongings.

That was it. No deep, dark secrets. Nothing that would destroy a man's life or give him cause for murder.

Maybe the Alpha thought that Malik's video had ended up in Dougie's hands, and from there had come to me. I was sad to disappoint.

I picked up the compass again. Shook it. Over the gentle tick of the needle, I thought I caught the faintest click of metal on metal.

Nik's voice came to me from a years-old memory. *I want you to see a few things.*

I stood abruptly, startling Clyde. I grabbed Dougie's compass and went out into the hall and down to the room that Nik had shared with Ellen Ann before his death.

Nik had been dead for six months, but his box still sat on their dresser. I opened it and searched through his war-related treasures for his compass. Not the one that had been issued to him before he left for Vietnam. Rather, the older one his father had carried.

I found the compass, an almost identical match to Dougie's with its nicked casing and the letters **US** stamped on the outside. When I popped open the lid, the inside was also a near-duplicate of Dougie's. But when I eased my fingernails beneath the mechanism, it readily separated from the casing and dropped into my hand.

A smooth hollow lay beneath.

I set aside Nik's compass and opened Dougie's again.

Maybe I'd been too tentative before, afraid to destroy what little I had left of him. Now I went to the garage for the smallest flat-head screwdriver I could find, and when I returned, I pushed the end into the narrow gap and pressed.

With a pop and a sprinkle of fine desert sand, the mechanism fell free.

I stared.

In the hollow space was a cloud of cotton, and inside that, a small key. The top of the key had been sawed off so that it would fit. I knew a few things about keys, a gift from my railroad career. This key had **XL7** stamped on the face, which meant it was originally a blank made by Ilco. Heart pounding, I returned to Gentry's room and grabbed my personal laptop from my duffel. I did a quick search. The XL7 blanks were primarily used for mailboxes manufactured by four companies. I could exclude US Postal Service keys, which would be designated as such. But that still meant that this key went to one of roughly a million mailboxes in the United States.

Assuming the mailbox was even in the United States.

Assuming it went to a mailbox.

I looked at my watch, calculating.

I had thirty-nine hours remaining. More or less.

CHAPTER 11

We were the Marines the other Marines avoided. The pariahs,
the bad-luck charms. The ones no one wanted to risk being
near. As if we didn't just process death. As if we brought it.

—Sydney Parnell. Personal journal.

Back in the truck, Clyde watched squirrels through the open window
while I checked my phone for messages—none—and tried once more
to call Hal. Straight to voice mail.

I adjusted my rearview, checking the street behind. Two houses
down, a little girl rode a tricycle along the sidewalk, feet pumping,
braids flying. Her mother watched from the driveway, coffee cup in
hand, her powder-blue waitress uniform wrinkled and baggy, as if she'd
just gotten off work.

I returned my attention to the view out the windshield. Next door
to Gram's, a teenage boy stood on the concrete stoop, texting madly.
Beyond that, the street baked quietly in the rising heat, lawns brown
and half-choked with weeds, paint peeling like a bad sunburn. Royer
was a dual- or even triple-income kind of place, and by now most
people would be at their first job. Around five, they'd knock off and go
on to toil at the next minimum-wage sweatshop.

I stared down at the small key cupped in my palm. The same questions kept running through my head. If this was the "intel" the Alpha sought, how had it come to be in Dougie's possession? And why had he hidden it instead of turning it over to someone who would know what to do with it—whoever that might be?

Instead, he'd left the compass with me. And later that night he'd died.

The key taunted me with its mute simplicity. Perhaps this was the key to a storage bunker holding Saddam's gold. Or an entrée into the location of those weapons of mass destruction we never found. If I stood in front of Cohen's home with a sign that said **FOUND IT**, would the Alpha relieve me of the key and tell me Malik and I were safe now?

Olly olly oxen free.

Right. If I kept this up, pretty soon I'd find myself hunting alligators in the sewers or watching for the mother ship.

A block over, someone fired up a lawn mower. Clyde and I both jumped. I looked in surprise at my partner. Clyde could sit through a barrage of artillery fire and not twitch a muscle. That was part of his training.

But a lawn mower set him off?

"Buddy, we gotta go see your trainer. I think you're coming down with a case of nerves."

Clyde kept staring out the window as if ready to take on the lawn mower if it got close and made an aggressive move.

"Exactly."

The little girl and her tricycle zipped by on the sidewalk.

"Kaylee! Kaylee, you turn around right now," her mother called.

The girl kept going, her head thrust forward like she was hoping to break Danica Patrick's record at the next Indy 500.

Somewhere behind us, an engine growled to life. I looked in my side mirror. A black SUV came around the corner and rumbled down the street at the pace of a fast walk. I shoved the key into my pocket and my Glock into my waistband. Clyde and I got out of the Land Cruiser.

The mother had ditched her coffee cup and was moving at a fast trot down the sidewalk. The truck kept pace with her. The little girl was still far ahead of both of them.

Clyde's eyes were already on mine, ready for a command. I gestured toward the girl, then shouted, "Guard!"

Clyde took off like a rocket. As soon as he began to run, the truck driver revved the engine. I heard the gear drop into place, and the driver accelerated.

"Kaylee!" screamed the mother.

I broke into a run, heading toward Clyde and the little girl. Clyde had all but closed the gap. No doubt he would terrify both the girl and the mother. But my concern was the truck. I threw a glance over my shoulder.

The SUV popped up onto the sidewalk and swerved toward me.

I yanked my Glock free from the small of my back and pivoted on my heel, racing into the nearest yard. As the truck pulled alongside, I spun and went into a crouch, gun up.

"Police!" I yelled.

I caught a glimpse of a shadowy figure in the cab as the driver yanked the wheel in the opposite direction, dropped off the curb, and accelerated back onto the street.

At the end of the block, Clyde had corralled the girl on her tricycle and herded her onto the grass. Her eyes were wide with terror.

I ran after the truck, but the driver gunned the engine and sped down the rest of the block, racing past Clyde and the girl and disappearing around the corner with a squeal of tires and not so much as a flicker of brake lights.

The mother and I reached the girl at the same time. I called Clyde back to my side while the woman snatched up her daughter from the tricycle. The little girl burst into tears.

The mother looked at me and then Clyde with a mix of horror, anger, and gratitude.

"I'm sorry if we scared her," I said. "Clyde is trained to protect."

"That's his name? Clyde?"

I told Clyde to offer a paw. The woman—her name tag read Sandy—squatted and turned the little girl toward Clyde.

"See, sweetie? He's a guard dog. Like a guardian angel."

The little girl wiped her nose and stared at Clyde. Clyde kept his paw out, and Sandy reached around her daughter and shook it. When she stood again, I ordered Clyde back a couple of paces.

Sandy stroked the girl's hair. "Jimmy would have grabbed her."

"What?"

"My ex. He's been threatening to take her."

"That was your ex-husband?" So sure was I that this was a move by the Alpha that I struggled to recalibrate.

"Thank you so much. I don't know what I would have done if you hadn't been here." She swept the girl's hair back. "You probably scared him off for good."

"You need to report him," I said. "Get a restraining order."

"I will." She looked sincere.

I pulled out a business card and handed it to her. "Call me if I can help."

As Clyde and I walked back up the street toward the Land Cruiser, I glanced at the house next to Ellen Ann's.

The teenager was still on the front stoop.

Still texting.

I wondered if he'd ever looked up.

◆ ◆ ◆

The next item on my list was to go to Denver Pacific Continental head-quarters and talk to my boss. Since I was going to pursue Kane's killer, I might as well try to make it semi-legit.

Going into work would also give me the chance to catch up on the latest buzz surrounding Kane's murder. All cops feel the murder of another cop. But railroad cops form their own unique clan, regardless of whether we're freight or passenger, and Kane's death would hit hardest among my fellow bulls.

But I had to take care of something first. Clyde's and my close encounter with Jimmy made me determined to know if the Alpha had actually put a tail on me. I rolled down the windows—the Land Cruiser didn't have air-conditioning—then got back on the highway, heading away from work. Ten minutes later, I exited and detoured to a theme park in northern Denver known as Water World. At the entrance, I joined the line of cars filing into the immense parking lot. The place was packed with thrill seekers, but I drove to the outer edge of the lot and backed into a spot.

A steady stream of cars followed, packed to the gills with families or teenagers. Fifteen minutes after I'd parked, a brown sedan caught my eye. It drove up and down the lanes, passing multiple parking spots. When it drove directly past the Land Cruiser, I spotted two men in buzz cuts and polo shirts sitting in the front. The man in the passenger seat turned to look straight at me.

They drove past and parked a few spots down. The driver shut off the engine and lowered windows, while the passenger reached a hand over the seat and came back with a white McDonald's bag. He pulled out four red boxes and handed two of them to the driver. They chatted and ate.

I got the message. Intimidation, not stealth, was the point of this game.

I considered marching over, telling them to get the hell away from me. But it felt too much like crushing cockroaches. I looked at my watch. Cohen should be on the ground by now. I keyed his number, but the call went straight to voice mail.

"Call me," I said.

As the day's heat seeped into my bones and the last of the adrenaline trickled out of me, I resisted the desire to put my seat back and take twenty. I didn't know when I'd picked up the tail, or who would take over for these guys when their shift was over. I felt outmanned and probably outgunned.

I leaned over and pressed my face against Clyde's warm back. He shifted until we were sitting forehead to forehead.

"Just one more day," I told him. "One more day, and we'll end this."

Unless the Alpha ended it first.

I pushed myself upright. Clyde gave me a tongue-lolling grin and went back to people watching. His tail thumped as a squirrel bounded across the asphalt and ran up one of the handful of trees in the lot. He gave a happy, I'm-not-on-duty bark.

One thing about my partner—he made a rich life out of little things. And he didn't sweat the big stuff. I should learn from him. For the moment, I'd make better progress if I focused on squirrels and ignored the wolves.

I started the engine.

The sedan followed us out of the parking lot. I watched as they tailed me onto the on-ramp, but once on the highway, they dropped back and let a few cars get between us. They didn't seem overly concerned with keeping me in sight.

Interesting. My truck had been locked in Cohen's garage while I was gone—safely stowed behind the guarded gates of Cherry Hills.

But the same could be said of Cohen's home. And that hadn't stopped them.

After a stop at Travelli's Deli and fighting noontime traffic the entire way, I turned into the parking lot of Denver Pacific Continental headquarters. I waited. A few minutes later, the sedan drove past the DPC gate and parked half a block down on the public street.

I pulled into a spot between my boss's new red pickup truck and a dark-blue BMW sedan that belonged to the new guy, Greg Heinrich. Heinrich was five months into the job and—in my humble opinion—lacked a certain commitment to the profession. Plus, I didn't trust his car. Why would the kind of guy who could afford a Beamer take a job as a railroad cop? Was he just making time between gigs? Or lording it over us blue-collar trash?

Clyde and I got out. My faded tan Land Cruiser looked embarrassed to be next to such shining examples of modernity.

"It's a muscle play," I told my car. "You'll give the fancy guys the shudders."

When Clyde and I walked into the small office area that housed the railroad police, my boss was nowhere to be seen. But Heinrich sat at his desk, which faced mine, chatting into his Bluetooth. He looked up and waved when we walked in. I dropped into the chair at my desk and signaled for Clyde to sit. Judging by the slow thump of his tail, Clyde was happy to be back. A working dog is happiest on the job, squirrels be damned.

"I'm on it," Heinrich was saying into the mouthpiece as he tilted back and stared at the ceiling. His face was red. "Yeah, yeah, it's covered. Don't worry. I got it. See you tonight."

He finished his conversation and turned to me with a tired smile. The candle burning in his eyes didn't match his haggard expression. Coffee or Red Bull, I figured. The rocket fuels of cops everywhere.

"What are you doing back?" he asked. "Not that I'm not happy to see you. But aren't you supposed to still be on vacation? And what's with the hair? And the shiner?"

I'd worked out my story ahead of time. "Took a fall by the pool and decided Mexico isn't for me. I just came in to talk to Mauer and get the buzz on Jeremy Kane."

"Kane. What a tragedy." For a moment, Heinrich looked like he'd be sick. I offered him my trashcan, but he swallowed hard and gave me a weak smile. "I should never have looked at the recordings. I'm going to have nightmares for months."

Wait until he got his first jumper. "Any news that's not in the papers?"

"Nothing I've heard. Denver Major Crimes says it looks pretty cut and dried. Guy was a few trees short of a forest, and something triggered him. God knows what. Maybe he just didn't like Kane's looks. Next thing you know . . ." He swallowed again. "We're on Level 2 security, but nothing's come across the wire."

"What about links to similar crimes?"

"One tramp shoved another in a town in New Mexico. And another guy fell asleep on the tracks after his friend dragged his sleeping bag there. Just another day in the life of drunken hobos. On the other hand, the regular cops aren't exactly sharing with us cinder dicks. Ask me, Major Crimes is a bunch of self-righteous assholes. Here"—he reached back around to his desk and picked up a printout—"is the Daily Intelligence Briefing. There's some buzz along the eastern seaboard from the homeland guys. Talk of a threat." Heinrich shrugged. "I don't pay too much attention. Homeland Security would have us going up and down like yo-yos if we tracked too closely. Tracked. Get it? And anyway, don't see any link with our guy."

I scanned the printout. "And no one has suggested Kane's death had anything to do with a bigger danger?"

Heinrich gave me a look like maybe I'd drunk too much of the terrorist-threat Kool-Aid.

"Nah. Like I said—" He cocked his head, and I could tell he was getting a stream of information through his Bluetooth. He murmured a confirmation, then pushed back his chair and stood.

"We got a trespasser," he said. "Same schmuck keeps standing on the tracks down near Hogan's Alley. I better get on it."

I stood as well, and Clyde came to his feet, his eyes on me.

"I like the new look," Heinrich said, heading for the door. "Always did prefer brunettes."

I didn't punch him. But it was a close thing.

◆　◆　◆

Mauer still hadn't returned, but the door to his office stood open, so Clyde and I went on in. My ass had barely hit the chair when I heard my boss's voice.

"The hell you doing back?" he said by way of greeting as he breezed in.

"It's good to see you, too."

He went around his desk, smiled at Clyde, then shot a scowl at me. He looked as ferocious as a teddy bear with constipation.

"I gotta be honest with you, Parnell. I'm kinda pissed to see you here. Thought you'd be slamming tequila and baking on a beach about now. And what's with the shiner?"

"Mexico City doesn't have beaches."

"Whatever. Why are you sitting in my office instead of letting some rich señor buy you a nice dinner? And forget the shiner. What's with the hair? Trying to blend with the locals? Never mind. I don't want to know. Go ahead and have a seat." He glared at me. "Oh, yeah, I see you already did."

I smiled at him, and he rolled his eyes. When it came to his officers, Deputy Chief John Mauer was all bluff and no bite. Around the office he acted more like a den mother than a leader of men. We would have walked on live coals for him. About six months ago he'd suddenly dropped more than sixty pounds. Over the last two, I'd watched with relief as he regained a third of it. Whatever demons he'd been battling, he seemed to have bounced back.

"I want to work the Kane case," I said.

"The thing about you, Parnell, is you beat around the bush too much."

He opened a drawer and pulled out a treat, which he tossed to Clyde. Clyde caught it in midair and waited hopefully.

"That's all I got, maligator," Mauer said.

Clyde huffed and sat.

Mauer scowled at me. "I'm gonna ignore what you said."

"Sir, I heard about Kane while I was in Mexico, and I—"

"Do not tell me you came back because of the murder at Union Station." He stabbed a finger at me. "You need to drop the Columbo act and play at being a railroad cop once in a while."

"Who's Columbo?"

"Jessica Fletcher, then."

"I'm not big on pop culture."

"I can tell. Just stop trying to solve every damn crime in the county. How's the therapy going?"

"You aren't supposed to ask." I'd been in DPC-mandated therapy ever since the Hensley investigation went south and a lot of people died. A number of them at my hand. "Kane was a Marine. He was in Habbaniyah when I was."

"I know he was a Marine. What the hell does it matter that you guys were in-country at the same time?"

"It's—"

"And don't give me any Semper Fi bullshit, Parnell," he plowed on. "Denver's finest is already on it. It's not." He pounded the desk. "Your." And again. "Job." A final slam.

I let him go on for a bit, grousing about people knowing their place and not sticking their necks out or their noses in. With Mauer, once the cork came out of the bottle, it was hard to fit it back in until it was damn ready to go. I waited until he wound down enough to take a breath, then stepped in.

"I went to Mexico because I'm trying to figure out something that happened in Iraq when I was there."

"Parnell, you're giving me whiplash. What the hell does Kane getting killed by some asshole bum have to do with Iraq?"

"It probably doesn't. But I need to be sure."

He pressed his fingertips to his temples like he'd just gotten a headache. "You will be the death of me."

"Is that a no?"

"More of a hell no."

"Okay then." I stood.

"Ah, for—" He dropped his hands. "Sit your ass back down. You told me when you applied for this job you wanted a little quiet."

I remained standing. "Maybe I wasn't meant for quiet."

"Everyone but DJs and stuntmen needs downtime."

"And Marines."

He muttered a string of words I was pretty sure weren't in the dictionary, then took a breath and sat up, propping his elbows on the desk. "Explain it to me."

I dropped back in the chair. "I just want to poke around a little. Ask a few questions. Make sure I'm wrong."

"Iraq and Kane. I'm not tracking."

"It's probably nothing."

"You're still on vacation. Helluva way to spend it."

I waited, unsure whether to give him my pearly whites or puppy dog eyes. I would go outside the lines if I had to, but this job would be easier with official backing.

We had a stare down for thirty seconds. I blinked first. I got to my feet a second time. "I'll be back in the office next week, when my vacation is officially over."

"Goddammit, Parnell." He unlocked a drawer in his desk and reached inside. "Helluva way to run a railroad."

He held out a key fob and an extra set of keys. "Your new chariot. If you're going to go all Sherlock Holmes on me, you might as well drive it instead of that deathmobile you call a car."

I raised an eyebrow. "We got new vehicles?"

"Homeland decided it was time to drag us into the twenty-first century. New SUVs for everyone. More horsepower, cellular, and a satellite linkup. And your K9's digs are pretty cushy, too."

My fingers itched to take the keys. "I'm not on duty yet."

"The detailing ain't done yet, either. Fair trade. You'll be undercover. Seems to me it's a good idea to get used to the vehicle before you're officially chasing bad guys. Move your Land Cruiser to a corner spot until you can come back for it. Or better yet, hide it in that pile of junk by the garage. We got an image to uphold."

I took both the keys and the implied approval. "Thanks, boss."

He grimaced. "Pick up your work laptop on your way out. Now get out of here. Both of you. And don't let me see you in the news."

Outside, the heat bore down like a bad mood. The sun had burnished our famous Colorado blue sky into a dull hollow, like an upturned fry pan.

I drove around to the far side of headquarters and across a series of tracks to the garage. One of the mechanics, Mason Reese, saw me coming and waved me in. Here was where they serviced not just our police cars, but also the crew trucks, our little putt-putts, the high-rail vehicles, and assorted other track maintenance equipment.

"Hey," he said when Clyde and I got out. "Your truck's not done."

"Good to see you, Mason." We shook hands. "Boss told me to go ahead and take it. Give it a test run for a couple of days."

He thought about this, then shrugged. "Okay."

Mason gave the sense that all human activity was mysterious and better left unexplored.

"You mind if I leave my Land Cruiser here for the next day or so?"

He swiped his nose with the back of his hand. Shrugged. "Okay."

"Would you take a look at it first? I need to check something."

"Can't service personal vehicles."

"I'd never ask. I just want you to look at the undercarriage, see if you spot anything unusual."

His eyes finally met mine. "You mean like, is there a leprechaun hiding behind the muffler?"

I'd never heard him string together so many words, and I wasn't sure if he was serious or not. "Or something. Do you mind?"

Another shrug, slightly more elaborate than the first two. He told me to wait. He disappeared into the bowels of the garage, then returned with an inspection mirror. This one came with a light, which he switched on. He began moving along the vehicle, making a tsking noise with his tongue. He clearly thought I was one sandwich short of a picnic. But he was the one who'd brought up leprechauns. He went around the rear of the Cruiser to the far side, then stopped, squinted, and went back a step.

"Hmm," he said. Mason-speak for, *Wow, there's something really strange and unusual here.*

I joined him on the far side, and we both bent low. Mason pointed to a small black box. "Tracking device."

He yanked the thing free, and we stood up to inspect it.

"Magnetic case," he explained. He slid the device free of its housing. "They can track you anywhere on their phone or computer."

Mason was positively gushing, but it was as I had suspected.

He held it up. "Put it back?"

"Um, no." I pondered my options, then held out my hand. "I'll take care of it. Where's my new truck?"

"Out near the gate."

151

"Would you mind driving it over here? I don't want to be seen getting in."

"You said your boss approved it."

I hefted the tracking device. "It's not my boss I'm worried about."

Mason scratched his head. "But whoever's tracking you on their computer can't see who's in the cab."

"Maybe he isn't just tracking me on his computer. Maybe he's parked out on the street, and he plans to follow me. I don't think he means good things, Mason."

Mason grunted. Then shrugged. "Okay."

After he left, I walked out to the tracks. I slapped the tracker in its magnetic housing underneath a coal car that would be leaving in an hour for the US-Mexico border. The Alpha's men wouldn't be fooled for long. But if I got lucky, it might take them an hour or two to figure it out. By then, I'd be buried in the city.

I wedged the Land Cruiser between some utility vehicles so that it was out of sight on the north side of the garage, then grabbed a few personal belongings—the contents of the glove box, the polar fleece jacket I'd appropriated from Cohen, Clyde's and my Kevlar, my toolbox and backup pistol—then locked up. When Mason pulled up in a dark-blue Ford Expedition, I nodded my approval. This was the first brand-new vehicle I'd ever driven, and as I circled it and kicked the tires, I felt like a grown-up.

"Check it out, Clyde."

Mason left the engine running.

"Tank's full," he said.

"Thanks."

"Don't let 'em get you," he added and stalked off.

I opened the rear hatch to show Clyde his designated area. It was roomier than the old Ford, with a removable padded bed, built-in food and water dishes, and some pretty sophisticated environmental controls.

"All you need is a screen and a Wi-Fi connection," I told him. "You could catch up on *The Adventures of Rin Tin Tin*."

Picking up on my excitement, Clyde barked. He was a big fan of the crime-fighting German shepherd. In Iraq, Dougie had found the old episodes online. He and Clyde and I used to watch them together.

"I'm kidding, pal. You should be catching up on training videos. Let's check out the cab."

I opened the front passenger door and was delighted to see that someone had installed a dog harness in place of a regular seat belt. I wondered if that bonus had come from my boss or Mason.

I signaled Clyde to hop up and buckled him in. "Try not to shed too much." I walked around and got in behind the steering wheel. I opened my duffel and took out my work laptop, popped it into the swivel mount near the dash, and powered it up. The internet came up along with an application to link to dispatch and another program that would run searches on a slew of databases.

"Welcome to the twenty-first century," I told Clyde. "You think this will make it easier to catch bad guys?"

Clyde cocked his head at the screen, unsure. He was more of a traditionalist, I think. Teeth and claws.

I fist-bumped his paw.

CHAPTER 12

A war in five senses. Blood, sweat, tears, dust, pain.

—Sydney Parnell. ENGL 0208 Psychology of Combat.

Union Station, where Kane had been murdered, was overseen by the Regional Transportation District. Their cameras would have caught Kane's death from different angles. I planned to force myself to watch the recordings as many times as it took to get something to shake out.

The Transit Watch Command Center served as the RTD's headquarters, and that's where Clyde and I headed next. We'd been there a few times before. Denver Pacific Continental and the RTD share information and data, and we have a Memorandum of Understanding to help each other out. DPC was especially interested in using some of the RTD's camera technology to monitor critical areas on our own lines.

I'd called on the drive over and offered my help to Transit Police Chief Ryan Taft. I told him I knew a lot of the homeless, and maybe I would recognize our killer if I saw him in motion. It turned out I didn't need to sell myself. Taft muttered something about me being a celebrity and said he was happy for the help.

He met us at the door to the single-story, bland brick building situated in a quiet neighborhood of small businesses. In his early sixties, tall and well built, with a thick head of gray hair and kind eyes, Ryan had a way of leaning in when he talked that made you feel like his coconspirator. Today his expression hovered between harried and pissed, but he waved us in warmly, bent and shook Clyde's paw, and—good man that he was—said absolutely nothing about my black eye. He led us through the warren of offices to the center of operations.

"Anything specific on this case caught your eye?" he asked as we walked.

"I haven't seen anything yet but newspaper articles."

"Let's fix that."

The control room was a high-ceilinged space, dimly lit, with workstations and a bank of monitors showing all of Denver's railway stations, the interiors of buses and trains, and key points along the commuter tracks. The RTD—Denver's mass transit system—was a network of commuter lines, light rail, and buses that served much of metro Denver and the airport.

All five of the workstations were manned. Normally, this time of day would only require a couple of people on task. But Kane's death had everyone on high alert. Taft introduced Clyde and me to the men and women watching the monitors, who barely looked away from their screens, then led me to a door in the back and ushered me into their computer room.

"You want to see the recordings from that night, I assume," he said.

"That's right. If we're lucky, I'll have seen this guy before."

Taft waved me toward a chair, then took a seat in front of a monitor. Clyde sat next to me, but kept his eyes on the chief, as if he understood that the game was afoot and he might have a chance to nail a bad guy in the near future. Taft punched a few buttons, images appeared on the screen, and soon he had the recordings up from that night.

"It's damn difficult to watch." Taft's voice sounded like cement hardening.

Kane came into view. I recognized his red hair and the faint limp from our encounter last winter.

I watched as he moved into the range of one camera, then out, then into another. The RTD had cameras mounted at every station, giving 360 degrees of coverage. Two thirds of the trains were also outfitted with internal cameras.

Through the camera's eyes, I spied over Kane's shoulder as he spotted the homeless guy and headed in that direction.

"How long was the transient there before Kane went to him?" I asked. "Can you back up and show me when he got into that space?"

"You bet." Taft pushed some buttons. "It was just under four minutes between the time the killer showed up and Jeremy went to roust him."

"And Kane had just come on duty. Was it normal for him to get outside that fast?"

"It's SOP. He'd be rotating locations with the rest of the security team. Kane always liked to establish a baseline. A leftover from his time in the military, I guess. Whenever he came on duty, he'd take a walk through the station, then head out to the platforms and give them a good visual. Here it is."

We watched as the killer hobbled into view, entering the platform from the northeast, in the direction of the tracks. He was hunched over and favoring his right leg, muttering to himself as he moved. Periodically he would stop and stare at something that caught his eye, then mutter some more and shuffle on. He carried a dirt-stained backpack, and, even in the heat, he had on a zippered sweatshirt with the hood pulled up and a blanket wrapped around his shoulders. He wore gray sweatpants torn at the knee and laceless sneakers. Both knees looked red and scraped. Immense sunglasses covered half his face, making me think of the famous sketch of the Unabomber from the mideighties.

The man on the video looked very much like the drawing that had been in the *Denver Post*. Other than the dirty clothes and scabby skin sported by a lot of homeless people, nothing about him looked familiar.

"The media is calling him the Pushman." Taft rubbed the back of his neck. "A pun on the old Pullman railcars. It's as good as anything, I guess. But I hate it. I just keep thinking of how Kane must have felt in his last moments."

We watched as the Pushman settled into his spot.

"Stop it there for a sec," I said. "How many security officers were on duty with Kane?"

"We had our usual seven guys. Three were down below, at the bus terminals. Two were inside Union Station. Sadler was outside with Kane. But he was around at the front of the building, answering a complaint about panhandling."

"Anything suspicious about the complaint?"

"You mean as a diversionary tactic? Sadler doesn't think so. It was the kind of standard grievance you get when vagrants brush up against the well-to-do. LoDo is famous for it."

LoDo was short for Denver's Lower Downtown, a hip part of the city that drew tourists, locals, and cool people from all up and down the Front Range. It also attracted the homeless, the desperate, and opportunists of all stripes. In a typical year, LoDo had a crime density of almost four thousand offenses per square mile.

"Let's keep going," I said.

Taft hit play again and slowed the speed. We moved forward in slo-mo, watching in painful increments as Kane approached his killer.

"He followed protocol," Taft said. "Gave the guy a warning for lying on the floor in the station. If anything, Jeremy erred on the side of leniency. He hated arresting these guys."

"Maybe because he knew some of them are vets."

"Probably. Anyway, he gives this asshole a warning, then a second warning. If he'd had the chance, the third time would have been a charm. Kane would have issued a final warning. Then if the guy still refused to move, he would have arrested him for trespassing."

"Sometimes," I murmured, "that's what they want. Three hots and a cot."

We watched as something caught Kane's attention and drew his gaze away from the Pushman. Taft hit pause and swiveled his chair to face another monitor.

"Another possible diversionary tactic?" I asked.

"Doesn't seem like it." He pulled up the recording from a different camera, and we were looking at a panorama of the people standing on the far side of the tracks. "In a case like this, it's standard procedure for an officer to periodically check his surroundings. Make sure no one is getting too close. Or that the homeless man isn't himself a diversion."

I studied the faces of the Saturday-night crowd, looking for anyone familiar or anything unusual. Maybe I was hoping a man would be standing there in a ball cap that read **ALPHA**.

No such luck.

Most people were engrossed in their phones. A few looked in Kane's direction; watching a cop roust a homeless guy probably served as entertainment while you waited for your train. It looked to me like a typical weekend crowd—a lot of young people on their way in or out of the clubs and a few middle-aged couples probably just done with dinner in one of the nearby restaurants.

Of course, if the Alpha had sent someone to tail Kane, it would be someone who could blend in, just like Rooftop Thomas in Mexico. But why bother with a tail? Assuming Kane wasn't leading a nefarious double life, he would be traveling to and from work and home and going to visit friends or run errands.

Whoever it was, they'd definitely caught Kane's attention. His gaze was focused.

"We ran the faces of everyone on the platform," Taft said. "Sixty-seven people. I've got our boy genius trying to triangulate and narrow it down. Ah, speak of the devil."

A man with a beard, his bare arms sheathed in tattoos, stuck his head in the door. He looked all of nineteen as he waved a piece of paper at us. "I got it down to five names."

Taft took the paper. "Give me a rundown of your process. The condensed version."

"Sure." He shrugged. "It's straightforward trig. From where Kane stood, I extrapolated his line of sight across the platform. That told me which cameras covered the zone where he was looking. Lines of sight from those cameras gave me the three sides of a triangle—the two lines extending from the cameras and a baseline I calculated by walking between them. Then I just determined the angles and extended the lines until they crossed. That narrowed Kane's view to the five people who appear on both cameras."

"Remind me not to ask about the math next time," Taft said. "But I think I followed enough to say you've earned your Superman cape."

"A raise will do." He winked and disappeared back out the door.

Taft flattened the paper and we looked at the list of names.

Laura Almasi. Sonia Lopez Martinez. Kenneth Riley Napierkowski. Leroy Parker. Thomas Wilson.

"Any of the names mean anything to you?" Taft asked.

"No." *Dammit.*

"Not to me, either. I'll run them and send you photos and profiles if you wish."

"Yeah, thanks."

"I'll get them to Detective Gorman as well."

We went back to the other monitor, and Taft played Kane's final moments. The man surging up from the ground, the flash of the knife. Kane turning in what must have been stunned surprise.

Then the final act, which had earned the Pushman his moniker from the press.

I forced myself to keep my eyes open.

"Play the clip again where the guy first gets up," I said. "Did you see that tattoo?"

"We saw it." Taft rewound, then froze the image.

What we could see of the Pushman's face was a rictus of rage. Lips drawn back to expose white teeth, the barely visible forehead wrinkled with his snarl. He had his right arm up, the knife clearly visible in his hand. On the inside of his arm was a tattoo of a star and crescent and below that, Arabic writing.

"The crescent and star. That's a symbol of Islam," I said.

"Right. The script is Arabic—the words mean Five Pillars. This sent us off chasing rabbits, thinking this might be a terrorist act. But the theory doesn't hold. Not so far, anyway. No one has stepped forward to claim the death. And those assholes always step forward. That's not to say the guy didn't see himself as the Lone Hassan. But that makes it a hate crime, not an act of terror. Hard to imagine this guy having political or social objectives."

I studied the tattoos. "The five pillars."

"You know what it means?"

"They're the basic tenets of Islam. Faith, prayer, charity, fasting, and pilgrimage."

Taft folded his arms. "Looks like this dipshit lost out on all of them."

A woman poked her head through the open doorway. "Chief, you got a call on your landline."

Taft stood. "Excuse me a minute? Feel free to play with the buttons while I'm gone."

I took Taft's seat and replayed the scene over and over. But if I'd been hoping to recognize the guy, to maybe prove to myself that he was just what he appeared to be, I had to admit defeat. I was certain I'd never seen him before.

He could still be a mentally disturbed vagrant.

And I could be a nun.

Aside from the tattoo, the most striking thing about him were his teeth, which were visible when he went after Kane.

They were straight. And perfectly white.

Maybe Dentists Without Borders had come to Denver.

When Taft returned, I vacated his seat and asked if he could give me stills. "Two of the killer, close-up and full body. And another one of the crowd."

"Sure thing." More button pushing. The printer on the desk began to whir.

"What do we know from gait analysis?" I asked.

The ability to watch for criminal activity in public places had gotten a huge leg up when someone realized that humans can be identified on surveillance cameras by how they move. A person's walk was as unique as a fingerprint, and one of several biometric markers used by law enforcement to track suspicious activity. The RTD had sophisticated gait-analysis software built into every camera—a total of ten thousand cameras placed on the RTD's trains, platforms, and buses.

The system worked by building computer images—avatars—of every person recorded by its cameras. The computer could then use that avatar to find all the locations a person had traveled to within the RTD system.

It was one of the coolest gee-whiz high-tech things to come along. But it was still just software.

"Gait analysis hasn't given us anything," Taft said. "We found no matches to Pushman's avatar. This is the first time he's been on RTD property."

"What are the weaknesses of the software?"

"Not many." Taft tilted back in his chair and folded his arms. "Simply feigning a limp won't fool it. Neither will slowing down or speeding up. This guy's heavy clothes are a deterrent—especially that blanket. But we still have a high level of accuracy."

I dropped my elbows to my thighs as I ran down a mental list of possibilities.

"What if we're making the wrong assumption?"

Taft cocked his head. "What do you mean?"

"What if the guy isn't homeless?"

"That would make him a hell of a good method actor."

"Maybe it's a good costume. Maybe he even spent a few months building the persona—the dreads, the beard, that shuffling walk. If he did that, he would have created a completely different avatar from his normal one."

"Meaning he's been on RTD property in the past, but we've got him marked as a different person."

"Right."

"Why would he go to such lengths?"

"So he could scope out the place. He might be a local who rides the trains and knew he could be recognized. Or . . ." A little buzz built in my skull. "Or he didn't want to be tracked once he left the station. Maybe he didn't disappear. Maybe he became someone else."

Taft rubbed his jaw. "You're talking a lot of work and some serious premeditation."

"But it's possible? The hunch and the shuffle, the heavy clothes—those might be enough to fool the software?"

"Maybe. Our software doesn't look at externals, so the hair and beard don't matter. But those other things . . ." His voice trailed off as he replayed the tape. "It's possible to create a gait that can fool the system. But it's not easy. Our killer would have to know specifically what elements to adjust. Just switching from a walk to a shuffle wouldn't do it."

"What if his backpack was weighted? Would that matter?"

"Probably not. It changes your walk, but in ways we can predict and correct for."

"How's that?"

"When people gain weight naturally, over time, their body adjusts, and they maintain their normal stride. Thus, if a man went from a hundred and fifty pounds in January to two thirty the following December, he'd still have the same gait. But a person's walk changes if they suddenly pick up a heavy load. Their feet strike the ground harder. It's physics, and it's not something you can easily compensate for. Our cameras will catch the change. It's how we watch for backpacks with bombs."

"So not easy. But doable."

"In theory. If our guy was a pro, he could have practiced carrying the load off camera or even gradually increased the load, again off camera, without giving himself away. Now you're back to premeditation."

I considered the Alpha and the resources he might have. "If you figured the guy knew exactly how to fool the system, would your software be able to accommodate for that?"

Taft's eyes went soft. "I know you want this to be more than a random tragedy, Sydney. We all do. But what you're suggesting sounds like a conspiracy. Or a professional hit. Why would Kane be a target for something like that? It's ugly and pointless, but the homeless angle makes a lot more sense."

"Can we take ten minutes to play pretend?"

If the look in his eyes went any softer, I'd be tempted to hit him. I told myself it was sympathy, not pity.

He shook his head. "It's not that simple. We can build the avatar based on certain assumptions—weight, height, skeletal structure. But if you want us to build a database of possibilities, we'll have to go through thousands of data points."

"When you created your avatar and ran it, did you find any outliers? People the computer pinged on but rejected?"

"I'll ask our analyst, Meredith. And I'll run your idea by her. But if she didn't find any outliers, I don't see how we could do this."

"Can you at least try?"

"It isn't the best use of our resources."

I made my voice as soft as the look in his eyes. "This guy killed one of ours, Ryan. This man pushed Kane—"

"You're preaching to the choir. We'll look. We're all hands on deck with this, Sydney."

I looked down at my feet for a moment, then stood. "Thanks, Ryan. Let me know what you find."

◆ ◆ ◆

Back outside, instead of getting in the truck, I grabbed Clyde's dish and some water from the cooler and took him into the shade beneath a small grove of dispirited sumac entrenched at the far end of the asphalt lot. I poured water for him and, after a moment's hesitation, dug out a cigarette from my rainy-day stash in the glove box and lit up. Two steps forward, ten back.

While Clyde enjoyed the water and the breeze, I worked to annihilate my lungs as I watched the street for a brown sedan and checked my phone for a message from Cohen. Nothing.

He was busy, I told myself. He'd call later.

Clyde finished drinking the water, then stretched out in the shade, his tongue lolling. I stuck the cigarette in the corner of my mouth and squatted beside him. I reached under his vest and scratched. His tail thumped. I scratched harder, and his tail matched my tempo.

"Good boy!" I said in the high-pitched voice he loved.

Nothing like a little dog therapy.

I stopped after a moment but stayed on my haunches while I smoked and thought. Clyde gave me his pitiful look.

"Later, buddy. I can't think and scratch at the same time."

He huffed and rested his head on his outstretched legs.

I'd learned a few things. Kane's killer wasn't homeless, whatever the Denver PD might think. And I'd be willing to bet he wasn't Muslim, either. My guess was the tattoo was another distraction, on top of the homeless ploy.

What I couldn't figure out was why the Alpha would go to such lengths to kill Kane in public when it required so much subterfuge. There would be a hundred ways to murder Kane quietly. Maybe even in a way that didn't look like murder.

I wondered if the Alpha was sending someone a message. Or making a point.

I had two things to hope for. That Taft's analyst would find some possible matches to the Pushman. And that whoever had caught Kane's attention long enough to cause him to keep his back to his killer would give me a lead.

I ran over the names again in my mind. Laura Almasi. Sonia Lopez Martinez. Kenneth Riley Napierkowski. Leroy Parker. Thomas Wilson.

Nothing shook out. Maybe it would once we had more information about them.

I finished smoking and stubbed out the cigarette on the ground. I pocketed the butt and stood, stretching out the kinks in my back. Clyde watched me through one eye, waiting to see if we were really going anywhere.

Overhead, puffs of clouds wafted by. Traffic rumbled on the nearby road. The roots of the trees around us had broken through the concrete, creating a series of cracks in the asphalt.

"It's like a ball of yarn," I said to Clyde. "We'll just keep pulling on threads, seeing where they take us. But why do I feel like there's a bomb ticking at the center of this particular ball of yarn?"

Clyde yawned. Perspective.

"Yeah, I know. All in a day's work for you. Let's go, boy."

We were thirteen hours in.

CHAPTER 13

Sometimes you have to define yourself outside the expectations of the system.

—*Sydney Parnell. Personal journal.*

"You want what?"

Detective Bill Gorman gaped at me across the restaurant table. He had a beer bottle halfway to his mouth, his hand paused in midair as if someone had shouted "Freeze!" during a game of statue.

I repeated myself, but spoke more slowly this time.

"I want to help with the investigation," I said. "I know a lot of the homeless. If Kane's killer is really living on the street, I have a shot at finding him. Just bring me up to speed so I've got some background."

"Yeah?" Gorman's hand finished its trajectory, and he took a swig. "I already talked to every 'person without residence' in a two-mile radius of Union Station. Half swear they know the guy, half swear he's never been around. And all the bastards want money to talk."

Act like a dick, it's what you get back. "Can't hurt for me to try, right?"

We were sitting at an upstairs table at the Irish. I'd called Gorman an hour ago, reminded him who I was, and offered to buy him a late lunch and a beer. He'd told me he was buried with the Kane case, but agreed he did have to eat.

The Irish was a police hangout, but right now we had the upper floor to ourselves. This time of day fell in that no-man's-land between the end of the lunch rush and the start of happy hour. Seemed like Gorman was willing to sneak up on happy hour. I was happy to oblige.

The light was dim, and the only sounds were piped-in Celtic tunes and an occasional bang from the kitchen downstairs.

Could be that today it was extra quiet because the air conditioner was on the fritz. Bill Gorman's face was shiny with sweat. He'd shed his suit coat and rolled up his sleeves. Under his arms, damp darkened his light-blue button-down.

Gorman was in his late fifties, but my guess was he'd started going to seed years back. The softening came from within, like an apple left too long in the bin. Still nice and shiny on the outside, but it gave under a gentle squeeze.

The flat expanse of his square face and heavy jaw was just this side of a caricature of a 1940s screen idol a few decades past his prime. Thick black hair swept back from his forehead in a flourish. His teeth were commercial-grade white. He even had a dimple in his chin. It was the eyes that ruined the effect—they were small and speculative.

He jerked his chin toward my face. "What happened?"

"Racquetball. So about Kane . . ."

"Shame to see a shiner on a pretty face."

"The case," I said.

He sighed. "Look, Cohen told me I should talk to you, but I don't have much to share."

"Start with what isn't in the papers."

"There's nothing."

I narrowed my eyes. "Nothing?"

He shrugged and spread his meaty fingers apart, as if to prove he wasn't hiding anything. "Asshole's a white rabbit who popped up out of nowhere, then disappeared down his rabbit hole. Nothing useful on the cameras. Knife was the kind sold by every damn sporting-goods store in the city. Witnesses got nothing to add to what the cameras caught. And I already told you how it went with the tramps."

The waitress approached with Gorman's burger and fries and another Michelob. Clyde sat up, thrusting his nose into the hamburger's scent cone. His nostrils flared. I gestured him back down.

"Sure you don't want anything to eat?" the waitress asked as she set my seltzer water on the table.

"I'm good."

Gorman watched her leave, then rolled his eyes at my glass. "Last time I saw you, you were drinking whiskey like it was water. Now you're just drinking water?"

"Times change." I pulled my glass toward me, as if protecting it. "An RTD guard named Sadler went after the killer. What did he see?"

Gorman pounded ketchup onto his fries. "I'm telling you, rabbit. Witnesses told Sadler the asshole took off northeast, heading along the tracks. Sadler went in the same direction. Traffic cams tracked the suspect to that construction area along Wewatta Street. Then he just went . . . *poof*."

"Not like a slow-moving homeless man to be that good at disappearing."

"I'll bet you dollars to donuts these guys have hidey-holes we can't even guess at."

I pulled up a mental map of the area around Union Station. "What if someone picked him up? He disappeared near all those office buildings and parking garages. And he wasn't that far from Commons Park."

"That's exactly why I talked to the homeless there. And why I had patrol go door to door. Hell of a lot of doors, too. No one saw anything. For all I know, he might have made it to the Platte River and thrown himself in. I should be so lucky."

I propped my elbows on the arms of my chair. "Did you look in the trash cans? If the clothes and hair were a disguise, maybe he dumped them."

"A disguise?" Gorman's breath wheezed in and out as he laughed. "You think he took a shower and picked up a pair of shoes, too? Maybe stopped for a shave?"

"Or maybe he had a car stashed. Did you look at cameras in the nearby garages?"

Another wheeze. "Now you think this joker had a getaway vehicle?" He leaned back and rubbed at his chest as if he had heartburn. Half his burger and all the fries had disappeared. "No way."

"Why not?"

"The correct question is *why*." He pulled a business card out of his shirt pocket and used a corner to pick at his front teeth. "Let's take a walk down fantasy avenue and say this nutcase has a hard-on for cops. Let's even say he's been eyeballing the security guys and Kane gave him the chance he'd been dreaming of. Okay, maybe. But if you walk a little further out on that limb and say it was *so* preplanned he had a disguise and a getaway car? That he's Mr. Sophisticated? Then you'd at least figure the guy had been to Union Station before to scope out the place, right? Am I right? But no." Gorman looked triumphant. "He's never been there. Trust me, I checked."

I ignored that. "Did you run down any vehicles that were nearby when it happened? They'd be on camera, wouldn't they?"

Something dark slithered into Gorman's eyes. "If I didn't know better, I'd think you were trying to tell me how to do my job."

Seemed like someone had to. "I'm just throwing out ideas."

"Genius choo-choo cop, is that it?" He laughed and relaxed. "Look, I'm sure you're good at what you do. Guarding trains and chasing trespassers and all. But this is a little outside your ball-i-wick."

"*Bail*-i-wick," I enunciated, unable to resist.

"What?"

"Never mind."

He flushed. "Whatever." He finished with the business card, started to put it back in his shirt pocket, then glanced at it and changed his mind. He slid it into the inside pocket of his suit coat.

I finished my water.

"My opinion," Gorman said, "it's just a tragedy. One of those pointless things. Cases with these fucking religious freaks usually is."

I perked up at this tiny tidbit. "What makes you say he's a religious freak?"

"His tattoo. That wasn't in the paper. Some Muslim shit."

"You mean the star and crescent?"

His small eyes went smaller. "How'd you know about that?"

"I just came from RTD. So you figure the tat makes him a zealot?"

"How would you interpret it? You see his picture? The guy is a few pubic hairs short of a full snatch." He winked. "Not that that's always a bad thing."

I resisted the urge to ask him if he made his mama proud. "Plenty of people have religious tattoos. Crucifixes. Bible verses. It doesn't make them zealots."

"Look, I got nothing against being devout," he said. "I'm on Team Jesus myself. But these Muslims, they're a whole different breed. Cop killers."

I didn't grab the bait.

Gorman pushed his empty plate aside and wiped his fingers on a napkin. His eyes went past speculative and turned suspicious. "So level with me. What exactly is your interest in this case?"

"He was a cop, Gorman. And a veteran. He deserves the best."

Gorman's eyes showed a spark, like an arsonist's match. "And you don't think that's me."

I swallowed my own anger. "That's not what I mean. Kane was a Marine. I owe him."

The match flared, then went out. "Semper Fi, eh?"

"Right."

"Okay. So now *I* got some questions. You probably think I met you out of the goodness of my heart, right?"

And here I thought it was for the free meal.

"But what I want to know is, what does it mean that your number showed up in Kane's phone records? Is that some Marine shit, too?"

The sweat cooled on my neck. "Kane tried to call me?"

"Check your phone. I got his number here." Gorman pulled a folded piece of paper from his breast pocket and pushed it across the table.

I powered up my phone and went to the list of recent calls. There it was. Not once, but five times. The calls had come while I was on the run in Mexico City. I'd never even noticed.

"He tried to call me when I was on vacation," I said.

"You want to tell me why?"

"Six months ago I helped a friend of his beat a murder rap. Maybe it had something to do with that."

"I remember that case." Gorman nodded. "You chased down a rattler's nest of assholes. Shot most of them. I heard about that, and I'm thinking, this chick never heard of due process? So did Kane leave a message?"

"No." If I'd noticed the call and picked up, would it have made a difference in what happened? Would Kane still be alive? I touched my temples, fighting the headache that comes with feeling like a screwup.

"Look, the guy can't hide forever. And when he comes back out—" He made a fist with his right hand and slammed it into the palm of his left. "We get him."

That was Gorman. A lot of theoretical gung ho.

He finished his second beer. "I gotta shake the hog's leg. Be right back. Then it's off to the salt mines."

As soon as he disappeared down the stairs, I reached over and grabbed his suit coat. I pulled out the card. Three of the four corners were blunt from toothpick duty. On the face was printed VALOR INDUSTRIES.

The address was in the Denver Technological Center in the southeast part of town.

On the back, someone had written in black ink **100K**.

A hundred thousand what? Maybe it had nothing to do with the case, but I'd take a look at Valor Industries. I replaced the jacket and sat back in my chair as Gorman reappeared.

"Thanks for the food and the beer." He grabbed his jacket. "Let me know if you ever want to do it again. Could be fun. Oh, and if you figure out why Kane called, let me know."

I watched him make his way down the stairs.

Sure, pal. Got you on speed dial.

CHAPTER 14

Hope is not a game plan.

—*Sydney Parnell. Personal journal.*

After I left Gorman, my blood still boiled under my skin. My hope was that he was doing more than he admitted to. And even if he had his head up his ass, I had the consolation that he wasn't on his own. He'd be working alongside men and women who were still breathing clean air.

Regardless, I'd continue on my own path to find Kane's killer.

When Clyde and I got into the truck, I ignored the option for air-conditioning and powered down the front windows, then headed west toward Littleton and the home of Sherri and Jeremy Kane. Clyde gleefully watched out the window, his tongue hanging out the side of his mouth. He looked like a kid who'd reached the front of the line at the ice cream truck.

Soon, Mason would stencil the Expedition with the same wording that appeared on my old vehicle: **STAY BACK! K9 ON DUTY!**

Anyone who read that and saw Clyde would have a good laugh.

"You should work on your image," I told him.

Clyde wasn't the least bit concerned about his image. He could switch from tongue to teeth in an instant.

I snapped on sunglasses, then took off my ball cap, fingered loose my braid, and let the wind sweep away the sweat from the roots of my hair. This was what passed in my life as communing with nature.

I'd visited Jeremy and Sherri Kane's home once before, when I'd needed information about a case involving a member of Kane's fireteam. I'd been impressed with Jeremy Kane on that visit because—despite a likely permanent disability due to an injury in Iraq—he was still hanging tight to his goal to become a medical doctor. It would be excruciatingly difficult, given his memory issues, but he'd been determined, and his wife had been supportive. Maybe he'd started working toward that dream before the end came.

I was less fond of Kane's wife, Sherri. The daughter of a medical doctor and a socialite, she'd been born with a silver spoon in her mouth and clearly thought when she married Kane that she was going to maintain her social status. But if there's anything I've learned, it's that life will explode one land mine after another, even when all you're trying to do is walk from the couch to the refrigerator. The war and Kane's injury had thrown Sherri a grenade no one could catch with grace. Her husband had come home a hero. But he'd also come home with memory issues, a limp, PTSD, and a huge ration of cynicism that he hadn't had before.

Jeremy had told me his wife didn't like to hear about the war. But as far as he was concerned, that was okay. He hadn't wanted to talk about it.

I took the Bowles Avenue exit from C-470 and headed back east. So far, there had been no hint of anyone following. At a traffic light, a couple of kids in a minivan waved at Clyde. He drooled and they squealed.

The light changed.

When I pulled to the curb in front of the Kanes' split-level home, the first thing I noticed was that their house had gone from run-down-but-on-the-mend to just run-down. The wheelbarrow I'd noted on my last visit still sat on the side of the driveway, but it was now rusted. The dirt that had been piled next to it had vanished with the winter winds and summer rain. Since Kane had just died, the downward trend wasn't because a widow was overwhelmed. It looked like Kane had been busy elsewhere.

Or maybe he'd given up.

The only positive note to the general dreariness was a gray Mercedes-Benz parked on the driveway as far from the wheelbarrow as possible, as if rust were contagious.

I turned off the engine and moved Clyde to his air-conditioned crate in the back. The Kanes had a pit bull, and I didn't want to rock anyone's boat. As I walked up the drive, I did some quick math. Sherri had been eight months pregnant the last time I'd seen her. Their second child would now be five months old. Their oldest, Haley, was three or four.

From the backyard, the pit bull unleashed a volley of barks. I glanced over my shoulder at Clyde. He was watching out the window, no doubt ready to break through it if the dog came after me. I gave him a thumbs-up. He kept watching.

The pit bull cranked up the barks.

I rang the bell. I waited a few minutes, then rang again. I wondered if Sherri could hear the bell over the barking. Then the dog fell silent, and the tread of footsteps sounded on the other side of the door.

The woman who answered was twenty-five years older than Sherri, but otherwise looked much like her. Her chin-length bob was bright silver, her casual but fashionable clothes impeccably tailored. She had a ring on her left hand with a diamond the size of a small country.

Sherri's mother, I assumed. The owner of the Mercedes.

I said, "My name is Sydney Parnell. I'm a friend of the family. Is Sherri at home? I'd like to express my condolences."

The woman's face was a perfect blank. On closer inspection, I saw that her lipstick was smeared and her mascara had flaked.

"Sorry, who?" she asked.

"A friend of the family."

"Oh. All right." She unlatched the door and waved me in. I stepped into the living room, which was empty of furniture and filled with moving boxes.

She closed the door behind me, then came to life slowly, as if her battery had just reached enough capacity for her to function.

"Sherri is changing Megan's diaper," she said. "I'll let her know you're here."

"Thank you. I didn't catch your name."

"Oh. I'm Sherri's mother, Krystal." She blinked a few times. "Would you like some coffee? We've got muffins, too. Blueberry."

"Coffee would be great," I said.

I followed her down a hall stacked with more cardboard boxes and into the kitchen. Here, someone had clearly been hard at work, scrubbing away all semblance of dirt. Many of the cupboard doors stood open, the shelves empty. More boxes were stacked in the corner.

"Is Sherri moving?" I asked. Master of the obvious.

"She and the girls are coming home to her father and me," Krystal said. She pointed toward the table. "Please, sit down. Do you take cream and sugar?"

"Black, please."

She set a mug of steaming coffee in front of me along with a buttered muffin.

"I have coffee cake, if you'd rather. The neighbors have been bringing food. I'm sure they mean well. But it's just too much."

"The muffin is wonderful."

"I'm sorry it's so hot in here. We offered to help Sherri and Jeremy with air-conditioning." She stopped and blinked at the moisture in her eyes. "But Jeremy . . . that boy had too much pride."

"I know this is a terrible shock."

She looked at me and frowned. The battery hit 100 percent capacity, and the skin around her pale eyes tightened. Maybe it was the dog hair on my pants.

"How did you say you know the family?"

At that moment, Sherri walked into the kitchen carrying a baby. The baby was round and soft, with wide eyes and a pink hair band holding back her soft frizz of hair. She smelled of talcum powder. Hard on Sherri's heels was her first child, Haley. Haley had been zoned out on cartoons the last time I'd seen her, but now she was as wide eyed and alert as her sister, staring at me from behind her mother's leg.

Sherri herself looked like she hadn't slept since she got the news. Her eyes and the tip of her nose were red. The rest of her was white as a sheet. She saw me and managed to muster a little outrage.

"You," she said.

"Sherri?" her mother asked. "She said she's a friend of the family."

I stood. "I'm so sorry for what happened, Sherri. I came to see if I could do anything to help."

Sherri's anger whooshed out of her like air from a popped balloon. She handed the baby to her mother and sank into the chair across from me. When Haley climbed into her lap, Sherri absently wrapped her arms around the girl. Haley studied me with her father's intent gaze and blue eyes. She had his red hair, as well. Kane must have loved that.

"Mommy, can I have a blueberry muffin?" Haley asked.

Without waiting for permission, I slid my untouched plate across the table. Haley smiled at me.

"Thank you." She looked up at her mother. "Mommy?"

Sherri's gaze settled on me. "Why are you here?"

"To help, if I can."

"Yes, you were such a help when Elise died." She wielded sarcasm like a knife. Sherri had been livid during the Hensley case when I'd dragged Kane into it. "Mother, would you take the girls upstairs to watch TV?"

Krystal looked like she would protest. But then she nodded and shifted the baby to her other hip. "Of course. Haley, honey, let's go upstairs. We can play dress up if you want."

"Can I take my muffin?"

"Food stays in the kitchen."

"Mother. It doesn't matter anymore, does it? Haley, you can take your muffin."

Haley slid off her mother's lap, balancing the plate in her small hands. The stairs creaked as she and her grandmother and the baby disappeared from view.

Sherri turned to me, narrowing her own eyes down to slits in perfect imitation of her mother. "Why are you really here?"

"Jeremy tried to call me five times the day he died. I'd like to know why."

"You didn't pick up?"

"I was in Mexico. I didn't see the calls."

Sherri's mouth went slack, and her hands fluttered up as if to ward off my words. Her hands were pale and slender, fragile in a way the rest of her was not. They settled on her chest, fingers spread like a cage over her heart.

"Why would he call you?"

"I don't know," I said gently. "I thought you might."

"No. I don't."

I walked out onto the ice. "Something to do with the war, maybe?"

"Damn the war."

She lowered her hands to the table, flattened her palms, and pushed herself up. She poured herself a mug of coffee.

Every time I'd seen Sherri in the past, she'd been flawlessly put together in a way I couldn't fathom how to achieve. Money was part of it—the perfectly tailored clothes, the expensive hair. Attitude was the other half. Sherri had been raised to believe the world was her oyster and, if you were patient, life gave you pearls.

Now she looked as if she'd been shattered from the inside and pieced back together with bailing wire and Xanax.

She groped for her chair and sank into it.

She said, "For a long time, Jeremy was doing all right. He loved his job with the RTD. Standing watch was what he knew best, and because of that, he also thought it was what he *did* best."

I understood. Why not monetize your anxiety? A lot of us did.

"But a week ago," she went on, "he started acting the way he did when he first came home from Iraq. Those horrible nightmares. He'd wake up screaming, and his screaming would wake the girls, and then *they'd* start crying. On the nights he didn't have nightmares, it was because he never went to sleep. I'd find him walking the house or standing at the living room window. I thought he was having a . . . a breakdown. I begged him to go back to his therapist."

"You have any idea what triggered this?"

"I know when it started. I'd gone out with my girls group. Dinner and a movie. Jeremy was fine when I left. But when I got home, everything had changed."

"What did he say when you asked?"

She flushed. "I didn't. Not at first. I just thought he was mad that I'd left him alone with the girls." She gave me a plaintive look. "I keep telling him I'm sorry. I'm sorry I didn't understand. I'm sorry I got mad. Do you think he can hear me?"

"I'm sure he knew that, Sherri."

"I need him to know *now*. I need to know he can hear me."

She tilted her head back as if she couldn't get enough air. I gave her a moment. Then I said, "So when you got home that night, he was angry."

"Not angry. Not exactly. Agitated."

"Later, did you ask him what had made him agitated?"

Her flush deepened. "I asked Haley. She said someone called, and Daddy was on the phone for a long time. After that, he put the baby down with a wet diaper and sent Haley to bed without reading her a story. Megan was soaked when I got home."

"He was distracted."

Her gaze roamed the room as if she wasn't sure where she was. "He was terrified."

"Of what, Sherri?"

But she'd jumped tracks. "Detective Gorman told me Jeremy was killed by a lunatic. A bum. A . . . a random stranger. How can this happen? My husband defended his country in Iraq. He survived a bomb blast. And then he comes home to be killed by a madman." Her fingers curled into fists. "Tell me where there's any justice in that."

There wasn't, of course. I remained mute before her rage and grief.

"If they find him," she said, "I hope they fry him. *That* would be justice."

Part of the Xanax had given way, exposing the cracks, and tears poured unheeded down her face. I spotted a box of tissues on the counter and passed it to her. She pressed a tissue to her eyes and sat silently for a moment.

My chest aching, I waited her out. In the backyard, the pit bull loosed a broadside of barks that tapered off to a cranky growl. He whined at the door, then gave up on that, too.

A siren whoop-whooped in the distance.

Sherri shook herself and pushed up from the table. She moved around the kitchen, touching boxes, closing cupboards and reopening them. She stopped by the window.

She said, "War never ends, does it? Even after they sign peace agreements or armistices or cease-fires or whatever the hell it is the politicians do. It just goes on and on. You can't escape. You can't rewind. War changed Jeremy, and when he tried to fix things, it sucked him back in."

"Is that what he said?"

Forgetting her half-full mug on the table, she yanked another out of one of the boxes and splashed coffee into it. She didn't seem to notice when coffee spilled on the counter. "He thought I needed to be protected. He decided for himself that I couldn't take it. But that was all on him—he wouldn't talk to me."

"I'm sorry." And I was.

"You're with someone, aren't you?"

"Jury seems to be out at the moment."

"Things come and go. Doesn't matter what you plan." She blew her nose. "Do you talk to him about Iraq?"

"No."

"And here I thought women were smarter than men."

A weight settled onto my chest. *Weight with a capital* W, Nik Lasko used to say. Heaviest pounds you'll ever carry.

"So what made you think this was about the war?" I asked.

"He finally told me it was Lester Crowe who called."

"One of his fireteam members."

"Crazy Crowe. That's what Jeremy called him. Not in a mean way. In a . . . a Jeremy way."

"He and Crowe talk often?"

"Almost never. But that's Crowe. He disappears for months at a time. Pops back up like nothing happened."

"And did his calls always upset Jeremy?"

"Not like this one. They made him sad and worried. But not angry. And not scared. Then . . . this."

"Did he tell you what they talked about?"

"No. But whatever it was . . . things got weird after that."

"How so?"

"Jeremy is—Jeremy *was* always protective of us. But after that night, he got paranoid. First he tried to get me and the girls to move in with my parents. When I refused, he ordered an alarm service we can't afford. And twice I found him up in the middle of the night. He said he couldn't sleep. But he had a gun. We agreed we wouldn't have guns in the house." Another plaintive look. "I think he was going crazy."

"No, Sherri. He wasn't."

"How can you possibly know that?"

I decided it was time she understood a little of what her husband had been through. If I ever managed to crack this case and expose the Alpha, it was better she heard it from me, not on the five o'clock news.

Plus, I didn't want her thinking Kane had been crazy.

"What you said about war never ending, it's true," I said. "The war is still here. There's something you need to know. A group of us were involved in something in Iraq. Jeremy and his fireteam. My commanding officer and me. It was something we should not have done. Something wrong."

She held up a hand like a stop sign. "That's not possible."

I trotted out the same words I'd used with Cohen. They were starting to feel thin. "We thought we were saving Americans."

"No." She set the coffee down on the counter and folded her arms. "You're wrong about Jeremy. He would never be involved in anything wrong."

A memory rose.

The Sir and I climbed out of our vehicle, and the Sir's flashlight caught the faces of the men. They were all masked. Until they'd spoken, I'd thought they were Iraqis.

"This is fucked," one of them said.

"Who cares?" one of the others asked. "They killed Renks. And Haifa."

That's when I realized they were Marines. I'd looked at the Sir, bewildered.

But all he'd said was, "Let's get this done," before he led me into the house.

I shuddered.

Sherri was looking at me like maybe I didn't have full ownership of my marbles.

"He was trying to do the right thing," I said. "We all were. War . . . it jumbles up what's right and what's wrong. You get tunnel vision."

Fury flared in her eyes. "Is this why you came here? I've lost my *husband*. Are you trying to destroy his memory, too?"

"His death wasn't random."

"Why would you do that? Take what little I have?"

"Sherri, please. I'm not trying to take anything from you."

Her nostrils flared. "You need to leave."

"Sherri—"

"Now."

I stood. "It's the truth. You need to know."

"Get out!"

We stared at each other across the bright and shiny kitchen—Sherri's domain that the exterior of the house couldn't match. I had to admire her righteous anger. But she was picking the wrong fight. I wasn't the enemy.

Krystal appeared in the doorway, armed with her own look of righteous fury.

"What are you doing?"

Mama bear. Now I knew where Sherri got it.

"You need to leave right now," she said.

"No." I approached her. "Your daughter and I need to finish this conversation."

Krystal stepped back a pace, and Sherri's expression shifted from fury to astonishment. Quite possibly no one had ever stood up to her mother.

Krystal tried to look over my shoulder. "Sherri?"

We both looked at her daughter. Sherri's face played like a flip-book, racing from one expression to another. Finally, her eyes showed the realization that what I offered was a thread she could pull. A thread that might provide answers her husband no longer could.

Her face settled into a look half of grief, half of resolve.

"It's all right, Mother. She's right. We have to talk." She gently pushed her mother toward the stairs and watched while Krystal disappeared down the upstairs hall. She turned to me. "You really think Jeremy's death wasn't just . . . just bad luck?"

"I do."

"Oh, fuck." The words sounded all wrong coming from her refined lips.

But grief breaks down all barriers. Death is the great equalizer.

"Fuck," she said again. "Tell me how I can help."

◆ ◆ ◆

An hour later, I walked out to my truck carrying a large manila envelope. I let Clyde into the front, then got in with him and slid the key into the ignition.

I hadn't learned a lot from Sherri. I'd hoped to find information on Kane's laptop, but it turned out Gorman had taken that as well as Kane's phone.

And I'd failed to learn anything about the people Kane might have been looking at on the platform just before he died. Sherri didn't recognize any of the names.

But what I had learned felt important.

First—Kane had lost touch with Sarge, who'd disappeared. *Gone underground* was how Kane put it to his wife. He'd worried that his old friend might be up to no good. Since this was the same Sarge who claimed his orders to kill me came from a man with the CIA, I was inclined to agree. Kane had the key to Sarge's apartment in a desk drawer. When I asked, Sherri gave it to me. This was a coup—the chance to go through Sarge's apartment might turn up all kinds of interesting information. Maybe even the cell phone Malik had given him. The one with the video Malik had taken of men unloading weapons in Iraq.

Second—although Kane loved his job with the RTD, he'd been looking for something with better benefits. Two weeks ago he'd scored an interview at a private, family-owned intelligence firm called Vigilant Resources. When Sherri mentioned that Vigilant was a subsidiary of a precision-weapons manufacturer named Valor, I recalled the business card Gorman had so elegantly used on his teeth. *Valor Industries.* And the number 100K.

Presumably, Gorman had gone to talk to Valor as part of the investigation. Maybe the 100K was the salary Kane had been offered by their subsidiary, Vigilant. But when I asked Sherri if Kane's job hunt had come up in her conversation with the detective, she said no. When I asked if any of Kane's friends knew about it, she again said no, not to her knowledge.

The news about Gorman wasn't a five-alarm fire. He could have learned about Vigilant any number of ways. Maybe the business card in his pocket had nothing to do with Kane's job hopes. Gorman was probably thinking of retirement. Could be he had job hopes of his own.

Weapons companies hired former cops for security. I could be poking my stick at a nest of twigs, not vipers.

Maybe.

Sherri said her husband was especially excited about the job because the president and CEO of Vigilant, a man named James Osborne, had served in Iraq. He and Kane had been in-country at the same time. Osborne was with the State Department, not the military. But military and intelligence intermingled all the time in a war zone. We were all on the same team.

Prior to the interview, Kane had collected information about Valor and Vigilant, mostly in the form of a couple of glossy brochures and some printouts of internet searches. That was what Sherri had given to me in an envelope. Jeremy, she said, had wanted to be fully prepared for his interview. What was strange was that he'd hidden the envelope, taped it inside a dresser drawer. She'd only found it when she was emptying everything into boxes.

A magpie scolded from a nearby tree, popping me out of my reverie. I reached into the glove box for a cigarette, then stopped myself. Self-control begins at home.

I thought about Sherri and Kane, and the end of their dream. We always say live for today and don't waste time worrying about tomorrow. But what keeps us up at night is knowing that tomorrow is roaring down on us like a tsunami, and a lot of us don't know how to swim.

For a moment I let my mind wander into forbidden territory. How would I feel if something happened to Cohen? Or if, now that he knew what I was, he walked out of my life? Would I have the strength to pick up and go on again, the way I had after Dougie died?

Of course you would, the Sir said in my mind. *That's what we do. We go on, no matter what.*

I looked out the window and saw him standing by the curb. He nodded.

Of course we go on.

Maybe even after we're dead.

I pulled away from the curb and headed north.

CHAPTER 15

Most of us—maybe all of us—are broken in some way.
Depending on who we are, those cracks can either let in the
darkness or the light.

—*Sydney Parnell. Personal journal.*

No one answered when I knocked on the door to Sarge's second-floor apartment.

I counted to twenty, then used the key Sherri had given me. Clyde and I slipped in, and I closed and locked the door behind us.

Clyde gave no indication that anyone else was in the small apartment. But I signaled, and we went fast together through the space, clearing it. The apartment was deserted.

It was also a wreck. Someone had gotten here first.

The other time Clyde and I had been here, the place had been a misery of dirty clothes, dirty dishes, and takeout boxes. There had been a sense of desolation I found depressingly familiar. Maybe without the stabilizing influence of Grams, my childhood home would have looked like Sarge's.

Lonely knows lonely. And Sarge—Max Udell—seemed pretty damn lonely.

But now that I knew a little about him, I had to wonder if the version of extreme bachelorhood he'd created was a mirage. A cover for this man who claimed to work for the CIA.

The current wreckage of his home, though, wasn't part of any cover. Someone had torn the place apart.

Clyde and I did a second walk-through.

The same kind of pizza boxes and empty beer bottles that had covered the kitchen counter on our last visit were on the floor, crushed and broken. The sofa had been gutted, the mattress and box springs dismantled, the contents of the closets rifled and tossed to the floor.

Once again I had the sense that mysterious forces swirled around us. Invisible, but active and dangerous. If this were a chess match, Clyde and I were unquestionably the pawns. I wasn't sure what piece Sarge played.

I returned to the front room and signaled Clyde to guard the door. Then I went back through the rooms a third time, searching more slowly. I scrutinized the living room, kitchen, and the first bedroom before heading into the last room.

This second bedroom served as Sarge's office and a place to exhibit the artifacts he'd collected in Iraq. On my last visit, it had been the only clean and organized space in the apartment.

Now it was a ruin. The bookshelves had been toppled, the clay pots and cuneiform tablets smashed. Copies of *National Geographic* and *Archaeology Magazine* covered the floor. I yanked open the drawers to the filing cabinet, which had been packed full of folders. Now, all that remained were utility bills, a rental agreement for the apartment, and a few flyers. Sarge's desk was likewise empty, the drawers wrenched out and thrown to the floor.

Above the desk, where Sarge had pinned hundreds of photographs, rose a wall empty of everything except a constellation of pinprick-size holes. The wall of memories was now mute.

My hope of finding Malik's phone or a copy of the video vanished. In all the mess there were no phones, no media disks, no thumb drives. Not even an old VHS tape.

But there wouldn't be. Whoever had torn the place apart was probably after the same thing.

On my way out, I stopped to scope out the bathroom.

The linoleum floor was covered with broken bottles of cold medicine and mouthwash. The air reeked of cough syrup and hydrogen peroxide. But now that I was in the room, I detected something else beneath the medicinal odors. A sharp, familiar stench.

I looked at the blue-plaid curtain hiding the bathtub.

Unease slithered through my stomach. There was no one, living or dead, hiding behind the curtain. Clyde would have let me know.

But there was something.

My eyes went to a splash of reddish brown on the bottom corner of the curtain.

Reluctantly, I reached out a hand and drew back the fabric.

The tub was filled with an inch of dried blood. More blood spattered the tiles, halfway to the ceiling. Smears painted the inside of the curtain.

I dropped the curtain and backed out of the room, my boots crunching over the debris.

Unless Sarge had slaughtered an animal, someone had died in that bathtub. You could not bleed that much and live.

But was Sarge the victim? Or the perpetrator?

◆ ◆ ◆

In light of that discovery, I decided Clyde and I should head to Joe's Tavern in the Royer district.

I told myself it wasn't because I needed a drink. Clyde and I wanted a safe place to work, and I needed the company of normal.

I kept an eye on the rearview mirror, but we appeared to be traveling solo.

Joe's was the kind of neighborhood bar where the regular clientele showed up year after year, aging quietly like books fading in the sun. The place had a soft patina, as if the patrons' hopes and dreams and sometimes their ruin had rubbed into the tables and floors. I'd gone to Joe's first as a child towed by my parents, then later with the kids I'd grown up with. Now Clyde and I were regulars.

Paul Porter, a Royer local and the latest in a long line of owners, had kept the familiar wood paneling and red-vinyl booths when he took over five years earlier. But he'd brought in free Wi-Fi, replaced the felt on the pool tables, and introduced a pretzel-and-wasabi mix to go with the popcorn. The old guard groused about the changes until Paul hired a short-order cook and added a bar menu. With the addition of a grill and a prep line, the hard-liners didn't even have to leave to eat, which made drinking all the easier.

As Clyde and I walked in, Paul glanced up from his stool behind the bar. Hitting the far end of his fourth decade, he had kept the cool, casual hip of someone twenty years younger. Today he wore his trademark look—skinny jeans, an untucked button-down, a small earring in his left lobe, and a permanent five o'clock shadow. He looked like he belonged behind the mic at a poetry slam.

Paul had hit on me a few times. Always in the southern way—with such careful politeness, I had to think twice to make sure I knew what was happening. I'd turned him down with a lot less polish. You can take the girl out of Royer . . .

"Well, look who's here." Paul smiled and came out from behind the bar to give me a hug and silently appraise my wounded face. Then he dropped down to rub Clyde behind the ears.

Clyde nosed Paul and closed his eyes with pleasure.

Paul got back to his feet.

"How you been?" I asked.

"You hear my knees pop? Pain in the ass getting older. But I deal. Sit yourself down, and I'll pour you something. Got an outstanding batch of green chili on in the back, too."

"Chili and a drink sounds great. But would you mind if I hide out in your office?"

"Fighting with your old man?"

"Who says *old man* anymore?"

"He *is* older than you."

"So are you, Paul. Case you hadn't noticed."

"Sucker punch to the ego, Sydney."

"You can handle it. But it's nothing like that. Cohen's out of town. I need to get some work done, and I don't feel like keeping my own company. Clyde's a true friend, but when we're home he mostly sleeps and snores. Farts a bit."

Clyde glanced up at me as if wondering what was wrong with sleeping and snoring. And the occasional gas.

"*Mi casa es tu casa,*" Paul said. "Help yourself. You need internet?"

"Depends. How secure is your router?"

"Hey." He thumped his chest. "You forget who you're talking to? I got the best money can buy."

"What I forget is that you're paranoid."

"What I am is smart. You see this crowd?"

I glanced around. "There's no one here under seventy."

"The old guys are the worst. They practically rioted when I bumped happy-hour drafts to a dollar. If I don't watch them, they find their way online and buy all their tighty-whities at Walmart.com, then figure out how to charge them to the tavern and ship them here."

"Underwear in bulk in one easy click. Wait until they discover Amazon."

"Stop."

"So I can hop on your network for a while?"

"Not a problem." He grabbed a piece of paper from a stack at the end of the bar and wrote down a long string of numbers, letters, and assorted characters. "Just don't share."

I took the paper. "Should I eat this when I'm done?"

He handed me a bottle of a local brew. "I'd stick with the chili. Shredder is under the desk."

Paul's office was located at the end of the hall that also held the bathrooms, a janitor's closet, a storage room, and a door to the outside where Paul went to smoke when he wanted something other than the occasional illicit cigarette. While I settled at the desk with my personal laptop, Clyde sniffed around the ten-by-twenty office. When he was sure we were safe, he found a place to his liking beneath the window.

"You doing okay, boy?"

He rested his head on his paws and sighed. I was sure he missed Cohen. More exercise, better food, and some decent outdoor time. I checked my phone to see if I'd missed a call from Cohen, then shoved away the pain that thinking about him brought.

"Sorry, boy. You're stuck with me."

He yawned.

"Very subtle. If you're not sure I got the message, you could go to sleep."

He closed his eyes.

"Okay, boy," I murmured, feeling guilty. "Point made."

I opened my duffel and pulled out a sealed bag with one of the dental bones I'd gotten from Clyde's trainer. The things looked like real bones and—frankly—also stank the way I imagined fresh caribou must. But Clyde scrabbled to his feet, tail wagging. He waited until I offered the treat, then took it neatly from my hand and resumed his place under the window with a contented huff.

No doubt the bone made him feel like he was one with the wolves again. And we could all use a little taste of the wild.

While Clyde gnawed happily, I shook out the contents of Sherri's envelope onto the desk—these were the items Kane had gathered as part of his background research before his interview.

On top were two brochures, one for Valor Industries and another for its subsidiary, Vigilant Resources.

The brochures promised potential recruits an exciting career with companies working at the leading edge of weapons and intelligence operations. Headquartered in Dallas, but with offices all around the globe, Valor had been founded by Sheldon Osborne after WWII, and was still owned and run by his descendants. They specialized in precision weapons, mainly missiles and torpedoes.

Vigilant, with its clever open-eye logo, had opened its doors in 2005. It didn't overtly state what it specialized in.

Standard marketing—all fluff and no stuff.

I unfolded the rest of the papers. Based on what Kane had told his wife, I was expecting printouts from internet searches. But these looked like downloads from a digital camera, printed on regular paper so that the quality was only so-so.

The first was a daylight exterior shot of a strip joint.

The place was abandoned. My first clue was the word on the marquee below a stylized drawing of a nude woman: *Closed*. And not just for the day. Weeds choked the parking lot, and a sheet of plywood had been nailed over the front door.

I studied the photo, trying to come up with even one theory that could explain why a closed-for-business strip joint would help Kane in a job interview. Then, still clueless, I set the photo aside.

The remaining pictures were even less forthcoming—multiple long-range shots of a building and a few smaller structures on a flat stretch of prairie, God knew where. The photos were almost identical, and were taken from such a distance that I had to stare at them for a while before I could see anything in them at all. Faint geometric forms, the same color as the prairie. When I squinted and used my imagination, I thought I could make out the wings of a small plane on the far side of one of the structures. Or maybe it was another building. Or a bit of fuzz on the camera lens.

I leaned back and rested my clasped hands on my head, trying to imagine Kane's interest in these places, and why he had hidden the photographs. Defeated, I set the pictures and brochures aside and decided to see what I could learn online.

I powered up my laptop.

The screen flashed, and a cartoon video of a beheaded woman appeared, blood pumping in spurts from her severed neck.

Underneath were the words *This could be you.*

I slammed the lid down.

"Shit," I said.

Clyde opened one eye.

I squeezed my own eyes shut. I saw Haifa's and Resenko's severed corpses in Habbaniyah. Saw Malik weeping in the front room, only feet away from his murdered mother. I saw Angelo's body in the alleyway, his face a ruin.

No one should die the way they had.

But maybe someone thought it was my turn.

Whoever had broken into Cohen's place had found my laptop. The cartoon clip was only for shock value. But it meant he'd no doubt copied everything on the hard drive and placed a Trojan horse inside to monitor key clicks and take screen captures. Since he'd chosen to advertise his invasion, I figured this was part of his ongoing campaign to remind me who was calling the shots.

I opened my eyes and looked over at Clyde, still enjoying his bone.

"They don't get to win, Clyde. Not this time."

If the Alpha had hoped to intimidate with that clip, he'd failed. All he'd done was piss me off. Reinvigorated by rage, I shut down the computer. Reluctant to take Clyde away from his bone, I told him to wait, then went back out to the truck for my work laptop.

Outside the door to the tavern, I paused to take in the parking lot.

The sun had just set, and dusk bathed the world in lavender. Moths flapped at the light over the tavern door, and a few mosquitoes buzzed. Nothing else stirred.

Moving quickly, I unlocked the driver-side door and reached under the seat for my work laptop.

A whisper of movement, and something hard jabbed my ribs.

"We have to talk," a man said.

Only four words, but I knew that voice. I should have shot Sarge last winter when I had the chance, then chopped his body into pieces and fed the parts into a wood chipper.

It worked in the movies.

I raced down my list of options. They were distressingly few. Scream. Give in. Fight back.

"Didn't expect you to be this careless, Parnell."

I knew I should be afraid. Sarge was dangerous. Even deadly. But I was too far into my anger to back off the cliff.

"I'm in the mood to hurt something, Udell," I said. "And you just pissed me off."

Sarge snorted. "Not asking to be your friend. Just need a few minutes of your time. I figure coming at you this way means we can have a conversation without your dog trying to take off my face."

Vowing to never leave Clyde behind again, I pushed aside the laptop and groped for the backup pistol I'd taken from the Land Cruiser. "You want to talk, then get away from me."

"Fucker killed Kane," Sarge said. "Now he's chasing Crowe halfway across the country. This shit ends now."

My fingers scrabbled against carpet. Where was the damn gun? "Give me a name. I'll pass it to the police."

"I don't have a name. That's why I'm here."

My fingers brushed cool steel. I worked my hand around the grip.

Another dig in my ribs from Sarge.

"I figure you've got a gun under that seat," Sarge said. "But you shoot me, and every answer I have dies with me. Think about that. I'm going to step away now."

I slid the gun free. Sarge's feet kicked against gravel as he moved back. I swung around with the weapon up.

He had his own gun raised.

We stared at each other over the barrels.

"Now what?" I asked.

"Truce?"

"Fuck that."

"Fuck all." Sarge lowered his weapon.

"Toss it," I said.

He did. I let it hit the ground.

"Hands on the truck," I said. "Spread-eagle."

When he complied, I patted him down, but found nothing.

I bent and scooped up his weapon.

Around us, the parking lot remained quiet save for a dove cooing its satisfaction with the warm evening. No one came or went.

"Where's Malik's video?" I asked, curious to see if he knew.

"Ah, fuck." Sarge closed his eyes. "You don't have it? Word was you ended up with it."

An image of Dougie's compass flashed in my mind. The key was safe in the duffel in Paul's office, guarded by Clyde.

"Malik gave that video to you," I said.

"And I passed it straight up the chain of command. Way too hot for me to hold on to."

"What's on that video, Sarge? What's the Alpha so damned determined to hide?"

Sarge opened his eyes. Or rather, his one good eye. The other, I now saw, was swollen shut. The rest of his face didn't look great, either.

"The Alpha," he said. "I forgot that's what you call him."

"The video, Sarge. Tell me."

"American weapons." He let loose a long, melancholy sigh that sounded like it came from somewhere deep. "Sold illegally to Iran by an American company, smuggled into Iraq, and used to kill American troops. All with the blessing of a goddamn prick the devil has kept alive for his own mean purpose."

A breeze gusted up, licking the sweat from my skin. My tongue clicked against the roof of my suddenly too-dry mouth.

I said, "He killed everyone who knew about it. Malik's mother. PFC Resenko. Murdered them in cold blood."

"And he killed your man, Doug Ayers. He killed them all. He's *still* killing people." Sarge's jaw went tight like he was working through something he couldn't swallow. "And now, Corporal, it's us. Your number and mine are about up. Only chance we got is to put our heads together and figure out who this asshole is. Then we send a three-hundred-pound mortar straight up his ass."

"My number was up six months ago. Remember that, Sarge? You were the one who was going to call in my ticket, until I got the upper hand."

Sarge nodded. Then he tilted back his head and stared at the sky for a moment. When his eyes once again met mine, the storm of anger had quieted into a pensive calm.

"I was fed a lot of bad information about you, Parnell," he said. "Some seriously fucked-up shit. Told you were a threat to national security because you were endangering the mission. That you had intel you'd use to bring down the good and protect the evil. I swallowed their lies like I was swallowing good scotch. Thought I was some hot-shit superhero." The calm sputtered out, and his voice came like a growl. "Took me a long time to realize I was on the wrong team."

The image of Sarge beating me in my own kitchen broke free from the compartment I'd stowed it in. "Do you even remember how much you hurt me?"

"I remember. As I recall, you got in a few licks of your own."

"There's more where that came from."

"Well, then." He chuckled. "Damn good thing we're on the same side now."

CHAPTER 16

When the dog has a chance to bite, he will.

—*Effie "Grams" Parnell. Private conversation.*

"Explosively formed penetrators," Sarge said. "EFPs."

He sat in a chair in Paul's office in the back of Joe's Tavern, his body pitched forward as if ready to run, his eyes on Clyde.

For his part, Clyde looked intently interested in chewing off Sarge's feet and then moving up to more sensitive areas. Max Udell was a lot more entertaining than a dental bone.

"Dog's making me nervous," Sarge said. "Doesn't he know we're on the same team?"

"Clyde's not really a team player."

"Shit."

"Plus, I need a little time to decide if we *are* on the same side."

"I gave you my gun! Put myself at your mercy."

"You could be a mole."

"Ah, fuck me, I'm not a spy."

"Because you'd tell me if you were."

But in truth, I believed him. The vibes Sarge gave off felt right. And sometimes you have to trust your gut.

That didn't mean I was going to kiss his ass.

"Clyde knows we've called a truce," I said. "He won't take off your face unless you do something stupid."

"Define *stupid.*"

"Anything that pisses him off." I opened my work laptop and hit the power button. "Now go on with what you were saying."

Sarge leaned back in his chair. Clyde adjusted his haunches. They rolled eyes at each other.

"These EFPs were nasty motherfuckers," Sarge said. "They could be launched from a distance, rather than buried in roadside trash. Easier to use. More flexible. And way more lethal. The only thing the bad guys had that could blow up an M1 Abrams tank. The penetrators started showing up a week before Haifa and Resenko were killed."

"We were getting some bad shit in Mortuary Affairs then," I said. "The bodies—it wasn't good."

"Like I said. E-fucking-Ps."

"How do you know so much about them?"

"Rick Dalton."

"Your favorite spy."

"Rick was a good guy. He got involved with the EFPs because he was monitoring reports from Special Operations Command— SOCOM. The SOCOM guys noticed an uptick in American casualties near the border with Iran. It looked like the weapons were coming in across the border. But Rick knew these ordnances were way too sophisticated for the insurgents or even the Iranians. He went to SOCOM and started asking questions."

"What did he learn?"

"Nothing. After a few weeks, the bad guys stopped using the EFPs. All traces of them disappeared. No unexploded ordnance, no fragments. Nothing. Like they'd never been there."

I heard Angelo's voice in my mind. *Dalton. They wanted to know . . . about him.*

"Where *is* Rick Dalton, Sarge? Are you sure he isn't the Alpha?"

Sarge shook his head, then dropped his elbows to his knees. "Remember when you told me he was dead?"

A shiver hitched a ride up my spine. I'd seen Rick's ghost—or a chemical response to stress, per my therapist—months ago, back when everyone else thought he was still alive and well in Iraq.

Sarge rubbed a hand over his mouth. "You had that one pegged. He's dead. He's been dead. Turns out he went down during the same mission that nailed your pal, Ayers."

A layer of goose bumps rose on my over-hot skin.

Maybe I actually had seen Rick's ghost. Which would be an argument in support of my sanity.

I'd share with my therapist: *I really* do *see dead people.*

I startled when the computer pinged, signaling it had finished with diagnostics and was ready to do my bidding.

I handed Kane's brochures over to Sarge. "Before he was killed, Kane was looking into two companies—Valor and Vigilant."

Sarge glanced through them. "You think one of these companies sold the EFPs to Iran?"

"Valor specializes in large precision weapons."

"These brochures all you got on them?"

"So far. Let's see what I can find online."

I logged into the router, then opened up a browser and entered Valor Industries in the search field.

Sarge scooted his chair close to mine.

"Clyde's still watching," I said.

"Don't I know it."

We tracked my search together.

I found a metalworks company and a packaging business. Not so much as a whisper of a weapons industry.

"Try another browser," Sarge said.

I tried three more. Same result.

Sarge rubbed his chin. "If they were responsible for the fuckup in Iraq, maybe they decided to get out of the business."

"I'm guessing companies like Valor don't close their doors when things get a little hot. More likely they get their customers through word of mouth." I opened another browser. "Let's try Vigilant Resources."

Clyde swiveled toward the door just then, and Paul called out, "Dinner is served."

I pushed back my chair and opened the door. Paul stood in the hallway holding a tray with a bowl of green chili and tortillas wrapped in foil along with a glass and a bottle of dark beer.

His eyes landed on Sarge, taking in Udell's battered face. "Didn't know you had company."

"Brought him in through the back. You mind doubling up on the food and drink?"

"Sure. Clear some space, and I'll set this on the desk."

Bless Paul and his easy nature. I moved my computer to one side, and he set down the tray with a flourish.

I forced a smile. "The food smells wonderful."

"Best green chili in Denver. Hell, in Colorado." He offered Sarge his hand, and they swapped names. "You look like you could use a drink. What's your poison?"

"Whatever she's having. Thanks, man."

"No problem."

Paul departed. A minute later he was back with another bowl of chili and several more bottles of beer.

A glance at me. "Get you anything else?"

"You're too good to me."

"Remember that when you finally dump the cop."

Or when the cop finally dumps me.

"Holler when the beer runs out," Paul said on his way out.

I closed the door behind him, spooned some chili into my mouth, then returned to the computer.

Vigilant Resources's website came up at the top of the search. We read silently while I clicked around the site.

Vigilant offered intelligence, security, and consulting services in both the physical and cyber arenas, their services geared more toward corporations and government entities than private citizens. I zoomed in on a photo of a man in Arab dress standing next to an unsmiling man in black with the caption SAUDI ROYALS VISIT NORWAY. Maybe a few private citizens, if you counted Arab princes with billions at their disposal. Services listed included bodyguards, discreet investigations, K9 training, software solutions and cyber countermeasures, and access to a worldwide network of professionals.

"Holy shit," Sarge said. "These guys got it all."

A line buried under a Managed Support menu option caught my eye. I pointed with my spoon.

Sarge read aloud. "'We work with government and intelligence services, here and abroad.'"

"Services like the CIA?"

Sarge nodded. "I'd figure. And NSA, DHS, NIC, NCS, DNI. Etc., etc. Abroad, you got everyone from the Saudis to the Slovenians. Want me to go on?"

"You know how much I hate alphabet soup?"

Vigilant's main office was in Washington, DC, which made sense for a company with US government contracts. Their lone satellite office listed an address on the south side of Denver, in the Tech Center. That office had opened six months ago.

Sarge and I looked at each other.

"Why Denver?" Sarge asked. "Why not bigger places like, I don't know, New York or Chicago?"

"Maybe those government contracts include military work. Colorado is second only to Washington in the number of military personnel."

"No shit?"

"No shit."

I ran through the list in my head. In metro Denver we had Buckley Air Force Base. Colorado Springs boasted Fort Carson, Peterson, and Schriever military bases along with the Air Force Academy and the North American Aerospace Defense Command—NORAD. Farther south was the US Army Pueblo Chemical Depot. The number of personnel rose even higher if you added nearby Wyoming, with its F.E. Warren Air Force Base, nuclear missile silos, and training areas.

I knew from a recent training session on Colorado's terror risk that we also had four hundred contractor companies that were part of the military-industrial complex and cleared by the Department of Defense. Even more mom-and-pop subcontractors serviced the big guys.

The Disaster Management Institute, which provided intensive training for military and law-enforcement personnel from all over the country, was also based in Denver.

"I can buy that they'd have an office here," I said finally.

"That's why you're so sweet," Sarge said. "Cause you're fucking naive. If these are our guys, they ain't in Denver to play patty-cake with soldiers."

I ignored that and returned to scrolling the website.

As Kane had told his wife, the president and CEO of Vigilant was a man named James Osborne. Given his last name, James was presumably a member of the family who had founded Vigilant's parent company, Valor. He looked barely north of fifty, and handsome in a spy-novel sort of way with a craggy face, cropped salt-and-pepper hair, a measured half smile, and a confident tilt to his chin.

I say, old chap. I suspect you've got a mole in your outfit. I can fix that for you.

Osborne listed his admittedly impressive credentials on a secondary page, along with that of his top staff. His CV included time spent working for the State Department in the Foreign Service, with postings in Ethiopia and Iraq. He boasted an impeccable education at Georgetown University's School of Foreign Service, graduating summa cum laude with a master's in international affairs. He was a career army officer who'd done a stint during Desert Storm before ultimately retiring as a full bird colonel.

There were no personal details at all. No mention of a family or hobbies or his golf handicap. Osborne wasn't running the kind of business where you shared that sort of thing.

If Kane had learned something about either Valor or Vigilant that cost him his life, he hadn't gotten it on the internet.

Sarge finished off his first beer and moved on to the second. "If this Osborne asshole worked in State, like it says here, he could have been either a diplomat or a spy. A secret squirrel, as we grunts like to say. Rick worked with a lot of secret squirrels."

"The Alpha tortured a man to death in Mexico City. He wanted to know about Rick Dalton."

Sarge stopped with the bottle halfway to his mouth. "That makes no damn sense."

"Maybe he doesn't know Dalton can't hurt him."

"Which means he doesn't know he's dead."

"We never processed his body." Once again, the memory surfaced of the ghost I'd seen in Sarge's apartment. "How do you know he's not still walking around, doing whatever it is secret squirrels do?"

"I got the word."

"From who?"

"That's as much as I can say."

I glared at him, but he didn't relent. I looked back at Osborne's picture. Why would the Alpha care about Dalton? Unless this particular secret squirrel could expose the Alpha's nuts.

And no man wants his nuts exposed.

If I were casting for a movie, Osborne would make a great Alpha. Handsome, confident. A good dresser with precisely the right arrogance in his square jaw.

"So we got one candidate for the Alpha," Sarge said.

"Maybe more if we can learn anything about Valor."

A headache had been pirouetting on the corners of my brain; now it waltzed into the middle of the dance floor. I rifled through Paul's desk until I found a bottle of ibuprofen, and dry-swallowed four caplets. I pushed the photos toward Sarge.

"Kane's," I said. "He had them in with the brochures."

Sarge went through each photograph, then gave a low whistle.

"They mean something to you?" I asked.

"Not the ones of the buildings. Fucking piles of rocks in the middle of nowhere. But the strip club." He looked up. His eyes carried a lot of steel. "Damn."

"What?"

"When I was on the inside of the Alpha's organization, or at least, as far as I ever got on the inside, I heard that he had a boarded-up club somewhere here in Denver. I wasn't in the circle who knew where it was. I just heard the talk."

"Why would he have an old strip joint?"

"For hiding things. Weapons. The occasional asset. Scuttlebutt was they also use it for doing things they don't want anyone to know about. Like when they need to break someone who can't be bribed or threatened. Men like your friend in Mexico."

"They *kill* people there?"

"What I heard. The Alpha runs a mean business. But I guess you learned that the hard way."

"And you worked for him."

"You don't shit gold bricks, either, princess. I didn't believe the rumors until after they sent me to nail you. Everything changed after that."

We both looked at the picture of James Osborne. Sarge gave him a sardonic salute with his beer.

"What ugly fucking freak show," Sarge said, "did our man Kane walk into?"

CHAPTER 17

The past leaps out without warning and grips you by the throat.

Forget trying to stay on your feet. You can't even breathe.

—Sydney Parnell. Personal Journal.

Clyde and I walked Sarge out to his pickup. Sarge pressed his key fob, and the truck flashed its lights.

"I'll call as soon as I know something," he said.

"Likewise."

We'd formulated a plan. For the time being, I would keep digging, see what I could learn about Vigilant Resources and James Osborne. I'd try again with Valor Industries, too, see if there was anything floating around on the Dark Web.

Sarge, meanwhile, would drop in on a friend who was still in the business. This friend, Hutch "the Handler" Voss, was closer to the inner circle of the Alpha's organization than Sarge had been. But the two of them were tight. Hutch might, with half a bottle of Jameson's inside him, be willing to cough up information about the Alpha. We figured every little bit would help.

I'd stayed quiet about the key in Dougie's compass. Sarge might have a few guesses what box that key would open. But I wasn't ready to cross that line with him. Not yet. He had to prove himself.

Sarge opened the truck door, then turned to me.

"I appreciate the trust," he said.

"Why don't you explain it to me, Udell. What you did last winter. And why you never came back to finish the job."

He frowned. He looked bad in the fading light. Whatever he'd done to someone to cause the blood in his apartment, he'd taken a few licks of his own. One eye swollen shut, his lower lip split. A bandage over his left cheek. We were a pair, I supposed, with our injuries and our anger. But while we stared at each other, something softened in his face. After a moment he closed the door and leaned against his truck.

"Fair enough."

I crossed my arms.

He nodded. "Like I said, I was told you were hiding intel that could affect the state of the free world. I had a new mission. You can take the boy out of the Marines, but you can't take the Marines out of the boy. Then . . . fuck." He ran his hands over his stubbled hair. "When you said you weren't hiding anything, you were pretty damn convincing. Plus, you let me go free when anyone else would have laid me six feet under. And there was the fact you got one of my guys off a murder charge. Tucker Rhodes, man. He'd have been in a bad way, otherwise. So no way I was going to hurt you any more than I already had. Not what I signed up for when I set out to save the world. I believed you didn't have the goods, and I backed off. Later . . ." He sucked in a long breath of air, eased it out. "Later I learned they were still after Malik. I got out."

"And then did what?"

He gave a rueful shake. "Oh, I played like I was still in the game, but I didn't do anything useful. I ditched my phone, lost myself in Texas for a time. Then they killed Kane. I've spent the last couple of days shaking the tree, trying to roll something loose. Haven't won myself any friends that way."

"The blood in your shower."

"I sent some questions up the chain. The Alpha answered with a cleanup man."

"Who you killed."

"Law of the jungle."

"You know I will kick your ass, then put a bullet in your brain if it turns out you're lying to me about any of this."

"What I like. A girl who knows how to sweet-talk a man." His teeth flashed in the dark. "Now let's get down to business. We got us some Alpha ass to fry."

Back in Paul's office, with the jukebox in the bar bellowing out Led Zeppelin, I scrounged once more through his desk until I found a crumpled pack of cigarettes. With a book of Joe's Tavern matches, an apologetic shrug toward Colorado's smoking ban, and a promise of never again, I lit up. I filled my lungs and carried the half-empty beer bottle to the window. Clyde resumed his spot under the window and sprawled across my feet.

"Hey, buddy," I said softly.

Clyde twitched his ears and closed his eyes.

Darkness pressed against the glass.

My mind kept tossing up images of the Marines who'd been brought into MA during the time Sarge had talked about, the time of the EFPs. Young men, barely past being kids, ripped apart so that putting them together was like working a macabre jigsaw puzzle with half the pieces missing.

The Sir standing in the bunker telling us to pencil in the missing parts.

Shade it black.

I swallowed. My throat and chest burned like someone had poured acid down my windpipe. I finished the beer and tapped ashes into the empty.

There was no reason under the sun for Iran to have weapons or technology from an American firm. At least, no good reason. We'd severed diplomatic relations with Iran and put the country under economic sanctions in 1980, after they'd taken fifty-two of our embassy people and held them hostage for over a year.

Plus, there were all kinds of checks in place to prevent American companies from selling to the bad guys.

Selling legally, anyway. Throw away the rules, and anything's possible.

I inhaled. Exhaled. Gently, I tugged my feet free of Clyde's bulk and went back to the desk. I set down the beer bottle, leaned against the chair, and nicotined my way through my thoughts.

Then again, the laws hadn't stopped a lot of people. Flip through the DOJ's periodic summary of companies and individuals who violated the Arms Export Control Act—required reading for my job—and you'd be astonished by the number of people found guilty of trying to smuggle intelligence and goods to foreign powers. Hundreds, maybe thousands.

And those were just the stupid ones. The ones who got caught.

But that list of felons was a far cry from suggesting that seemingly upright companies like Valor and Vigilant were selling to the bad guys. I picked up Kane's glossy brochures. Valor remained a black hole outside of their pamphlet. But judging by Vigilant's expanding real estate and a client list that included nations, the companies appeared to be doing just fine. There was no reason for them to take the kind of risk involved in violating sanctions.

I circled back to James Osborne. A diplomatic posting to Iraq likely meant Baghdad, a mere two hours away from our FOB. If the timing was right, it could mean that Osborne was in-country when CIA agent Richard Dalton was there and during the time Dougie had been sheep-dipped—pulled into covert activity—by the same intelligence agency.

I dropped the remains of the cigarette in the empty bottle, picked up my phone, and called a friend in the State Department.

I'd met Alison Handel in Kuwait before we'd entered Iraq. She was on her way to join the embassy staff in Saddam's palace, while I was headed to a military base in the middle of the desert. We were the only American women in town for a few hours, and we'd become fast friends over airline bottles of vodka. We'd stayed in touch through career changes and family drama, and now I reached her at her home in Delaware. After the formalities, I told her I was looking for information about James Osborne.

"That low-life, scum-sucking, pecker-headed, bottom-dealing, swindling asshole? Makes me happy I'm not in the business anymore. What do you want to know?"

Asshole. That sounded promising.

"Did James Osborne work in the embassy in Baghdad three years ago?"

"That's no secret. He worked in DAS."

The Defense Attaché Service. The men and women in DAS assisted the US ambassador on military matters. They also handled political and military matters within their area of jurisdiction.

Even more promising.

I said, "He travel out of the Green Zone much?"

"Probably. Hold on." The click of a lighter, then the exhale of smoke came across the miles. "What I remember most about him is that he spent a lot of time entertaining visiting Saudis."

Grooming future clients, maybe. "Does that fit with the job description?"

"That's above my pay grade. But whatever Osborne's deal was at the embassy, he'd made it pretty sweet."

"What do you mean?"

"For one thing, most of us lived in reconstituted shipping containers. But Osborne had gotten himself ensconced in one of the villas along the river. Downright luxurious. Clearly the man had high-level connections. I used to jog along the Tigris, and I'd see him and a few other staffers on the patio having drinks and cigars. I recognized the Americans he socialized with—three guys whose paths crossed mine now and again, usually at embassy parties. Didn't know their names. But they and Osborne must have been friends, because none of them worked together."

"What do you think they were doing?"

"Um, drinking and comparing golf scores? Sometimes a cigar is just a cigar. But sometimes . . ." A pause while she drifted off.

"Spill it."

She cleared her throat. "I'd see them in the Residential Palace now and again, heads together, talking quietly. Not that it was a crime. But something felt off about it. The only other people I ever saw that group with were the Saudis."

"How do you know they were Saudis?"

"I was in logistics, remember? Somebody always wanted something. Especially when it came to entertaining foreign dignitaries. One of the Saudis was at our embassy quite a bit. He was one of the royals, probably looking to cut his own path, independent of his family. We were contracting out a lot of business back then."

I thought of the picture of the Saudi prince on Vigilant's website.

"What else can you tell me? About Osborne, I mean."

"Oh, he was a smooth operator, that one. Popular with the women. Good looking. Family money. Had that mystique that surrounds anyone you suspect works in intelligence. But way too arrogant for my taste. One of those guys who'd go down with a sinking ship because he'd never actually believe his ship could fail. When a guy like that falls— and I hope to Christ he does—he takes a lot of good people with him."

Her voice had gone flat.

Ever astute, I said, "There's something else."

"Yes. Maybe."

She fell silent, and I prompted her. "Alison?"

"A friend of mine in the Defense Attaché told me about a weird thing that happened. She was running during her lunch break, going through the residential area. Not the villas where Osborne lived, but the slums. You know about them?"

"The Green Zone has slums?"

"It's where a bunch of locals took up residence after Saddam's forces fled. They never caused any trouble, and we never evicted them. Going there wasn't exactly unsafe, but my friend said it did tend to keep her on her toes, which she liked. Bit of an adrenaline junkie. Anyway, she told me that one day she saw Osborne there with another man, someone she hadn't seen before. The two were standing in a doorway, as if they were about to part. When my friend spotted them, she ducked behind a car. She said she didn't know why. The whole thing just seemed odd enough that she decided it was better if they didn't see her. She caught part of their conversation. Not any specific words. Just their voices. They were speaking Farsi."

"Farsi? This guy with Osborne was Iranian?"

"Maybe. Don't read too much into it. He could have been Iranian American, maybe a civilian contractor."

"Or he could have been in Iraq to help out the Shia militias. You know Iran was backing those guys."

"If that were true," Alison said, "he'd never have gotten into the Green Zone."

"Then why speak in Farsi?"

"A way to have privacy while among the Arabs, maybe? Of course, we were cutting deals with the Shia militias back then, so when my friend told me about it, I guess I wasn't totally surprised. This man could have been a go-between. He wouldn't have been one of the guys on the wanted posters, but he could have been lower level."

"She ever see him again?"

"Nope."

"Interesting." The Iranian connection sent my mind to Zarif, hiding Malik all the way down in Mexico. "You think you can get me the names of the staffers Osborne hung out with?"

"I'm not in the biz anymore, remember? I'll ask around, but people don't tend to talk to those who aren't on the inside."

"Whatever you can find. And thanks. You've been a help."

"Always ready to do my part for the free world. I find those names, I'll let you know."

We chatted a few more minutes, then hung up. I returned to my place at the window. The headache sent up a last flare, then faded to a dull ache under the influence of the pills.

So okay. As Kane had already checked, Osborne had been in Iraq at the right time. That bit of intel had value only as a strategy to narrow my list of potential Alphas from one to . . . well, one. But a lot of people had been in-country during that time. Not all of them got villas, but some did. Any number of people could have worked to cover up the arrival of the weapons or arranged for the murders of Haifa and Resenko.

Then again . . .

Probably not too many were holing up for furtive talks with staffers in unrelated departments. Or carrying out secret meetings with Iranians in the slum area where they were unlikely to be spotted.

Did Valor/Vigilant have an arrangement with Iran?

That would be treason. The kind of treason worth killing people to hide.

The hair on the back of my neck rose.

A song from the jukebox filtered through the door—a Frank Stallone song about things being far from over. I reached for the second beer, and realized that it, along with the chili, the tortillas, and the first beer were history. Mindless eating and drinking. I looked at the clock display on my computer and was startled to realize I'd been at this for a couple of hours.

I was halfway through my designated time, and all I had was a weak theory and zero proof.

That much had gotten Kane killed.

CHAPTER 18

The problem with trauma is that it opens up a world of the possible you wish you'd never known about. Once you know that trash conceals IEDs or homes burn down, or friends die young—once you know these things, you cannot unknow them. And that's when you realize we're just fish in a barrel.

—*Sydney Parnell. Personal journal.*

The Dark Web is the underbelly of the internet. It's the home of illicit marketplaces, activist chat rooms, and in its darkest iterations, a place to indulge your worst vices. I was just setting up Tor Browser to hide my IP address—a requirement for Dark Web access—when my phone buzzed.

Ryan Taft with the RTD.

I answered with, "Any news?"

"I got a definite maybe on an avatar for the killer."

"You're a king among men. Tell me."

"We actually got a lot of definite maybes. Like you and I talked about, it is conceivably possible to disguise your walk, but there are certain consistencies we can hone in on once we remove other factors. With any luck, I should be able to get a shortened list to you in under an hour."

"There's a place in heaven for you, Ryan."

He laughed. "From your lips to God's ear. In the meantime, I just emailed you some information on the five people on the platform, the ones Kane might have been looking at. I'll be back in touch soon."

We disconnected, and I clicked on Taft's email. As promised, he'd highlighted five names. Three men and two women, along with their ages, addresses, and the fact that none of them had a criminal record.

I stared at the list, hoping for a flash of recognition or at least a glimmer of familiarity that had eluded me the first time I'd first seen the list at the Transit Watch Command Center. Still nothing.

I read the names aloud.

"Laura Almasi. Sonia Lopez Martinez. Kenneth Riley Napierkowski. Leroy Parker. Thomas Wilson."

I did a property-tax search. One of the women, Laura Almasi, had paid taxes on a property in Lindon, which was in eastern Colorado, two hours outside Denver. Not much out there. Maybe she was a rancher. She and Wilson still had out-of-state driver's licenses for Texas and New Mexico, respectively. Leroy carried an outstanding parking ticket. Nothing about the other two seemed even that noteworthy.

Hoping for something more useful, I opened up the Department of Motor Vehicles photos Taft had attached.

Two of the five were white, two black, and Sonia Martinez was Latina. They ranged in age from eighteen—Leroy—to Napierkowski's sixty-seven.

None of them looked like psychopaths.

Correction. They all looked like psychopaths. These were DMV photos, after all.

Sonia Martinez, age thirty-two, was soft eyed and pretty. Maybe Kane had been doing nothing more in his final moments than letting his gaze rest on an attractive woman.

Pushing away my frustration, I mentally filed away the five candidates and returned to the Dark Web. But while I knew my brief foray into the back alleys only scratched the surface, I didn't have any better luck searching for Valor there than I'd had on the sun-splashed streets of the regular internet.

Agitated, I closed my laptop. "Let's get some air, boy."

The desk was between Clyde and the door, but he still beat me there.

Music and laughter filtered from the bar into the hallway, and the clash of pans in Paul's tiny kitchen suggested a busy night. Things were rocking and rolling up front. Stallone had given way to the Bee Gees. Tonight's clientele must have celebrated their youth during the heyday of the disco era. I imagined there were a few gold lamé jumpsuits and metallic halter tops in the narrow space that passed for a dance floor.

Clyde and I pushed through the back door into a balmy night filled with the chirp of crickets. In the distance, headlights flowed like a halogen river on the interstate, the whine of traffic muffled by the kings of disco and the wind breezing through nearby trees.

"Scout," I said to Clyde. He dutifully trotted in a widening half circle out from the building until he was thirty yards away. Nothing caught his attention. I whistled him back.

"Good boy." I gave him a treat from my pocket.

While Clyde checked out the local flora and fauna, I stretched and ran through some light calisthenics in the faint light falling from the windows, disregarding complaints from my assaulted ribs. I wanted another cigarette the way a baby wants a bottle, but I ignored the siren call. No one but me was going to clean up my act.

Finished, I leaned against the bricks in the shadows, propped a foot flat against the wall, and folded my arms. Inside, the jukebox took a break, and I soaked in the sounds of a normal neighborhood. Kids shouting, a dog barking, the thump of a basketball, and the rise of cheers from a nearby court—the locals enjoying a pickup game. Clyde nosed through the weeds, tail wagging.

"Just don't eat anything," I called.

My phone buzzed. Taft.

"I have those names," he said. "People who might be a match for the Pushman."

I dropped my foot and pulled my notebook and pen from my pocket. "Ready."

"Before I read them to you, you need to know that this is just speculation. You understand that, right?"

"Absolutely."

"So no going all *Kill Bill* on these people once I send the list."

"Going what?"

"Uma Thurman. She kills a bunch of people after they kill—never mind. Just tell me you'll coordinate with Gorman."

I had another flash of Gorman holding a business card from Valor. He'd clearly found someone to talk to. I bet he could fill in a few of the blanks on my page.

I crossed my fingers. "Pinkie swear. Just give me the names."

I jotted the names down as he spoke. None of them looked familiar. Taft gave me addresses for three of the four. The fourth person, a man named Mark Fadden, wasn't in the Colorado DMV—his most recent address was Atlanta, Georgia. Taft had flagged him because a few years earlier, Fadden had been convicted of a crime by a military court and given an eighteen-month sentence and a bad-conduct discharge.

Bingo.

"This Mark Fadden, how often does he use public transportation?"

"The other three are regular users. But Fadden has ridden an RTD bus exactly four times, twice into Union Station and twice out. Each time, he walked up and down the upper-level platform a couple of times, then went into the station and bought a beer and a newspaper. After that, he sat at a table for an hour."

"A guy goes to Union Station for a beer and a paper?"

"I'm crushed by your cynicism. The place has ambiance."

"Sounds to me like he was scoping things out."

A pause. "That's how I read it."

"What about the day of the murder?"

"No sign of him on any buses or trains that day. Which is a strong argument against him being our suspect."

"Unless someone dropped him off and he put on his Pushman persona."

"Sydney, be careful with this. Don't read too much into the biometrics. We've crossed a line by matching up Fadden and these other men with a theoretical avatar. We don't know that any of these guys are the one we're looking for."

I glanced at my watch. "I got it, Ryan. But it doesn't hurt to poke around a little. Did Fadden take the same bus both times?"

"Number fifteen to and from East Colfax. He got on and off at the Tower Road stop." Taft spoke slowly, like he was picking over his words. "If he's our guy, and I mean *if*, there are a lot of places for him to hole up out there. Used to be the only things living that far east were prairie dogs. But there's a bunch of subdivisions now. Tower Triangle. Friendly Village."

I pulled up a mental image of Kane's photo of the strip joint. There were a lot of clubs like that on Colfax. And a lot of them had gone under.

I thanked Taft and disconnected. My skin tingled, as if my bones were electrified. I whistled Clyde in.

Back inside, I collected my belongings and left cash on the desk to cover the food and drinks. Clyde and I found Paul in the bar setting up shots for a group of women about my age. The ladies were pimped out for a night on the town in short skirts and high heels, and one of them wore a shoulder-length bride's veil. A Royer girl, enjoying her last night of freedom before her walk down the aisle.

Watching the bride-to-be's giddy excitement, I experienced a strange twinge in my stomach. The woman was taking a lot of selfies,

---

half of which involved holding up her engagement ring and blowing a kiss, presumably to her fiancé.

Another pang. I pressed a hand to my stomach. It had to be the chili.

I waited while Paul finished pouring and added the drinks to a tab. He turned to me. "Still working?"

"I'm done. Thanks for the use of your office."

"Anytime. I mean it."

"See you later, then." Clyde and I headed for the door.

"Hey, Sydney," Paul called.

I turned. Something in his voice.

"You look tired," he said. "You should give it a rest sometime."

"I'll—"

"I know. Sleep when you're dead." His face had slumped, lines and creases I'd never noticed carving new shadows on his skin in the dim light over the bar. He looked crushed, as if an anvil had dropped on him when he thought there was nothing overhead but blue sky.

Maybe men got pangs about engagement rings, too.

"Have a good night, Sydney Rose," he said.

"You, too."

I walked out the door with images of bridal veils and late-night whiskeys banging through my mind like doors on a deserted house.

CHAPTER 19

*The only way you feel safe in a relationship is if you feel free
to leave it.*

—Effie "Grams" Parnell. Private conversation.

A full moon shone down on Denver as we exited the interstate and
turned east onto Colfax Avenue. Silver light flooded the city; it was
as if we moved through mercury. A yellow-and-black checkerboard—
Denver's downtown high-rises—patterned the sky. It was a flawlessly
perfect night, the kind that invites contemplation over action, peace
over vigilance. A perfect night to live and the wrong kind of night on
which to die.

But I had murder on my mind.

And Kane's photo of the strip club on the dash.

The man on the RTD recordings, Mark Fadden, had exited the
Route 15 bus at Tower Road, the very last stop. From there, he'd presumably headed straight south on Tower—the cameras hadn't picked
him up on the sidewalk or crossing the street.

It was just this side of midnight, and traffic was light. I reached
Tower Road in a few minutes, and after cruising along Colfax for
another four blocks in search of the club, I decided to start my reconnaissance in the same direction Fadden had disappeared. I pulled a

U-turn and went south on Tower Road. There wasn't much. Storage facilities, the Colorado Department of Transportation offices. Further south, the buildings vanished, and the land flattened into a two-dimensional plane of pure black. My headlights picked out a rabbit as it darted across the road and disappeared into the grass.

I reversed course and drove along the northern stretch of Tower. On my left were a few scattered businesses, none of them dance bars. To the right, a sprawling residential area. If Fadden was renting a home or staying with a friend in one of those houses then, short of a door-to-door search, I'd never find him.

Working from the premise that Fadden was the Alpha's hit man, I figured he'd still be in town—an assassin on retainer, waiting for his next job. My biggest worry was that Fadden wasn't even our guy. That I was not only looking for a needle in a haystack, but it was the wrong needle and the wrong haystack.

I turned right and went another block east, drove down Himalaya Road, and worked my way back to Colfax, heading toward the bus stop. There was only one street between the RTD stop and Tower Road. Zeno ran south from Colfax, taking a straight shot through a run-down neighborhood of dilapidated businesses before making a ninety-degree turn east and relabeling itself 14TH STREET.

Fingers crossed, I went south.

Just before we reached the ninety-degree turn, the headlights picked out a strip joint on the right.

Wary of being watched, I drove by without slowing.

The club looked every bit as lonely as it did in Kane's photograph. The sign said CLOSED. The front door was boarded up. Someone had taken a rock to the sign, partially destroying what had once been an artist's rendering of a stylized woman clinging to a pole.

No lights, no vehicles. No movement of any kind.

I went around the corner and doused my headlights, then waited five minutes before making a U-turn and coming back around. I pulled to the curb a hundred yards down and on the opposite side of the street, killed the engine, and stared through the windshield.

The building, a play of silver and shadow in the high moon, was two stories tall, fronted by the weedy lot I'd noted in the photograph. The lower floor jutted out from a narrow upper story like an obstinate jaw. The entire place gave off an aura of dreary resignation. Probably not much different from the way it had been when it was open for business.

Maybe the resignation was cut through with despair.

Maybe I was projecting.

The area immediately around the club was hard-packed dirt; the place had a lot of exposed flank. Even from this angle, no lights showed in the solitary upper-floor window, which still tossed back a glaze of moonlight from a full pane of glass.

The rest of the neighborhood lay quiet. The only other moving vehicles were back on Colfax, the lone sounds the occasional thrum of a car engine from the same direction.

I pulled out my phone and dialed Sarge. When he didn't answer—presumably he was in the midst of getting his friend Hutch "the Handler" drunk and malleable—I sent a text telling him I'd found the club and that Kane's killer might be inside. I sent the location and ended with, I will wait for you here.

I adjusted my seat and leaned back, prepared for a quiet stretch of surveillance. If the place was as empty as it appeared, we'd be able to do some reconnaissance. If not, then better that there were three of us—two handguns and a set of teeth. I folded my hands across my lap and practiced deep breathing.

When my phone buzzed, I figured it was Sarge, giving me an ETA.

What greeted me instead was a picture of Cohen.

He was in a chair, hands wrenched behind his back, his head held in place by a strap across his forehead. The left side of his face was bloodied, the eye swollen, his ear scraped raw. His good eye glared at the photographer.

He'd been gagged with his own tie. His white button-down was red with his blood.

A second text lit up the phone.

23 hours.

Below it was a smiley face.

My entire body went hot. The bones holding me upright turned to liquid, and I crumpled in the seat.

No. No, oh no, no.

I sucked in air and threw the phone to the floor. Then snatched it back up. I shot back a text.

Hurt him, you won't get your intel.

The answer came immediately.

Keep the intel, he dies.

I let loose a long, low moan. My stomach flipped, and I squeezed my hands together, telling myself I could throw up later. After we had Cohen. After he was safe.

"I'm so sorry, Mike," I whispered. "I'm so sorry."

Clyde pushed against me, licked my face, answered my moans with his whimpers.

In my mind I heard Sarge's voice.

Scuttlebutt was they also use it for doing things they don't want anyone to know about. Like when they need to break someone who can't be bribed or threatened.

There were no cars on the property, no recent tracks, no indication that this was where they were torturing Mike. But that didn't mean he *wasn't* here, either, on the other side of a single door.

Hurt. Maybe dying. Hoping someone would come.

I sent a final text to Sarge. They have my friend. I'm going in.

I buckled Clyde's Kevlar vest under his belly and yanked my own vest over my shirt. I racked a round in the Glock and put the backup pistol in a holster. Ignoring the way my hands shook, I grabbed a flashlight and my lock-picking kit and jammed them into the pockets of my jacket along with the silenced phone. I zipped the pockets closed.

The thought of calling the police rode across my mind. But the notion quickly vanished, chased away by an image of Gorman holding a business card from Valor. It may have meant nothing.

It may have meant everything.

Outside my window, Angelo materialized in a silver haze. His ruined face carried a single message of warning. *Move fast.*

Beside me, Clyde was a coiled spring, ready to explode.

We slipped into the dark.

◆ ◆ ◆

Clyde and I crossed the street in the shadows, then sprinted across the open space to the strip joint. We hugged the walls and did a fast jog around the building, looking for a point of entry.

The front door was boarded up tight. No ground-level windows. The plywood over the back door was a ruse—it swung aside when I pushed. But the door was held fast by a hefty lock body, suggesting a dead bolt of industrial strength. My kit could not manage that.

We went around to the front again, where a few feet of roof fronted the single window.

A drainpipe clung to one end of the building. I gave it a test shake. Solid.

We could do this.

I jogged Clyde out to the edge of the parking lot and signaled for him to stay. Then I ran back to the building, stopping a few feet away.

I bent at the waist, making my back as flat as possible, and signaled Clyde.

He surged forward, racing toward me across the lot, gathering speed.

We'd done this trick numerous times at Avi's training center. But this was our first real-world application. My heart was in my throat at what might go wrong. Clyde could slip. The roof might be weak.

Whoever was inside could hear us and come out shooting.

And then Clyde leapt. His paws hit my back with the force of a falling boulder, and just as suddenly, the weight was gone. I straightened and looked up.

Clyde grinned down at me from the roof. I ordered him to his belly, then it was my turn. I got a running start toward the drainpipe and jumped as high as I could. I gripped the pipe, planted my feet on the wall, then worked my way up.

At the top, I hauled myself onto the roof and dropped flat beside Clyde. Together we belly-crawled to the building's single point of vulnerability.

An old double-hung window. It was set low in the wall and looked solid, the glass reinforced with wire mesh that obscured whatever lay on the other side.

We froze when a car drove by. Headlights swept the lower floor as a sports car raced past without slowing. It rounded the corner with a squeal of tires, and the sound of its engine faded into the distance.

The club remained quiet.

I removed a flat-head screwdriver from my kit, then rose to a crouch on one side of the window. The wind had died down, and the only sound was the gentle seesaw of crickets. I jammed the screwdriver between the sash and the sill. The window resisted for a moment, then slid up a quarter inch.

I paused, listening for any indication that our arrival had been noted. The building creaked in another gust of wind, then quieted.

The rest of the world stayed silent.

I wriggled my fingers in and raised the window, then reached in my pocket for the flashlight. I bent my knees and shone the beam into the room. The space was large, the floorboards clotted with debris. The beam caught a sleeping bag and a lantern. In one corner, someone had created a rudimentary kitchen out of a portable electric burner, a pan, and a stack of paper plates. To my immediate right stood an old filing cabinet. I played the light across the room, then leaned in and angled the flashlight down to make sure the floor was clear of anything that would hurt Clyde's paws.

The filing cabinet crashed to the floor. Fingers gripped my wrist and jerked me forward. My head cracked against the sash as I was yanked through the window and thrown to the ground. My attacker spun toward the window and slammed it shut just as Clyde lunged for the space. My partner hit the reinforced glass and fell back. His barks rolled through the night.

The world was swimming. The flashlight beam ghosted in and out from somewhere nearby. I yanked my gun from the holster. Before I could bring it up, a sneakered foot stomped on my wrist. My fingers went numb, the weapon dropped, and my attacker kicked it away. I scrabbled for the second gun, but the man wrenched it free and sent it flying after the first.

One weapon, then the other, hit the wall.

He stepped back, and I glimpsed a man's form, tall and lean. A flash of moonlight revealed his face. The same face, minus the dreads and the beard, I'd seen on the RTD recordings.

Mark Fadden. The Pushman.

Clyde kept barking.

I rolled to my side and scissored my legs, trying to catch Fadden's ankles. But he sidestepped me and brought his hand up. He aimed a pistol at my head.

The flashlight winked out.

He said, "Be still."

I froze. I heard the man back off a few steps. Outside, Clyde's barks turned to growls.

"Where is Cohen?" I asked. "Let me see him."

A faint clank. A battery-powered lantern flared on, filling the room with cold white light. Fadden squatted just out of my reach, his gun now aimed at my chest. He cocked his head and studied me as if I were something that had stuck to the bottom of his shoe.

I said, "If you hurt him any more, I *will* kill you."

The look in his eyes was an abyss—deep and empty. Then he grinned, the expression holding the same dark vortex that hollowed his eyes. "I know you. You're the girl with the intel. You've walked right into my parlor, my sweet little fly."

I wondered how fast I could move, but decided he could shoot faster.

"What, not familiar with the poem? Here's the best part." He moved the muzzle in a tiny circle, as if scratching a line around my heart. "Up jumped the cunning spider, and fiercely held her fast. He dragged her up his winding stair, into his dismal den, within his little parlor—but she ne'er came out again!"

I pulled up an image of Kane's face just before Fadden shoved him in front of the train. Rage boiled and cleared my head. "You killed Jeremy Kane."

"It's what I do."

Keep him talking. If he was talking to me, he wasn't hurting Cohen. "Who gave the order?"

"Who's holding the gun? I get to ask the questions. Now, I'm going to look outside. Move an inch, and I'll take out your left kneecap. It's also what I do."

Keeping his gun on me, he rose from his squat and went to the window. Clyde threw himself against the glass, and Fadden jumped back.

"Bet I could train that dog," he said.

"Let him in and see."

"Or . . ." He hawked up phlegm, then turned his head to spit. "I could shoot him."

I could see Fadden better now. He was tall and rangy in a way that suggested a rock climber or swimmer. His skull was shaved, his face all angles. He wore jeans and a T-shirt, and on his inner arm were the star and crescent and two lines of Arabic script that I recognized from the RTD recordings. Part of the star had been erased, and the script was smeared—the tattoo was only surface ink. He'd added it to throw off the investigators.

Clyde disappeared from the window.

"The police are onto you, Fadden," I said. "They know you killed Kane. But what they really want is the man who hired you. Let me go. Let the cop go. Cut a deal while you can. You hurt us, you'll lose that chance."

"Take off your jacket," Fadden said, walking back. "Slowly."

"Your boss won't want me hurt. Call him. He'll tell you."

"Jacket. Or left kneecap. You decide."

I did as he ordered, sliding my left arm free and wondering if the tool kit in the pocket gave it enough weight that I could knock him off-balance.

But as I swung the jacket around with my right arm, he lunged forward and propelled a foot into my stomach just below the Kevlar. Heat drilled through my gut, and I retched. He jerked the jacket free and stepped back, then went through the pockets. He found my phone, keys, and the tool kit. He slid the phone into his pants pocket and threw the rest in the same direction he'd kicked the guns.

He sank back to a squat and gave me a dead smile, showing those clean white teeth I'd seen on the recordings. His eyes and face remained as devoid of emotion as a blank sheet of paper.

"I don't often get a lady caller," he said. "Especially a hot one." With his left hand, he tugged a pair of metal handcuffs from his pocket. "It's a dilemma. Should I rape you first and then kill you? Or would you rather I did the shooting first? Or"—he flexed his free hand—"maybe I can change methods and give you both. Choking does heighten sexual pleasure."

I curled around the pain chewing through my stomach.

"Let him go," I managed. "I'll stay. I'll do what you want."

In the white light, his eyes glittered. "Can't decide? Then I'll make the call. Lift your wrists and hold them together."

"Can't."

"You won't like it if I do it for you."

I raised my arms.

"Together," he snarled.

I did as he said.

"If you so much as twitch, I'll shoot you."

He rose and approached me from behind. His sneakered feet squeaked on the tiles. When I felt the first brush of metal against my skin, I grabbed the handcuffs and pulled, jerking him forward.

As he toppled, I rolled, throwing myself clear. His gun went off, the bullet whizzing by so closely, I felt the mortal whisper of its passage.

I kept going, pushing through on my momentum. I made it to my knees, got one foot planted.

A blow on the left side of my skull made my brain catch fire. The room tipped sideways, and I hit the floor. Pain flared across my ribs as I landed. He outweighed me by at least fifty pounds. I couldn't let him get on top of me. I put my palms on the floor and tried to regain my feet.

Fadden's shadow approached, followed by the man. His shoes stopped a few inches from my face. Then he kicked me in the ribs, hard, and I was on my back.

"You're a slow learner," he said.

The pain in my ribs was paralyzing. I couldn't breathe. Dark spots blossomed in my vision, and my head felt like it was full of wet sand. I knew I should get up—*There's something bright and strong in you again*—force my limbs to move—*Haven't seen it since before the war*—to fight, but the floor rose around me, cool and inviting, and I drifted toward a promise of no fear, no pain, a promise I wanted more than anything to be real.

Someone moaned. And I was back in the room, ribs on fire, something bright leaking back into my muscles.

Fadden set the gun on the floor. I reached a hand toward it, and he laughed before he straddled me, then lowered himself to his knees.

My fingers kept scrabbling for the gun.

"It's a foot beyond your reach," he said. "Just so you know."

He grabbed my wrists, shoved my hands up above my head, and shoved a knee between mine. I bucked under him and jammed my trapped leg into his groin. He shifted his weight, forcing my leg back down, and his body came between me and the lantern.

"Clyde!" I screamed. As if he could do something. As if he could come through reinforced glass.

But Fadden jerked around in surprise, maybe thinking I'd seen something. His grip on my wrists eased, and I twisted free.

He whirled back, his hands grabbing for mine.

My thumbs found his eyes. Pushed.

He let out a roar, his hands going to his face.

I threw him off, scrambled to my feet. I sprinted for the door, sliding into the wall as the room tried to upend itself. The floor shook with footsteps. Something clamped around my ankle, and the floor rose and slammed into my face.

My breath left my body.

Fadden dragged me back into the room. Dropped his weight on me. Worked a knee between my thighs again.

A breeze rushed into the room. The trash swirled along the walls.

"Parnell?" Sarge's voice.

The weight lifted, and Fadden flew into the wall, propelled by a burst of tan and black as Clyde hit him like a wrecking ball and sank his teeth into Fadden's flesh.

Fadden shrieked.

I rose to my knees. The working part of my brain remembered the electric burner I'd spotted in Fadden's makeshift kitchen. I started crawling.

From somewhere, Sarge was yelling, swearing he'd shoot the dog if the dog didn't get out of the way.

I yanked the burner's cord free and crawled back across the floor toward where Clyde had Fadden pinned down. I caught a glimpse of Sarge trying to get a bead on Fadden.

Fadden's right arm flailed free. He still had his gun. Clyde shook him like a doll, but Fadden kept working to bring the gun around.

My scream tore through my guts. "No!"

A bullet puffed into the drywall above Fadden's head. Sarge taking a shot.

"Out!" I shouted at Clyde. "Out!"

With a furious growl, Clyde released Fadden. Fadden found his knees and brought up the gun, jerking it toward me.

"Out of the way, Parnell!" Sarge yelled.

But I'd gotten to my feet and was already stepping in. I used the cord to swing the burner in an arc, putting everything I had into the blow. It slammed into the side of Fadden's head with a meaty crunch just as the room exploded with gunfire and the top of Fadden's skull vanished.

He dropped. His gun slid away, and I snatched it up in my left hand.

The bottom half of Fadden's face was white and empty. Most of the rest was gone.

Clyde pressed against me.

"Sydney." Sarge's voice. "Hey, you okay?"

I ignored him, edging closer to Fadden, my chest heaving, gun up and ready should he twitch a muscle. His remaining eye glared at the ceiling while blood pooled beneath him.

I nudged him with my foot.

"He's dead, Sydney. It's okay. He's about as dead as it's possible to get."

I looked at the burner still dangling from my hand, my fingers in a death grip around the cord. The heating element was matted with hair and blood.

I dropped it. It exploded when it hit the floor, springs and screws and shards of metal flying out. The sound echoed through the room like a cannon shot. Pieces rolled or bounced across the floor and eventually came to rest. All went quiet. The only sound was that of my heart, slamming blood through my ears like a jackhammer.

Sarge gripped my shoulder.

"We needed him," I said. "Why did you shoot him? We needed him."

"Seemed like it was him or you. Although I have to say, I never seen anyone so handy with small appliances."

As I stood over Fadden, chest heaving, the images that rose in my mind, slotting into my brain like pinballs slamming home, were of Sherri Kane. And Haley, and the baby, Megan.

And Jeremy Kane, walking his beat. Standing on the wall for all of us.

"Let's move," Sarge said.

I backed away from the corpse. I blinked and looked around the room. My brain stuttered, then connected a few wires.

"Cohen," I said.

Sarge stopped. "Who?"

Clyde was trotting back and forth near the doorway, agitated. I called his name, and as soon as his eyes were on mine, I raised an arm, then thrust it out.

"Find him, boy. Seek!"

Clyde thrust his nose into the air, taking scent. He raised his tail like a flag, and raced out of the room. His barks came back to us, echoing off the walls until it sounded like an entire pack of Belgian Malinois baying on the hunt.

I grabbed the lantern and ran after him.

CHAPTER 20

Marines don't cry.

—Sydney Parnell. Personal journal.

Clyde disappeared down the stairs.

Sarge and I plunged down the stairwell after him. No need for silence. If there was anyone else in the building, they must already figure World War III had just played out over their heads. Either they'd been smart and run . . .

Or they would go the way of Mark Fadden.

Sarge said, "What friend of yours are we looking for?"

My feet slipped. I grabbed the banister, which gave beneath my hand.

Sarge grabbed me.

"Cohen." I got my balance.

"The cop?" He whistled between his teeth. "Christ on a sandwich."

Ahead of us, Clyde reached the bottom. He paused to sample the air, then his back paws skittered on the tiles before he righted himself and sped left, toward the rear of the building. The lantern flared over walls scabrous with flaking paint and wires hanging in clots from the ceiling.

Clyde disappeared. The stairs went on forever.

Images clicked through my head with the speed of a shutter snapping.

Angelo gasping out his last in a Mexican alley.

Kane disappearing beneath the train.

Haley's shy smile as I pushed the muffin toward her.

Cohen propped on his hands above me, his eyes languorous, afternoon sun spreading golden bars across our skin.

I skipped the last few stairs, landed badly, and felt blood seep from the reopened wound in my side.

"Mike!" I shouted.

I raced down the hallway past closed doors and followed Clyde, who darted through a doorway. I set down the lantern so that the light spilled out ahead of us, and Sarge and I went in with shooter's stances.

No one waited for us.

The room had been a kitchen. The countertops were pulling away from the walls; pale squares on greasy paint showed where appliances had been. An industrial-size double sink overflowed with empty food cans. A door directly across from us led to the outside.

At the far end of the kitchen was another door. This one was closed and secured with a steel drop bar.

Clyde trotted back and forth in front of this door, whining.

"Mike!"

My gaze fixed on the countertop next to the barricaded door, where someone had spread a white towel. Carefully arranged on the clean white space was a bottle, a syringe, and a bloody rag, neatly folded.

Adrenaline hurled me across the room. I lifted the drop bar from its brackets, tossed it aside. The handle turned easily, and I yanked open the door.

Clyde flew inside.

I blinked. A hundred-watt bulb hung from the ceiling, an orange extension cord leading to wherever they'd tapped into the grid.

A man sat in a wooden chair. His wrists were duct-taped tightly to the arms of the chair, his ankles bound by nylon rope. More tape covered his mouth.

My heart jerked as if I'd been shot, and I gripped the doorframe to keep from falling.

This was not Cohen.

This man had thick blond hair and a shaggy beard that reached his collarbone. Familiar blue-green eyes set in a web of wrinkles. Face and neck and forearms tanned a deep desert brown, the veins prominent in a physique stripped of anything unnecessary. He was so still I couldn't hear him breathe, yet even bound to the chair, he was a coil of energy. I sensed, deep inside him, a clock ticking invisibly, ready to trigger an explosion.

His eyes met mine.

My knees sagged, and my breath caught in my throat. This wasn't possible. It wasn't. He was dead. I knew he was dead. I'd seen his corpse.

My mind hurtled into the past. I saw this same man sitting at a metal folding table in a grove of gum arabic trees, his long legs stretched in front of him, his left hand waving away the droning flies as he chatted with an old tribesman while Clyde and I kept watch. In my memory, dust rode languidly into the air and hung there, white as talcum in the desert light. The man twirled the old lion's head ring he wore on braided leather around his neck.

Sarge squeezed in next to me. "What the—?" he started. Then, "Holy fuck."

Clyde's tail was wagging hard enough to take the rest of his body with it. He barked and circled the chair in a mad scramble, butting the man's legs.

The man never took his eyes from mine.

Sarge pushed past me and ripped off the tape covering the man's mouth.

The man said, "Rosie."

Sarge produced a knife and went to work on the ropes.

"No," I murmured. "You're not real. You're dead. I saw you."

He shook his head slowly, his eyes sleepy from whatever drug they'd been giving him. "It wasn't me."

"I *saw* you. I have your ring. It was on your *body*."

"Rick Dalton. Not me."

"Get her out of here!" the Sir shouted.

Gonzo took my arm. "Come on, Lady Hawk."

I shook him off, intending to go to Dougie's corpse where it lay on the table, still in the body bag. His lion's head ring caught the light and tossed it back. His face was covered with sand. I took a step, then collapsed to the floor. Dougie. I turned my head and vomited.

"I'll take her," the Sir said.

Clyde was whining now. I blinked. Sarge helped the man rise unsteadily to his feet. He was tall, over six feet, dressed in black fatigue pants and a sleeveless T-shirt. His legs shook, and Sarge braced himself beneath the man's left arm.

"Maybe you should sit back down," Sarge said.

"Not here," the man answered.

"I never saw your ghost," I said. "Never. Not once. You never came to me."

"My dear, sweet Rosie."

I was drowning. I must have sounded crazy to him. But the dead were all right with crazy. "Why now?"

He took two shaky steps and reached out to touch my face.

I remembered those long fingers. The calluses. The white-blond hairs and the knuckles and veins and the scar on his right wrist where he'd snagged it on barbed wire when he was a kid.

"No," I choked. "It's impossible."

He pulled me to him. His flesh was warm and solid against mine. His heartbeat echoed in my ears. His beard tickled my face before he pressed his forehead to mine.

Doug Reynauld Ayers.

Back from the dead.

CHAPTER 21

I've killed people. I've tortured people. Sometimes under orders. Sometimes to stay alive. I need to be clear on this, Sydney. So you know who I am.

—Doug Ayers. Personal conversation.

"Panic won't help," Sarge said to me from where he sat.

Above us, trees rustled in the county park where we'd fled. The moon spilled silver. I stopped my pacing long enough to glare at him. "That the kind of bullshit platitude you peddled during the war?"

"It's pure truth."

"Yeah? Well, fuck that."

But I took a deep steadying breath and hoisted myself up on the retaining wall. If I leaned back, I could see the basketball court at the far end of the park. The lone hoop was lit by a single streetlight.

Sarge was right. If I couldn't get a grip, everything would go up in flames.

Across the two-lane country road from the park was the Coach Motel, a place as gray and devoid of character as a metal bucket. Except for an older couple in the room at the end—ranchers judging by their mud-splattered pickup and worn cowboy boots—we were the only customers.

Dougie stood in the lighted lobby, paying cash for two rooms. We'd left the body of Mark Fadden behind for someone on Team Alpha to find. We'd searched the place but found nothing of Fadden's that was personal. Nothing that pointed toward who had hired him or what he intended next. What we *had* found was the Alpha's arsenal—we'd helped ourselves to enough weapons and gear to equip an LA street gang. While I retrieved my belongings and Dougie got the backpack he'd had when he was taken, Sarge went through and wiped down every place the three of us might have touched, erasing our presence as much as possible. We stocked up on groceries and beer at a strip mall and finally came here, to this tiny roadside inn and a deserted park on the edge of nowhere.

I'd gotten one more text from the Alpha. Our original deal was off. At noon the next day, they would begin removing pieces of Michael Cohen.

By two in the afternoon, if I hadn't delivered, they would kill him.

The temperature had dropped to the fifties, but my skin burned as if I'd dunked myself in acid. Under my jacket, blood seeped through Gram's bandage. Every molecule of adrenaline had dissolved, and now my body sent up flares of pain strong enough to make the world spin.

But my pain was nothing against what Cohen would endure if I could not find him.

I leaned down and ran my fingers through Clyde's fur. "You learn anything at all from that friend of yours?"

"Hutch?" Sarge sighed. "Nothing. Man drank my whiskey, but he was scared as shit to talk."

I curled my hands into fists.

My mind could not find a place to roost. It lit on the feel of Fadden's weight on my body and the sight of his crushed skull, then flew to Clyde's desperate barking. It circled about and landed on the fact of Dougie's sudden return from the dead, and my struggle to figure out how I felt about that—relief, rage, joy, and shock were all good candidates.

It bumped up against the photo they'd sent of Cohen.

And there it lingered before finally wandering into the past—Cohen in his living room, his shoulders up, his voice ripping a hole in my flesh.

I don't know if I can trust you to have my back.

The mantra I kept coming back to was the fact of Dougie's key. On the drive over, I'd taken it from my duffel and placed it in my pocket. Every hope I had for Cohen hinged on that.

The key, and the weapons locked in the back of my SUV.

I nodded toward a paper sack. "I'm ready for another."

Sarge popped the top off a bottle of beer and handed it up. I hesitated, then placed it on the wall next to me. Probably good to take a breather.

With his own drink, Sarge gestured toward the lobby. "That is one messed-up dude."

"You don't know him."

Sarge's chuckle was as dry and mirthless as bones rubbing together. "Knew him then, know him now. War turned that boy inside out."

"Didn't seem like it did you any favors, either."

He glanced up at me. In the faint light, he was a silhouette, solid against the night.

"Ditto for you, sister," he said after a moment.

A breeze flicked against my flesh, tangled my hair. I registered the sensations as if they belonged to someone else.

"Least we got one thing," Sarge said. "We got the fucker who nailed Kane."

We did have that.

I held my head in my hands to keep it from flying off. "When you guys were driving here, did Dougie tell you how they got him in that strip club?"

"Just said he was tired and he got careless. Wouldn't say anything else. Point of pride, I think." Glass clinked as Sarge got another beer. "What I want to know is what he's been doing since everything went down in Iraq."

Lying to me. Hiding from me. Breaking my heart across years of silence.

But the camera in my brain clicked through old images, and I thought I knew at least some of it.

A man calling himself Strider leading Malik to safety in Iraq. *Snap.*

Delivering him to another man in Mexico City. *Snap.*

A different man in the airport, his throat slit. Big fucking *snap.*

I lifted my head as a lone car whizzed by, speeding toward the horizon. The dark soon swallowed it.

I picked up the beer, drained half of it.

Across the street, Dougie came out of the lobby and moved through the parking lot toward our two vehicles. Even his walk had changed in the years since I'd last seen him. In Iraq, he'd been a force—his six-foot-three height, his optimism, his booming laugh. Back then, he'd taken over every room he went into.

This new Dougie was quieter. And much more dangerous.

He got a backpack out of the trunk of Sarge's car and disappeared into one of the rooms.

"Why did Rick Dalton do it?" I asked. "Go along with destroying Haifa's and Resenko's bodies? Why did he pass along the Alpha's order and start all this?"

"Only thing I can figure is that he thought it was the right thing. Just like you and me and the rest of us poor dumb schmucks. All of us trying to fit one big fucking genie back into the bottle."

"It didn't bother you, what we did?"

He shot me a look; I felt the heat coming off it. "Bothered the hell out of me. We were choosing the many over the few, which I get. Sometimes, that's how the play goes down. But Resenko was one of mine, and Haifa saved our lives more than once. Still . . ." He fell silent for so long I thought he'd had his say. Then he added, "Parnell, you'd better learn to move on. We all got things we wish we hadn't done. But God sees everything in our souls, and even with that, He believes in forgiveness."

I thought about that for a time.

Dougie came out of the hotel room and walked across the parking lot toward the park. He'd changed into a pair of jeans and a black short-sleeve tee. His wet hair gleamed.

Clyde got to his feet, tail wagging, straining toward Dougie. I held tight to his lead in case he forgot there was a road between us and his former handler.

I nudged Sarge's shoulder with my foot. "Did he tell you what intel he hid?"

"Said he never *had* any intel. Didn't know what the hell I was talking about."

"What?"

"Don't panic, Corporal. We'll figure it out."

But the key was Dougie's. He *had* to know. The key would take us somewhere, give us something with which to buy Cohen's life.

I nodded. "You're right."

But I felt like I was climbing Everest with a flashlight and a pack of chewing gum. I didn't like the odds, and it was Cohen's life I was gambling with.

Sarge must have heard something in my voice. He squeezed my foot. "I filled him in on the way over. Told him about Osborne. About the video. The fact they took your man. You watch, Parnell. Between the three of us, we'll put it all together."

Dougie reached us. He scooped a beer out of the paper bag, ruffled Clyde's ears, and sat next to me on the wall. He touched his hand to my knee for only a second. My skin went hot. He looked and smelled the way I remembered him in Iraq, the way he'd been in my dreams.

I had a thousand questions for him. A million. My mind buzzed with them, a nest of hornets careening off the inside of my skull, drilling me with their need to know. I wanted—craved—a rundown of everything that had happened to him since he'd kissed me good-bye three years ago and walked away to join his team.

But not now. Now all that mattered was Cohen. And Malik.

I took the key from my pocket and pressed it into Dougie's palm. He stared. "What's this?"

My heart stepped onto an elevator and pressed B for Basement. "It was in your compass."

He turned it over in his hand. "I don't understand."

Sarge got to his feet and took his own look.

I stared at Dougie. "The Alpha says you have what he wants. Isn't that right, Sarge? You had what he wants and then you gave it to me." My voice rose. "The key has to lead to Malik's video."

"Rosie, I'm sorry. I've never seen this key. And I didn't hide any intel."

"You gave me your compass." My skin was on fire. "That last day before you—before I thought you'd been killed. Didn't you mean for me to find it?"

Dougie made a fist and popped it softly against his thigh. "Rick Dalton."

Sarge looked from me to Dougie. "Say what?"

"Rick and I worked together. When we were in the field, we usually shared a sleeping space. A tent, or a room in the house of a friendly. A lot of times it was just the two of us deep in enemy territory. You develop a lot of faith in someone when they have your back. I even trusted him to look after Clyde. He could have left the key, no problem."

"That's why the Alpha was asking about Rick Dalton," I said. "He knew Sarge and Rick Dalton were pals and that Sarge sometimes worked for him."

"That's right," Sarge said. "The Alpha would have known I'd give Malik's video to Rick."

"And the Alpha," I went on, "also thought the same thing everyone else did—that Rick was still alive." I turned to Dougie. "Rick hid that key in your compass so you would have it if something happened to him."

"I don't suppose he left an address, too," Sarge said.

Dougie stirred. "He was going retire to Vegas. He bought a condo there."

"But he wouldn't have mailed the video there," Sarge said. "He would know that's the first place the Alpha would look."

"A postal store, then," I said. "There have to be a lot of them in Vegas."

But Dougie shook his head. "You have to think like a spy. If you want to hide something, you don't bury it in your backyard."

"Where, then?"

"Somewhere anonymous. Close but not too close. And a place you'd have a reason to visit."

"That narrows it down." Sarge made a disgusted sound. "Sounds like mission impossible."

"It's meant to be."

"Why didn't he just upload the video and email it somewhere?" I asked. "And for that matter, if he trusted you so much, why didn't he tell you about Osborne and the video? Or just give you the key and say something like 'in the event of my death'?"

"Maybe he didn't trust anyone at that point," Dougie said. "You realize somebody on the inside is a traitor, how can you believe anyone? As for uploading the video and emailing it somewhere, likely he did. Rick would have wanted multiple copies in multiple places. Assuming he dared. The Alpha would have been monitoring communications— by sending that video, Rick would have risked exposing himself."

"Not only that," Sarge said. "Malik's phone was an old piece of shit. Maybe Rick *couldn't* upload the video."

"Okay," I said. "So he would have needed to send the original somewhere. And not to family, because the Alpha would look at them."

Dougie laughed. It was a faint flicker of the big booming laugh I remembered so well. This laugh was dry and sharp and came from a place I didn't know. But it still counted for something.

Clyde must have thought so, too. He rose from where he'd sprawled below Dougie's feet and leaned against his legs.

Dougie said, "Rick made a big deal one day of telling me he had a half sister. It was the family secret, because Rick's parents were still married when his dad got involved with a Las Vegas showgirl. Rick only found out about it after his parents died and he read their letters. He waited years, he said, and finally reached out to her after he was in Iraq. She was his only sibling."

Sarge laughed softly. "I'll be damned."

"He was planning on visiting her after the war. Then a week later we were ambushed, and he was killed." Dougie's hands staccatoed against his thighs. "He had this planned. He knew what was on that video. Knew he had to get it out of the country."

I slid off the wall, then regretted it as the world wobbled. I reached out a hand to steady myself. "Where is she, Dougie?"

"Bullhead City, Arizona. A hundred miles south of Las Vegas. She manages a copy center there."

Sarge's laugh grew louder. He grabbed me and gave me a bro hug. "How much you want to bet she has mailboxes there, too?"

I pushed Sarge away and told myself that pain makes us stronger. "Let's call her."

"No," Dougie said. "It's safer for her if we keep her out of the loop. We go in, find the mailbox, and leave without her knowing we were there. Then we use it to get your detective out of danger."

I leaned carefully against the wall. The world stopped wobbling, but my back burned with a thousand agonies. "This is our one shot, isn't it? If the video isn't there, we've got nothing else."

"That's optimism for you," Sarge said.

Dougie roughed Clyde's fur. "What's odd is that this key is all Rick left. Rick was Mister Triplicate. He always had a plan B, usually a plan C."

"Maybe there wasn't time." I frowned. "Or maybe, like you said, he couldn't risk it."

Sarge spread his feet and clasped his hands behind his back. "You want me to go to Vegas? You trust me enough for that?"

"You can't go alone," I said. "Too dangerous."

"Yeah, well, we don't exactly have an army to help. The two of you need to find Cohen. I'll move fast and keep my head low. Agreed?"

Dougie and I exchanged glances. But Sarge was right. There was no one else.

"Agreed," we both said.

Sarge said, "Okay, good."

But Dougie and I were still looking at each other.

In that moment, it was as if no time had passed. As if we were still young and in love, carrying faith that the war would soon end and there would be room enough in the world for our dreams.

That we would always be together.

Sarge said, "Why do I suddenly feel like I'm interrupting something?"

Dougie startled, and his face folded in on itself, overcome by a sadness so profound it was visible even in the dull glow from the streetlight.

I knew the feeling.

Dougie shook himself and said, "You feel you can manage Bullhead City on your own, Udell, then we'll trust you to bring back that video. After all, Malik trusted you with it when all this started. Seems only right for you to bring it back. While you're gone, Rosie and I will work on figuring out where her friend is. And tracking the man you guys call the Alpha."

"James Osborne," I said.

Dougie nodded. "Sarge told me your theory. What you guys learned about Valor Industries and Vigilant Resources."

"There's more." I told them about my call with Alison Handel, my State Department friend. When I finished, Dougie fisted his hands one atop the other and tapped them together, thinking. Then he nodded.

"Rick worked with Osborne. I don't know in what capacity. But Osborne gave the order to allow the weapons and the Iranians into Iraq, then set up the mission for us to capture them."

"Then he really *is* our Alpha," I said.

"He definitely sounds like a good place to start." Dougie flattened his hands on the wall. "For now, I suggest we get a few hours of sleep and start fresh. Not much we can do until Sarge can get on a flight to Vegas."

"We can look for Cohen," I said.

His look was soft. "You have any ideas where?"

I had to shake my head.

Sarge collected the empty bottles and took the room key Dougie offered. "I'll book a seat on the first flight out. And arrange for a rental car. I'll let you know what time I'm heading out." He headed toward the motel, then turned back. "Have you two thought about how this is going to play out? We turn over the intel, what's going to stop him from whacking us?"

"Nothing," Dougie said. "The only hand we have right now is that video. Soon as we turn it over, he'll kill us."

"Nice. And if we don't turn it over?"

"He'll kill us."

"I hate suspense," Sarge said. "Why don't we lie down on that highway right now and get flattened by a semi?"

"We'll figure out something."

Sarge eyeballed us in a way that could only be described as skeptical. "Don't take this the wrong way, but 'we'll think of something' don't get my heart fluttering. I might take my chances with the semi."

"Just get the video."

Sarge glared at us another minute, then shook his head and crossed the road to the hotel, stopping long enough to grab a backpack from his car before disappearing into the room.

The moon sank behind the mountains. A gust of wind set the swings to swaying.

Dougie looked up, and I followed his gaze. The night was a spangled glory, ablaze with silver light, magnificently indifferent.

"Perspective," Dougie said.

My heart wasn't fluttering, either. "The kind of perspective that says our lives mean nothing? That none of this matters?"

"No. The opposite of that."

I held out a hand, and he hoisted me back atop the wall. I was starting to get used to the pain. Like having a tracking monitor on your ankle. At least you knew where you stood.

"I don't understand," I said.

Dougie's heels drummed against the wall. "After I nearly died in that ambush, I spent a long time in Iraq. Every day for six months I walked a line between death and life, moving back and forth across that line with every hour. Then for another six months, even as my body grew stronger, I wondered if going on was worth it. My men and I had been betrayed by our own countrymen. Most of us had died. Dalton had died." He folded his arms. "I'd seen the worst this world has to offer."

"So what changed?"

"All this time I was hiding in the home of a man who took me in for no reason other than that he believed God expects all of us to care for anyone in need."

I remembered Zarif's words. "The hadith."

"That's right. A source of guidance for Muslims. This man took me out into the countryside, to the home of his wife's brother. The brother and his wife took care of me, and the man visited as often as he could, at first bringing medicines and bandages. Later other things. Books. DVDs. Fruit from the market. Little gifts to keep up my spirits. Every day, these people risked their lives and the lives of their families to help me. Me, an invader. One of those who brought death and destruction down on their country."

He stopped, and I waited out his silence. After a moment, he went on.

"Then one night, when it was near my time to leave, the man who'd first taken me from Habbaniyah asked me to walk with him in the desert. We walked for a long time. I was much stronger by then, and I kept up with him. Even when we went so far out into the desert that I thought he had changed his mind and meant to kill me."

"What happened?"

"When we were out of sight of all man-made light—campfires, lanterns, lights from the generators—he led me up a hill and pointed to the same sky you and I are looking at now. He said that even though there are many stars, each one is glorious. Each star has a place in the heavens. And no star is greater or lesser than any of the others. And that is why he helped me." He dropped his head, kept drumming his feet. "It sounds corny now. Stars in the heavens, for fuck's sake. But when I was with him in the middle of the desert with my life hanging by a thread, it didn't sound trite at all. It made perfect sense. He also said that eventually every star goes out. And the thing for us to remember is that when our own time comes, there will be others to carry on. Others to pick up the sword or plow that we dropped. And we'll always have our place in the heavens."

My tears were unexpected, rising from a place I'd barricaded shut long ago. I turned my face away so that Dougie wouldn't see me weep.

"It sound corny to you?" he asked.

253

I forced a laugh. "I wish it did."

"I'm asking for just a few hours with you." He became so still that for a moment it was as if he'd slipped away into the dark. "Just tonight. And I'm not talking about sex. I know you love someone else, and I'm glad for you. I just . . ." He pulled in a deep breath. "I just need to hear you breathe. Need to have my eyes on you for one night. You were always my compass rose."

I looked up once again at the glittering canopy of stars. Blinked away the last of my tears.

Then I reached over and took his hand in mine.

CHAPTER 22

There is no place in war for love. But I loved anyway.

—Sydney Parnell. Personal journal.

In the hotel room, I closed and locked the door behind us and fastened the chain. I heard one of the beds creak as Clyde jumped on top.

When I turned around, Dougie hadn't moved away from the door.

Our bodies were only inches apart. In the gloom, the heat rising from his skin flared over me like the signal arc from a radar beacon. His scent, both foreign and familiar, filled my nose and mouth. Memories swirled through my head like leaves caught in a storm, urging me to a distant place, another time.

Beneath this longing was the drumbeat of my fear for Cohen.

I dug my nails into my palms and pressed my back against the door, grounding myself. In the faint light, I searched Dougie's face, trying to read his expression. The single overhead bulb merged his shadow with mine. We seemed more dream than flesh.

"You've been covering it well," he said, "but you're hurt."

"It's not so bad." Not for my body, anyway. In my soul, an existential battle waged.

"Let me see to it."

"I'll be fine."

"You need to be at your best. For whatever's coming down the pike."

Panic surged, and I pushed it down. But it was like trying to drown an elephant.

"I'm afraid of you," I whispered. "Afraid to be too close."

"Rosie." His voice cracked. He pulled back, and the light fell between us, dull and fly spotted.

"Don't touch me."

"I want to help you. Only that."

I remembered the bloody rag at the strip club. Neatly folded and spattered with blood. "They hurt you, too."

"He hadn't really started."

The room was overwarm, the air as thick and languid as the tropics. My blood throbbed under the weight of my confusion. For a few moments I let my mind run along a path into a future that included both of us.

"Maybe it's not you I'm afraid of." I touched a single lock of Dougie's hair. "Maybe it's me."

I sat on one of the beds, my feet flat on the floor and my back snugged against Clyde, who lay sprawled down the middle. Dougie returned from the bathroom, drying his hands on a towel. He switched on the table lamp so that the light fell across the bed, then knelt in front of me.

I'd long ago removed the Kevlar. Now I stripped off my filthy T-shirt. Dougie's eyes swept past my bra and came to rest on my ribs. Gently, he turned me so the light slanted over my skin.

His fingers left burn marks where they touched.

Tenderly, he peeled away the blood-soaked bandage. He studied the wound for a moment, then rose and went into the bathroom, returning with more towels and a damp washcloth. He opened his backpack.

I stared. "You have medical supplies?"

"I've spent the last two years running deep ops in remote places. Had to be ready for anything."

"The kind of secret ops that meant you couldn't pick up the phone and call me?"

"Exactly those kind."

"Three years, Dougie."

His eyes met mine. "Having me back in your life would have brought you the wrong kind of attention. I wouldn't risk it."

"You should have given me a choice."

"No." He closed his eyes. Opened them. "Not even that."

A storm surge of hurt washed up against me.

What kind of man chooses to remain dead to those who love him, just so he can get the job done? And how far into the covert world had he stepped by the time I met him in Iraq?

Maybe the Dougie I thought I knew had never existed.

"It was a mistake," I said. "Falling in love with me."

"It wasn't in the plan." His mouth ticked up. "But it was never a mistake."

So perhaps even the strongest among us have an Achilles' heel. Who would turn away love?

An image of Cohen rose, along with another surge of pain. Cohen didn't know about Dougie.

Another part of my past I hadn't shared.

As Dougie worked, I studied the top of his head, the thick, dark-blond curls. In Iraq, he'd worn a bandanna to keep his hair back from his face. Or a *keffiyeh* when he needed to move in secret. In the desert, riding horseback, he'd been exotic. Mesmerizing. A man both at home in the wilderness and startlingly alien.

Here, in this dreary hotel room, he was even more so.

I said, "How long have you known about the Alpha?"

He shook his head. "I knew we had a traitor in Iraq. But I didn't know he was still active until I pulled Malik out of that shit-hole spy school. The Alpha knows more about me than I do about him."

A needle bit my skin, and I jerked.

"Anesthetic," he said. "Stay still."

He was much as I remembered him. Still tall, of course. Still strong. Eyes brilliant in the semigloom, the blue-green of tropical seas. There were new wrinkles—crow's feet around his eyes, two vertical lines like slashes on each side of his mouth. And the expression in his eyes had shifted from optimism to something darker.

I gasped when he pulled a different needle through my skin. He murmured an apology but didn't stop.

Could a person be of two hearts? Could you walk through life loving one person as much as another? Or, with the sides irreconcilable, would your heart eventually break beneath the load?

I closed my eyes and focused on the pain.

"Done," he said after a time.

I glanced down. He'd closed the wound with tight, neat stitches. "It looks good."

His fingers smoothed a bandage over the wound. He ran one thumb up my rib cage, and the air shifted as we both sucked in our breaths. He removed my ball cap and fisted a tangled lock of my hair.

"You could have died in Mexico," he said. "I should have stopped him sooner. I was afraid to show my hand."

Gently I disentangled his fingers. "We should sleep now."

"Just give me this moment."

His thumb stroked the side of my face, his touch as light as if he had no more substance than one of my ghosts.

He said, "What kept me alive was the thought of being with you again."

"Sh."

"Every day in Iraq, a movie played in my mind. A movie of what our life would be when we were together again. You'd be a teacher, like you always wanted. I'd stay home and cook. Tend a garden."

Despite everything, I laughed. "You? A house husband?"

"I'm ready for it, Rosie. It's all I want as soon as I finish with the covert work." His face lit up. "That and about five kids."

My laugh came smaller this time. "Kids."

His fingers brushed my jawline, trailed down to my throat where my pulse ached. "Every day and night for months while my body healed, I imagined you next to me. I'd close my eyes, and there you'd be. Telling me that I had to live. Nothing more. Just live."

My shoulders shook with my sobs.

His hand moved to my bare shoulder, the calluses across his palm like brands upon his skin. "I never gave up on us. I always imagined that in another year, two at the most, we'd be together."

"All I had were memories. And those hurt so much." My breath shuddered. "I tried to let you go. Lately . . . it's been a little easier."

"Because of the cop." His voice was filed down to an edge.

"Michael Cohen." Saying his name brought fresh pain. My eyes strayed to the clock on the bedside table, calculating the hours. "I'm not the same woman you loved."

"I'm not the same man. Everyone changes."

How easy it was to see that. His confidence hardened into hyper-vigilance. Optimism buried by anger. The man I loved had been washed through a cycle over and over, until what remained was a hard core of qualities that almost mocked the man he'd been.

And yet. The gentleness remained.

He said, "Is he a good man?"

I remembered our bedroom that morning, a million years ago. The silence between us. Would that be the last thing we shared?

"He's a very good man."

"And you love him."

I'd already searched my heart. "Yes."

"More than . . . ?" He pulled his hand away and dropped his gaze.

"Don't ask," I whispered.

Silence hung in the air.

But when he lifted his eyes to mine, he pulled up a smile that must have cost him almost everything he had left. "Then we'll bring him home to you."

◆ ◆ ◆

Sarge came by to let us know he'd booked a 6:00 a.m. flight. The three of us sketched out a rough plan for the next day, I gave him Rick Dalton's key, and Sarge bid us goodnight. After he left, I washed up in the bathroom. When I came back out, toweling my hair, Dougie had removed his shirt and shoes and settled atop the covers next to Clyde. Clyde slept with his head tucked under Dougie's shoulder.

The soft light from the bedside lamp illuminated a network of thick scar tissue that webbed Dougie's stomach.

I stopped. "When did that happen?"

"During the ambush."

I sat on the other bed. "That's when you decided to switch places with Dalton."

"I didn't make that decision, Rosie. I was gut shot. I woke up twenty hours later and miles away. I assume it was one of my sources in the village who made the switch in order to protect me, and another man took me out of the city. When I came to, I was in a house in the middle of nowhere. The man and woman who lived there took care of me for almost a year."

"So much pain."

"Life *is* pain. There or here. No matter who we are."

True that. "How are we going to find Cohen?"

"Sleep. Something will come to us."

"That part of your secret-ops training?"

"Sometimes the best way to solve a problem is to walk away from it. I'm guessing you know that. You just don't know how to do it."

"Maybe not." Not when it came to Cohen.

He reached over the edge of the bed into his backpack and tossed over a few protein bars. "Better to use this time to eat and rest, Rosie. So we can be on our game at first light."

As I turned down the sheets, Clyde lifted his head. But when Dougie cooed a few words to him, he resettled. They both closed their eyes, and soon my partner's quiet, even breathing joined Dougie's.

Dougie was right. I should sleep. Come dawn, I needed to be in the zone, ready to find Cohen and spirit him away before he ended up like Angelo.

But as tired as I was, I could not rest. Not with Cohen beaten and in pain, wondering if the next day would bring his death. I stared through the gloom at my laptop and asked myself if the key to his location lay buried somewhere on the internet. Something I'd missed. Some clue I'd failed to pick up.

I threw off the covers and opened my computer, curling my feet beneath me as I sat at the table. Using multiple browsers, I hunted down virtual alleyways and surveyed electronic vistas. I pursued James Osborne as if he were a rabbit to my wolf, diving down holes, digging through layers, searching for a scent.

Since I didn't think Osborne would take the risk of hiding Cohen on Vigilant property or at his personal address, I looked for ties to other locations.

But Osborne was too smart for someone with my skills. He'd erased all footsteps save for those on the broad avenue of his website.

He was a ghost in the machine.

After an hour, with my eyes closing against my will, I had to admit failure.

Determination is not a plan, desire no substitute for strategy.

I rose and went to the window, edging aside the curtain.

A gossamer veil of clouds covered the stars. Only a soft yellow glow from the streetlamp held back the dark.

Clyde roused himself, shook, and hopped off the bed. He padded over and stood next to me at the window. He put his paws on a chair, and we stared through the glass for a time, until I released the curtain.

In the dark, Dougie gave a sharp, sudden cry and swung a fist. He muttered something and turned to his side.

How had he and I gotten to this place? How was it that even our love had been corrupted by war?

For three years I'd played out this impossible reunion in my mind. Now here it was, lost before I'd grasped it. Dougie and I didn't belong together. We'd changed. Our lives had moved onto separate paths. Water had flowed not just under the bridge, but over it until the bridge was no longer even there.

Dougie yelled again. Beside me, Clyde let out an agitated whimper.

I rested my hand on his head.

"I know, boy," I whispered. "I know."

Clyde looked up at me, and I ruffled his ears.

"We're not alone. Sarge will find the intel, and we'll bring Mike home. I can't think past that."

I set aside my fear. I locked it in a box and threw away the key and dug out my combat face, the one I'd discovered in Iraq my first day out of the wire. Then I ate a couple of protein bars and crawled back into bed for a couple of hours.

Food, then sleep, then war.

CHAPTER 23

Everyone is the hero of their own story.

—*Sydney Parnell. Personal journal.*
Paraphrased from John Barth.

It was still dark when I woke to the sound of water running in the next room. A television set murmured on low volume. A drawer slammed, and something thumped against the wall.

Sarge, getting ready to head out.

I sat up and checked my phone—4:00 a.m. and nothing more from the Alpha. My eyes were gritty with sand, my body a mass of pain. I swung my feet to the floor, dry swallowed more of Dougie's over-the-counter pain pills, and reached for my jacket.

Clyde hopped down from the bed. Half the night with Dougie. Half with me.

Split down the middle.

At the door, I paused. Dougie still slept, his arm thrown over his eyes, the sheets tangled around his waist, his muscles bunched even in sleep. I watched him for a moment, then grabbed my laptop, and Clyde and I slipped outside.

The predawn air was cool and clean smelling, the highway an empty ribbon unfurled across the prairie. Sometime during the night, the motel owner had shut off the single lamp in the parking lot. The only light came from the hint of dawn in the east and a thin golden glow leaking around the curtains over Sarge's window.

Clyde went sniffing for rabbits, his tail wagging and ears swiveling. He trotted past the rancher's truck where it was still parked at the far end of the lot, dew beaded on the windows and glistening on the back bumper with its GOD AND COUNTRY decal.

Clyde headed toward a clump of cottonwood trees.

I stretched for a few minutes and jogged in place, testing my body, stirring the sluggish flow of blood in my veins. Then I sat at the nearby picnic table, powered on the laptop, and opened Google Maps. I pulled up the addresses of the people who'd been on the platform when Kane died.

Dougie had been right. My brain, finally allowed to rest, had focused on the clue that had been in front of me all along. I was now sure that Kane hadn't let himself be distracted by a pretty woman. He was too much of a professional. The answer we sought was with one of the people who watched him die that day. One of them was the key. To the Alpha. To Cohen's location. To our way out of this maze. One of them would provide the link Osborne had not.

I zoomed in on the first address.

A few minutes later, the light in Sarge's room went out, and he came outside. He nodded at me and tossed his bag in the back of his truck.

"I'll call as soon as I know anything," he said, opening the driver's door. "And you let me know when you two yokels nail down some details."

I stood. Our eyes met over the hood of the truck. Sarge looked like he was thinking the same thing I was—that if everything went to shit, this might be the last time we saw each other alive.

I said, "For a man who tried to kill me, you're not a complete asshole."

"For a woman who kicked my ass *twice*, you aren't too shabby yourself."

I summoned up a smile.

If all went well, by the time Dougie and I were standing on Vigilant's doorstep ready to move against Osborne, Sarge would be on his way back to Denver with the video. As soon as Sarge confirmed, Dougie and I would walk into Vigilant and explain to James Osborne how things were going to go down.

He'd give us Cohen. We'd give him the phone. Promises would be made on both sides. Dougie and Sarge and I would remain silent. Osborne would leave us alone. Malik would be allowed to grow up and grow old without ever looking over his shoulder.

Like any good Mexican standoff, each side would be bound to its promises by the threat of mutual annihilation.

It had worked in the Cold War.

But it was bullshit, and all of us knew it. The only people who survived a Mexican standoff were the ones who fired first. Plus, there was no way I could let this asshole walk away free.

We needed our finger on the trigger.

My smile faded. "Stay frosty, Sarge."

"Eyes in the back of my head." He grinned and reached over the hood. We clasped hands. "Take care of yourself, Parnell. Never thought I'd say this, but it hasn't sucked being on the same side."

I nodded.

He cleared his throat, got in, and started the truck. Clyde came running back. I placed a hand on my partner's head, and we watched until the taillights of Sarge's pickup disappeared in the distance.

Then I returned to my laptop and got to work, searching for a trigger.

◆　◆　◆

Half an hour later, the sun had spread a red-gold fan across the picnic table. Clyde took a post-breakfast snooze at my feet. He opened one eye and thumped his tail when Dougie came out of the room carrying two cardboard cups of instant oatmeal and more protein bars.

"You let me sleep," Dougie said.

"You needed it."

He handed me one of the cups and a spoon, then sat across from me, his hair falling in untidy waves around a face still creased from sleep.

"I've been working." My knee jittered up and down.

Dougie's eyes went from my bouncing leg to my face. "What did you find?"

I pushed up from the table, unable to sit still. "I was looking for leverage to use against Osborne."

Dougie lifted the lid on his oatmeal. A cloud of steam rose into the air with the scent of maple. "Tell me."

I turned the computer around to show him the DMV photos of the people standing on the platform. "These five people were almost the last thing Kane saw before he died. He was handling a belligerent man who turned out to be his killer. But his last act was to turn his back to this man and zero in on one of these five people."

Dougie pulled the computer toward him, frowning. "Go on."

"I eliminated Martinez, Parker, and Wilson. There's nothing special about them other than their presence on that platform."

"Okay."

"I also eliminated Kenneth Napierkowski." Talking fast, I explained. "Neither he nor the fifth person, Laura Almasi, have any social-media presence. Rare these days, but not unheard of. Plus, Napierkowski lives in the Golden Triangle, which means he's wealthy, even though I can't find a job history for him. That's potentially suspect. But he isn't military. And as near as I can tell, he's never left the country. He's overweight and serves as president of an African Violet Society. He doesn't fit the profile."

Dougie nodded and moved his hand in a "go on" gesture.

I reached over and clicked on one of the photographs, enlarging it. "This is Laura Almasi."

"Tell me."

I moved around to his side of the table and scooted in next to him. "According to the Texas DMV, she lives in a wealthy enclave of Dallas called University Park. That's only forty minutes from Cedar Hill."

"And—?"

"Valor is headquartered in Cedar Hill."

He looked at me, eyebrows up, then used his forefinger to scroll through the information I'd pulled up on Almasi.

"This shows a PO Box in Colorado," he said. "Lindon."

"Right." My knee started bouncing again. "Lindon is on the eastern plains, an hour's drive from where we sit. It's a post office and a hundred and fifty people scattered around the area. But take a look at the satellite imagery south and east of the town."

I clicked on the tab I'd brought up for Google Earth. The screen showed an aerial photo of the Colorado plains centered around an area so pixelated and blurry that it was impossible to make out what was there.

Dougie gave a low whistle. "This kind of obstruction is extremely hard to get. Takes connections."

"Government ones?"

"Probably not. In the US, Google doesn't block even those sites that involve national security. A raft of public-access lawyers make sure of it. But a private entity can request masking. There's an entire city on the East Coast that did just that. It's rare, though. There must be something pretty damn interesting going on out there."

For the first time since we'd been back together, I heard the old excitement in his voice, like a line of quicksilver.

My own excitement bubbled up, and I forced myself to take a deep breath. We had very little time to find Cohen. I needed to be sure.

"Why else might this area be obscured?" I asked.

"There are a few possibilities." He zoomed in and out of the satellite photo. "Google occasionally blocks places for unusual reasons. Like protecting rare species from poachers."

"Last I looked, prairie dogs and cattle aren't on the endangered species list. Even more interesting—just two years ago, this area wasn't obscured. It was just a three-mile square stretch of grassland in the middle of nowhere. Then suddenly we get Almasi's PO Box, a land title held by a holding company that I can't dig into no matter what I try, and a flurry of construction permits. I even found a reference to the FAA, which suggests there's a runway out there."

"Fascinating." He looked up from the computer, his eyes bright in the morning sun. "You think Cohen is out there."

"It's remote, out of sight, and way off the beaten path. If you want to hurt someone, maybe kill and bury—"

I stopped.

Dougie dropped his hand on mine. "The most likely explanation is that a private company wants to hide what they're doing from their competitors, and they have the clout to make it happen." He withdrew his hand, leaned back on the bench, and folded his arms. "They wouldn't be in the assassination business."

"Unless they have something big to hide." I laid out Kane's photographs on the table. "Kane took these before he was killed. Somehow they learned he'd snapped them, which meant he might have connected the dots between Iraq and Valor. The Alpha had to eliminate him."

Dougie went through the pictures. "You're assuming that what's out there has something to do with Valor. We need a connection between Laura Almasi and Valor Industries."

"Let me show you." I clicked on another tab. "Laura Almasi barely exists in the virtual world. But someone digitized Cedar Hill's old newspaper. This came up when I ran a search on the family patriarch, Sheldon Osborne."

Dougie studied the scanned image while I swallowed down the oatmeal and mentally repeated a version of last night's mantra. Food, sleep, fight.

Dougie's eyes narrowed as he read.

> Catherine and Sheldon Osborne of Cedar Hill, Texas, are pleased to announce the engagement of their daughter, Laura Ann, to Arvin, son of Mr. and Mrs. Almasi of Dallas. Laura is a graduate of Rice University and is employed at the Osborne family business, Valor Industries. Arvin is a graduate of the Massachusetts Institute of Technology's Materials Science Program and is an intern at Valor Industries. An August wedding is planned.

I peered over Dougie's shoulder at the photograph. Arvin appeared happy, his handsome face creased in a wide smile, his rakishly long hair combed back from his face.

Laura looked quieter. Almost somber. She was young, but there was a no-nonsense air about her short, simple haircut, plain blouse, and un-made-up face. Her gaze was direct and almost challenging. But it also held a faint hint of something else I couldn't put my finger on.

As it had the first time I'd seen it, Laura's expression made me shiver.

I pulled up her DMV photo so that the pictures were side by side. It was clearly the same no-nonsense woman with the simple haircut and shirt. Only the look in her eyes had changed, flipping into something else.

An approaching madness.

"So there it is." Dougie curled a fist under his chin.

"The first time I saw Laura's name," I said, "I thought Almasi was Italian. But it means 'diamond maker' in Persian." I pushed away the cup with its remnants of oatmeal. "The Almasis are Jewish Iranians. Arvin and his parents came to the US in 1979, a few months before the fall of the shah."

"I'm not surprised. A lot of Jews didn't do well after the ayatollah took over. Some of them were executed as accused spies. If Arvin still has family there"—this time there was no missing the gritty enthusiasm in Dougie's voice—"then Laura—and through her, Valor—are vulnerable to blackmail."

At Dougie's confirmation of my thoughts, the excitement that had been building over the last thirty minutes shot a bolt of lightning from my brain to my gut. "She's part of what happened in Habbaniyah. Her brother, James, was in Iraq when all this went down, so he must be involved as well. You said he green-lighted bringing in the EFPs."

Dougie nodded. "And gave the order for us to go after them. It would have been a major triumph for him, capturing Quds forces and weapons inside Iraq. Then he suddenly put things on hold. When the order came to stand down, we just figured the intelligence was no good. That maybe there weren't any weapons."

"But Dalton knew otherwise because he'd seen the video." My excitement grew. "I'll bet Osborne talked to his sister. Boasted that he was about to bag some high-level Iranians. And she was forced to confess that she'd been selling arms to Iran."

"And those arms were now in Iraq." Dougie's expression flatlined into an icy, contained rage. "It was Osborne who sent us into that ambush. He couldn't run the risk that we'd realize the intelligence was good. That there really were weapons. His sister's weapons. If your theory is right, he was the one who betrayed us and meant for us to die."

"And he ordered the deaths of Haifa and Resenko. Anyone who knew about the video."

Dougie crossed his arms. "Osborne dropped a stone in the water. He had to catch all the ripples."

I touched a finger to the computer screen. "But I don't think he was the real instigator. I think she was. She set up the arms sales. Then she told Osborne to cover it up. Osborne was taking his orders from her."

His voice was a growl. "She does look half mad, doesn't she?"

"And she has Cohen." I pulled up the photo the Alpha had sent of Mike. "Look there, over his left shoulder."

Dougie took my phone and enlarged the image.

I pointed. "You see the letters?"

"*L A G E.*" Dougie enlarged the picture more. "Looks like part of a name. *L A G E C O N.*"

"Remember those construction permits I mentioned? If we fill in the missing letters, this could be Phlage Construction, which is one of the largest corporations in Colorado. Their website lists military-grade construction as the biggest part of their business. I think Valor hired them to build whatever it is they're building out there."

I brought my hands together like a prayer as Dougie's gaze met mine.

"James Osborne isn't the Alpha," I said. "His sister is. And somewhere beneath that dark cloud, she's holding Cohen."

It was all I had. I'd better be right.

CHAPTER 24

Find somewhere to put the fear, Rosie. A place inside where you don't have to look very often.

—Doug Ayers. Private conversation.

Wind buffeted the truck as we headed east. The sun came in hard through the windshield, slanting through the cab and flashing off our sunglasses.

Dougie drove while I rode shotgun, Clyde between us on the bench seat.

The engine in the rancher's truck we'd rented from the couple at the motel whined at a top speed of sixty-five—twenty miles over the posted limit. The truck bed smelled of hay and manure, the interior of coffee and cigarettes. Rips in the seats oozed stuffing, something loose rattled inside the dash, and a network of cracks splayed across the lower left corner of the windshield, glinting a rainbow of fractured sunlight.

The old Ford had been young when Elvis was. But it provided cover. A rancher and his wife, out for a drive.

Now why would you want to borrow this old bucket? the rancher had asked us back at the Coach Motel.

We'd spotted the Marine decal on the truck's rear window, and now Dougie all but stood at attention. *We need it, sir. It'll get us in.*

The old rancher's eyes narrowed as his gaze moved back and forth between Dougie and me, taking us in. After a moment, he gave a small nod. No doubt he'd seen faces like ours before. At Hué and Khe Sanh. In his own mirror. War faces. *Is this a matter of life or death?*

It's a question of both, sir.

He looked over the gear we carried. *Are you the good guys?*

Yes, sir. We are.

If my truck will do the trick, please take it. Bring it back if you can. He fished the keys out of his pocket and handed them over.

Appreciate it. Dougie jerked his chin toward the rancher's Circle F Feed & Supply hat. *That ball cap. Looks like it does a good job keeping the sun off.*

Consider it yours.

As we climbed into the cab, I heard the old man whisper, *Semper Fi, Mac.*

Fifteen minutes along, we exited the highway and moved to side roads. From there, we wound our way onto narrow paths carved out years earlier by the locals.

The prairie stretched out in undulating rolls of green and brown. The occasional herd of cattle watched our passage as the truck rattled over metal cattle guards and bucked through ruts deep enough to swallow the truck right up to the side mirrors.

"We're ten minutes out," Dougie said.

We'd studied online maps before we left. Highway 36 approached the Valor complex on a straight path from Denver—it was probably the road Kane had taken when he snapped the pictures. Way too risky for us to follow all the way east.

We would approach the complex from the north, staying on private property and hopefully eluding both the locals and anyone from Valor who might be keeping watch. The truck was the only disguise we had.

Per an old online topographical map, a thirty-foot-high ridge ran east-west just inside the blurred area. It would provide both cover and a good place from which to surveil the site, assuming it got us close enough to whatever was going on inside the pixels.

The transmission complained as Dougie dropped gears and we edged down a dry wash that cut across the road.

My phone buzzed. Sarge. I hit speakerphone.

"I'm twenty miles along the highway to Bullhead," Sarge said. "Zero traffic and no tail."

"We're heading to where we think they're holding Cohen." I filled him in on what we'd learned about Laura Almasi and Valor.

"The Alpha's a woman? I should have figured."

"Because women are tough and determined."

"Yeah . . . that's what I was thinking. I'll call back as soon as I've located Rick's box. Keep those fingers crossed. If it's empty—"

I locked the doubt away with the fear. "If there's nothing, then you'd better get back here and pick up our carcasses in case things go wrong. We're going in for Cohen no matter what."

As I disconnected I caught my reflection in the window. The woman who looked back at me wore her combat face—lips a thin line, eyes flat and cold.

Dougie wore the same look.

The only thing missing was war paint.

"We're inside the pixelated area," Dougie said a few minutes later as we jounced over another cattle guard.

I studied the grassland around us—360 degrees of empty beneath a flat sheet of washed blue. Just visible in the distance, a herd of pronghorn stood on dancer's legs. Closer by, a jackrabbit darted into cover.

"So far, so good," I said.

Five minutes later, we hit trouble.

Dougie tapped the brakes as we rounded a curve and a road-block came into view—an orange-and-white gate with a sign that read ROAD CLOSED. On the right was a guard shack. As we watched, a man appeared at the window, then strode outside. He wore a khaki uniform and carried a rifle.

"No time to backtrack," Dougie said. "We're going through."

He gunned the engine. The truck responded with a groan, creeping up toward thirty miles an hour. Ramming a barricade on a stretch of road like this felt as though we were running in slo-mo.

The guard signaled for us to stop.

"Take the wheel," Dougie said.

"He's just a contractor."

"No, he's not." He slid his foot off the accelerator. "Take the wheel."

I ordered Clyde to lie flat and reached over him to grab the steering wheel. It bucked in my hand as the truck slowed and the tires fought the ruts.

"Stop!" the guard yelled.

Dougie lowered the window.

The guard raised his weapon. A bullet punctured the windshield and thumped into the seat, missing Dougie by less than an inch.

He leaned out the open window and leveled his own rifle.

The guard's head burst apart in a red rain.

Dougie brought in the rifle, took the wheel, and stomped the gas pedal. We roared around the dead man and through the barricade, shattered wood flying into the air.

I stared out the back window at the man lying in the road.

"Shit," I said. My hands were shaking.

"He would have sounded the alert."

"What if he's expected to call in?"

"Then they'll be waiting for us." Dougie threw me a harsh look. "From here on, follow my orders. No questions. No arguing. We're heading into a kill zone. Do you understand?"

The dead man vanished in a swirl of dust. In his place stood a ghost—staved-in head, fingers gripped around the cord to an electric burner.

Fadden.

"I understand," I said.

◆ ◆ ◆

A few minutes later, Dougie pulled off the road and drove the truck behind a thick grove of cottonwoods growing on the bank of a shallow creek.

"Five minutes," he said. "Then we head out."

While he fieldstripped the rifles we'd taken from the strip club and checked the rest of our gear, I ran Clyde through a series of maneuvers we'd practiced with Clyde's trainer. I went through each of the most critical commands in English, German, and Hebrew, then ran through them all again using hand signals.

Clyde performed flawlessly.

I called him in, gave him his fill of water, then buckled his Kevlar vest around his stomach and chest and shrugged into my own vest. I slid on my thigh harness with my personal Glock and the shoulder holster with the stun gun and grabbed Cohen's jacket—the fleece I'd borrowed from him and never returned. I tied it around my waist. At the back of the truck, Dougie was loading his backpack. The last thing to go in were explosives and a few remote detonators.

"I thought this was a quick in and out," I said.

"Plan B. Things go wrong, we'll want leverage. I'll go in first and set things up. If Cohen can't walk, I'll acquire a vehicle."

"How long?"

"I'll be fast." He glanced down at my hands. They were still shaking. "Clyde and I can do this alone."

"It's Cohen. I'm going."

He gave me a measured stare, then handed over one of the suppressed M4s, a folding knife, and a pair of binoculars. I hung the glasses around my neck and slung the rifle over my right shoulder. The knife went into my pocket. We clipped on headsets and ran through a radio check. Then I whistled up Clyde, and the three of us headed south at a jog toward the ridge.

◆ ◆ ◆

The land stretched dry and golden brown around us, the day heating up as it moved toward midmorning. The stream soon trickled to nothing, but the dry arroyo wound steadily south. The wind became a beast, flattening the grass and swirling grit through the air.

Fifteen minutes brought us to the ridge we'd noted on the maps. I signaled Clyde, and the three of us dropped to our stomachs and crawled up the last few yards, not sure whether the compound would be a hundred yards away or almost three miles. And if they'd be watching for us.

We edged over the top and peered down.

The hill dropped steeply on the other side, flattening into a plain of tall grass and the occasional tree. A quarter mile away, a handful of man-made structures rose from the earth like ancient ruins.

Dougie and I eased up on our elbows and glassed the site.

I recognized it immediately. The angle was different. But this was the subject of Kane's photographs.

In the center of a large leveled area rose a two-story tan brick building, a plain rectangle whose only adornment was a series of narrow vertical windows up high, like those used by archers in medieval times. On the near side of the building, an obstacle course sprawled across a chunk of acreage. Rope ladders, a set of hurdles, muddy trenches covered by barbed wire. At the far end were scaling walls and a fifteen-foot-high wall used for rappelling.

"They're running a training center," Dougie said.

"But for who?"

"Good question." He kept panning. "I don't see any security cameras on the buildings or near the fence. They're probably still hooking things up."

Most of the rest of the site was still open prairie. But on the far side, just visible, a steel-and-concrete airplane hangar spread across a large area. A metal door covered the opening. Nearby, two private jets sat behind a chain-link fence. In one corner of the fenced area was a small collection of backhoes and tractors.

Next to the hangar, a concrete runway ran north-south.

"The planes are Cessna Longitudes," Dougie said. "Set you back twenty-five mil. They probably keep the really expensive aircraft inside the hangar. You see the green rectangle with the white sword painted on the sides of the jets?"

I turned the focus on the binoculars. "What is it?"

"Flag of Saudi Arabia, minus the Muslim creed. Whatever's going on out here, it's a big deal. Saudi involvement would explain why this area was blurred out on the maps. It was probably done at their request."

"Friend of mine who retired from State said that James Osborne kept company with the Saudis in Baghdad. Maybe he was wooing potential clients." I lowered the glasses and palmed sweat from my forehead. "I heard on the news maybe a month ago that an unnamed US company employing ex-CIA officers is negotiating with the Saudis to help them create their own spy empire."

Dougie moved the binoculars from his eyes. "It's true. The organization will be modeled on the Special Activities Division of the CIA. But the fact that there are former CIA officers involved has some people in Washington questioning its legality."

I didn't ask him how he knew all this. I was sure he had connections. "You think the company is Valor?"

"Looking at this complex? I think it's Valor and Vigilant. Vigilant trains the men and builds the organization. Valor supplies it with weapons. They have some damn powerful backers."

This could explain the Alpha's recent aggression in her efforts to hide Valor's treasonous arrangement with Iran. A multibillion-dollar contract with Saudi Arabia would float the company for years. Even decades. And provide entrée to Saudi Arabia's allies—the United Arab Emirates, Bahrain, Qatar, Oman, Egypt, and Kuwait.

The wealthiest countries in the Middle East.

A cash cow, there for the milking.

Unless someone could prove that Valor Industries also worked with the Saudis' deadliest enemies—the Islamic Republic of Iran.

I lifted the binoculars.

Scattered around the rest of the complex were twenty construction trailers arranged in four clusters. A large *P* was stenciled on their sides, presumably for Phlage Construction. They all had a single central door flanked by two windows covered with aluminum blinds. Roughly ten feet by thirty-six, the trailers looked like matchsticks next to the rest of the complex.

Unless they'd moved him, Cohen had to be inside one of those matchsticks.

A road from the distant highway entered the complex from the southwest, a guard shack just visible. Another road ran between the compound and the runway.

Eight vehicles sat in a large paved lot a short distance from the brick building—seven black SUVs, their sides streaked with dust, and an incongruous red Mercedes sports car. Allowing four people per SUV and two in the sports car meant somewhere between eight and thirty potential threats inside the complex. More, if people were bunking down on-site.

But only two men were visible. One on patrol, walking the perimeter. And another on the far side of the compound, standing guard atop a twenty-foot-high wooden platform.

We timed their activity. The guard on the platform made a slow rotation of the area every ten minutes, watching the horizon through his binoculars. He seemed less concerned with anything that might be happening closer by—maybe that was the purview of the guard on the ground. Between his scans of the horizon, the man occupied himself with his phone, eyeballing something on the screen.

The second guard made a complete circuit of the area every fifteen minutes, walking just inside the chain-link fence that encircled the compound. The first time he walked the perimeter, he stopped and spoke with the guard on the tower. On his second circuit, he didn't pause.

Dougie said, "Watch the trailers farthest away."

I shifted the binoculars. A door to one trailer stood open. A man came down the stairs, talking on his phone. He crossed to one of the other trailers and disappeared inside.

"Five to ten men, probably," Dougie said. "Or there could be an army inside that building. But no workers. Maybe because they've got Cohen here."

We divided the area into sectors and assigned labels to each cluster of trailers from T1 to T4, and designated the large building as Country Club and the hangar as Zeta. This would allow us to communicate our whereabouts inside with a minimum of talk and no chance of being understood by eavesdroppers.

My phone vibrated. Sarge again.

I ducked out of the wind below the ridge line. Grasshoppers pogo-sticked around me.

"I've got the phone," Sarge said.

My heart smacked against my chest. "You're holding it?"

"Affirmative. It's an old Nokia, just like I remember. Sealed in a manila mailer with all kinds of interesting postage."

Relief swept through me. "It's working?"

"Battery's dead. We'll have to find a charger. Want to know what else was in there?"

"First, are you back on the road?"

"Yeah, I'm driving. And I left behind about half a million dollars, all tightly packaged in bundles of hundred-dollar bills. TSA would throw my ass in jail if they caught me carrying that much money. But now you know I love you. I could be hanging out poolside in glorious Bullhead as we speak, getting drunk and enjoying some female companionship. A half-million fucking dollars."

I processed the news, wondering if Laura Almasi was also looking for the cash. But five hundred grand didn't seem like enough to interest her. Not against Saudi billions.

"Get on that plane," I said. "I'll text you the coordinates of our location. We're going in."

"I'll call when I'm about to board. You don't answer, I'll try again when I land. If you still don't answer, I'm calling the Feds."

We disconnected, and I elbow-walked back to Dougie and filled him in on Sarge's news.

"We're going to nail her." He lowered the binoculars and reached for his backpack. "I'm going in now. Wait ten minutes, then follow me once the guard is on the far side. As soon as Clyde locates Cohen, notify me. Then find cover and wait."

"Got it."

"If I'm not there in ten minutes, extricate Cohen and get to the truck. Keys are on the driver's side front tire. Then get the hell out. I'll follow as soon as I can."

"Check." As if I'd leave him.

"No heroics. You wait for me, you could die."

I crossed my fingers. "I won't wait."

"Go in fast and go in hard. Don't give them time to react. Anyone sees you, take them down."

The thought of more deaths made the air in my lungs evaporate.

"Lethal force, Rosie. If we don't extricate your friend, they'll kill him. Even if they've kept him blindfolded and drugged, he's too big a risk. He's a *cop*. So don't hesitate. Because they won't."

I sucked in air and gave him a single clipped nod. "Chin up, head down, one round in the chamber. Let's do this."

His grin was fierce. "See you on the far side."

I watched through the binoculars as Dougie crouched in the grass at the base of the ridge, waiting for the man on the tower to finish his study of the horizon. Waves of heat flickered up from the ground, turning Dougie into an apparition.

As soon as the man put down his binoculars, Dougie sprinted toward the complex.

At the fence, he knelt and used bolt cutters to snip an opening in the metal. He wriggled through and darted to the nearest structure—the first trailer in the section we'd designated T1—then began working his way around the complex in the direction of the airplane hangar.

I watched him until he disappeared behind the training center—the Country Club—then coordinated my own approach with the actions of the guards. As soon as the tower guard returned to his phone and the grounds patroller was out of sight, Clyde and I took off at a full sprint. At the fence, we dropped to our stomachs and wriggled through the gap. When we reached the cluster of trailers designated T1, we snugged up to the closest. I signaled Clyde to stop and crouched next to him.

The wind moaned around the buildings. I heard a door and a snippet of voices, but they quickly faded. The wind caught something on the obstacle course, a plastic flag maybe. It snapped over and over.

"I'm in," I whispered on the radio.

"I'm at bravo," Dougie answered, letting me know he'd made it to his first destination. We'd decided to skip what would normally be our term for the first designation—*Alpha*.

Alpha had a whole different meaning for this operation.

Now for the hard part. Staying out of sight while Clyde did what he did best.

I gripped his harness to signal the start of his work. He watched my face, ready.

Game on.

I gave him a hit from Cohen's jacket. His tail wagged.

I said softly, "Seek!"

CHAPTER 25

Sooner or later, we all come to the ultimate contest, when it's just us and the devil.

And the devil hates to lose.

—*Sydney Parnell. Personal journal.*

Clyde lifted his head, scenting the air. My heart crawled all the way up into my throat while I waited. What if I was wrong? What if Cohen was a hundred miles away, his hand splayed on a table, his torturer standing over him with a knife, ready to butcher him?

The seconds ticked by as the wind continued its incessant moan and the nearby crack-snap of plastic on the obstacle course sounded like small-arms fire. Clyde worked against the wind, struggling to pull out every scent molecule that whirled by.

Then his ears perked, and his tail rose like a flag.

He had a hit.

Relief swept through me. Cohen was here.

I kept my grip on Clyde's vest and signaled him to go slowly as we clung to the cover of the trailers.

We moved east.

◆ ◆ ◆

"Charlie," came Dougie's voice in my ear. And a few minutes later, "Delta."

That was three targets, wired and ready to blow if we needed that. The big stuff, probably. The training center. The airport hangar. Maybe the Saudi planes.

Leverage.

Clyde and I moved forward, staying at a good pace despite our stops to duck behind cover and avoid the guards. Clyde halted at the corner of each structure and waited for my go-ahead before proceeding. After the third perfect performance, I took him off the lead.

Twice he lost the scent in the boom and shudder of the wind.

Each time my heart stopped. And each time he found the scent again, and we kept moving.

Our next dash took us to the training center. I caught a glimpse of the sign over the front door as we sped around to the back.

VALOR INDUSTRIES
TRAINING CENTER

At the back of the building, a section of the airplane hangar was just visible. Beyond that were the two jets parked outside and the runway. I kept my eye on a single door set smack in the middle of the otherwise featureless exterior wall.

"Frosty on," Dougie said. "They know we're here."

As if in response, the door flew open. Clyde and I slipped back around the corner and then to the nearest set of trailers. We crawled underneath. A minute later, two men walked by, accompanied by radio static.

"Fuckers blew him away," one of the men said.

Dougie's voice in my ear. "Six on patrol."

I waited until the sound of footsteps receded. "Roger. Proceeding to T3 and T4."

"I'm at Zeta."

The airplane hangar.

I peered out from beneath the trailer. No sign of movement. Clyde and I returned to the training center, sprinted past the now closed back door, and stopped at the far end.

The next cluster of trailers was a hundred yards away. No one was in sight. I gave Clyde the go sign, and together we dashed across the open space.

As soon as we reached the first trailer in the cluster, Clyde took a final sample of the air, then lay on the ground, his eyes on me, tail swishing through the weeds.

Just like that, he'd won the game.

He'd found Cohen.

We scooted into the dying grass that filled the two-foot space beneath the trailer. I shifted the rifle around to the front for accessibility, then pulled my Glock with the suppressor.

Voices floated down through the floor.

"You want me to keep going?" a man asked.

"Hold off," a woman said. "We might still need him."

Radio static. Then, "Ms. Almasi, there's a Detective Gorman from the Denver Major Crimes Unit to see you at Gate 2."

Well, that was certainly interesting.

"Get him the hell away." Laura Almasi. Her voice was a sexy rasp. A smoker's voice. "We have a situation here."

"I told him you weren't on the compound, but he says he saw your vehicle. Says he'll wait."

"He's been watching the road?" The rasp turned cold. "Tell him I'm in the middle of a meeting and will join him to go over his contract when I'm finished. Then suggest he and I meet at four o'clock at the Capital Grille instead. Let me know what he says."

"Roger that. Out."

Almasi said, "Cheap bastard like him, he'll want a contract *and* a free meal."

The man in the trailer chuckled.

With the man's laugh hanging in the air, I whispered over my radio microphone. "T3. Cohen is here."

Nothing.

The radio in the trailer crackled. "Ms. Almasi, the detective says he needs to ask you a few questions relating to the Jeremy Kane murder."

"Bastard's actually doing his job?" A pause. "Tell him I don't know how I can help, but regardless, he'll need to wait. These meetings can drag on. Don't offer any water or shade. If he insists on staying, let him bake for an hour or two."

"Roger. Out."

Overhead, the trailer creaked as someone moved.

"Bring him around," Almasi said.

There came the smack of flesh on flesh. A man groaned.

I gripped my pistol. The voices came from the north end of the trailer. I crept along the ground, heading toward the door set halfway down. I signaled Clyde twice to stay in place. *Stay. Really, stay.*

I didn't want him exposed during whatever came next.

"He's out," Almasi said. "Get some water."

The floor creaked as footsteps came down the length of the trailer and stopped directly overhead. Water splashed into a sink—the man was standing above me, a foot away from where I lay.

Time to act. Get the man while he was away from Cohen.

A lit fuse of adrenaline raced through my body and exploded in my chest. I closed my eyes and took a deep, steadying breath. I imagined Cohen and Almasi and the man she'd sent to get water. I pictured where they stood or sat, what weapons they might have.

Then I opened my eyes and slid through the grass, my passage covered by the sound of running water. I emerged near the door, stepped onto the first stair, and tried the knob.

It turned.

I wiped my sweaty palms on my thighs, then yanked the door open and leapt inside, pulling the door closed behind me and turning the lock even as I spun to the left. The man stood in a tiny kitchen, his left hand holding a water glass, his right working to free a gun. Beyond him, the trailer was empty.

The glass slipped from his hand and shattered against the linoleum floor. He brought the gun around.

I fired two shots with the suppressed Glock, center mass.

As he dropped, I whipped to the right. At the far end of the trailer a woman stood watching me, her mouth an O of surprise.

Two feet from her, Cohen sat with one hand cuffed to the chair, the other forced onto a table and duct taped at the wrist. He looked worse in person than he had in the photo. His eyes were closed, his head tipped back against the seat. My heart stopped until I saw the rise of his chest.

I told myself that later I would process how much they'd hurt him.

Right now, it was enough that he was alive.

My eyes went back to Almasi. Early sixties, iron-gray hair, eyes with an odd light in their gray-green depths.

"Hands up where I can see them," I said.

She raised her arms.

Behind me, the water still ran. The trailer was hot, the air close. Plumbing but no electricity. I looked over my shoulder. The man I'd shot was very dead. I moved to the end of the trailer, glanced at Cohen—who hadn't moved—then frisked Almasi. I stepped back, holstered the Glock, and snugged the M4 into my shoulder.

I centered the muzzle on her chest.

"Uncuff him," I said.

"I don't have the key."

"You can't spend all that Saudi money if you're dead."

The expression on her face changed, racing through a series of emotions that came and went so quickly I couldn't catalog them. Whatever else she was, Almasi was a complicated woman. But at the end, fury radiated off her like a furnace.

"Key is on the table," she said.

I held the gun between my shoulder and chin, swept up the key, and tossed it to her.

"Hurry," I said.

While she bent to Cohen, I lifted a slat on the blind. No one outside yet. At least not where I could see them.

"I have the bird," I murmured into the radio microphone.

Silence.

Cohen groaned.

"Mike," I said.

His eyes opened. "Sydney?"

To Almasi I said, "Now the tape."

She peeled the duct tape away from his arm.

"Help him stand."

She grabbed his wrists, braced herself, and pulled. Cohen slid forward an inch.

"Cohen!" I snapped. "On your feet!"

He jerked.

"Get him up," I said to Almasi, "or by fuck I will blow out your knees."

She pushed and pulled Cohen from the chair. He wobbled to his feet.

"Help him over. Bring the cuffs."

The anger in her face would have frightened Hades. But hell no longer scared me. Almasi draped Cohen's arm across her shoulders and braced her shoulder in his armpit. She grabbed the cuffs, and they hobbled toward me.

Cohen's face looked more battered than it had in the photo. The bruising ran down the side of his neck and disappeared beneath the collar of his shirt. The tips of three fingers on his right hand were taped.

His clothes were spattered with blood.

Process it later.

I peered out the slats. Two armed men now stood at the end of the corridor between the trailers.

When Cohen and Almasi were close enough, I took the cuffs and ordered her to bring her hands together in the front. I snapped on the cuffs and pocketed the key.

"Mike, can you walk on your own?"

His eyes met mine. The darkness I read there made me flinch. Maybe I was afraid of hell after all.

"Sydney." His voice sounded like they'd scraped down his vocal cords with a metal file. "Water."

I found another glass and filled it at the tap, my eyes on Almasi. He drank it down, and his eyes cleared a little.

I unslung the rifle and handed it to him. He took it with a nod.

It had been more than ten minutes since I'd told Dougie where we were. We needed a vehicle. I did not want to walk Almasi and an injured Cohen past armed guards.

I looked out the window again. The two men were conferring, and one pointed south, away from the trailer. They looked alert but not anxious. Given the size of the complex and the constant roar of the wind, they probably hadn't heard the shots. And since Almasi was using the trailer to torture a cop, my guess was she'd issued a do-not-disturb notice to everyone on the complex.

Her men didn't yet know I was inside.

I murmured into the mike. "T3."

Silence.

A third man joined the first two. They talked, and then all three moved away. *Now would be the perfect time to show up, Dougie.*

"All I want is the intel," Almasi said. "I assume you have it by now. Turn it over, and we can forget about all this. You go your way. I go mine. Nice and civilized."

She didn't look civilized. She looked like she wanted to hack out my eyes with a knife and then run them through a kitchen disposal.

But beneath the anger lay another emotion. I peered more closely at this woman who had occupied my nightmares for years. In my mind, I'd made her godlike—all-knowing, all-seeing, all-powerful. But here she stood in a sunbaked construction trailer in the middle of nowhere. A small, graying woman with age-spotted skin and a squint.

Nothing about her was what I'd expected, other than the rage.

Anger was often a cover for fear, or so my counselor said. I got that. I had plenty of both. But beneath Almasi's more obvious reactions I caught a flicker of something else.

"What?" she snapped at me, tired of my perusal.

Grief, I realized. What Almasi carried in her eyes was grief. The profound kind. The kind I'd seen at memorials and funerals and in the eyes of the chaplain when we carried bodies onto the base. The kind that breaks every bone in your body, but which you have no choice but to carry with you across a lifetime.

Something terrible had happened to her. Whatever it was didn't offer absolution for what she'd done. But it gave me a glimpse inside her armor.

I would give Dougie a few minutes more.

"Tell me about Kane," I said. "Was it the photos he took that tipped you off? Made you realize he'd connected Valor with the weapons smuggled into Iraq?"

She perched on the metal table where the keys had been. Probably she was okay with buying time, too. Give her men a chance to realize something was going down and move in.

The dice could roll either way.

Almasi cleared her throat. "The security cop? He was killed by a tramp."

"While you watched. Don't you trust your own people to do their work? Or do you just enjoy watching good men die?"

Cohen said, "She killed Kane?"

"She had him killed. Guy by the name of Mark Fadden did the dirty work."

Almasi said, "No one will believe such a crazy story."

"Fadden's dead," I said. "Just so you know."

"I don't know anyone named Fadden." But she smiled. Probably all to her benefit that her hired hand was dead. Hard to testify from the grave.

"What I'd like to know, while we're standing around being civilized"—my voice was thick—"is *why*. Why you told your brother, James, to allow those weapons into Iraq. Why you told him to send a special-ops team on a mission and then let the bad guys know they were coming. Why you had to kill innocents like Malik's mother, who was only trying to help us."

I was guessing about who'd given the orders, but it sounded right. I felt a cold satisfaction when I read the truth in her eyes.

She was—in fact—our Alpha.

I stole another glance out the window. The stretch of grass lay empty.

Almasi said, "*Why* is a complicated question."

I looked at her cold face, the arrogant confidence that she would not only get away with her crimes but profit from them. In that moment I didn't care what tragedy might have motivated her. Rage exploded through me, unspooling lines of fire through my veins like heated wire.

I pushed her back down the length of the trailer and into the chair where Cohen had been sitting. I yanked my knife from my pocket and opened the blade. Her eyes went wide, and her pulse leapt in her throat.

I looked around, found the roll of duct tape, and sawed off a length, which I slapped over her mouth.

Her face turned ashen.

I grabbed the table they'd used with Cohen. The surface was red and sticky.

"Sydney," Cohen said. "We need to go."

"Not yet. We're waiting for a ride."

I looked on the floor and found the pliers she'd dropped.

"Is this what they used on you?" I asked Cohen.

He looked at me, then at Almasi. He nodded.

I leaned my weight into her, pressing her into the chair, and grabbed her manacled hands. I forced them onto the table.

She bucked in the chair, curling her fingers tight into her palms, her skin slick with sudden sweat. I wrenched her left ring finger free and pressed it down, holding it in place.

Cohen moved to the other side of the table. I didn't risk a glance, afraid of what I might see in his face. Approval or condemnation. Both terrified me.

Then he took the duct tape, used his teeth to tear off a length and strapped down her wrists above the cuffs. She kicked her feet against the floor and rocked her body. The chair banged against the floor.

"She killed Jeremy Kane," Cohen said.

"And a lot of other people."

"And she's the one who wants to kill the boy you went to find. And you."

"That's her."

A muscle jumped in his cheek. "I'll do it."

"This won't look good in a trial."

"Doesn't matter." He held out his hand. "I know exactly how it's done."

I glanced at his bandaged fingers, then gave him the pliers.

He pressed the tip just under the left side of her fingernail. A bead of blood appeared. She gave a muffled scream behind the gag.

I leaned in. "You feel ready to talk now?"

She nodded hard, her breathing labored, the pulse in her throat galloping with her heart.

"Smart woman. I'm going to remove the tape. Make a sound, you lose the nail. Understand?"

Another nod.

I kept my grip on her finger while I peeled back the tape, ready to slap it on again if she drew breath to scream.

Her eyes stayed on the pliers.

I said, "Let's start with your husband."

"What?" Her eyes darted to me, and two spots of pink appeared on her cheeks.

"Arvin Almasi. Let's talk about him."

"We haven't been together in years."

"But you're still married, aren't you? Still protecting his family in Iran."

"His family can rot in hell."

"Not his family," Cohen said. "Her child."

Almasi's lips drew back, and she made a guttural snarl. But side by side with her wrath came a flicker of panic.

"Shut up," she said.

"I heard her on the phone," he went on. "She has a daughter in Iran."

She snapped her teeth. "You're wrong."

But pieces of the puzzle jostled into place, the outline of a picture taking shape.

Not greed. Blackmail.

I said, "Is she Arvin's?"

She lifted her chin and stared us both down. "Fools. Both of you."

"He's blackmailing you with the life of your child." Here it was. That grief. Some of my rage ebbed before a dull gray sweep of horror. "You and Arvin married just before the 1979 revolution that put the Islamists in power. He was an engineer who claimed to be madly in love with you. You had a child together."

"You're wrong."

I nodded to Cohen, and he brought the pliers back to her finger. She squirmed. "Stop! Please."

"Then explain it to us," I said.

"Yes. Just please stop."

Cohen lowered the pliers.

She said, "When I met Arvin, I was a widow living in Iran with my daughter. I was there to help my father negotiate a contract with the Iranian government. This was two years before the revolution." Her eyes turned red, and she blinked. "Arvin was home after studying in the US. We fell in love. Got married. At first, everything was good. Arvin adopted my daughter. We were happy. Then we began to hear rumors of rebellion."

"And Arvin was part of that."

"Not at first. But he changed. As an engineer, he was highly respected. Useful. Men came to him shortly before the shah fell. They flattered him, told him how important he was. But what they really wanted was Valor's weapons. I told Arvin this, but he was a fool. He listened to their flattery."

I let loose of her and straightened. The flat light of the sun filtering through the blinds felt oddly cool. "If you were worried, why didn't you leave?"

"I meant to. I was going to walk away from Arvin and take my daughter and get out of there. But I had to close down our offices, get our staff out of the country. I thought I had time." Her gaze went away, staring into the past. "Then the embassy fell."

The picture came into focus. "Much later, he let you leave. But he kept your daughter."

"Miriam," she whispered. "He took her from me."

Her shoulders dropped, and her fear for herself slipped away. In its place came an expression I'd seen once or twice on my own mother's face. A naked panic you find only in a parent's eyes.

"He placed her with a family. I was allowed to see her only every month or so. He promised it was just for six months. Then a year." Her head sank to her manacled hands. She spoke into her fingers. "Then three. I was helpless. I had no rights in the new Iran. After three years he sent me back to Texas. He needed me to make sure the ayatollah's government got what it wanted. He kept Miriam so that I would do as he asked."

"And did you?"

"What choice did I have? Miriam. . . . she and I talk. She doesn't understand why I left. She has no idea what Arvin did. But she is healthy. Happy."

I looked at her bowed head. The sensible haircut and shoes. The heavily veined hands with the neatly trimmed nails I'd been angry enough to actually rip out. This woman had permitted the deaths of American troops. Had ordered the torture and deaths of who knew how many others. By any definition, she was a monster.

But for a few moments, she was also a mother. And what wouldn't a mother do to save her child? What wouldn't she sacrifice, even if what she ransomed wasn't hers to give?

A terrible story of treachery and deceit, with a child standing on each end. Miriam, the first bargaining chip. Malik, the final pawn.

And Laura Almasi in the middle, determined to sacrifice one to protect the other.

Cohen handed me the pliers and moved away to look out the window.

"Anyone?" I asked him.

"Not yet."

To Almasi I said, "And Arvin is still in Iran?"

"Mexico. He left three months ago."

My heart was already racing, but it managed to find the accelerator. "He's hunting for Malik."

"Yes. But I imagine he's also recruiting for one of Iran's terrorist organizations. That's what he does."

I pictured Zarif's compound. The privacy. The security. His determination not to be seen with me, and his insistence that I leave the country. Maybe he, too, was a hunter, looking for men like Arvin Almasi.

"Given how many people you've killed," I said, "I'm surprised your husband is still breathing."

"He dies of anything but natural causes, Miriam dies, too."

Of course.

"You've done as he's asked for years," I said. "Would he really hurt Miriam now? You could take this to the Feds. Offer a plea deal—Arvin for you. Expose him for what he is. Then take it all the way to the White House and have them demand your daughter's return. Why keep making this worse?"

"He *will* hurt her. When she was twenty, I told Arvin this had to stop. I said I would tell Miriam what he'd done. He hired a man to snatch her off the street, to rough her up. A warning." She was blinking faster now, holding back the tears. The rage had dissolved, and pain held full sway. "She has her own life now. A husband and children. My silence buys her life and that of her family. Valor is all I have left. And my brother. If I am in prison, we lose everything. And the Iranians win."

"This place here. You're training men who will turn around and train the Saudis?"

She lifted her chin. "The enemy of my enemy is my friend."

"Meaning what, exactly?"

"James will win that contract to help the Saudis. We will teach them. Arm them. I cannot guarantee Saudi Arabia will try to destroy Iran. But with James's help, I can promise that Iran will never get the thing it most craves. It will never be the leader of the Muslim world."

Cohen spun away from the window. He bore down on us, his eyes ablaze with murder. He thrust out his hands, and I thought he would slam the table into Almasi.

Then he stopped abruptly. He lowered his hands and gave a soft shake of his head.

He said, "You killed Jeremy Kane because he discovered what you were doing out here. He was connecting the dots, and that threatened to ruin your plans."

She stayed silent.

He leaned on the table and thrust his face into hers. "And if the Feds learned of your agreement with Iran, you'd lose everything. Your daughter. Your business. Your aspirations. You'd spend a couple of decades in prison and come out so old you'd piss yourself every time you rolled over in bed."

She reared back. "Miriam. Arvin would—God knows what he would do."

"You'll never stop, will you?" He grabbed her head. "You'll keep killing and killing, knocking everyone out of your way as if they were nothing more than pieces on a chessboard."

His knuckles whitened, and the tendons stood out as his hands tightened against her skull.

She moaned.

Part of me wanted him to kill her. Part of me knew he wouldn't be able to live with himself if he did.

I touched his shoulder. "We need to go."

He looked at me, his chest heaving with his rage. "If we leave her, she'll kill us."

"No, she won't. She knows that if we die, the video she wants goes to every news agency in the country." I touched him again. "Come on."

Cohen held on a moment longer. Then he shuddered and dropped his hands. He shot me a look I couldn't read and returned to the window.

But Almasi smiled, a straight seam in the granite of her face, as cryptic as the *Mona Lisa*'s.

"What video?" she said.

My hand brushed the pocket holding my phone. I hadn't heard from Sarge, who should have boarded the plane by now.

And nothing from Dougie.

"We have company inbound," Cohen said. "Two men."

"Guards?"

He nodded. "That ride coming?"

"I don't think so."

My gaze met his. A question stood in his eyes as clearly as if he'd spoken. He was asking who I was. What I was willing to do. Which lines I would back down from and which lines I would cross.

I knew he was asking himself the same questions.

"This is your show," he said. "You've been fighting this battle as long as I've known you. I'll play it however you want."

I nodded.

We could throw open the door and shoot the men before they knew what happened. Dougie would have told us to do just that.

He would have been right.

But every death leaves a mark, no matter the justification. No matter what you might tell yourself. Ask any combat veteran. Or any cop who's had to fire on someone.

My eyes went to the man I'd killed, lying on the floor of the tiny kitchen.

We all have to live with our ghosts.

I dropped the pliers, returned to Almasi, and pushed aside the table. "Looks like you're our golden ticket."

I yanked away the tape and lifted her out of the chair. She wasn't a big woman, but she seemed made of iron—rigid and strong. I pulled her close and pressed the muzzle of the Glock to her temple.

"Know this," I told her. "Your life means nothing to me. Less than nothing. Because as long as you're alive, I'm dead. So if you don't convince your men to let us pass, I will blow your brains out." I shook her. "You still have something to lose. Remember that when you're talking to those men out there."

Her throat moved as she swallowed. "I understand."

Cohen went to stand by the door. Our eyes met again, and in his I saw an echo of my own rage, formed by his realization that darkness was not only ever present, but also wide reaching.

For a moment, I thought the dark would swamp him.

But he shook it off. "We're going to fix this."

"Yes, we are. But first, we've got to get out of here. Don't leave my side."

"Like shit on a shoe."

I thought he had the shoe and the shit mixed up, but I didn't argue.

"Okay," I said. "Here we go."

I half dragged Laura to the door. "Tell your men to hold their fire. Shout it so they can hear you. We're going out."

"You want to be Butch Cassidy?" Cohen asked. "Or the Sundance Kid?"

CHAPTER 26

You can do everything for the right reasons, and still fuck it up.

—Sydney Parnell. Personal journal.

"Don't shoot!" Laura said as I kicked open the trailer door.

I shook her. "Louder."

"Hold your fire!"

We emerged from the trailer into the heat and wind. The sun stood almost directly overhead, casting everything in high relief and giving the world an over-bright feel of unreality, as if we were actors on a studio set. The only sounds were the unrelenting distant snap of plastic and the creak of Cohen's footsteps as he moved down the stairs and took a position to my left, the M4 comfortable in his arms.

Clyde remained beneath the trailer. Silent.

Safe.

Another man had joined the first two. All three had their weapons tight on us, fingers in the trigger guards. Their eyes moved back and forth between me and Cohen, assessing.

"Nobody panic," I said.

I dragged Almasi down a couple of feet to the section of the trailer that held the kitchen. The refrigerator would provide extra coverage in case someone decided to try a shot from the other side.

Cohen followed.

The men swiveled, tracking us.

They were professionals—early to midthirties, athletic builds, all of them wearing a casual uniform of cargo pants and black T-shirts. No Kevlar—which suggested a careless degree of confidence. They stood with their feet apart, rifles snugged comfortably into the meaty part of their shoulders as they leaned ever so slightly forward, mirrored sunglasses glinting in the light.

Only their taut jaws betrayed any uncertainty.

I tightened my forearm against Almasi's throat. "Their weapons. Tell them."

Almasi said, "Put down your guns."

"Bad idea, ma'am," said one of the men. A Latino with close-cropped hair and a tattoo that snaked out from under his sleeve and twined around his forearm and wrist.

"Almasi." I pressed the gun harder against her skull. "Be convincing."

"Put down your weapons!" she said in a voice that promised to flatten everything in its way.

"Ma'am, we can't—"

"Now!"

The men eased their guns to the ground—at least the guns we could see.

"Now, flat on the ground," I said. "Good. Lace your fingers behind your heads and cross your ankles."

The men complied.

"Any of you so much as breathe hard," Cohen said, "I will shoot you."

I imagined Dougie's voice in my head. *Shoot each one. Back of the head. Do it fast and get out.*

I pushed Laura down to her knees and crossed to the two closest men. I collected their rifles and slung the straps over my shoulder. Then I patted them down and found three more pistols. I cleared the guns and tossed the ammo in one direction, the guns in the other.

I approached the third man. He lay farther away, near the end of the passageway between the trailers, where the corners led to blind spots. As I approached, he looked up.

"Eat dirt," I said.

He lowered his head.

With the Glock extended, I checked each corner—nothing. I turned back toward the third man, then heard a faint scuff in the dirt behind me. I spun around as a bearded man moved into position from the far side of the trailer, his location blocked from Cohen's line of fire.

He grinned at me over his pistol. "Drop the gun. Now, hands up."

I lifted them. Strapped across my back, the rifles clanked together.

Cohen said, "Don't move," to one of the men. Then, "Sydney?"

"I've got this."

"Bit of a troublemaker, aren't you?" The bearded man was still grinning. Maybe thinking about his bonus in next week's paycheck.

Training, I told myself. It was all in the training.

I kept my eyes on the man as I curled my fingers in toward my palms. A crease appeared between his eyes. But he didn't have time to puzzle it over.

Clyde rocketed out from beneath the trailer and sailed across the ground, his lips peeled back in a silent snarl. The man screamed as Clyde leapt and sank his teeth into flesh. My partner's momentum drove them both to the ground, Clyde a furious storm on top.

The man yelled a string of curses. He still had a grip on his gun and was trying to work it under Clyde's belly.

I scooped up the Glock.

"Out!" I yelled to Clyde.

The man kicked and thrashed, his heels pounding the ground.

"Clyde, out!"

Always the toughest part of the job—getting a Belgian Malinois to let go of his prey. But Avi and I had drilled Clyde on this over and over, and this time Clyde heard me. Or maybe he heard my desperation.

He released the man and danced away.

The man raised his pistol, his focus still on Clyde. I fired. The bullet plowed into his navel, ran up his chest, and exploded out the back of his spine. I fired again. The second bullet entered below his ribs and exited his shoulder in a bloody spray.

He twitched, then lay still.

I spun around. The other three men remained prone. Someone muttered, "Shit."

"You good?" Cohen said as I approached.

"I'm good."

I hauled Almasi to her feet. She was red faced and sweating, strands of hair clinging to her damp cheeks, her eyes bright with fury.

"I need the keys to one of the SUVs," I said.

"Fuck you."

"I still have those pliers."

Her eyes promised one thing. That someday I would be at her mercy. And she would have none.

She pointed with her manacled hands.

Clyde and I walked over to the man she'd indicated, a hulk with white-blond hair, and dug my toe into his stomach. "Keys?"

He ground out the words. "Right front pocket."

His right hand edged down.

I pressed the Glock to the back of his neck. "Don't." I crouched, slid my hand into his pocket, and pulled out the keys. Clyde and I returned to the trailer.

"Let's go."

I was looking back at the three when a hole opened between the shoulder blades of the man with the white-blond hair, accompanied by the meaty smack of high-velocity metal drilling flesh. From somewhere east of us came a soft *pock*, like the sound of champagne popping.

The man twitched, then lay still.

Almasi dropped to a crouch, hands over her head. Cohen shoved me against the trailer wall. "The hell?"

The white-blond man didn't move. Two more swift *pock*s and neither did the others.

Dougie's voice sounded in my ear. "We've got movers coming in from the east. Get out. I'll cover you."

"Sydney?" Cohen said.

I unshouldered the M4s I'd collected and laid them on the ground. "Company's coming. We have to move fast."

I ordered Almasi to her feet. "Slow us down, I'll shoot you."

She rose without protest. Her face said all the fight had gone out of her.

We moved along the cluster of trailers, not stopping to clear the corners. The periodic burst of gunfire told me Dougie was true to his word.

He said, "Get across the field."

"Cut left," I told Cohen as we approached the end of the row. "Sniper's got us covered."

We burst into the sunshine. The parking lot was two hundred yards away across a stretch of weedy ground. A quick sprint for everyone except maybe Almasi.

I glanced to my left. Three vehicles heading our way, still distant but closing the gap. Sunlight glinted off their bumpers and mirrors, their headlights hazy in the undulations of heated air rising from the ground.

"Move," Dougie said.

Almasi stared at the field, then sank to a crouch and buried her face in her hands.

"I'll get the car," Cohen said.

I squinted in the direction of the approaching vehicles. Still a long way off. I tossed him the keys, and he snatched them out of the air. Our eyes met briefly, and in his I saw a riot of conflicting emotions. Fear, understanding, anger. And beneath all of it, what I chose to see as love.

Then he spun on his heel and took off across the field.

Clyde, sensing the game was changing, had his eyes on mine.

"Go with Cohen," I said, wanting my partner out of reach of the reinforcements.

Clyde raced after the detective.

"More movers to the south," Dougie said. "I need you to get across that field in the next five."

"Roger that."

I jammed my hands under Almasi's arms and hauled her to her feet. She sagged against me, and I pushed her upright. She was weeping. She staggered forward a few steps, then stopped. Her head drooped, and her chest heaved as she sucked for air.

"Can't," she wheezed.

I pushed her again. "Can. And will."

She lifted her head. Her moist eyes held a dull cast like those of fish laid out on ice. A froth of spittle glistened at the corner of her mouth.

"Move," I said. "Or you'll never see your daughter again."

She moved.

The parking lot seemed a thousand miles away, the world vaster than it had been an hour earlier. The field carried the exposure of mountaintops. My spine drew as tight as a piano wire, waiting for a bullet.

Halfway across the field, Almasi stumbled and went down.

"Get up," I said.

She rose to her hands and knees, head down, body swaying.

"Come on," I said.

But she stayed in the weeds. "Go ahead. Shoot me."

Dougie said, "Leave her."

"She's our protection," I said.

I bent over and grabbed her around the waist.

She twisted at the hips as I pulled, and her arms came up fast. Her manacled hands slammed into my temple. Pain burst in my head like a bomb going off. I staggered, then went down hard, my head striking the ground. My gun flew into the weeds.

Then she was on top of me, her knees pinning my elbows as she pressed the handcuffs against my throat. In her right hand she held a knife. My knife.

"How's it feel?" she snarled.

The blade was a whisker's breadth from my eye. Sunlight glinted on the steel as she turned the tip toward my eye.

I raised my knees and hips to buck her off. My own momentum pushed the knife forward. It slid into my flesh at the cheekbone. Pain roared its fire across my face.

"First blood," Almasi said.

On the edge of my vision, I caught a blur of gold and black. Clyde. He had seen me go down and now was running toward us, his body a bullet arced in our direction.

The knife bit a second time.

"Second blood," she said. Her eyes bulged, wild and savage, her lips peeled back from her teeth, spittle slicking her chin. She shoved all her weight against my throat.

I got one arm free and grabbed her wrist.

Then I heard Clyde yelp. An instant later, the sound of a rifle cracked across the world.

The bastards had shot Clyde.

Rage fizzed across my brain, popping and sparking behind my eyes.

I let go of Almasi's wrist and scrabbled for the holster on my belt, my hand soft with sweat and sliding around the leather as I dug for steel. My fingers found the handle, and I worked them around the grip of the knockoff TASER I'd gotten in Mexico. I jerked it free, pressed the gun against her ribs, and squeezed the trigger.

Her body jerked and flailed as the twenty thousand–volt jolt hit. Her eyes went wide, and a guttural shriek tore out of her throat. Fire licked up my own arm—the knife making its final mark against my flesh as she convulsed.

I shoved her off, rolled over, and crawled toward Clyde.

"I'm coming, boy," I whispered.

He lay on his side in the weeds, his right leg tucked under him. When he saw me, he lifted his head and whined. He tried to get up.

"Stay down."

A puff of dust rose as a bullet struck the ground twenty feet away. A second one came closer. The lead SUV roared toward us, but now another vehicle cut across the field from the parking lot, tires slewing in the dirt, the horn blaring to make sure we knew he was coming.

Cohen.

I curled next to Clyde, my body between his and the oncoming vehicles. His tail gave a single thump, and he tried to lick my face.

Blood streaked his fur, just outside the protection of the Kevlar vest.

In my ear Dougie said, "Get up. Get out of there."

Cohen brought the vehicle to a shuddering stop, placing the SUV between us and the Alpha's reinforcements roaring toward us. The driver's door flew open, and Cohen jumped out.

I rose to a crouch.

"Come on, boy, we gotta go."

Clyde tried to rise, but his right hind leg folded beneath him.

Cohen crouched on the other side of my partner, and we slid our arms under Clyde's belly.

"On three," Cohen said.

Clyde stayed quiet as we lifted him. He turned his head, licking the tears where they mingled with blood on my face as we carried him to the truck.

Around us, the rattle of gunfire filled the air. Dougie, laying down covering fire.

"How close are the SUVs?" I asked Cohen.

"Close." Then, "I got him. Open the door."

I slipped my arms free and yanked the back door open. I scooted in to help Cohen ease Clyde across the seat and rested my partner's head in my lap.

"You're going to be fine, boy," I told him.

He closed his eyes.

Cohen closed the door and jumped into the driver's seat. He slammed the truck into gear and spun it around to face east. I wiped blood from my face and watched through the rear window as the lead SUV swerved to the left while the one immediately behind peeled off to the right.

"They're going to try to head us off," I said.

"We'll outrun them."

Cohen accelerated across the field. The truck jounced on the rough terrain, dust pelting the windows and lifting in a plume behind us. I caught a glimpse of Almasi off to the right, struggling to rise.

A line of holes appeared in the windshield of the SUV on our left. The vehicle swerved sharply, then rolled to a stop.

"Running low on ammo," Dougie said.

"We'll be at the back door of the Country Club in three." To Cohen I said, "Get us to the rear of the brick building."

I braced myself with one hand and held Clyde in place with the other as Cohen rocketed the SUV across the open space and along the side of the building. At the corner, he slammed on the brakes and took the turn wide, the tires jittering in the dirt. He accelerated again along the back of the building.

The back door burst open, and Dougie ran out. Cohen hit the brakes again, bringing the SUV to a stop in front of the door. Dougie threw himself into the passenger seat, and Cohen accelerated away from the building toward a narrow dirt track that led south to the airplane hangar.

Clyde lifted his head and softly moaned. I rubbed his ears.

Dougie leaned over the back seat, his face a thundercloud. "How is he?"

"He can't put weight on that leg." My mind was screaming down a list of things that could be wrong. Shattered bone, severed nerves, bullet fragments grinding their way through soft tissue.

"Soon as we get out of here, I'll take a look." Dougie ran a light hand over Clyde's flank. Clyde flinched and pulled away.

"You're hurting him," I said.

"He can move his leg. That's good." Dougie looked at me. "He'll be okay, Rosie."

Behind us, one SUV and then the second came around the building and accelerated in our direction.

Dougie dropped back in his seat. "They must be the guards from the security booth near the highway."

Ahead of us, sunlight glinted off a chain-link fence—the one Dougie and I had seen from the ridge.

Cohen's eyes were on the rearview mirror. "They're gaining."

"Turn left," Dougie said. "There's a gate farther down."

I leaned forward. "Can't we ram the fence?"

Dougie shook his head. "The airbags will deploy, which could cut off the fuel supply. Plus, we want to funnel them through the gate."

I didn't ask what he had in mind.

Cohen made a hard left, and we sped along the fence. The pursuing SUVs left the track and angled across the field.

"I can't outrun them," Cohen said.

Dougie rolled down the window and picked up the M4. "Just get us through the gate."

He half crawled out the window with the rifle, braced his legs, and began firing over the roof as our car bucked on the rough road. The staccato rattle of the gun sounded like an earthquake.

Behind us, weeds and dirt flew into the air, and headlights shattered. The SUVs dropped back but kept coming.

"Get inside," Cohen yelled as we reached the gate.

Dougie dropped back into the cab, and Cohen jerked the wheel hard. We skidded through the opening and bounced onto the road that ran to the runway.

"They're going to reach us," I said.

"No," Dougie said. "They won't."

As the first SUV reached the gate, a ball of flame exploded into life with a savage boom, red-orange flames licking out, the mass roiling with dark clouds. Sections of fence appeared in the sky like startled crows. Our truck shuddered as dirt and debris pelted glass and metal.

Leverage.

The first vehicle leapt into the air as if from a catapult and came down on its side. A second later, the driver's door popped open, and a man crawled out. He reached back to help a second man as fluids in the engine ignited.

Cohen accelerated onto the runway.

A series of booms echoed across the prairie. Beyond the SUVs, smoke poured from the high windows of the training center, and a tongue of flame licked out. A fissure appeared halfway up the wall; then, in slow motion, the building collapsed in a cloud of dust.

Two seconds later, one of the construction trailers shot into the air on a current of flame. Then a second one.

"How much explosive did you have?" I asked.

"I found additional supplies."

Now I knew what had taken him so long.

I glanced back at the airport hangar and felt something cold in my stomach as I imagined multimillion-dollar jets exploding, the flames sweeping across the dry prairie. "Is there more?"

Dougie wore a look of grim satisfaction. "Not for the moment."

Cohen cut the wheel, and we left the runway and went cross-country, barreling over the fields toward the highway. Behind us, flames shot into the air.

We hit Highway 36 and skidded onto the asphalt, burning rubber.

A minute later, we pulled into the lane of oncoming traffic and shot around a brown sedan trundling toward Denver. I glanced over as we went by.

Gorman sat behind the wheel, eating a sandwich while the world burned behind him.

CHAPTER 27

God teaches forgiveness. But he first cleaned house.

—*Avi Harel. Former Mossad K9 Trainer.*

"I'm worried about Clyde," I said.

"Swap places with me," Dougie said. "I'll take a look."

Cohen pulled over to the side of the road. We'd traveled at least twenty miles from the compound with no sign of pursuit. Dougie's bombs were keeping Almasi's people busy—the billows of smoke and ash rising from the bombed structures looked like a huddle of frightened sheep on the horizon.

"I'm not going far, buddy," I whispered to Clyde as I eased out from beneath him.

I'd removed his vest and harness, given him all our water, then held his head and murmured prayers while Cohen and Dougie sat in the front and swapped name, rank, and serial numbers.

I was pretty rusty when it came to having any kind of conversation with God. The last time we'd chatted, I might have said a few unkind things. But if he was listening, I hoped maybe he'd just be happy to hear from me again. Like getting a phone call from a child you'd all but written off.

Clyde moved his head to watch me as I opened the door and stepped out into a searing heat so dry it felt like poison filling my lungs. A swirl of wind and dust entered the cab, and Clyde whimpered.

Then Dougie appeared at the door. "Hey, pal, we're okay."

Clyde quieted.

I held the door open against the wind as Dougie climbed in.

"I haven't heard from Sarge," I said. "And he isn't picking up."

Dougie looked at his watch. "He's probably boarding. We'll talk to him as soon as he lands."

I thought of Almasi's *Mona Lisa* smile, the one she'd shown when I mentioned the video.

"You're probably right," I said.

Dougie heard my uncertainty. "One thing I've learned, Rosie. Worrying won't help."

I felt a slap of anger. "This is Sarge we're talking about."

He leaned in and touched his forehead to mine. "The more we care, the more we need to tell ourselves we don't. It's how we keep our feet."

Lessons from the war. If it matters, shove it into a box.

I caught Cohen's eyes on me as I stepped away. He had to be wondering how Dougie and I knew each other. And why we were together.

As soon as I was in the front seat, Cohen put the vehicle in gear and popped back onto the road. A mass of tumbleweeds hit the front bumper, pulled free, then went sailing past.

In the back seat, Dougie opened his backpack. He'd brought the same supplies he'd used to treat me at the hotel, and now he went to work.

"Okay, pal," he said. "Let's see what we're dealing with."

I unbuckled and leaned over the seat. Dougie snapped on disposable gloves, then gently examined the wounds while Clyde turned his head and rolled his eyes, trying to watch.

"Near as I can tell, it's a clean shot through the muscles on the back side of his femur," Dougie said. "Lateral entry and exit wounds. He needs surgery, but I don't think any bones are involved."

"That's good," Cohen said.

"It's better than good. Turn off the a/c. We need to keep him warm." He braced himself as the road curved. "Let's start with a happy pill."

He reached into his kit, pulled out a blister pack, and broke the foil.

"Thirty milligrams of morphine," he said.

He crouched on the floor. In a single deft motion, he grasped Clyde's snout with his left hand and used his fingers to pry open Clyde's mouth. He placed the pill on the back of Clyde's tongue, then rubbed Clyde's throat to get him to swallow.

"Good job, pal."

Clyde looked betrayed.

"What's next?" I asked.

"Pressure bandage." He removed a plastic bag labeled EMERGENCY BANDAGE—TRAUMA WOUND DRESSING. He applied gauze to the injuries, then gently placed the compression bandage and began unfurling the mesh wrap. Clyde moaned when Dougie reached underneath him and pulled the wrapping around. But Dougie moved too fast to give Clyde much chance to object. He pulled the wrapping through a clip, then wound the bandage back around the other way and tightened it.

All the while he talked reassuring nonsense in a soft voice.

I stared at the bandage. Some things you can't shove into a box. "Will he be able to use that leg again?"

"As long as the bullet didn't hit the sciatic nerve. That's the biggest risk, I think. But I'm hopeful. We got lucky—the round passed laterally and front to back. The most important thing now is to keep him stabilized and get him into surgery. We're heading to a veterinarian, right?"

"In Denver," I said, getting a nod from Cohen.

Dougie rubbed my partner's head until Clyde drifted off on a morphine cloud. Then he made room for himself against the door and leaned his head on the seat back. "I'm going to catch a few."

He closed his eyes and settled in. It was a gift he'd had as long as I'd known him. The ability to sleep on a dime.

I turned back around. A gust of wind rocked the truck and slapped dust against the windows.

"Sounds like Clyde's doing okay," Cohen said.

"For now."

"And Superman? How's he doing?"

I read between the lines. "Dougie is an old friend. From the war."

Cohen opened his mouth. Closed it. Finally said, "Okay."

We left it at that.

Cohen drove with a heavy foot and a deft touch. He had to be in incredible pain, but he shouldered that just like he shouldered everything else. Like he could just keep taking bricks, no matter how many life piled on.

The right side of his face didn't look bad. But on the left, the bruises were a vivid purple, his left eye a slit against the swelling. His injured ear seeped blood. My eyes were drawn to the taped fingers on his right hand where—I assumed—Almasi had ripped out the nails.

I should have taken the pliers and used them while I had the chance.

"How about you?" I asked.

"Just need a few bandages and some lidocaine."

"Tough guy."

"Learned from a master." He took in my face and then tipped his head toward my arm. "She got you."

I looked down at angry flesh that was only now beginning to hurt. My side and face burned.

"She played me," I said.

"She played us all." He rubbed the back of his neck. "I think I really would have done it. Ripped out her fingernails. I just needed an excuse.

If she hadn't talked—" His voice sounded like flesh tearing on a hook. "All I could hear when we were standing in that trailer was my blood, roaring in my ears. Like having a hurricane in my head. I had no idea I was that person."

"You aren't that person. You can't judge yourself because for a few minutes you wanted to hurt someone who hurt you. She was going to *kill* you. If you want to be angry at someone, be angry at me. I'm the one who put you in that position."

"You didn't put the pliers in my hand."

"But I brought a shitload of violence into your life."

He was silent for a time. Then he said, "I've been mad plenty of times. But I've never been so angry that I couldn't trust myself."

"Mike. Stop." I took off my cap and shoved back my sweat-dampened hair. "I should have told you sooner what was going on. If I had, maybe this wouldn't have happened."

"Ah, Christ, I don't know. I'm the one who pushed you into a relationship." His eyes went to the rearview mirror, and I knew he was looking at Dougie. "Could be I pushed too hard."

"You were right to push. I needed to be pushed. I hope—" I pressed the heels of my hands to my eyes, then dropped them and looked him full-on. "I hope you don't regret that."

He tapped his palm on the steering wheel and didn't meet my eyes. "It's been a rough couple of days. I just need a little time."

"You kicking me out?"

His laugh was weak. "Fucking Marine. I'd be afraid to try."

Not the answer I was hoping for. I snugged my cap back on and turned away, staring out the window at the land rolling past, at the miles and miles of empty ground stretched like an offering beneath the faded wash of sky. The prairie was starkly beautiful with its spikes of yucca, its shimmering hues of gold, the occasional splash of emerald where groundwater seeped.

But the vast reaches of its desolation felt like a metaphor for an empty heart.

"I was kidding," Cohen said so softly I wasn't sure I heard him.

I summoned up a nod because one seemed required.

"Sydney." His voice was still raw. From what he'd suffered or from what all this had cost him, I wasn't sure. "I was angry that you didn't trust me enough to tell me the truth. But that doesn't mean I don't love you."

He loved me.

That was the good news. But something weighted his voice, and I finally realized it was the other shoe, poised to drop.

"Go on." I looked at him, because that seemed required, too. Like refusing the blindfold at your execution.

He flattened his hand, ran his palm along his forehead. "I just—you bring a lot with you. And not all of it is good."

Another nod. Me, being agreeable.

Behind us, the horizon smoked and burned—fire and ash and dust.

I called Avi and told him about Clyde, and shared what Dougie had said about the injury.

"Call me when you are ten minutes out," Avi said. "Then bring him around to the back. We will be ready."

A while after that we hit Denver and pushed through the early start of rush hour, weaving through traffic, sometimes using the shoulder when we hit an impassable snarl. Dougie and Clyde snoozed on, oblivious. I directed Cohen to merge onto I-70 and keep heading west to the exit for Washington Street. From there, he should proceed north toward East 58th.

"The North Washington area? We'll be heading into warehouses."

"It's where Clyde's trainer has his center. No neighbors to bother when the dogs bark."

"And he's a veterinarian?"

"The best. He used to train and care for K9s for Mossad. I wouldn't trust anyone else."

As soon as signs for the National Western Complex building appeared, I called Avi and told him we were fifteen minutes out.

Twelve minutes after that, Cohen pulled into the parking lot of a vast, nondescript warehouse surrounded by an eight-foot fence and without a single sign to give away what happened inside. I directed him to drive along the side of the structure and into a second lot in the back. Dougie woke as we parked, switching immediately from crashed out to full-on alert.

Avi met us with a gurney and two techs wearing surgery gowns and caps. Gently we eased Clyde out of the vehicle and placed him on the stretcher. The techs rolled him into the building, and the rest of us hurried after.

Inside, another tech joined in, and Avi's team jumped into action. They got oxygen on Clyde, inserted an IV catheter into his front leg, and checked his vitals while Avi examined the wound.

Awake now, Clyde rolled his eyes toward me, probably more bewildered by the attention than the pain. He was still on a morphine high. I couldn't get close enough to touch him, but I put everything I had into my eyes.

He quieted.

Avi finished his exam and stepped back. He glared at me, then softened as he took in my wounds and Cohen's. "I thought you were on vacation."

"Things got out of hand."

"You seem to have that gift." He turned to Dougie. "You are the medic?"

"Yes, sir. All handlers are taught basic veterinary care."

Avi looked at me, then back to Dougie, connecting the dots while Dougie filled him in on what he'd done to treat Clyde, including the morphine.

"You can stay," Avi said to Dougie. Then he pointed at me. "You go to the hospital."

"It's not an option right now."

"Then go to the other examination room. I will send one of my techs to take a look. Him, too. Cohen, right? This is your detective? What were you guys doing today? No, do not tell me. Do not ask, do not tell, good policy." He rounded on one of the techs. "We need X-rays. What are you waiting for?"

"You're going to be fine, Clyde," I said. "I love you."

The last thing I saw before Avi closed the door was Dougie in a disposable cap and mask standing next to my partner.

Handler and K9, together again.

Cohen and I took seats in the next room. It smelled of antiseptic and anxious dog. Posters advertised deworming medicines and vaccines. A barrage of barking echoed through the room from the training center on the other side of the wall.

Under the stark fluorescents, Cohen's bruises looked even worse. I worried that maybe there were other injuries—broken bones, damaged organs.

I shifted in my seat. "You look like shit."

He laughed. "You look in a mirror lately?"

But the laugh was faint, and he was holding a hand to his ribs.

A young woman with an auburn ponytail came in and closed the door behind her. "I'm Sara. Avi has asked me to take a look at you."

We introduced ourselves. She smiled, eyeballed us, then gestured Cohen onto the surgery table.

"Remove your shirt, please."

She and I both sucked in a breath at the bruises that purpled Cohen's chest and left side.

Sara rolled a lamp over to the table. "You are in a lot of pain?"

"I've been better."

"One to ten, with one being the lowest and ten being unbearable."

"Call it a four."

She raised an eyebrow, and I said, "He's being macho."

"We'll go with six." She snapped on latex gloves and ran her fingers along his ribs.

He gritted his teeth. "Maybe seven."

Sara was efficient as she moved around him. "Does this hurt? How about here? What do you feel when I apply pressure to this area?"

When she finished with his face and chest, she moved on to his hands. She rolled a tray table over and asked him to spread his fingers. He did so, but I read in his eyes what it cost him—too much like what he'd undergone in the trailer.

Gently, Sara removed the tape. She scowled. "This was no accident."

"We fell in with the wrong crowd."

Her gaze went from Cohen to me. "There's a story I probably don't want to hear."

She gave him acetaminophen, apologized that she couldn't give him something stronger, then applied ointment to his wound and rewrapped the fingers with gauze and tape. "Have you had a tetanus shot in the last five years?"

He nodded.

"Okay, good. You need to see your doctor. I suspect you've cracked a couple of ribs, and you need to make sure there aren't any internal injuries. Plus, you'll want something stronger for the pain. You'll be hurting for a while." She turned to me. "Your turn."

I took Cohen's place on the examination table and stripped off my filthy shirt. She clicked her tongue as she had with Cohen while she cleaned and bandaged the wounds on my face and arm, then peeled off the now-filthy bandage on my ribs that Dougie had applied earlier. She examined the assorted other injuries, shone a light in my eyes, announced that I should get a tetanus booster, then gave both of us lab coats to wear in lieu of our shirts.

I slipped on the coat, grateful for something clean. "How are things going in the other room?"

She finished washing her hands. "I'll check for you."

After she left, Cohen sat and leaned his head back against the wall. I pulled out my phone and dialed. If Sarge turned on his phone as soon as the plane landed, he should pick up.

The connection went through.

"Sydney Parnell," said a voice I didn't recognize. "I've been told to expect your call."

The hair on the back of my neck rose. I put the call on speakerphone. Cohen opened his eyes.

I said, "Who is this?"

"Wrong question, Ms. Parnell."

"Where's Sarge? Put him on."

"That's more like it. But I'm afraid I have bad news."

I started shaking. Couldn't stop. I set the phone on the examination table and shoved my hands under my arms.

"Do you want to hear what it is?" the man asked.

Cohen got to his feet.

"You fucker," I said. "Put Sarge on."

"Sarge," the man said, "has a communication problem right now. Hard to talk when you're at the bottom of a river. But thanks for locating that video for us. You've been most helpful."

"I will find you," I said. "And when I do, I'll—"

"Oh, you won't need to find us, Ms. Parnell. We'll come to you."

The connection went dead.

I backed away from the phone as if it could keep hurting me. As if it would deliver the terrible news over and over like a viral tweetstorm. I barely felt it when Cohen put his arms around me and turned me so that I could press my face to his shoulder.

In my mind, I saw Sarge as he headed out that morning.

For a man who tried to kill me, you're not a complete asshole.

For a woman who kicked my ass twice, you aren't too shabby yourself.

My knees gave way. Cohen half carried me to a chair.

I couldn't feel my body. Not my hands or my feet. Neither legs nor arms. I couldn't feel anything at all except a vile, bitter lump in my mouth that wanted to slide down my throat, to close off my air and stop my heart.

I shut my eyes for a moment and saw Sarge's hand clasped in mine. His grin.

Eyes in the back of my head.

"Here's some water," Cohen said.

I looked at his face, tried to see him through the watery film smeared across my eyes.

The door opened, and Dougie came in. He took one look at me and stopped as if he'd run into an invisible wall. I saw the despair in my mind reflected in his eyes.

"They killed Sarge," I said. Even though he already knew.

CHAPTER 28

It is not over until God says it is over.

—Avi Harel. Private conversation.

We sat around a table in Avi's shaded courtyard.

Avi had created the patio as an oasis inside the industrial complex of warehouses, alleyways, and parking lots. Trees lined the slate-floored space. A fountain played in the corner. This time of year, terracotta pots of geraniums and marigolds lined the cement-block walls.

The table was loaded with what Avi called the food of Jerusalem. *Kofta b'siniya*—lamb-and-beef meatballs in tahini sauce. Pita bread. A tomato-and-cucumber salad. And, on ice, a bowl of milk pudding—*muhallabieh*.

It was all beautiful and smelled fabulous.

But none of us ate.

Clyde had come through the surgery with flying colors. The wound involved only soft tissue—no skeletal injuries—and no damage to the sciatic nerve. Avi predicted Clyde would be mostly healed within three weeks and would enjoy a full recovery by eight. While the others gathered on the patio, I'd slipped in to see him.

He lay in an ICU crate, the IV still dripping fluid into him and three ECG leads clipped into place. His fur was shaved, and a Penrose drain drew blood and fluids from beneath the incision. He wore an e-collar to keep him from chewing on the surgical site. The cone of shame, we called it.

It used to make me laugh.

I pulled a chair over to his crate and sat with him, just the two of us. He opened his eyes and watched me sleepily. The room was cool, the lights dim, our mingled breathing and the beep of machines the only sounds. I held his paw and apologized. Promised it wouldn't happen again. I thanked him for being the best partner anyone could have and told him that if he wanted to go with Dougie, I'd understand. But that if he didn't, it would make me very happy.

After a time, I was done with my tears, and Clyde had drifted back to sleep. I knuckle-bumped his paw and joined the others on the patio.

While we stared at the food and waved away the occasional wasp, I listened to Dougie fill in Cohen and Avi on the events of the last few days and tell them about Malik's video—what it was and how we'd tracked it down.

What it meant to lose it.

"Even if we can't prove Valor's relationship with Iran, we can put Almasi behind bars," Cohen said. "Kidnapping and torturing a cop, for starters. And if we can link her to Fadden, she'll go to prison for Kane's murder."

"It's good," I said. "It's necessary. But it isn't enough. What she did is treason."

"So we build our case piece by piece." Cohen pushed food around on his plate. "We start with Kane and the motivation for his death and work back through time."

Dougie gave a soft snort. He stretched out his legs and crossed the ankles. The aviators were back in place as sunlight found a way through the trees.

I knew what he was thinking as clearly as if he had spoken. When the system failed, you took justice into your own hands. The idea was as old as civilization, as common as yesterday's news.

Cohen honed in on Dougie, his eyes sharp. He'd picked up on it, too. "You're thinking about extrajudicial means." He paused. "Execution."

Dougie folded his arms.

"That's nothing but vigilante justice." Cohen's smile was bitter.

"But," Dougie said, "it *is* justice."

"It makes us no different from her."

Dougie uncrossed his ankles and sat up. "She's killing innocents. We aren't."

"We don't have the right to be judge, jury, and executioner."

But Dougie and Avi exchanged glances. Mutual understanding and a bond over similar battles. Some of which, I imagined, they were still fighting.

I watched Avi from beneath the brim of my hat. There was something contained about him. Like a sheath over a knife. He was tightly controlled in a manner that suggested if he were to move just a fraction faster, you would lose your wallet and maybe your life before you even knew he'd shifted position.

I'd never seen Avi in this light. Now I shivered in the warm breeze.

Cohen was looking at me. "You haven't said anything."

"I'm a cop," I said quietly. "That should be enough." But I was thinking of my ghosts. Fadden and the Six. I'd passed judgment in the wink of an eye. What did that make me?

Agitated, I scooped an ice cube out of my water glass and pressed it to my neck. "So what do we do?"

"We think on it," Avi said. "What you Americans call brainstorming. But for that we need a little help."

He went into the building and returned a moment later with a bottle of clear liquid and four shot glasses. He poured until the glasses were filled almost to the rim, then passed them around.

"I'm not exactly in a drinking mood," I said.

"It is arak. It will feel like a fresh breeze through your mind. Then we will determine our next step."

We each picked up a glass.

"To Sarge," I said.

"To Sarge," said the others.

We clinked glasses and slammed down the liquid. It blazed a line down my throat, then popped up into my sinuses and swept through my head like a storm. For a second I couldn't breathe. Then I felt like I could breathe better than I ever had.

I also felt as though someone had applied a welding torch to my insides.

Cohen placed a fist to his chest. "Are you trying to kill us?"

"Usually, we mix arak with water. Or perhaps grapefruit juice or lemon. But medicinally, it is best this way."

I set the glass down and let my eyes water.

Only Dougie looked unfazed.

"Now we will come up with our answer," Avi said.

Sara, the tech, appeared in the doorway. "If you guys aren't too busy, I have a question."

"Of course." Avi pulled out a chair and gestured for her to sit. "What is it?"

She dropped into the seat and grabbed a piece of pita bread. "I was looking at the X-rays."

A flutter of panic. "Is something wrong?"

"No, no. Clyde is fine. But I've worked with several combat assault dogs. MWDs. They all have microchips, right?"

Dougie and I nodded.

"But just one chip."

"Go on," Avi said.

"Clyde has two chips. As you may know, chips are normally injected under the skin between the shoulder blades. That is where one of Clyde's chips is. Now, occasionally a chip might migrate down a dog's body. But this second chip is located under Clyde's right hind leg. It's an odd place for it to end up."

My eyes met Dougie's. A whisper of hope ran a finger across my skin, light as a feather.

"Has Clyde had another owner?" Sara asked. "Someone else who would have chipped him?"

"No." I was still looking at Dougie. "You said you trusted Clyde with Rick Dalton."

"I left him with Rick several times."

"And you said Rick was Mr. Triplicate."

A light had come into his eyes. "Always."

"So what I'm hearing"—Cohen looked from me to Dougie—"is that this guy Rick had a second chip placed in Clyde."

Avi clapped his hands together. "It is as I said. The arak is magic."

We all stood and moved toward the building.

I struggled to sound matter-of-fact. "Who could have done it?"

Dougie opened the door and held it. "The CIA had a veterinarian in Baghdad for their K9s. Or it could have been someone on the base. Maybe even a local vet—that would have been safest. No questions, no explanations."

As we walked into the room, Clyde opened a sleepy eye. He wagged his tail when we approached.

"Good boy," I said in my squeaky voice. "Good boy, Clyde."

He got the other eye open.

"How do these chips work?" Cohen asked.

Sara held up a scanner. "Every microchip has an identification number. The number is unique for every chip and thus for every pet. If someone brings in a stray dog, we scan the number, then call the manufacturer and notify them we've found the animal. They look up the identification number in their database and contact the owner."

She opened the door to Clyde's crate.

"Like this." She held the scanner between Clyde's shoulder blades, then showed us the screen. "This one's a nine-digit number, and the chip is manufactured by HomeSafe. This is the chip Clyde had when you took ownership, is that right?"

I nodded. "I just updated the owner information on their database."

"Here is what I get when I scan the second chip." She reached farther into the crate and held the scanner over Clyde. "Another nine-digit code. Standard. It also has ISO code 368, which usually indicates where the chip was manufactured. But in this case, I think it's almost like a message."

Avi said, "What do you mean?"

She closed the door to the crate. "I'm familiar with the more common ISOs—I've seen them often enough. But this code I had to look up."

"Iraq," I breathed.

She gave me a surprised look. "That's right. And since Iraq doesn't manufacture microchips—"

"Someone was telling us the chip was placed in Clyde in Iraq," Cohen finished.

"That's what I'm thinking," Sara said.

Avi opened a laptop on the counter. "Because of our animal rescue work, I have access to a national pet-registry database. We should be able to find the contact information for whoever placed that chip."

We crowded around him while he opened up a database and logged on. Sara read off the identification number and Avi typed. A minute later the system chimed, and a box appeared.

Avi rubbed his chin. "Curious."

We were looking at:

BLOWFISH.COM

Maninthefield
*&5MANI#N#THE)$5^fie4ld678

"It's a cloud account," Cohen said. "He uploaded files to Blowfish. That must be his username and password."

Avi opened another tab and navigated to the Blowfish website. When prompted, he entered the rest of the information. Another screen appeared, this one with a list of file-folder icons. We peered over his shoulder while Avi read the labels out loud.

"Email. Audio. Video."

He clicked on the icon labeled "Emails," and a list of file names appeared. He scrolled down. And down. And kept scrolling.

"There must be a hundred emails," he said. He double-clicked on one, and the email opened in a second tab. We stared at an unformatted string of upper and lowercase numbers, interrupted by an occasional symbol.

"It's gibberish," I said.

"He used encryption software," Avi answered. "The Feds will be able to decode it."

"Maybe."

"They will use something like BULLRUN or another decryption software. No problem. And you see, you can read the sender and receiver. OsborneJa to LAlmasi." He looked up at me, his sun-creased face jubilant.

"I hope you're right." I pointed. "Open up the video folder."

Avi clicked and a single file popped up. *BorderTapeMalik*. Another click, and a window opened with the video. Avi enlarged it to full screen and clicked play.

We watched in silence as the video opened with the interior of a truck. It was clearly night, the footage grainy. A man's face shone faintly in the dashboard lights. This, presumably, was Malik's uncle.

He turned toward the camera and murmured something in Arabic.

Avi translated. "He says to put away the phone. It is best to not take any video. Not tonight."

The action stopped. When it started again, Malik's uncle was now helping other men move wooden boxes from the back of one truck and into the other. The action took place in the white wash of headlights, the men talking softly, their voices faint in the rush of wind against the microphone. The filming was jittery and at a bad angle, as if Malik had tucked himself on the other side of his uncle's truck, afraid to be caught.

I counted eight men in addition to Malik's uncle. Seven of the men and the uncle helped move the boxes, their arms and shoulders straining, their steps slow. The eighth man appeared to be in charge, pointing at the others and directing them with his hands to move quickly.

Ten crates in, one of the men lost his grip. His end crashed into the ground as both men leapt back with a shout. The crate splintered on impact and the man in charge yelled.

Avi said, "He is telling them to fix it. To hurry with another box. And also a few other things I should not translate."

The two men who'd been carrying the box moved away, and the camera panned to the ground, then to the side of the truck. I caught a flash of a door handle.

Malik, moving to a different spot.

I glanced at Dougie. He was pensive, his index fingers pressed to his lips, a crease between his eyes. Then he leaned toward the screen and his hands came down.

"There it is," he said. "Pause it."

I looked back at the computer.

The camera had zoomed in on the crate. Avi rewound a few seconds, then hit play. He paused the video just as the camera closed in on the shattered crate and two large cylinders with copper-lined concave faces sitting on the ground.

Cohen drew a deep breath. "What are they?"

"Warheads," Dougie said. "For Explosively Formed Penetrators. The explosive is inside the case. The copper face becomes the actual weapon. Now look closer. You see the winged V on the side?"

"Valor's logo," I said.

On the video, the man in charge snapped out a command.

Avi said, "He is asking for the boy. He wants the boy to help."

A few seconds later, the camera went dark.

Around me, the room was utterly quiet. A clock ticked on the wall. The dogs next door had stopped barking, training done for the day.

I placed my hands on the back of Avi's chair and leaned into it, no longer trusting my legs to hold me.

Avi broke the silence. "Clyde is the hero."

"And Rick Dalton," Dougie said.

I pulled out my phone. "You guys ready to call the Feds and loose the dogs of war?"

"Do it," Cohen said.

I pulled up my contacts and dialed a friend at the FBI, Madeline McConnell.

She answered with, "Sydney, where the hell have you been? It's been weeks. We were supposed to have drinks."

"I need you to copy down something, Mac. It's the access to a cloud account."

"This isn't a joke, is it? Today has been long and frustrating."

"No joke. And your day is about to get brighter." Or maybe darker. I gave her the name of the cloud company and read off Rick Dalton's username and password.

"Okay. Let me take a look."

There came a long silence. Then a whistle. "The hell is this? Emails. Videos."

"Just look at it."

Through the phone I heard Malik's video play again as Mac started it up. I closed my eyes and thought about Marines and soldiers in Iraq.

About Dougie's shattered life and Cohen's injuries, and Clyde's. My mind pulled up pictures of those who had paid the ultimate price. Haifa and PFC Resenko. Jeremy Kane. Angelo Garcia. Sarge.

Mac came back on the line. "Who took this video, Sydney? This is in Iraq? What does it mean?"

I thought about Malik. A boy who'd lost everything.

But who now, with this, might get a little bit of it back.

"Justice," I said. "What it means is justice."

ONE MONTH LATER

CHAPTER 29

Wisdom is earned trench by trench, street by street, from one battle line to the next.

—*Sydney Parnell. Personal journal.*

I stretched out my legs in the Mexico sun and watched Malik dribble a soccer ball down the grass at Parque Tezozómoc. The shouts of the other children echoed through the air as the game went back and forth across the grass.

Malik was good with the ball. But maybe his greatest skill was his speed. He was a boy who knew how to run.

At least now he was running toward something. Not away.

Overhead, leaves rustled. Shadows stretched across the park. A squirrel darted across open ground and vanished up a trunk into the safety of high branches. Seven o'clock in the evening, and the light was long and low. But even with the approach of twilight, the sun held a warm embrace. In Denver, it was officially autumn, and the nighttime air would swirl with the promise of winter.

But here, in *la ciudad de México*, it still felt like summer.

Beside me on the bench, Ehsan Zarif sat with his elbows on his knees, watching the game. When one of the opposing players knocked an elbow into Malik's chest, Zarif leapt to his feet and shouted, "Foul!"

No one looked over, and he sat down with a self-conscious smile. "It is just a practice match. I get carried away."

"It's because you care. You can be forgiven."

He pulled out a pack of cigarettes and turned them around and around in his hands.

"I am grateful for what you have done," he said. "Malik is like a son to me. And now he has a life again."

I'd been in Mexico for three days. Time enough to visit with Jesús and take him and his friends out to dinner. To meet with Angelo's widow and put her in contact with David Fuller, who had promised to help the family. And to give Señora Torres a check, courtesy of a fund-raiser I'd run in Denver. It wasn't nearly enough to cover the lost tunnel. But it was a start.

Mostly I'd spent the time with Malik, who was heartbreakingly relieved to see me. This time I hadn't lied when I promised him I'd be back. His world was a little more stable.

Zarif told me that Malik had been doing better, even in the few short weeks since I'd seen him. I've heard that our happiness level remains mostly stable throughout our lives, no matter what happens. Win the lottery, and whatever happiness the money brings will fade. Lose a loved one, and we bounce back. According to the psychologists, we have a happiness set point. We don't deviate too far from it.

Maybe trauma was the same way. If we are not continually retraumatized, perhaps we eventually claw our way back to normal. Start sleeping through the night again. Regain our optimism.

Lose our ghosts.

Across the way, the Sir gave me a nod.

"This is the first time Malik has been outside a wall since he got here," Zarif said.

"Freedom looks good on him."

Zarif laughed, and I joined in. I pushed my sunglasses up on my head. "Did that sound theatrical?"

"Normally, I would say yes." He slid the cigarettes back in his breast pocket and draped an arm across the back of the bench. "But with Malik . . . maybe it sounds exactly right." He let out a sigh. "I was worried you were coming to persuade him to go to America with you."

"I never wanted to claim him. I just wanted to give him a life."

"On that you have succeeded." His gaze returned to the game. "I've been following the news."

The intel we'd provided the FBI had been a bombshell. A week after I picked up the phone and called Mac, Laura Almasi was arrested on what looked likely to be a long list of charges—kidnapping, torture, murder, money laundering, various tax crimes, conspiracy to defraud the United States, violations of the Arms Export Control Act and other statutes, acting as an agent of Iran, violating US sanctions, providing material support to terrorists, and conspiracy.

Her brother, James Osborne, faced similar charges. Authorities were also investigating some of the men Osborne had associated with at the embassy in Baghdad.

Whatever the Saudis had to do with Valor Industries, and whatever was sitting in the airplane hangar near Lindon, remained a secret. That, apparently, was information provided only on a need-to-know basis.

Cohen and I didn't make the cut.

Cohen, Dougie, and I had been grilled for three full days. On the fourth day, Dougie hadn't appeared at FBI headquarters. By noon the same day, Cohen and I were also cut loose. An investigation by the Denver Major Crimes Unit, led by Detective Gorman, was still ongoing, but looked certain to conclude that I had not used excessive force when I killed Fadden in self-defense or shot Almasi's security guards while assisting in the investigation of Jeremy Kane's murder. My interrogation had been brief. Bill Gorman was too busy basking in the applause he'd received for solving Kane's murder and coordinating the investigation into Sarge's death with the Nevada police. He stayed calm and matter-of-fact, even after I told him he was a self-aggrandizing cockroach who couldn't solve a murder with a video of the deed and the killer's signed confession. I'd withheld further opinion about his inability to tell his ass from a hole in the ground.

I was asked only a couple of times about the deaths of several guards both in and out of the complex and about the explosions that had rocked Almasi's compound. When I said the details were fuzzy, that line of questioning petered out and then stopped.

As they say, it's who you know. And Dougie, apparently, knew the right people.

Cohen and I were hailed as heroes in the media storm that broke after the arrests. And even as the military machine revved up to look into leveling charges against me for my actions in Iraq, I was assured in private that I would not face trial. If pushed, they'd play the "only following the orders of a superior officer" card. What it meant, reading between the lines, was they had bigger issues than a former Marine corporal to worry about.

I was okay with that.

Dougie had retrieved the rancher's truck from the copse of trees where we'd stashed it. He told me the man never asked any questions. But with the story splashed all over the news, he didn't have to. All he'd said to Dougie was, "I've never been wrong about a fellow."

Dougie had also phoned Dalton's half sister in Nevada and told her that her brother was a hero. He mentioned she might want to check the postal box, and left it at that. We didn't know where the money came from. But Dougie said Rick would want his sister to have it.

Two weeks after my phone call to the FBI, Arvin Almasi was arrested in Mexico City. Two days after that, he was found dead in his cell, an apparent suicide. I'd considered asking Zarif if he'd played a role in finding Arvin, but decided some stones were better left unturned.

Some questions better left unanswered.

Now, in the park beside me, Zarif pumped his fist as Malik approached the end of the makeshift field and kicked the ball neatly past the goalie.

"He has a future, that boy," Zarif said.

Indeed he did.

I stood. "I should get going."

Zarif also rose. "You want to say good-bye to Malik?"

I shaded my eyes and watched his teammates crowd around him. "Don't interrupt him. I'll be back. And you've promised you'll bring him to Denver."

"I will." He held out a hand. "It is a pleasure knowing you, Sydney Parnell."

I looked at him. "You aren't going to stab me again, are you?"

He laughed and kissed my cheek.

I carried my sandals in my hand and strolled barefoot through the grass, enjoying the quiet breeze and the soft shift of light from gold to purple.

I had one more person to see before I flew home.

He was standing near the park's lake. I didn't see him until he stepped out from beneath the trees.

When I drew near, he held out his hands and took mine. We stood that way for a few moments, my fingers soft in his calloused palms. I studied the back of his hands, the life written there in overlapping scars.

Then he released me and stepped back. We started walking.

"Clyde's doing good?" he asked.

"He's doing great. He misses you."

"He had my back for a long time."

"Dougie—"

"It's okay, Rosie. You two are partners now. Much as I miss him, I'd never break that up. Plus, it wouldn't be fair to him. Like I said, I go into some rough places. And he's not getting younger."

"Don't say that. Clyde has a lot of good years left in him."

I stopped, then Dougie did, and we gazed across the lake. A flock of geese was coming in for the night, their great wings sweeping inches above the water, their white bodies reflected like puffs of cloud in the deep green of the lake.

I nudged his shoulder. "So what's next for you? Still dark ops?"

"A few days on a beach. Then, yeah, back to work." His gaze went soft, focused on something I couldn't see. "It's what I know."

I tried to make my voice light. Failed. "I probably shouldn't ask where you're going."

"I probably wouldn't tell you."

"I half expected Laura to have committed suicide." It was a question. As close as I would come to asking him about extrajudicial execution.

"Unless I'm very wrong about the afterlife, Laura will be far more miserable alive than dead."

I had to agree. As she had predicted, she'd lost everything. Career, reputation, the family business, her brother. Her freedom. I didn't know Miriam's fate, but I had to assume that with her stepfather dead, she was free to continue with her own life on her own path. I wished her luck.

On the far side of the lake, the geese settled on the shore, their quiet honks drifting over the water like sleepy goodnights.

I glanced at Dougie. His face was carefully carved into an expression that gave away absolutely nothing.

I said, "Are you haunted?"

"By the people I've loved? Or by the people I've hated?"

"Both."

His gaze stayed on the lake. "I see my brothers from Iraq every night. The men who lost their lives in that ambush. Men like Rick Dalton."

"In your dreams, you mean?"

"Yes."

"What about the people you've killed? Do you see them?"

"Never." He looked at me. "You?"

"I see those I processed in MA. And those whose lives I've taken. But not—" I stopped, wondering how much of my madness to share. "I don't see them just at night."

"Ghosts." He nodded. "The fallout of war."

"My therapist says they're manifestations of my anger and fear."

"I think the poets would say something different." He turned to me, and his face softened. "If I'm lucky, someday I will see ghosts as well. You took what happened to you and used it to become a better person. But me . . . I survive by walling off everything. I'm not haunted. But maybe I should be."

There was something tight in Dougie, a part of him that withheld things he might never be able to let go of. A man of violence both suffered and meted out. He seemed meant for solitude now.

But I said, "The Dougie I knew is still in there."

"Maybe. Like Han Solo, frozen in carbonite."

I toed a stone and kicked it toward the water.

Dougie asked, "Have you told your detective much?"

"Some. What happened. But not how it felt."

"It's hard with civilians. Even cops." He found his own stone and scooped it up, putting all of his arm into the throw. Across the lake, the geese rustled when the rock hit the water. "When I was in that village in Iraq, close to death, one of the things that kept me going was what I needed to say to people. The things I hadn't said yet. Things that seemed important."

I turned to him. His eyes were far away. As blue as ever, but with a distance in them that told me he would never fully be back.

My throat tightened. "What did you want to tell them?"

"In some ways, I wanted them to understand. But that wasn't reasonable. Mostly I just wanted to tell them I loved them." He turned to me finally, his gaze—for the moment—very present. He raised his fingers to my face. "It's not too late, Rosie."

I sucked in a ragged breath.

"With him, I mean."

I exhaled. "I know."

I turned, and we began walking back in the other direction. I said, "When will I see you again?"

"Maybe soon." A shrug. "Maybe never. We had . . ." He looked past me, seeing something I couldn't share.

I nodded. "I know. Our time."

"And that's forever."

When he moved away, it was with his old, familiar walk. Tall. Confident. A man who could steer the world. He headed toward the trees, his dark clothing blending with the growing night. At the last moment, he stopped, and our eyes met across the distance.

He raised a hand and gave me a small wave.

We had our forever.

My hand was still up when he disappeared into the shadows.

As I headed back in the direction of the car that Zarif had arranged for the airport, my phone pinged. A text from Cohen.

You still coming home tonight?

Home. A beautiful concept. I typed, Yes. Howz Clyde?

Little thief ate my burger

I smiled. See you soon

We will be at the airport

I stared at the phone, the screen swimming in front of me.
Some things will not do themselves.
Some things you have to do yourself.
I typed the hardest seven letters of my life: Love you
Then I prayed the phone would die before I did.
Ping.

Love you too. Now get your ass home.

So that was that. I smiled and slid my phone into my pocket.
Cohen and I still had plenty to figure out. But he hadn't kicked me
out. And I hadn't left.

Bad happens to all of us, of course. But if we are fortunate, the good
in life balances those things we might wish to forget. We are able to pick
ourselves up and brush ourselves off. We carry on.

We're still good.

The last light of the sun turned the grass into emeralds. I walked
back through the park, behind Zarif still on the bench, past the soccer
game. I paused for a moment, watching as Malik kicked the ball. It
soared into the heavens in an arc that seemed long enough to reach from
Iraq to Mexico. From one side of the world to the other.

Ultimately, the universe is a moral place. And while the arc of the
universe is long, as Martin Luther King Jr. said, it bends toward justice.

Always, it bends toward justice.

ACKNOWLEDGMENTS

The list of men and women willing to help me with the Sydney Parnell novels continues to grow. It's one of the greatest things about pursuing this writing gig—the people I meet.

First, to my beta readers. All outstanding writers, they each bring terrific insight and great skill to the editing task. They are patient, forgiving, and generous with their time and creative talent. My deepest and most appreciative thanks go to Michael Bateman, Deborah Coonts, Ron Cree, Kirk Farber, Chris Mandeville, Steve Pease, Michael Shepherd, and Robert Spiller. All of them improved the book immensely, and my gratitude knows no bounds.

To Danielle Gerard and J.R. Backlund, who sat with me in the bar at ThrillerFest and helped me plot murder and mayhem. You guys are genius.

This book would not have been possible without the knowledge and insight of the following people. Career Intelligence Officer Steve Pease. Army Major Thomas E. VanWormer (retired). FBI Special Agents Gerard Ackerman and Matthew S. Harris. And Doctor of Veterinary Medicine Doug Schrepel. I am grateful for the time and wisdom of Denver RTD Chief of Police John F. Tarbert (retired).

And, as always, my thanks to Denver Detective Ron Gabel (retired). Ron, you are truly one of the good guys.

To the veterans I met through Creative Forces. You guys have opened my eyes, expanded my mind, and touched my heart. I know you hate hearing this, but to me, you're all heroes.

A special thanks to my agent, Bob Diforio of the D4EO Literary Agency, and to my fantastic editors, Liz Pearsons and Charlotte Herscher. My gratitude to the team at Thomas & Mercer—all of you exemplify the best.

Finally, to those who support me in so many ways. Lori Dominguez, Maria Faulconer, and Cathy Noakes (who went above and beyond). To my children, Kyle and Amanda, and to Steve. Always.

AUTHOR'S NOTE

In writing this novel I took certain liberties in how I portrayed some of the countries, cities, and institutions. The world presented here, along with its characters and events, is wholly fictitious. Denver Pacific Continental (DPC) is a wholly fictional railway. Any resemblance to actual events and corporations, or to actual persons, living or dead, is entirely coincidental.

That said, the technology I used in this novel, primarily the gait-analysis software, does exist and is changing the way law enforcement operates in the ongoing hunt for criminals and terrorists.

An intelligence source told me about the brief appearance in Iraq of a weapon that the manufacturers—the Russians, he thought—wanted to test against the US Abrams tank. This sparked the idea for Valor's Explosively Formed Penetrators. The EFPs described in these pages are real. It is true that Iran was smuggling weapons and personnel into Iraq during the Iraq War, and that some of these weapons were thought to be too sophisticated to have been built in Iraq. If you're curious, the following articles provide a start:

- Fahim, Kareem and Liz Sly. "Lethal roadside bomb that killed scores of US troops reappears in Iraq." *Washington Post*. October 12, 2017.

- Conroy, Scott. "US Sees New Weapon In Iraq: Iranian EFPs." *CBS News.* February 11, 2006.
- Gordon, Michael R. "Deadliest Bomb in Iraq Is Made by Iran, US Says." *New York Times.* February 10, 2007.

The line about the arc of the universe used at the end of *Ambush* appeared in a 1958 article written by Martin Luther King Jr., where he placed the line in quotes to indicate its previous use in other sources. The original metaphor appeared in 1853 in a collection of sermons written by abolitionist minister Theodore Parker.

A number of Americans are working with various Middle Eastern countries, including Saudi Arabia, to provide training and even armed forces. For one example, see Jenna McLaughlin's article "Deep Pockets, Deep Cover" (*Foreign Policy*, December 21, 2017).

If you are concerned about the plight of Iraqi citizens who aided US and coalition forces during the war in Iraq, I recommend the book *To Be a Friend Is Fatal: The Fight to Save the Iraqis America Left Behind* by Kirk W. Johnson. If you're looking to make a difference, several organizations like my fictional Hope Project could use your help. These Iraqi men and women—mostly men—risked their lives and the lives of their families because they shared the same dream for Iraq that Americans hold: to create a free and fair democracy.

AMBUSH READING GROUP GUIDE

1. What is the significance of the title?
2. Sydney feels guilty for leaving Malik behind in Iraq. Do you think Americans should be responsible for the safety of the men and women who helped us in Iraq? What about their families?
3. As a Marine veteran, Sydney carries psychological scars from her time in war. What scars did you notice? What other characters were changed by war?
4. Do you think Sydney's ghosts are real or manifestations of her post-traumatic stress disorder?
5. Sydney's K9 partner, Clyde, is an intricate part of the novel. How might things be different for Sydney and for the story without him?
6. The Alpha did terrible things, but for a reason. How do you feel about the Alpha's motivation?
7. One of the characters supports using extrajudicial punishment—going after suspected wrongdoers outside the normal legal system. Do you think that in some cases, the results justify doing things that might be considered bad or questionable?

8. Did any of the events in the book shock or surprise you?
9. Did the book make you curious about the Iraq War? Do you want to know more about America's relationship with Iran and Saudi Arabia?
10. Was the ending satisfying?

ABOUT THE AUTHOR

Photo © 2017 Trystan Photography

Barbara Nickless is the author of the Sydney Rose Parnell series, which includes *Blood on the Tracks*—a *Suspense Magazine* Best of 2016 selection—and *Dead Stop*. Both novels won the Colorado Book Award and were finalists for the Daphne du Maurier Award of Excellence, which *Blood on the Tracks* won. Her essays and short stories have appeared in *Writer's Digest* and *Criminal Element*, among other markets. She lives in Colorado, where she loves to snowshoe, cave, hike, and drink single malt Scotch—usually not at the same time. Connect with her online at www.barbaranickless.com.